MW01615564

Wheels of Fire

HOLLYWOOD DEMONS #3

USA TODAY BESTSELLING AUTHOR
AUTUMN JONES LAKE

WHEELS OF FIRE

Hollywood Demons #3

AUTUMN JONES LAKE

Your love stories never end...
AN USA BESTSELLING AUTHOR AUTUMN JONES LAKE
AUTUMNJONESLAKE.COM

COPYRIGHT

Hollywood Demons #3
Copyright ©2020 Autumn Jones Lake
Digital ISBN #: 978-1-943950-54-6
Paperback ISBN #: 978-1-943950-58-4
Large Print Paperback ISBN #: 978-1-943950-59-1
Audio ISBN #: 978-1-943950-60-7

Cover Models: Megan Napolitan and Zack Bradford
Cover Designer: Lori Jackson Design
Photographer: Wander Aguiar Photography
Edited by Angela James

This is a work of fiction. Names, characters, organizations, places, events, and incidents are either products of the author's imagination or are used fictitiously and are not to be construed as real. Any resemblance to actual events, locales, organizations, or persons, living or dead, is entirely coincidental.

No part of this book may be reproduced, or stored in a retrieval system, or transmitted in any form or by any means, electronic, mechanical, photocopying, recording, or otherwise, without express written permission of the publisher. This copy is intended for the purchaser only. No part of this book may be reproduced, scanned, or distributed in any printed or electronic form without prior written permission. Please do not participate in or encourage piracy of copyrighted materials in violation of the author's rights. Purchase only authorized editions.

The Lost Kings MC is a registered trademark of Ahead of the Pack, LLC.

ALSO BY AUTUMN JONES LAKE

THE LOST KINGS MC SERIES

Also available in audio

ACKNOWLEDGMENTS

This trio of books has been such an adventure and a joy to write during such a challenging time. As much as I've immersed myself in Mallory and Chaser's world, their story wouldn't have come alive without several key people.

Thank you to Angela James for helping me tame this story and for your valuable input.

Lauren McKellar, thank you for the weekly check-ins and keeping me sane during the writing process. I absolutely adore this story, and I wouldn't have pulled it off without you guiding me along.

Thank you so much to Lori Jackson for creating three beautiful covers and capturing what was so special to me about these books.

Wander and Andrey thank you for being so patient and helping me bring the images in my head to my covers.

Many thanks to LK Shaw for appreciating my snark, making me laugh, and always being willing to listen.

Sue Banner, Sophie Ruthven, Melissa Machado, Tanisha Franzese, Athena Stephenson, Shawna Wood, Jennifer Furr, Laura Knowles, Elizabeth Kelley, Tammy Dalton, Sirenda McNece, Kathryn Linke, Tanya Skaggs, and Brittany Lehnhoff—

there really aren't enough words to thank you for sticking with me through so many books. For being so patient when I drop a book on you last minute or you have to remind me about promo graphics. I'm not sure how I got so lucky and I probably don't deserve you, but I appreciate you so much.

Jessica Alcazar, thank you for traumatizing—oops, I mean kindly pointing out a few flaws and suggestions on how to polish them. Thank you for your *plot twists!* and reminding me when I'm running behind.

I really need to thank Samara, Rob, Lance, and Samantha for bringing Mallory and Chaser to life in the audiobooks. Deciding to produce my own audiobooks for this series was scary and I can't thank you enough for making it such a smooth process.

Last, and never least, thank you to Mr. Lake who is my rock. You never hesitate to kick my ass into gear or reassure me that I'm awesome when I'm in a spiral of self-doubt. Thank you for keeping me fed, caffeinated, rolling out my yoga mat every morning and doing...well everything else around here while I'm in deep writing mode. In a year full of so much uncertainty and distress, you continue to be my anchor.

DEDICATION

"Love does not consist in gazing at each other, but in looking outward together in the same direction."

—*Antoine de Saint-Exupéry*

CHAPTER ONE

Chaser

Sometimes the path to harmony isn't in the doing of stuff, it's in the *un*doing of the things that leave you unbalanced. The releasing of the people hanging around your neck. The albatrosses who drag you under. It's a lesson I should've learned a long time ago.

Instead, thanks to my druggie bandmates, I'm sitting in an austere six by eight cell. With no idea whether Andrew is alive or not.

Fear digs the deepest graves. That's why I'm keeping mine in check.

I'm innocent.

This is all a big mistake.

I'll be out soon.

"Adams!" an officer shouts.

Please let that be someone coming to their damn senses and letting me out of here.

I stand and wait by the cell door. The officer approaches, almost apologetically. "I gotta cuff you."

I hold my wrists out as he slides the gate open. "Do what you gotta do."

"Lot of us are fans," he says in a low voice as he walks me through the corridors.

"Thanks." What the hell else do I say? You'd think growing up in an MC, I'd have a healthy hatred of law enforcement. And I do, to a certain extent. But my father always impressed upon me the importance of showing respect until it's no longer an option. Law enforcement's just doing their job.

The grim vibe of the building doesn't improve as I'm led away from the cells, down a corridor with painted cinderblock walls. All windowless and free of decoration. We stop outside a small room. Inside, a square metal table is bolted to the floor. A crabby-faced detective waits to interrogate me on the other side.

He scowls as the other officer walks me to a chair.

The guy is most definitely not a fan.

Once we're alone, he sits forward. "Let's go over your story again, Mr. Adams."

"This is ridiculous." I spread my hands on the table in front of me. "Test me for gunshot residue."

"You seem to know an awful lot about the process."

I roll my eyes. "While you're wasting time busting my balls, the person who *actually* shot my friend is running around free."

"You and Andrew Lane are friends?"

"Yes." Most of the time I want to kill the guy but I haven't made a serious attempt, yet.

It's probably better to keep those sentiments to myself.

"A number of witnesses say you had an argument yesterday. Over your girlfriend."

"She and Andrew had a mild disagreement. We resolved it. Hell, I played on stage with Andrew last night."

"Another witness says you threatened to shoot Mr. Lane a few nights ago."

"Bullshit." One of the only "witnesses" was Alvin and there's no way he'd rat me out to anyone. Jacob and Garrett technically

2

didn't see anything. I can't imagine the girl Andrew brought on the bus spilling the story so fast. And Mallory would never talk to the cops. That leaves someone who wants to feel important spreading second or third-hand information.

"So you didn't threaten to shoot him?"

"We get into disagreements all the time. We're a bunch of guys on the road cooped up on tour buses."

Unimpressed, he flips through his notebook. "That doesn't answer my question."

I shrug.

"Does Andrew Lane have a drug problem?"

Does he ever.

"No idea."

"What about Jacob Whitfield?"

He's the whole reason we're in this mess.

"You'll have to talk to Jacob."

"We will once we locate him." He leans forward. "But come on, he's *your* singer. You don't know his habits?"

"I'm not his babysitter." Big, fat lie there.

"He's the one who called you and asked you to meet him and Andrew?"

"Yeah."

"Any idea what they were doing in that part of town?"

"I assumed they'd gotten lost." *While trying to score heroin.*

"Then what?"

"When I got there, Andrew was already on the ground bleeding out." I squeeze my eyes shut for a second, drowning in the helpless feeling of possibly watching a friend die.

"And?" he prompts.

I take a deep breath. "I put pressure on the wound and slapped Jacob to snap him out of his shock and told him to call 911." Furious over the whole situation, I may have punched Jacob a little harder than necessary. But I'll happily take the blame for the crime I actually *did* commit if Jacob has the urge to press charges.

3

"Who else was there?"

I close my eyes again, trying to remember details lost in the chaos. I'm pretty sure Vinnie and Garrett took off as soon as I arrived. It's not in my nature to snitch or volunteer information to cops, though. "I'm not sure. Everything was crazy. I focused on getting Andrew help and didn't pay attention to who was around us."

He rolls his eyes at what I'm sure sounded like a self-serving statement. "Where was your girlfriend during all this commotion?"

Unease prickles down my spine. Mallory doesn't need to be brought into this. "Asleep in our hotel room."

"Are you sure about that?"

"Yes."

He stands and knocks on the door. "All right."

"Are you letting me go?"

"I'll attempt to verify your version of events." He jerks his chin up. "Someone will come in and test your hands."

"Good."

Raised voices in the hallway, draw our attention to the door a few seconds before it's flung open. The detective barely has time to jump out of the way.

"If you're done violating my client's rights, I'd like to have a word with him," the intruder says.

I drop my head, suppressing my laughter. Knew my girl would come through. After her initial confusion, when I called to explain what was happening, she bucked up and promised she'd track down my father. And fuck knows, Dad wouldn't waste time finding me a lawyer the second he found out I was in jail.

After the detective leaves, the man extends his hand to me. "Sloan Paxton, your father hired me to represent you." He drops into the seat across from me. "I'll need a little time to get caught up on your case. Speak to the detectives. See what I can find out. The victim is in critical condition—"

4

"Andrew's alive?"

He pins me with a stare. "Yes."

"Thank God," I breathe out.

"These are still serious charges."

"I know that," I spit out. "I was worried my friend was dead. No one's told me anything."

"I'm not going to ask if you did it—"

"I didn't."

He holds up one hand and shakes his head. "Don't." He glances down at the papers in his hands. "Who's Peter Carson?"

"The band's tour manager."

"Andrew's band, or yours?"

My brows draw down. Why the fuck's he so interested in Pete? "Mine. Why?"

"He's the one who told the cops you tried to shoot Andrew the night before."

"Are you shitting me?" I jump up, stabbing my fingers through my hair. "Why the fuck would he do that?"

"You tell me." He studies a legal pad covered in chicken scratch that must only be legible to him. "Your girlfriend states Peter told her he had no idea where you were."

"That piece of shit."

"Easy. Let's get you out of this jam." He consults his notes again. "Do you own a gun?"

"Yes," I answer carefully.

A slight downward twitch at the corner of his mouth says that's not the answer he hoped for. "Where is it now?"

"Locked up on the tour bus."

I swear he breathes a sigh of relief. "You never made it back to the bus last night?"

"I see where you're going with this. No. The cops arrested me at the hospital."

"Good. Okay."

"Is Mallory okay? Have you talked to her?"

Paxton shifts and won't meet my eyes for a second. "She's

5

worried about you. She came down here with me but they won't let her see you yet."

"She's *here*? Get her back to the hotel. I need her to stay clear of this as much as possible." Damn, knowing she's so close kills me.

"Is she involved?"

"No and I want to keep it that way. She doesn't need the bad press." When will my shitty life decisions stop putting Mallory's career in jeopardy?

"Let's continue. What is your relationship with Andrew Lane?"

"We're friends. We've collaborated on some songs. Our bands are touring together." I shrug. That tour might be over. Hell, Kickstart's entire career might be blown if the whole world thinks I tried to kill the legendary Andrew Lane.

"There's no animosity between you?"

"Sure, he pisses me off all the time. Then he does something nice and makes it hard to be mad at him."

"And what's his relationship to Mallory?"

"Why?" I growl.

He stabs his pencil in the air. "That right there is a problem." He leans in closer. "They're going to try and paint this as a love triangle that got out of hand."

"That's pure bullshit. She's friends with his girlfriend. They work together. The four of us hang out back in L.A. sometimes."

"Girlfriend." He taps his pencil against the table. "Name?"

"Pamela Scott."

He scribbles down her name without a twitch of recognition. Guess he's not a *Playboy* fan. I sit back and assess my attorney. My father chose well for being an emergency-over-the-phone situation. Guy seems serious and sharp. Two things I'll need if there's any hope of extracting myself from this mess.

MALLORY

6

Waiting around the police station while the lawyer talks to
Chaser is torture.

"Miss, I'm sorry. Only his attorney's allowed to see him right
now." The officer glances over his shoulder quickly and in a lower
voice adds, "Paxton's a good lawyer. He'll have Chaser out by this
evening."

"I hope so." My gaze strays behind the counter. Chaser has to
be somewhere on the other side of that sad, gray cinder block
wall. Pain gathers in my chest. I can't get to him.

I drift over to an empty wooden bench and sit, watching the
door for the lawyer. The second he returns, I jump up to
greet him.

"How is he? When can we get him out?"

"Easy. Not here." He takes my elbow and guides me outside.
Heat simmers through my thin canvas sneakers, snaking up my
legs. We cross the busy street and into a small, municipal parking
lot before he'll utter a word. "The cops have nothing. No
weapon. No clear motive."

I let out a long, slow breath. Not that I ever doubted Chaser.
"What can I do?"

"He wants you to go back to the hotel."

"And do what? Sit on my butt while he's in jail? No."

The corners of his mouth twitch. "I figured that would be
your answer."

"What can I do?"

"I know you said Peter's a weasel, but can you talk to him?
Flesh out why he might have pointed the cops in Chaser's
direction."

"He's not a big fan of mine, but I'll do my best." I glance over
my shoulder toward the police station. "I was planning to go to
the hospital next."

He hesitates before answering. "Mallory, I need you to be
honest with me. Is there anything between you and Andrew
Lane?"

"God, no. Why would you ask that?"

"Because if this continues, the cops need a motive. And a love triangle between you, Chaser, and Andrew will sound nice and juicy."

"That's ridiculous. Chaser spends more time around Andrew than I ever have. Working," I add just in case he has other ideas. "Andrew's girlfriend and I work together on the same show."

"Chaser mentioned that. The four of you are good friends?"

"Sort of. Pamela can be prickly."

"Is there a reason for that? Is there a possibility she and Chaser...?" He lets the suggestion hang in the air, staring at me with two raised eyebrows.

It takes me a second longer than it should to understand his meaning. "No way."

He holds my gaze.

"I understand why you have to ask, but Chaser and I...we're close. We don't lie to each other." I take a moment and consider the way to phrase my next thought. "And Pamela, if she was having an affair with my boyfriend, I don't think she'd be able to stop herself from bragging to all of Hollywood."

He chuckles. "So, she's *that* kind of person."

"Competitive. I don't know why, since she's way more ahead of the game than I am."

"Is there a reason for that?" He holds up his hand. "I believe you when you say there's nothing going on between you and Andrew. But is it possible she's aware of feelings Andrew has for you?"

Feelings for me? I stop and consider Andrew's wacky behavior. His strange compliments and random moments of sweetness. His pervy questions. "Deep, specific feelings for *me*? No. That I'm a female he'd like to bang and add to his list? Possibly."

"And that doesn't bother Chaser?"

"He trusts me." I stop and stare over his shoulder at the brick wall with faded lettering that I can't decipher. "We haven't been together long. But we've been through a lot in that short time."

His sharp lawyer demeanor softens. "I can sense that, Mallory. Chaser's lucky." He glances over at his car. "Do you need a ride?"

"If you don't mind dropping me off at the hospital?"

"Not at all." He opens the passenger side door, then hesitates. "Be careful who sees you there, though. We don't want word to spread that you're sitting vigil at Andrew's bedside."

"Trust me, that's the last thing I plan to do." No, I want to find Jacob and choke him. Then whap Peter upside the head with my purse a couple dozen times.

"It'll help to have you there, so you can call me if Andrew wakes up. If he can make a statement, exonerating Chaser, I'll move on that. If not, then we'll need to regroup."

There's no "if not" in my head. Andrew better wake up and clear Chaser, or I'll kill him myself.

CHAPTER TWO

Mallory

Determination and anger fuel me as I walk into the hospital. On the way over, Mr. Paxton gave me some general ideas of questions to ask Peter and Jacob if I see them. Having a task to do doesn't make me want to strangle those two jackasses any less.

As I pass what looks like a waiting room, I recognize one of the people slumped over in a chair. My steps falter and I back up.

"Jacob, what's going on?" I ask, treading closer. His rumpled, dirty clothes and skin suggest he's been run over by a garbage truck.

"Mallory?" He glances up and blinks at me.

"What the hell happened?" I lower my voice to a harsh whisper. "Chaser's in jail. What are you doing here?" I don't bother mentioning that the cops want to question him. I can't afford to have Jacob bolt.

"Waiting for Andrew to wake the fuck up so he can tell the cops Chaser didn't do it."

His answer deflates a fraction of my anger. For once Jacob's trying to be helpful.

He searches the nearly empty waiting room like he can't believe he's still sitting there. "Where are the other guys?"

"I don't know. I just met with Chaser's lawyer."

"Shit." He drops his gaze and shakes his head. "You had to get him a lawyer?"

"He's in *jail*, Jacob," I remind him. "I called his father and he found him a lawyer."

"Aw fuck." He rakes his fingers through his already messy hair. "Chaser's going to kill me."

My boyfriend might have to get in line. I'm feeling murderous myself at the moment. "Jacob, what happened?" I ask in my most patient voice.

"It's all my fault."

You don't say.

"She shouldn't be here!" Peter yells from behind me.

"What the fuck, man?" Jacob snarls, jumping out of his chair.

"Her boyfriend's accused of shooting Andrew." Peter backs down under Jacob's raging bull face. "She shouldn't be here."

"Fuck off. You work for *us*, dickwad."

"*You're* the one who accused Chaser," I point out, calmly.

"You did what?" Alvin asks, stepping into the waiting room. His arm brushes against mine, filling me with relief that someone I trust is here. "Why would you do that?"

Peter backs up a few steps and shrugs. "Chaser pointed a gun at him. Andrew got shot. Two and two." He looks a little less sure of his theory. "Equals four. You know?"

"You fucking moron!" Alvin plants his hands against Peter's chest and shoves him hard enough to slam into a row of chairs on the opposite wall.

"Don't," I warn, pressing a palm against Alvin's shoulder. "We don't need you in trouble too."

I reach out and grab Jacob's arm as he attempts to go around us to get to Peter. "You too."

Jacob hangs his head. "I deserve to get in trouble."

"Well, I can't argue with that."

Alvin slips his arm around my shoulders. "Did you just get here?"

"Yes. Chaser's lawyer dropped me off." I flick my gaze at Jacob. "The cops are looking for you."

"Shit. Why?"

"Why do you think?"

Alvin lifts his head, throwing a glare Peter's way. "How about you do something useful and find a lawyer for Jacob?"

"I didn't do anything. I don't need a lawyer."

"Shut up." Alvin elbows Jacob.

Peter eyes the three of us warily and it's a good thing Alvin's still hanging onto me because my urge to rip out Peter's lying tongue hasn't abated.

"What happened, Jacob?" Alvin asks once Peter slinks away.

Jacob's gaze shifts my way. He *should* be worried. If he's in any way responsible for this, I won't hesitate to hand him over to the cops in order to save Chaser.

"Nothing. Some guy robbed us."

"Why'd you call Chaser?" I ask.

"I called him before we got robbed. I thought he could help."

"That's as clear as mud."

He gives me a helpless shrug.

Alvin leads me over to a chair in the corner. "You get any sleep last night?"

"No," I admit.

"Let's chill. The lawyer knows where you are, right? And the nurses know where to find us if Andrew wakes up."

"Thanks," I whisper, resting my head on his shoulder.

"Everything's going to be okay, Mallory."

I wish I believed him.

"Mrs. Lane?"

Someone touches my shoulder. "Mallory Lane?"

"What? No." Groggy, I shake my head and search the room. Alvin's passed out in the chair next to me. Jacob took up residence on the nubby old couch across from us. His deep snores fill the silence.

"I'm Mallory," I finally answer.

"Andrew's been asking for you," a nurse in a white uniform and gentle smile says.

I jump up, jostling Alvin in the process. "Hmm. What?" he mumbles.

"Andrew's awake?" I ask the nurse.

"The police are in there interviewing him now." She tilts her head and studies me. "But he's been asking for you non-stop."

I don't have a response. Why would Andrew ask for me over, well, anyone else?

Alvin nudges my shoulder. "Go," he urges. "We'll stay here."

The nurse leads me down the hall. "Your husband's quite the character."

"Andrew's not..." I open my mouth to correct her. But, what if only family members are allowed to visit him? I have to see him. He has to tell the police Chaser's innocent. "...a fan of hospitals," I finish.

"No one is." Abruptly, she stops and peers inside a room. Two men in cheap suits are stuffed inside the small space, blocking my view of everything except two big feet sticking off the end of the bed.

"No," Andrew insists. "I told you. I didn't get a good look at the guy. He jacked my cash, shot me, and ran." Something metal screeches against the floor. "Ow. Fuck. Get me out of here."

"Mr. Lane." The nurse leaves my side, rushing into the room. "Please, settle down."

"Oh, hey. I don't suppose you can give me a sponge bath?" Andrew asks in such a normal way, that if the two detectives

14

weren't still blocking my view, I bet I'd be able to see the flirty smile Andrew added to the request.

I roll my eyes toward the ceiling. Even recovering from a bullet wound, he's ridiculous.

"Mr. Lane," one of the detective snaps. "We're not finished."

"What more do you want from me?" His hand peeks out between the two detectives, fingers flicking toward the door. "Go catch the guy and let me heal. I have a show to do tonight."

"That's not going to happen, Mr. Lane," the nurse says.

"Are you sure it was a stranger?" one of the cops insists. "What about Russell Adams? We heard he had plenty of reasons to shoot you."

"Russ—*Chaser*? Fuck no. Why would you say that?"

Oh thank God.

"But you said you didn't see the person who shot you," the other detective persists.

"I said I didn't get a *good* look. Never saw the guy before. Fuck, I've seen Chaser every day for the last three months. You think I don't know what he looks like?"

"All right." One of the detectives shifts and Andrew's face comes into view. His eyes widen.

"Mallory!" He waves me into the room with frantic hand gestures. "Get me out of here."

"Uh." My gaze darts around the space, landing on the detectives, the nurse, and finally Andrew. He's bandaged from waist to nipples and a few shades paler than normal, but otherwise intact. "Are you okay?"

"No. Someone shot me."

I bite my lip to stop myself from the completely inappropriate laughter threatening to burst free.

"Did Chaser come with you?" Andrew peers around me. "Where is he?"

"He's in jail." I side-eye the detectives. "They arrested him for shooting you."

"Who are you?" the crankier detective asks.

"Mallory Dove." I nod to the nurse. "She brought me to see Andrew." Why do I suddenly feel the need to explain myself under their scrutiny?

"Oh, shit, Mallory. I'm sorry." Andrew glares at the detectives. "What the fuck are you bugging me for? Go let my friend out of jail, you dickwads."

"We still need information from you, Mr. Lane."

"Well, you're not getting any until you let my friend out." Obstinate as ever, he crosses his arms over his chest, then winces.

"I'm afraid I need everyone to leave," the nurse says, pushing us toward the door.

"Mallory can stay," Andrew protests.

I reach out and touch his arm. "I won't go far, Andrew."

His voice, begging me to stay, follows me down the hallway. Pay phone. Where are they when you need them?

Ah! Waiting room.

"What's going on?" Jacob asks as I race by him.

"Give me a second." I pull Mr. Paxton's card and a handful of quarters from my purse.

"Is Andrew okay?" Alvin asks.

"Andrew is...Andrew," I mutter. "Mr. Paxton, please!" I yelp as soon as his secretary answers the phone. "This is Mallory."

"Mallory?" Mr. Paxton's smooth voice comes over the line a few seconds later. "Is everything all right?"

"Andrew's awake. He told the detectives Chaser didn't do it."

"That was fast," he says. "Let me make some calls. Stay at the hospital. I'll pick you up on my way to the station."

"I'll be right here waiting for you." My voice trembles. "Will we get Chaser out today?"

"I'll do my best."

Honest, but not exactly the most reassuring answer.

Chaser

The loud clock on the wall across from my cell ticks my afternoon away.

Tonight's show is out. Stupid thing to worry about when Andrew's in the hospital. The whole tour is probably toast.

Hell, life as I know it might be over.

"Adams! You're out!" the guard from earlier shouts.

The metal cot squeaks as I sit up. Any glimmer of excitement stays on lockdown until he opens the cell door. Not until he motions me into the corridor without the handcuffs does a ray of hope perk up my spirits.

"Charges were dropped," the officer informs me.

"What happened?"

He shrugs.

I'm led to a small, boxy room with no windows. A less friendly officer shoves a stack of papers at me to sign. Then tosses my wallet, lucky guitar pick, and a few sticks of gum at me. My lawyer shows up as I'm finishing. Nothing like an attorney eager to earn his whole retainer.

"What happened?" I ask since the cops won't tell me a damn thing other than I'm "free to go".

"Your friend woke up. Gave the detectives an earful and demanded your release. Your girl made sure I knew about it right away."

"Where is she?"

"Outside waiting for you."

That's all I need to hear. I collect the rest of my stuff and head out the door with my attorney following.

The thick afternoon heat blasts my skin, a welcome relief after the cold, dark jail. Blinded by the sun, I hear Mallory rushing toward me before I actually make out her features.

"Oh my God." She buries her head against my chest and wraps her arms around me. "I've been so worried..."

"I'm okay." Fuck, it feels good to have her in my arms again.

"Chaser Adams! Did you shoot Andrew Lane?" someone shouts, breaking up our reunion.

Mallory clings tighter to me and I use my body to shield her from the intruder. Except, when I look up, there's more than one reporter descending on us.

"Did you fight over Mallory?" someone else shouts.

"No," I growl.

"All charges have been dropped!" my lawyer shouts back. "Mr. Adams has been exonerated by Andrew Lane himself. That's all we have to say on the matter." He drapes his arm over our shoulders and steers us toward a tan Volvo parked at the curb.

He opens the back door for Mallory before gesturing for me to get in the front seat. I'm so eager to get out of here, I don't question where we're going.

"Your father's taken care of my fees," he assures me as he gets behind the steering wheel. "Actually, I'll have to refund him a portion of the retainer." He stares at the police station. "You got lucky, son."

"Not feeling lucky at the moment, but thank you, sir."

"Counselor is part of my job description, you know."

My body tenses. After the night I've had, I'm really not in the mood for a lecture, no matter how well-intentioned it might be.

"Fire Peter Carson," he says. "He's as disloyal and incompetent as they come."

Can't argue with that. "Done."

"Distance yourself from Jacob." The older man glances over at me. "Everyone says you're talented. Have a promising career ahead of you. Beware of the ones who will drag you down."

I'm too stunned to be annoyed at him for the advice. It's nothing my subconscious hasn't been whispering at me for months. Abandoning the band I've spent so many years helping build doesn't seem right. But the lawyer has a point. I'm perfectly capable of getting myself into plenty of trouble. I don't need my bandmates to keep doing it for me. I've tried everything to help Jacob. But you can't help someone who doesn't want to help themselves. I'm stuck between loyalty to my friends and self-preservation.

"The band is...we've been friends for a long time."

"I understand that. Your loyalty is admirable but is it returned?"

Good question.

If I'm honest with myself, I already know the answer.

The car pulls up in front of the hospital and Paxton curses. "Fucking reporters."

"They weren't here earlier," Mallory says. "Or if they were, I didn't see them."

"Word probably spread that Andrew's awake." Paxton gestures to a road that curves around the side of the building. "There's a back entrance but you'll have to use the service elevator."

"Do you remember where Andrew's room is?" I ask Mallory.

"I think so."

So much for the back entrance. The tight line of shrubbery shakes and wiggles as the car comes to stop. As I study the dancing bushes, a reporter jumps out, camera in hand.

"No comment, Chaser," Paxton reminds me. "Don't give them anything."

"I won't."

"Call me if you need anything. Even if the tour continues and you're in another state, call me. If I can't help, I'll find someone who can."

I lean over to shake his hand. "Thank you. Appreciate everything you've done on such short notice."

"Take care of yourself." He tips his head. "Mallory's quite a woman. Be good to her."

One corner of my mouth curls up. Rock star, biker's son—I can only imagine what the lawyer thinks of how I treat women. "Trust me, I know what a lucky bastard I am."

I glance back at Mallory but she's staring out the window, biting her lip. Doubt she even heard the exchange.

"Good luck," Paxton says as we step out of the car.

19

I curl one arm around Mallory and use the other to block the man dogging us until we're inside the building.

"Don't they have anything better to do?" I grumble once we shake the reporter.

"It's a big story, I guess." Mallory runs her hands through her hair. "Pamela had already heard of it before I did."

"Really?"

"I was on the phone with her when you called me this morning."

"Fuck." This has been the longest damn day. Almost wish we'd gone back to the hotel instead of coming here. "I'm sorry you had to go through all this."

"I'm not the one who spent the night in jail, Chaser." She takes my hand as the elevator comes to a stop. "You know I'll do anything for you."

The door slides open before I have a chance to respond. This isn't a busy, bustling hospital. The hallway's empty and quiet. Mallory scans the corridor, trying to get her bearings. "The waiting room was this way, I think."

Sure enough, we find Alvin and Garrett in an otherwise empty room watching television.

"Oh, thank fuck!" Alvin jumps up as soon as he sees me. "You all right, bro?"

"I'm fine." I take his outstretched hand and allow him to pull me in for a hug and slap on the back.

I scan the room again. "Where's Jacob?"

"Cops took him for questioning." Garrett nods to the hallway. "I don't think they left the hospital, though."

Sure, me they lock up. Jacob will probably get a pat on the head.

"Vinnie's down in Andrew's room, trying to convince him not to leave," Garrett says.

"I'll deal with that in a minute." I raise my voice to get everyone's attention. "First, things, first, Peter's fired. I want him gone."

"Already done," Alvin says. "I called Thom after Mallory left and told him Peter better be on his way back to L.A. by the time you're out of jail."

"Thank you."

"Thom says he'll join us in Louisiana." Garrett shakes his head. "Not sure how that'll be helpful or if we're even going to make those dates."

"Vandals' management canceled tonight's show," Alvin says. "No way Andrew can play tonight. No matter what he seems to think. Next couple shows are up in the air."

"Fuck." I run my fingers through my hair. What a mess. All because Jacob skipped away on a heroin scavenger hunt last night.

Alvin jerks his head toward the hallway, inviting Mallory and me to follow him.

"Seriously, Chaser. You all right?" he asks.

"I'm fine. Glad Andrew's awake. No one would tell me if he was even alive until my lawyer showed up."

"He must have nine lives because somehow that skinny motherfucker's gonna be just fine."

I snort-laugh, which feels good after everything that's gone down.

Alvin has more info for us. "Heard the doctor say it was a peripheral hit that missed his vitals."

Could've fooled me. Thought he was going to bleed to death. "Figures."

Mallory pinches my side and I grin down at her.

"He was asking for you. Was really pissed when he found out you were arrested."

"I'm touched."

Alvin punches my shoulder. "Go see him. I'll be in the waiting room when you're done."

Mallory and I slowly walk down the sterile hallway, trying not to draw attention to ourselves.

"Chaser! Get me out of here!" Andrew begs, frantically waving his right arm at us.

Vinnie's got one hand on Andrew's chest, keeping him pinned to the hospital bed. "Can you talk some sense into him?" Vinnie pleads.

I cock my head. When has Andrew had any sense?

"Worth a shot." Vinnie cracks up.

"Not cool, bro." Andrew crosses his arms over his chest and winces. "Where are my fuckin' painkillers?"

Vinnie shakes his head. "I'll go ask if you promise to sit still."

Andrew raises two fingers and swears.

As soon as Vinnie's gone, Andrew tosses back his covers.

"Oh no you don't." Mallory rushes forward and presses her hands against his shoulders, pushing him back into bed.

Andrew grins at me over her shoulder. "If I'd known a bullet would get Mallory into my bed, I would've let you shoot me a long time ago."

"We can still make that happen."

Mallory lets out a disgusted snort and glares at Andrew. "You really do have a death wish, don't you?"

"I'll chalk it up to blood loss." I step closer and shove him back into the bed.

"Ow. Come on, Chaser. Get me out of here." He casts a suspicious look around the room. "Hospitals are breeding grounds for bacteria. I'm gonna catch something and my arm will rot off. I just know it."

"You're kidding, right? I've seen the filth you live in on your bus."

"Yeah, but that's *my* filth." He wrinkles his nose and scans the room again. "Who knows what's lingering in here."

"Christ." I pinch the bridge of my nose.

"Andrew." The extra patience Mallory forces into her voice draws a chuckle out of me. "You have to stay a little longer. Please."

"I need my arms, Mallory." He flails one in the air to

demonstrate. "I'll be better off at the hotel. I can hire a nurse to look after me." He whistles. "Ooo! Yes! A hot nurse."

"Good grief," Mallory mutters.

"Mr. Lane." An elderly doctor bursts into the room and Andrew recoils against the mattress.

I lean against the wall, crossing my ankles in front of me and Mallory slides up against my side.

"We cannot discharge you, yet." The doctor's stern tone finally seems to break through Andrew's desire to flee, he stops flailing and crosses his arms over his chest like a pouty kid. "You had surgery. This isn't a joke, Mr. Lane."

"Can I at least get some drugs? I'm in a lot of pain."

Andrew needs a chemical knock-out. The doctor flips through his chart and frowns. "I'll have something else brought up."

"What if I go to my hotel and hire a nurse to watch out for me?" Andrew asks. "Can I leave then?"

The doctor stares at him, obviously not used to dealing with annoying patients of this magnitude.

"We can discuss that option tomorrow. Right now, I need you to rest."

He pats Andrew's shoulder and whirls around, rolling his eyes at me on the way out.

"Are you okay?" Andrew asks me. "I'm sorry you got arrested."

"Not the first time. Probably not the last, either."

Mallory frowns at me.

"I knew you were a punk!" Andrew thrusts his fists in the air. "Seriously though, as soon as I found out, I told those dick cops to release you."

"Appreciate it."

"Is Jacob okay?"

"As far as I know."

"That was some fucked up shit, bro."

I hold up my hands. "I don't want to talk about it right now."

23

Andrew's gaze darts toward the open door. "Good call."

Mallory's busy tucking sheets and blankets around Andrew. I can't say I'm thrilled about her fussing over the jackass but I *am* amused that she appears to be trying to turn him into some sort of blanket burrito.

"You're going to stay put and let the doctors take care of you, right, Andrew?" she asks.

"Will you keep me company?"

"No," she answers in the same tone I imagine she'd use with a toddler or puppy. "I need to get Chaser back to the hotel and wash his jail stay off him."

Andrew scans me from head to toe. "You *do* look like shit."

"Back at ya, bro."

The corner of his mouth curls up and his wild eyes refocus on Mallory. "Are you gonna give your man a reunion fuck? Those are the best."

"Who says we didn't already?" Mallory arches a brow and taps her foot.

"I approve." His gaze strays to the phone, mouth hanging down like a damn basset hound. "Have you heard from Pammy?"

"She called this morning," Mallory says. "We couldn't talk long."

Andrew picks up his phone and slams it back down. "No dial tone."

"I'll ask the nurse if they can get it set up for you," Mallory promises.

"I don't want to be in here by myself." Andrew pouts.

"Vinnie's here." I'm actually not sure he stuck around but Andrew's whining is already working my last nerve. "Alvin's here too."

Mallory leans down and kisses Andrew's forehead. "We'll be back in the morning."

"Maybe," I add, wrapping my arm around her waist. "Come on, Nurse Nightingale," I tease in a lighter voice than I'm feeling.

24

"Chaser." Andrew's serious tone stops me.

He reaches out, grabbing my arm and pulling me closer. "Thank you, bro. I think you saved my life last night."

"Nah, doctors said the bullet barely touched you."

He points to his bandages. "This hole in my side says otherwise."

I reach out and slap his cheek. "Good thing you've been slacking on the workouts and had those love handles to catch the bullet."

"Fuck you." He slaps my hand away. "I could bench press your big ass right this second, motherfucker."

Laughing, we bid him good night and head back to the waiting room.

"That was mean." Mallory pokes my side. "He's suffering."

"Not your problem."

She curls an arm around my waist and leans into me. "True. I have all the man I can handle right here."

"That's right."

We stop in the waiting room and thankfully, Vinnie's still here. "You want to go sit with him so he doesn't run out?" I ask. "Doc's supposed to bring him something to shut him up soon."

"Yeah, I'm on it." Vinnie slaps my shoulder. "Thanks for coming down. I wouldn't have blamed you if you'd hopped a flight home."

"I'm here, bro."

Jacob shuffles into the room with his head down and hands in his pockets.

"You all right?" I ask.

He glances up and quickly averts his eyes, muttering, "Glad you're out."

"Surprised you're not locked up," Garrett says.

Jacob shakes his head. "I'm sure they'll be back. Told me not to leave town."

"Fuck that," Alvin says. "As soon as Andrew's cleared, we need to roll out."

"I'll call my lawyer and see what he can do," I offer.

Jacob nods but still won't meet my eyes. I'm too furious to deal with him right now, but Alvin's right, we can't leave our singer stranded here if the tour ever gets back on track.

Finally, Jacob picks up his head. "Are we leaving?"

"No." I point to Mallory, then myself. "*We're* leaving. You stay and keep Andrew company when Vinnie needs a break." I nod at Garrett. "You too."

"Whatever." Garrett waves me off. "We got this."

Alvin eyes the two of them. "I'm gonna stick around too."

"Thanks. We'll be back in the morning."

CHAPTER THREE

Chaser

In the taxi on the way to the hotel, I lean my head on Mallory's shoulder and fiddle with the hem of her T-shirt. "Did you mean what you said about showering with me?"

"I didn't say anything about showering *with* you."

"You promised to wash my jail stay off," I remind her.

"Well." The corners of her mouth twitch. "I saw a garden hose behind the hotel, I can turn it on and point it in your direction."

"Garden hose, huh?" I snicker.

At the hotel, I stop at the front desk and ask for messages. The clerk gives me an odd look. "Sir, you were scheduled to check out today. When no one answered the door or the phone, we had to clean the room. Your belongings are in the back."

"Motherfucker," I growl. "I'm not sleeping on that fucking tour bus tonight." I whip out my wallet. "You got another room?"

"Well, I...yes." He makes the arrangements while I impatiently tap my credit card against the counter.

Once we settle the room situation, I should go have a chat

with our bus driver, call Thom or do something business-oriented but I just don't have a fuck to give about any of it right now.

"You should call your dad," Mallory suggests on the way up to our new suite. "I let him know that you were probably getting out but that was hours ago."

"Let me take that shower first."

"Chaser, he was really worried about you."

"Trust me, he'll understand." I push into the room and set down our bags.

She sighs and follows me into the bathroom.

"What are you doing about work?" I lean into the shower and adjust the water.

Mallory hops up on the edge of the counter and bites her lip. "My flight to L.A. is tomorrow."

"Fuck, I'm sorry this trip got so messed up."

"My flight leaves from Dallas."

"I'll see if I can get it moved or I'll hire a car or something. Don't worry about it."

"I don't want to leave you after this."

I poke my head around the shower curtain. "Babe, there's nothing you can do by sticking around."

"I don't want *you* getting shot next."

"No one's shooting me."

"I'm sure Andrew thought the same thing."

"You're assuming Andrew thinks at all."

She snorts.

"Get in here."

"No pussy until you call your father."

"Who said anything about pussy? I need you to soap my back."

She slides off the counter. "Sure you do." But even as she's arguing with me, she strips her shirt over her head and wiggles out of her jeans.

"Fuck, you're hot." I hold out my hand. "Come here."

The second I get her in the shower with me, I back her up against the tile. "I lied."

"About?"

Instead of answering, I duck down and suck one of her tight nipples into my mouth.

"Oh." She runs her fingers through my hair. "Chaser."

"I'm sorry I made you worry." I latch on to her other breast and slide my hands over her hips.

"I was scared you'd be in jail in Texas for…" Her voice catches and I stop to peer up at her. "I felt helpless. Like when my father was arrested…I know it's not the same but…"

Shit.

"And Peter. That weasel." She squeezes her eyes shut and grits her teeth. "Not being able to trust anyone. I felt so…alone."

"I'm sorry."

"Mr. Paxton helped."

"Yeah, I was impressed with him too."

"I can't believe your dad found him so fast."

"All good criminals have a network of lawyers at their fingertips."

"That's not funny."

I slap off the water. "I wasn't kidding earlier, Mallory. I won't lie to you. You're smart enough to understand the club…my father's business, like *your* father's business takes a lot of *risks*."

"And look where my father ended up."

"He's a smart man. He'll do his time and come out the other side fine."

"Well, that's great for him." She stares at me for several beats. "I need you."

"I'll always make sure you're taken care of. My father and the club will take care of you. No matter what."

"That's nice but it's not the same." Her voice catches. "I need you *with* me."

This was the wrong time and place to initiate this particular conversation. It needs to happen in the future, for sure. But not now. "It doesn't matter. Right now, I'm just a rock star getting into regular rock star trouble."

"Hmm." She yanks a towel off the rack behind us and wraps it around her. "Go call your dad."

I run my gaze over her damp legs. "I wasn't finished with you."

She whips another towel of the rack and whaps me with it. "Call your dad."

Mallory

While Chaser's on the phone with his father, I dry off and slip into a clean T-shirt.

The phone in the other living room seems to be a separate line, so I call my agent.

"Mallory! What have you gotten yourself into?"

"What are you talking about?"

"There are a bunch of reports about your boyfriend shooting someone over a fight about you. What the hell is going on?"

"That's so stupid. Chaser was cleared. None of it had anything to do with me."

She's quiet but I can hear her fidgety nails tapping away at something on the other end of the line. "All right. I'll get someone on it. Squash those stories. We don't want your role on *Shallow End* jeopardized. You know they fancy themselves a family show."

"With the amount of cleavage and bouncing boobs showcased every week, how can anyone say that with a straight face?"

She ignores my critique of the show. "When are you back in town?"

"Tomorrow. I need to be on set for the table read Tuesday."

"Hmmm." I can clearly picture her beating one of her many green and yellow pencils against her scarred desk. "I have an opportunity I want to discuss with you."

"What kind of opportunity?"

"It'll be easier to explain in person. It's lucrative though."

"As long as it's not porn."

"Not porn."

"I'll call you when I get in, Marilyn.

"Just stop by."

"Okay." I hang up without another word and suffer no guilt. She's not usually big on goodbyes anyway.

From the other room, I make out Chaser's deep voice. Still on the phone with his father.

Chaser's on the edge of the bed, murmuring noises of agreement every few seconds. Deep into his conversation with his father, he only nods at me as I crawl into bed behind him. I rest my hands on his shoulders and knead my fingers into his muscles for a few seconds.

Without turning around, he reaches up and pats my hand. I'm probably being more annoying than helpful and I don't want him to cut his call short.

Exhaustion hits me and I stretch out on the bed, keeping my back to his. His rough hand skates up and down my leg. It's a soothing gesture. Between his touch and his low, rumbling voice, I end up falling asleep.

Chaser

"You feel like spending time in jail, I got plenty of stuff you can do for the club." My father's gruff voice can't hide his concern.

"Trust me, it wasn't how I planned to spend my night."

"Mallory okay? She was pretty freaked out when she called but she handled it well."

"She's fine. I'm so fucking pissed. She has to fly back to L.A. tomorrow. Not how I wanted our visit to go."

"I'm sure," he answers in a dry tone. "Jesus Christ, the story

31

was all over MTV. Half the girls were in the clubhouse crying their eyes out."

"For fuck's sake. The band needs the publicity but not like that."

"Who is this stupid son of a bitch?"

"Jacob's our singer."

"No, the other one."

"Andrew's the drummer for the headlining band."

"Does he have something going on with Mallory?" he asks in a sharp tone I don't care for.

"No. Fuck no." Guess the love triangle theory my lawyer warned me about reached my father's insulated bubble of indifference to pop culture.

"Just what the news guy said."

"It's bullshit." Is it though? Andrew's always been way too interested in Mallory for my taste. Then again, I pretty much want to murder any man who looks at her for more than two seconds. Still, I can't deny his interest in her is more than his usual disgusting admiration of the general female population. None of that matters since I'm not the one who shot Andrew. And we haven't fought over Mallory. Not yet, anyway.

By the time we end our call, Mallory's softly snoring behind me. I toss my towel on the chair in the corner and shift Mallory into the center of the big king bed, then crawl in next to her.

"How's your dad?" she murmurs.

I pull her into my arms and kiss her temple. "He's fine."

"Are you—"

"Shh, go back to sleep. I wanna cuddle with you."

Sleepy laughter. "Cuddle, huh?"

The last twenty-four hours punch me in the face as soon as I settle down next to her and close my eyes.

Mallory

The air conditioning clicks on and a cool breeze tickles over my shoulder.

I blink my eyes open and stare into the shadowy room. *Hotel room*.

Everything rushes back and I flip over, seeking Chaser. Scared getting him out of jail was just a dream.

But he's safe. Sound asleep. On his back. One arm flung to the side, the other resting on his chest.

My gaze travels lower.

No wonder I was cold.

The sheet's functioning as a tent instead of a cover.

Reaching over, I wrap my fingers around Chaser's erection, quickly glancing up to see if he's awake. His chest continues to rise and fall.

Two different impulses strike me. To softly stroke and run my tongue along his length. Or to straddle his hips and lower myself onto his waiting cock.

Taste wins. I drag my tongue down his shaft, from crown to base and back before closing my mouth over the tip.

He awakens with a gasp and groan. The rough pad of his thumb strokes my cheek, encouraging me to run my hand up and down before taking him as deep as possible.

"Ohhh, fuck. This is the best way to wake up." He lifts his hips and his head falls back against the pillow.

His cock hits the back of my throat and he groans. "Fuck, yeah. Like that."

I run my hands over his thighs, lightly scratching my nails against his skin and he shivers.

"Baby, come here," he urges. "I want to come in your snug little pussy."

I release him with a pop of my lips but continue stroking my hand up and down his length. "I know for a fact you're capable of doing both."

"I need to be buried inside you." He curls his fingers around mine and urges me up.

I lift my hips, positioning him and sink down, taking him inch by inch. He gives me a few seconds to adjust before curling his big hands around my waist. I wrap my fingers around his arms, leaning in and working him in and out. Hitting the perfect spot. My legs tremble. Tension builds inside me, ready to snap.

"That's it," he encourages.

"Oh," I gasp. "I'm—"

He lifts his hips. "Yeah, you are."

Pleasure fires through me and I dig my fingers into his arms.

He takes over, rocking my hips back and forth, helping me ride it out. "That's my girl," he whispers, dragging me down for a kiss.

When I finally open my eyes, he flashes a wicked grin. "My turn."

Holding me tight, he rolls us, raising himself on one arm. "Can you take more?"

"Anything you want to give me."

"Careful, little dove. What if it's everything?"

I wiggle my hips in desperation. "All of you. Please."

"What's your hurry? Got somewhere to be?"

Even as he teases me with playful words, he slides his hand under my ass, tilting me for a better angle to meet each slow, tortuous thrust.

Stroke after stroke, he steals my breath and words. Sweet pressure builds inside me again. Long and slow until I'm afraid I'll burst into flames.

Another thrust and pleasure rushes through every nerve ending.

"That's it," he whispers, watching but never slowing his hips. Panting and slick with sweat, he curses and empties himself inside me.

In awe of how I have the power to leave this strong, beautiful man weak and trembling, I can't stop touching him everywhere. Running my hands up and down his back, through his hair, down his arms.

34

Finally, he rolls to the side, pulling me with him. "Thank you for such an amazing wakeup."

I press kisses to his sweaty chest and nuzzle against his chin. One thought keeps repeating in my mind. I don't want to leave him.

OCT 18 3 1998

CHAPTER FOUR

Mallory

"I hate that I'm always leaving you." I curl my fingers into Chaser's jacket, trying to dislodge the awful feelings tearing me apart as I'm about to board my plane back to L.A.

He presses his lips to my forehead and inhales deeply. "I do too."

I pull away and slowly lift my gaze to his. "Tell me we'll get through this. I want...I like being on the show. It's why I came Hollywood." I wouldn't be able to admit this next part if he didn't look as broken as I feel. "But I want *you* more."

"Mallory." He brushes my hair off my cheek. "I've wanted this, where the band's headed, since I was twelve."

I swallow hard, willing my chin not to tremble.

"But I want you more too."

"What do we do?"

"I don't know, little dove."

"I want this *for* you too. I'm so proud of you, Chaser. I'm not trying to say I want you back in L.A. just to...I don't know..."

His mouth curls into a gentle smile. "Be your bodyguard?"

"Maybe."

"I want your success too, you know. Every week when I see you on television..." he pats his chest, "...I'm so fucking proud of you."

Still, I can't let go.

"You're coming to the New York show," he reminds me. "We'll have some time off to spend together after that."

"I'm worried about you too," I admit. This latest episode has done nothing to alleviate my existing fears.

"I'll be fine. This might have been the wake-up call the guys needed."

My mouth twists down but I don't want to contradict Chaser's optimism. He knows his band better than I do. Maybe Jacob's near-death experience will be the cure for his addictions.

Time ticks down way too fast. I squeeze my eyes shut and kiss Chaser one last time before boarding the plane.

The flight seems to take forever. I try to sleep but every time I wake we're still in the air.

Finally, the pilot announces we're touching down in Los Angeles.

My car's where I left it mere days ago. The thought of going to our empty home hurts too much, so I drive to Marilyn's office instead.

"Mallory!" She stands to greet me. "Funny you showed up now. I was just on the phone talking about you."

"I hope that's good news?"

"Yes, yes. I have a PR lady on the story about you and Chaser. That's a non-issue. I saw Andrew made a public statement."

I nod politely but I hadn't been that concerned about bad publicity from the incident. "Did you have something else you wanted to tell me about?"

"Yes!" She slaps her desk and grabs a folder. "How do you feel about Jazzercise?"

"What?"

"You as the star of your own celebrity fitness video."

Confusion leaves me shaking my head. "Celebrity fitness? *Me*? Why?"

"You're young, pretty, in good shape, and it's lucrative."

"But I don't know anything about fitness videos."

"Then it'll be like any other acting job." She waves her hand at me. "With some choreography thrown in."

"When?"

"They'll work it around your *Shallow End* schedule. A couple days to get the choreography down and two days max to film the whole thing."

"This is legit?"

She leans over, opens a drawer, and tosses a few VHS tapes on the desk, one-by-one. "Jane Fonda, Raquel Welch, Olivia Newton-John, Alyssa Milano—all legit actresses who have fitness videos. It's an honor to be asked, Mallory. Another revenue stream."

Nightmares of bopping around in bright-colored spandex, striped leggings, layers of colorful socks, and terrycloth headbands assault my brain. "Okay," I answer slowly. "If you think it's a good idea, I'll consider it."

By the way she works her jaw from side-to-side, she must have expected me to immediately accept the job with effusive gratitude. But it seems like such a strange job I want to talk to someone else about it before I agree.

It's probably not a good sign that I don't trust my agent's advice.

"This could be very lucrative, Mallory. The *Jane Fonda Workout* alone has sold almost a million copies."

"I said I'll think about it."

"We want to do it soon. Capitalize off your Video Vixen win."

Ah, the 'Candy Jar' video just keeps on giving.

As I leave her office, I consider who the heck to ask for advice. Pamela? No, she'd probably make fun of me, then try to steal the offer behind my back. Vickie? I haven't spoken to her in weeks, plus, I don't think she'd have any useful advice. Audrey's off in Paris and unless there's some emergency with the house, I don't want to bother her.

Really, there's only one person I want to talk to about this. Unfortunately, he's halfway across the country.

Feeling sorry for myself, I stop at the grocery store for a few items. As I'm standing in the check-out line, a copy of *Star Reports* with a rather unflattering photo of Chaser and me on the cover catches my eye. I flip it open to the "inside scoop" about the torrid "love triangle" I supposedly have going on with Chaser and Andrew. The photo of the three of us from the night of the Small Screen Music Awards, ripped in half with a bloody gun in the middle caps it all off nicely.

"For God's sake," I mutter, reading the completely fabricated bullshit. A lone photo of a forlorn Pamela tucked in the corner has me rolling my eyes.

"Do you think she forced Andrew to say Chaser didn't do it?" someone asks.

I glance up, frowning at the stranger. "Chaser *didn't* do it," I snap, tossing the magazine on top of the rack.

The woman's eyes widen with recognition and she slowly backs away.

As if anyone could *force* Andrew to do a damn thing.

Still furious when I finally arrive home, I unpack the groceries quickly. A copy of tomorrow's script is waiting for me in the mailbox and that gives me some comfort. I sit at the dining room table and flip through it, highlighting a few key lines and jotting down notes in the margins.

Around nine, the phone rings pulling me out of my reading. My stomach rumbles. I never ate dinner.

"Hello?"

"You get home, okay?" Chaser's voice warms the emptiness that settled in me the second I left him.

"Yup, I was just going through the script for tomorrow."

"This might be the only chance I'll have to call for a few hours."

"What's going on?"

"Andrew checked himself out of the hospital. He's determined not to cancel another show, so we're rolling out tonight and headed to Lafayette."

"Oh my God. Is he okay?"

He takes a few seconds to answer. "He's settled down since you saw him. Almost subdued. It's kinda weird, honestly."

"Don't get used to it. I'm sure it won't last."

"That's what I'm afraid of."

"What about Jacob? Was he able to leave?"

"Paxton said unless they want to charge Jacob with something, it's on them to come find him. Not like they can't figure out where we are."

I bite my lip. "I don't want you in any more trouble."

"I'm fine. Free to go." He lowers his voice. "What's going on with *you*? Did you meet with Marilyn?"

"I did."

"And?"

"I need your advice."

His rich laughter soothes my inner turmoil. "I'll do my best, little dove."

"She wants me to star in an exercise video." As the words come out of my mouth, I cringe. It sounds so silly.

"Like Raquel Welch?" he asks.

"That's one of the examples she gave me." I squint at the wall. "You came up with her name awfully fast. Why do you even know that?"

He chuckles. "Obviously, you were never a teenage boy."

"Gross," I mutter. "Oh! *Eww*. What if I end up being spank material for horny teenage boys across the country?"

He laughs even harder. "I think you've already achieved that status, 'Candy Jar' girl."

"It's not funny."

His laughter cuts off. "Did she say why?"

"To capitalize off the Video Vixen award. She says it could be another lucrative revenue stream if it does well."

"They want *you* specifically? This isn't an audition situation?"

"No, they want me."

"That's interesting." A soft humming sound comes through the phone and I have a vivid image of Chaser running his hand over his jaw while he thinks through the situation. "It's not a bad idea to have another asset out there making money for you. Are they offering you a one-time fee or royalties?"

That's something I hadn't thought of asking. "I'm not sure. Chaser, the bigger problem is, I don't know anything about choreographed sweating in front of a camera. I've been to like two step-aerobics classes in my life and all I learned is that I'm painfully uncoordinated."

He lets out a groan. "I bet you look hot in a leotard."

"Not the point."

"Mallory, you can do anything you set your mind to. I believe that with all my heart."

"Thank you."

"I don't think it hurts to find out more. Meet with the production company."

"I'll have to take dance or choreography lessons."

"You'll nail it. I have no doubt." He's quiet for a few seconds. "If you don't trust Marilyn, maybe it's time for you to find a new agent," he suggests, echoing my thoughts from earlier today.

"I trust her to find jobs for me. She's well-connected that way but she's almost too eager to have me accept anything that lands on her desk."

"That's not necessarily a bad thing. She wants her clients earning money." He pauses. "You might need a lawyer to look over these kinds of contracts, though. Someone to negotiate royalties and stuff. That really helped us out when we signed our first record deal."

A lawyer hadn't occurred to me yet. Most days, I still feel like an impostor in this business. Like a child prancing around in her mother's high heels and makeup. Not a professional who hires other professionals. "I'll ask around."

"Did you ask Pamela about the job? Has she ever been offered something like it? Would she do it if she had the opportunity?"

"I wanted to talk to you first. Besides, I don't trust her. She'll probably make fun of me."

"She better not," he growls. "Have you at least told her you're home?"

"Not yet. But we have a big scene together this week so I might hang out with her tomorrow to work on it after the table read."

I don't bother telling him about the tabloid. It'll only piss him off and there isn't much we can do about it anyway.

"Shit. Hang on." There's a muffled noise as if he's holding his hand over the receiver for a few seconds before he returns. "Dinner break's over. I gotta go."

"You didn't eat dinner?"

"I wanted to talk to you more. I'll grab something for the bus."

"I miss you."

"Miss you too, little dove."

My throat burns from holding back the emotions bubbling up as we say goodbye.

CHAPTER FIVE

Chaser

Talking Andrew out of tonight's show was a pointless effort. He's worried about disappointing the fans. I seem to be the only one concerned it's too soon. Everyone else is eager to get moving and making money again.

Unfortunately, tonight the fans aren't as eager to see Kickstart as they have been at every other show on this tour. When our crew lowers the banner with our name and logo, loud booing ripples through the crowd.

Bottles and garbage fly onstage, nearly missing the roadies hurrying to set up our equipment.

"What the fuck?" Jacob says, watching from the side of the stage. "What's Louisiana got against us?"

"Motherfucker," Alvin grumbles, glaring at Jacob.

"Guessing they still think I shot Andrew." Amazing I have to point out the obvious to Jacob. To say I'm still grouchy over the whole incident doesn't begin to cover our situation.

"Who kicked your puppies?" Andrew asks, slowly joining our unhappy gathering.

"Shouldn't you be resting until you go on stage?" I ask.

He dismisses my concern with a flick of his wrist and I flip him off in return. *Asshole*.

"What's going on?" Andrew peeks out at the crowd.

Alvin and I stare at each other, neither of us wanting to state the problem. Jacob wanders back to our dressing room. The whole situation's awkward as fuck.

Darren's grim as he approaches with my guitar to set me up for our show. "Rough crowd tonight," he mumbles.

"Yeah."

Ever the professional, Alvin marches out to his drum kit first. Instead of his usual excitement, his head's down, as if he's approaching a firing squad.

Since I'm not guilty of a damn thing and I've always been a defiant motherfucker, I stomp out on stage chin up, staring straight out into the crowd.

A beer bottle sails through the air, slamming into my thigh. It hits the stage with a loud *clink* but thankfully doesn't shatter.

"Motherfucker!" I shout, kicking it off the stage. Probably not the smartest move.

"Watch it!" one of the security guards yells at me.

"Watch the fucking crowd, asshole!" I shout back.

"Who's ready to rock out with my favorite band!?" Andrew screams into one of the mics.

I turn and find him storming our stage, coming straight for me. Before I can properly brace myself, he hooks an arm around my neck and hugs me to his side. "This badass motherfucker right here saved my fucking life!"

The crowd does this strange gasp-cheer thing.

"That's right," he continues. "Which one of you rowdy motherfuckers can scream 'thank you, Chaser' the loudest?"

The building shakes with the roar of a couple thousand fans yelling their gratitude.

Embarrassed as fuck, but relieved Andrew probably saved us from one hell of a shitty show, I tip my head and raise a hand to acknowledge their cheers.

"Woooo!" Andrew shouts, pumping his fist in the air.

"Andrew! I love you!" a girl screams.

"Show me your tits!" he shouts back.

He slaps my back a few times and runs off stage.

No more beer bottles are thrown at us. I glance back at Alvin. At least the *going to the morgue* look has been wiped off his face. He shrugs and pounds his bass drum a few times. His signal to Garrett and Jacob to get their asses out here.

Garrett strolls out, waving to the crowd. He throws me a wide-eyed *what the fuck* face.

Jacob runs on stage screaming into his mic. We launch into a rambunctious version of "Hammer to the Heart."

The rest of our show is tight. The audience probably can't tell but we're tense. Rattled by the earlier jeers. Jacob keeps his banter to a minimum. My guitar solo's short and perfunctory. Call me a moody creative, but I'm not feeling it tonight.

At least by the end of our set, we've won over the crowd. We take a bow and wave. Chants of "Kickstart, Kickstart, Kickstart" follow us off the stage.

Andrew's sitting on a metal folding chair off to the side. First time I haven't seen him jumping around or running up and down the hallways before his set. I hold out my hand and he grabs it, pulling me down for a hug.

"Thanks for doing that," I say, slapping his back.

"I feel so fucking shitty about all this," he says against my ear. "I'll make it right. Every night if I have to."

"Not your fault reporters have nothing better to do." I can't believe I'm trying to make him feel better about the situation.

Jacob backs away as if he has no culpability in any of this fuckery.

"You ready to go on?" Alvin asks, slapping Andrew's shoulder a lot more gently then he would've a week ago.

Andrew hesitates, glancing at the stage and then back at Alvin. "Yeah. Would you mind sticking around? If I can't finish, do you think you could take over for me?"

The request sends Alvin into a state of shock where he can't come up with a coherent answer.

Andrew seems to misread the situation. "I'll get you paid—"

"It's not that." I slap Alvin's back to knock him out of his panic trance.

"No, I mean, yes. I can do it," Alvin answers quickly. "I pretty much have your whole set list memorized."

"Thanks." Andrew blows out a breath. "Huge relief. I should've asked you sooner so you could've practiced...never mind." He glances down the hallway to where Kyle and Boner are waiting to go on stage. "They wouldn't have showed up for a practice anyway."

"I got you." Alvin straightens up and adopts a more reassuring tone. "But I'm sure you'll be fine."

"Thanks, bro."

Vinnie joins us and Andrew explains his contingency plan.

"Cool. Thanks, Alvin." He roughs his hand over Andrew's head. "You'll be stellar, lil' rock star."

I slap Alvin's shoulder and lean in. "You've got this."

He nods at me.

"I'll be back," I promise. No way will I let Alvin freak out all alone while he waits to see if he gets called to stand in for one of his idols.

I stop in our dressing room and find Jacob with a mug of tea and jar of honey. "You all right?"

He turns and shrugs, then points to his throat. I take in his appearance. Sweaty and shakier than normal after a show. I suspect his condition has more to do with heroin withdrawal than vocal issues.

"Need anything?"

He points to his arm and mimes shooting up.

"Not happening," I growl.

I get a shrug and a nod in response, which isn't all that reassuring. He must sense my mistrust because he holds his hand out. "I'm okay," he rasps. "I'm not going anywhere. Promise."

"Good, because Alvin might need to fill in for Andrew tonight. He needs our support."

"Give me a few." He gestures to the tea.

The bathroom door swings open and Garrett strolls out, a half-dressed blonde following behind him. He smirks at me and I lift my chin.

"Hey, Chaser," the girl coos.

"Hey." I turn back to Jacob. "Fill him in?"

Jacob starts some complicated sign language type gestures that seem to equate to "our drummer is filling in for their drummer." Satisfied the two of them won't leave the arena, I return to Alvin.

"You all right?" I ask.

He leans in close. "I'm freaked the fuck out."

"Knowing Andrew, he'll want to finish the whole show. But it'll make him feel better if he knows someone can take over."

"It's the least we can do after...everything."

"None of that shit's on you and me, brother."

He cocks his head. "Isn't it?"

"How do you figure?"

Before answering, he does a quick scan of the surrounding area. While it's crowded, no one's paying attention to us. "We have to keep a closer watch over Jacob. If he looks like he's about to fall, we need to catch him."

"How's that work long-term?" I'm not trying to be a dick. I genuinely want to understand Alvin's thought process. "We can't help someone who doesn't want our help."

"I think we should get him to see a doctor about his throat. Maybe hire a vocal coach to go on the road with us."

Why hadn't that occurred to me? Kyle doesn't have one but we've played with other bands who kept a vocal coach around. While we're not rolling in money, yet, we're certainly making enough to cover that expense if it means we preserve Jacob's voice.

"Let's talk to Thom about it before we approach Jacob," I suggest.

He holds out his fist and we tap knuckles. "Deal," he agrees.

At least it finally feels like we have a plan.

Mallory

"How was the show?" I ask Chaser as soon as he calls.

"Fucking horrible at first."

He gives me a rundown of the rocky beginning and how Andrew saved the night.

"Is he going to have to do that every night?"

"Probably. At least until word spreads and people stop believing the stupid gossip."

"I didn't want to say anything but, yeah, half the tabloids here are running a story about our torrid love triangle."

"Fuck," he mutters. "I'm so sorry."

"It's not your fault. It's no one's, really."

"Well, that's not exactly true."

"How is Jacob?"

"Off the junk for now. Seems like this incident scared him straight but I don't know..." He trails off and pain wraps around my chest. I wish I could be there for him.

So, I tell him exactly that.

"Hearing your voice helps. I miss you," he rasps.

"I miss you too."

He groans and I can almost picture him stretching out on his bed. "I can't stop thinking about waking up with your mouth around my cock."

My breath hitches. "Really?"

"Fuck yeah."

"I can't wait to do that again," I whisper.

"You'll get your chance soon enough."

CHAPTER SIX

Mallory

It's been a busy couple of weeks—busting some moves for the strange Jazzercise video, a handful of random auditions, and filming the increasingly weird *Shallow End* storylines. I am *so* ready for some alone time with Chaser.

"Let's go!" Pamela yells.

"I'm ready!" I rush out of the dressing room, almost knocking her over.

"We're going to miss our flight."

Somehow, my flight to New York to meet up with Chaser ended up being a girls' trip with Pamela. I guess she'd been planning to visit Andrew for the final show all along. No one told me we'd have to fly out together.

All my luggage is already in her car so we can go straight to the airport when we're done filming for the day.

"I'm so excited!" Pamela squeals as we hit the freeway. "I haven't been to New York since I was a little girl."

"You must be excited to see Andrew too."

She lifts one shoulder. "Sure. It's always weird after he's been on tour for a while, though. You know?"

I can only imagine. I wonder if she packed a can of Lysol to spray over his nether regions.

A thousand times, I wanted to tell Pamela what I'd witnessed on my last visit—Andrew nailing groupies backstage by the bucketload. But his warning that Pamela already knew but didn't want to be confronted with the information kept my mouth shut. Things are tense enough when we work together. Half the time I get the feeling she doesn't even like me. Telling her about Andrew's unfaithfulness won't improve our relationship. At least that's the excuse I keep giving myself for being a coward.

I'm almost tempted to give her the advice I was once given—make him wear a rubber—but I doubt that will be appreciated either.

Instead, we talk about the episode we just finished filming.

"I'm so happy we're on break. Landon keeps asking to suck my tits between takes." She pulls a gagging face. "I want to knee him in the balls every time I see him."

"*Eww*. He's old enough to be your grandfather." Thank God I rarely have any scenes with him.

"I know."

"Have you complained to anyone about it?"

"No way. You know who will get kicked off the show if I make waves."

"That's ridiculous." But even as I voice the complaint, I know she's right.

"That's Hollywood. Hell, that's everywhere." She parks the car and turns to me. "You're not a nervous flyer, are you?"

"Not yet."

"Good."

We unload our bags together. She huffs at my luggage. "How long are you staying in New York?"

"At least a week. We're going to visit his family." My mouth turns up. I'm actually looking forward to seeing Stump. I think I miss him more than my own father.

"You're from New York too, right?"

I nod, uncomfortable talking about my origins. "We'll probably visit my dad too while we're here." As much as I don't relish another prison visit, I can't be so close and not see my father.

Thankfully, she doesn't pry for more information.

CHAPTER SEVEN

Chaser

My need to see Mallory is a fever creeping over my skin. I'm irritable all day waiting for her, bummed she won't get in until late tonight.

I'm even more annoyed that I agreed to wait to go to the airport so Andrew and I could pick up the girls together.

When Andrew's finished with his set, he lopes off the stage, high-fiving everyone he passes. He takes his sweet ass time. When he finally makes it over to me, I'm ready to snap.

"We need to get going," I remind him, taking a step back as his sweaty stench clogs my nostrils. "You plannin' to take a shower?"

"Nope. Pheromones. Pamela digs it."

"I don't think that's the same...you know what, never mind. Let's go."

He stops at his dressing room door. "Give me two minutes." He holds up two fingers and shoves them in my face in case I can't count that high. "Stashed a little hottie in here for a post-performance BJ."

"Are you fucking kidding me?"

He disappears inside the room and I stare at the door. Am I really waiting for this asshole to get a blowjob from some random chick, while his girlfriend is waiting for him at the airport? And worse, delaying getting my hands on my own girl?

"Motherfucker." I slam my fist against the door and stalk away.

Jacob walks over and slaps my shoulder. "When Pamela breaks up with him, make sure you send her my way."

Next to him, Garrett chuckles. "What? You think she's gonna sniff his dick or somethin'?"

I spear my fingers through my hair. What was I thinking, agreeing to go with Andrew?

Fifteen minutes later—not the two he promised—he bounds out of his dressing room, sweater and more disgusting looking than before—if that's possible. "The fuck is wrong with you?" I snap.

He gives me that wide-eyed innocent puppy face that makes me want to punch him every single time. "What?"

"We're going to be late."

"Nah. We've got plenty of time." He turns and strides down the hallway to the closest door, his bodyguard, Benny following. "Let's go." Andrew waves his hand over his shoulder.

I have to jog to catch up with him. Sure, *now* he's eager to go. In the parking lot, he stops at a shiny, black stretch limo.

"What's this?" I frown at the fancy ride. "I thought we were borrowing one of the roadies' cars?"

"Nah, fuck that. That's no way to pick up your lady. You need to do it in style. Romance her."

"It'd probably be more romantic to pick up your lady without another woman's saliva on your dick," I point out.

"Don't be smug, Chaser." He wags his finger in my face. "Rock stars are supposed to *fuck*. You're an abomination to our species."

Maybe that's so. I'm okay with it.

The driver holds the door open and we climb in. Inside is all slick, shiny black leather seats, a bucket of champagne, and bouquets of big, fat pink roses.

None of those things occurred to me.

Not that I think Mallory cares about that stuff. And, given the choice between the guy who appointed himself the captain of team *fuck as many groupies as possible* or the faithful one who shows up empty-handed, I'm ninety-nine percent sure most women would pick the flower-less dude.

"What's all this?" I sweep my hand toward the flowers and champagne. "An 'I'm sorry I fucked every groupie who flashed her tits at me' apology package?"

"You gotta give the girl you're fucking on the regular *pink* roses. It's like a rule or something." He plucks one of the tacky bouquets out of its equally tacky vase and wags it at me, spraying droplets of water all over. "You can give one to Mallory if you want."

"No thanks." I shove the flowers away. No way would I give Mallory sloppy-seconds roses from *Andrew* of all people.

"You ever think of doing something outside of Kickstart?" Andrew jams the flowers back into their vase. "Like, totally different?"

"Sometimes. You?"

"Fuck yeah. I'd love to do something like, funky or rap infused. Just crazy, bonkers sounds. Something inspired the suits can't slap a label on. Sounds no one would ever expect from Vicious Vandals' drummer."

I don't have the luxury of money to pay for a project no one will know how to sell and haven't earned enough clout with the label to get them to fund a vanity project yet but it's a cool concept. "I grew up listening to a lot of the old outlaw country artists—Waylon Jennings, Johnny Cash—"

"Oh, fuck yeah! Cash is the man." Andrew punches his fist in the air, actually hitting the roof of the car. "Ow, dammit."

"Easy, cowboy."

"Aw man, those roadhouse blues... You could rock the fuck out of that, Chaser. It'd be totally rad."

I shouldn't be surprised Andrew's so open to adding a little country music to his fusion project. If I even mentioned it to Garrett or Jacob, they'd roll their eyes and turn their noses up. They're strictly rock-n-roll. Andrew appreciates every form of musical expression.

"One day." It's too hard to consider working on anything else at the moment. Especially when we're headed to the studio to record our next album after the tour. "I like where the band is headed right now."

"Yeah? You write anything good while you've been on the road? You sure fucking hide in your room enough."

"I've got a lot of material."

"Fucking awesome! You're gonna have the best time working with Cutter." He leans over and slaps my leg a couple dozen times. "So stoked for you guys."

"Thanks."

"We should do it, though."

"Do what?"

He waves his hands in front of him, avoiding the roof this time. "The rock-country-rap-jazz fusion. It will blow everyone's minds. Like get a whole bunch of different artists to collaborate with us. Maybe get a chick singer. No one would expect that from *me*." He giggles like a little kid.

Since it's totally bonkers and I don't see it happening anytime soon, I indulge him in his little musical fantasy. "It could be fun."

"You know who'd be totally off the wall? If we could get Crystal Gale to sing for us. Uh." He squeezes his eyes shut and thrusts his fists in front of his face. "I just want to wrap my hands in her fucking hair and—"

"Calm down." I cock my head. "Is there a woman you don't want to fuck?"

He shrugs and opens his mouth but I cut him off. "Never mind. Don't answer that."

"Don't worry. Pammy will keep me occupied. She's a freaky nympho when she hasn't ridden the D in a while."

"Charming," I mutter. "What makes you so sure she's not doing the same thing you are when you're on the road?"

"Fuck." The goofy grin falls off his face for a second. "Serve me right, I guess." He leans forward. "Why? Did Mallory tell you something?"

"No. Believe it or not, we don't spend a lot of time talking about your love life."

"You're on the phone with her for fuckin' hours every damn night." He actually seems offended. "Mallory never asks about me?"

"Yeah, she asks if your bullet wound has healed and if you're staying out of trouble."

"And what do you tell her?"

"That you're like the fuckin' Tasmanian Devil."

"Fuck yeah!" He claps his hands. "If I ever patch into a club, that'll be my road name."

Any club I've ever known would probably shoot Andrew before his crazy ass ever got near a patch. "You can't pick your own road name."

"Why not?"

"Your brothers have to give it to you. Sometimes, it's meant to be more of an insult than a compliment."

"Hah!" He points a finger at me and slaps his hands together. "You just said it. Done! You're my bro. Now you gotta call me Taz."

"Jesus." Why aren't we at the fucking airport yet?

"Nope, you gotta call me Taz."

The car glides to a stop at the curb and I don't even bother waiting for the guy to open the door. *Get me the fuck outta here.* Maybe Mallory and I can ditch the psycho limo and find a cab back to the hotel.

"Chaser!" Mallory's voice stands out to me above all the other noise.

Like a missile seeking the heat of my better half, I scan the area. It's dark and there's a crowd of people waiting to get picked up. The second our eyes lock, I'm shoving people out of my way. It still takes too long to get my hands on her.

No time for mundane greetings. Nope. I wrap her in my arms, lift her up and press my lips to hers. She clings to me, parting her lips, kissing me back with the same urgency. My tongue searches her mouth, stroking against hers, the insides of her cheeks, her teeth, exploring every bit of her. I want to breathe her in, consume her, until we're one and can never be apart again.

"Chaser," she gasps and pulls away.

"I'm not done," I murmur, dragging her closer.

I'll never be done with her.

CHAPTER EIGHT

Mallory

The strange vibe in the limo makes it hard to do what I really want to do—concentrate on Chaser.

Andrew and Pamela take up the entire back seat, kissing and licking each other. I swear if either of them gets naked, I'm tucking and rolling right out the door.

Chaser seems to sense my discomfort and pulls me into his side, kissing the top of my head. "How was your flight?"

"I thought it would never end."

He squeezes me tighter. "So glad you're here, little dove."

"Me too." I tip my head back to take him in, so happy to be in his arms after all this time. "You're all mine for the next few weeks."

He leans down and gently nips my earlobe. "I'm all yours forever."

My heart skips.

Is it crazy that we haven't been together that long but I feel the same way?

Pamela squeals and I shut my eyes. Chaser's laughter rumbles against my ear.

"I didn't even notice." Her shrill voice seems louder than usual in the confines of the limo. "How pretty. Ooo, smell them, Mallory."

A bunch of pink roses are shoved under my nose and I try not to gag. "Very pretty." I nod and do the obligatory sniff.

"Oh!" There's more squealing and a few seconds later, she waves a diamond tennis bracelet around.

Chaser leans down and whispers in my ear, "He could give her five of those and there still wouldn't be a diamond for every groupie—"

I press my finger against his lips. "Shh."

He sucks my finger into his mouth while staring into my eyes —a hundred promises of what's to come later. I lean up and brush my lips against his bristly cheek. "I have better uses for your tongue tonight, Chaser."

He groans. "I need you so bad, I'm seriously considering letting them watch."

My gaze skitters past Chaser. Pamela's busy mauling Andrew's face but his eyes are open, watching *us*. I quickly look away. "Not happening," I whisper to Chaser.

He's too focused on kissing the back of my hand to notice my shift in mood. How far is the hotel? This ride seems to be taking forever.

"Hey, Mallory," Andrew pushes Pamela away, "Chaser and I were talking about doing a country-funk-rock side project. What do you think?"

"A what?" I frown up at Chaser.

He rolls his eyes before turning to face Andrew. "We tossed some ideas around."

"That sounds lame." Pamela wrinkles her nose and slaps her hand over Andrew's face, pushing him away from her. "He's full of stupid ideas, Chaser. Don't let him distract you."

Something about her easy dismissal instantly makes me want to encourage them—even though I have no idea what a country-funk-rock whatever would sound like.

Andrew shakes off Pamela's hand. "You're not a musical person. Of course you don't get it."

"Neither is Mallory," she points out.

"Not true." Chaser brushes his knuckles over my cheek briefly. "Mal has a killer voice. Just doesn't let anyone hear it."

Heat spreads over my cheeks. "You're exaggerating. Once. You heard me sing a couple lines one time."

"I know what I heard," he insists.

Andrew's wearing a devious smirk and I brace myself for whatever absurdities are about to fly out of his mouth. Pamela must sense it too because she elbows him in the gut. A few seconds later, they're busy wrestling each other to the floor of the car.

The limo glides to a stop.

"Oh thank God," I mutter.

Chaser laughs at my obvious relief. "That's exactly how I felt on our way to the airport."

Carefully, we step around the still-wrestling couple and exit the limo. Chaser helps the driver grab my bags.

"Should we wait for them?" I ask, glancing back at the car.

"Hell no." Chaser's horrified expression pulls a laugh from me. "Let's escape while they're distracted."

He hustles us into the hotel without glancing back. Being on the road with Andrew for months would be exhausting for anyone. Sort of how I could use a break from seeing Pamela every day.

We're waiting for our elevator when high-pitched female shrieks draw our attention back to the lobby.

Please no.

"You son of a bitch!"

That's definitely Pamela.

The few people hanging out in the lobby this time of night, turn to stare. We're too far away to see the action but it must be quite a show.

"Pamela, wait! It's not what you think. Ow! Fuck!"

Chaser jabs the button for the elevator a couple dozen more times.

"Oh no," I mutter. "What happened?"

"I don't want to guess." He peers around me. "Do you see a door for the staircase?"

"We can't run away from them if something's wrong."

"Yes, we can."

The elevator door slides open and Chaser rushes us inside, stabbing the button for our floor over and over.

"Wait!" someone yells.

I lean over and press the "open door" button.

"So close," Chaser sighs.

I dig my elbow into his ribs.

Pamela jiggles over, all her perfectly applied makeup now nothing more than smeared-lips and a racoon-eyes.

"Pamela! What's wrong?" I've never seen her so...out of sorts before. We left them less than ten minutes ago in lovey-dovey land. What could've possibly happened in such a short amount of time?

"Did you know?" She pokes Chaser in the chest as the elevator doors slide closed behind her.

There's a thump against the elevator doors and a pathetic, muffled, "Pamela!"

Chaser glances down at Pamela's finger—still lingering on his chest—and carefully removes it from his body. "Know what?"

By the detached tone he uses, I suspect Chaser *did* know whatever it is Pamela's so upset over.

"That he was with...some...*skank* before you guys came to pick us up?"

"Pamela," Chaser says in his most calm and reasonable voice. "I'm not his babysitter."

She continues glaring at him and it occurs to me he didn't question her for details about whatever crime Andrew supposedly committed.

I side-eye him and he gives me a slight head shake in return.

"What?" Pamela says, gaze pinging between us.

"What happened, Pamela?" I ask. "You two looked so happy on the way here."

"I'm an idiot, that's what," she fumes.

The doors open and Chaser ushers us out of the elevator. The long corridor is quiet and softly lit with golden wall sconces reflecting off gold wallpaper. My sandals sink into the thick red carpet as Chaser hurries us along.

Pamela sniffs as she follows us. "Can I stay with you guys until I find a flight home?"

No, no, no. "Of course you can."

Chaser lets out a long breath. Clearly, he had a different answer in mind.

Somewhere behind us, a heavy metal door clangs open and shut. Chaser stops at a door and slides his key in the lock without looking up.

"Pammy!" Andrew shouts breathlessly. Panting and bent over, leaning on his knees, he calls out again, "Wait!"

"Fuck you!" Pamela whips around and flicks both middle fingers at him. "You cheating fuck!"

"Jesus Christ," Chaser mutters, pushing open our door. "Go on, hon." He gently touches Pamela's back. "You sure you don't want to talk this out with him?"

"I'm sure."

"Okay, I'll handle it. Stay here with Mallory."

Thanks a lot, Chaser.

I don't want to leave Chaser to deal with Andrew alone but I'm not sure what else to do, so I follow her into our suite. Chaser closes the door behind us. A second later, fists pound on the door hard enough to rattle the thick wood.

"Pamela!" Andrew's anguished scream rubs my nerves raw. "Please!"

Chaser's lower, but no less intense voice tries to reason with Andrew. One, two, three more bangs against the door. More talking. Then their voices fade.

Great. Now I'm stuck here alone with Pamela. Who knows how long it will take to tame Andrew.

"Are you okay?" I ask.

Pamela turns away from the window and dabs at her eyes. "No, Mallory," she snaps. "I'm not okay."

Ignoring her pissy tone, I drop down on the sofa. "Do you want to talk about it?"

"No, I don't."

Okay then. This isn't the romantic reunion night with Chaser I've been dreaming of for weeks but you don't see me bitching about it or kicking her out and telling her to find her own damn room.

Frustrated, I wait to see if she changes her mind and wants to talk.

"You want to know what happened? You really want the scoop on what kind of guy your buddy Andrew is?" Pamela paces in front of me.

I ignore her hostility. "If you want to tell me, I'm here to listen," I answer with as much compassion as I can at this hour.

She stops her furious pacing and kicks off her shoes. *Thwack, thwack.* They hit the wall by the door, landing in a pathetic clump someone's bound to trip over. "I went to blow that motherfucker and found lipstick rings on his damn dick!" she shrieks.

Afraid I'll laugh, which would be truly awful in this moment, I go over and pick up her shoes, dropping them under the long table in front of the couch.

"Are you sure?"

She plants her fists on her hip in a scary imitation of an evil comic book villain about to melt half a city block with the power of her laser eye beams. "*Cherries in the Snow* is kind of hard to miss."

Eww. Now I'll have to toss every tube of that color I've ever bought.

"God, do you know how many guys I've passed on because of that jackass? I could've fucked Davey Revolver."

Join the club. "He's gross."

She wrinkles her nose. "Andrew or Davey?"

Both of them. "Uh, Davey.

"Whatever." She lifts her head and a crooked smile twists her mouth. "You don't happen to know Kyle's room number, do you?"

"How would I know? We just got here. Why?"

"Because I've fucked him the last time Andrew and I broke up. And I have a sudden urge to do it again."

"Wow. Uh, okay." I can understand why it makes sense in her head but, *yuck.*

I glance at the door longingly. Is Chaser making out better than I am with Andrew? Or did we both draw short sticks tonight?

CHAPTER NINE

Chaser

"Chaser, I gotta talk to her," Andrew insists.

I keep pushing him down the hallway, but he's so damn loud, doors crack open and guests peek out to see what all the commotion is about. It's only a matter of time before security gets called. Strange that none of our bandmates have popped out to see if we need help. Not like we're all staying on the same floor or anything.

Every single one of those assholes is getting a five a.m. wake-up call for leaving me to deal with this fuckery on my own.

"Let her cool off for a minute and then I'll see if she wants to talk to you."

He stabs his fingers through his hair and tugs at the strands. "Oh, this is bad. This is *so* bad, Chaser."

"Give me your key."

He hands it over and I open the door, pushing him into the suite. Once he's securely inside, I stop and take in the room. Paintings ripped off the wall and broken. Television smashed by the window. Chairs overturned.

"What the fuck happened in here?"

He laughs. "Oh, we trashed the place earlier. I thought housekeeping would've cleaned it up by now."

"Are you fucking five years old?"

"What?" He shakes off the room stuff and grabs my shoulders. "You have to let me talk to her."

I cross my arms over my chest and put my back to the door. "Tell me what happened first."

He stops kicking debris out of his way, grabs his hair with one hand, and points at me with the other. "Don't you dare fucking laugh."

"That good, huh?" I'm already fighting to keep my mouth in a straight line. Can't help it.

"I'll punch your lights out if you laugh," he warns.

The struggle to keep a straight face is too much. "You can try."

He throws me a menacing scowl. "After you guys got out, Pammy was feeling frisky. She undid my pants." He reaches down to rub his crotch. "I was gonna get a little BJ action."

I groan, already suspecting where this is headed.

"I swear, if you fucking laugh—"

"Just finish your story. The suspense is killing me."

He glowers at me. "That banging little tart from the show left fuckin' lipstick all over my dick!"

Maybe it's exhaustion or disappointment that I'm not with Mallory right now when I've been jonesing for her for so long, but I fucking lose my shit. The sheer outrage in his voice is too much. I crack up so hard and fast, I end up sliding down the door till my ass hits the carpet, then fall over on my side, howling and clutching my stomach.

"It's not funny." Andrew's sneaker connects with my thigh. It only makes me laugh harder.

"Karma...she's a...brilliant bitch," I sputter.

"You jinxed me, Chaser! When we were getting in the limo, you called it!"

I stop laughing and stare up at him. "So it's *my* fault you

70

couldn't, I don't know, splash some water on your damn dick before picking up your girlfriend?"

"You were rushing me! We were late."

"Maybe you should've passed on the blowjob from the girl you just met?"

"Give up a free blowjob?" He blinks at me in confusion. "Why?"

"Not really free is it?"

"Fuck." He drops down onto the floor next to me. "That's deep, Chaser."

"Indeed."

He glances toward the bathroom. "I'm gonna take a shower. Maybe I can tell her it was just the limo's shitty lighting?"

While I question Pamela's intelligence for dating Andrew in the first place, the girl's not dumb. "You don't think she'll suspect you ran to your room and showered?"

"Fuck, what am I going to do? I told all my east coast girls not to come to our last show."

"Poor baby." I sit up and slap his leg. "Maybe use the extra time to think about what an asshole you are."

"Shit, man." He rubs his crotch. "She was *really* pissed. I'm lucky she didn't rip my dick off."

"Can you blame her? How'd you like to find some guy's cum in her panties?"

He actually seems to consider the scenario. "Yeah, I get your point." His gaze slides toward the door.

"Don't," I warn.

"Come on. I need to talk to her."

"Listen." I use his shoulder to pull myself off the floor. "I'll ask her but if she doesn't want to talk to you, let it go for tonight."

"Are you going to let her crash in your room?"

I'd rather not but I don't see another option. "If that's what she wants."

"If you fuck my girlfriend, I'm going to kick your ass, Chaser," he says with an absolutely straight face.

"Did that girl suck your brain out through your dick earlier?" I kick his leg, harder than a friendly bump. "I haven't seen Mallory in *weeks*. Your inability to control *your* dick has ruined *my* night."

"Fuck. I'm sorry."

I swear there's more remorse in his voice over interfering with my sex life than cheating on his girlfriend.

"That was a dick thing to say." He peers up at me. "It's just... Pammy's always talking about you. I know she only does it to piss me off but...she's into some freaky shit. Joining you *and* Mallory wouldn't bother her."

As if *that* wouldn't be the three-way from hell. "I'll pass, but thanks for the head's up. Even if Mallory were into the idea, I doubt she'd choose Pamela."

He raises an eyebrow. "You'd say no to two hot chicks?"

I'm done entertaining this train of thought. "Has it occurred to you that maybe you *wanted* to get caught?"

"No, why would I want this?" He raises his arms.

"So you can fuck everyone you meet without the guilt."

"Guilt?" He scratches his head. "I don't understand."

"Figures."

"Maybe." He's quiet for a few seconds, slowly tapping his fingers against the carpet. "I think maybe I want what you guys have."

"Who?"

"You and Mallory."

Apprehension prickles down my spine. "How so?" I ask carefully.

"Like, you guys are close. Pammy likes my money and my dick, but I'm not always sure she likes *me*."

"Can't imagine why."

He wraps his arms around his legs and rests his chin on his knees, looking so damn pathetic, I almost feel bad for the dig.

72

"It's so obvious that Mallory really *likes* you," he finally continues. "Actually listens to you. Wants to be around you and stuff."

Fuck knows I love being around her and I'm annoyed as hell that I'm not with her right this second.

"Maybe Pamela's not the one for you, then."

"But she's so fucking hot." He hugs his legs tighter.

Lord, I know I take your name in vain more often than I should, but this punishment seems excessive.

"There are beautiful women at our shows every night who love everything about you, right down to your stupid cock hammocks," I answer as non-judgmentally as possible.

"I can't date a groupie." He gags. "That's too weird." He spears me with a wounded look. "And my cock hammocks are awesome."

"Sure, buddy."

"I'm serious, Pam likes my money but, other than riding Kyle's dick, she doesn't give a fuck about anything to do with Vicious Vandals. And it's my whole life."

I blink and shake my head. "What?" No wonder he doesn't get along with his singer.

"It was a while ago. We were on a break." He waves it away. "She'd never even heard of us before I tracked her down. Took her forever to go out with me because she thought I was just a sleazy rock star."

"You *are* a sleazy rock star."

His eyes widen. "Shit, I guess she was right."

"Maybe this will be good for you." *It'll definitely be good for Pamela.*

"How is this good? When the tour's over, I'll be all alone again. Even if she's mean and never feeds me, I like coming home to someone."

"Well, if that's true, then treat the next girl better."

"I'm good to Pammy."

"Andrew, what I'm about to tell you isn't some cosmic

secret." I pause to make sure he's listening. "No amount of cars, flowers, or diamonds are going to make up for your woman finding lipstick on your dick. And if it does, you probably shouldn't be with that woman anyway."

"Damn. You're like a fucking philosopher or something, Chaser."

"I watched my dad do plenty of stupid shit while I was growing up. Taught me a lot."

"See, I didn't have a dad around to teach me the important stuff."

"Mine would've whooped your ass several times by now."

He snorts and holds out his hand for me to help him off the floor. "He still coming to our last show?"

"Far as I know." I glance at the clock. "Fuck, I was supposed to call him."

"I really ruined your night, huh?"

"In several ways. Yes."

"Thanks for sticking around, even though I'm an asshole."

I slap his shoulder. "I'll talk to Pamela but don't get your hopes up." I pause with my hand on the doorknob. "Don't go anywhere. Get some sleep. Stay out of trouble."

"I'll try."

Not all that satisfied with his answer, I escape out the door and into my room. It's dark but there's enough light to make out Pamela's body stretched out on the couch.

"Pamela," I whisper. "Are you awake?"

She sniffles and picks up her head. "Did he come with you?"

"No, I told him not to. Do you want to talk to him, though? I'll walk you down there if—"

"No, fuck him."

And that's the extent of my mediation. "All right. Night, Pamela."

She sits up but I pretend I can't see her in the dark and hurry into the bedroom, closing the door behind me. Mallory left a lamp on but she's curled away from the weak circle of light. I strip down and snap off the lamp before climbing into bed behind her.

"I'm back," I whisper.

"Oh." She turns over and kisses my chest. "Is everything okay?"

"No, Andrew's a mess. But it's his own fucking fault, so I'm low on sympathy for the fucker."

"Same here." She cuddles up closer to me. "This wasn't what I had in mind for our first night together in weeks."

I snort and kiss the top of her head. "Me either."

"Was Pamela still awake?"

"Yeah, I talked to her for a sec. Promised Andrew I'd try to get her to talk to him, but that was a no go."

"Did she ask you for Kyle's room number?"

"No, but I heard about that."

"Really? From Andrew?"

"Yup."

"You know I'd never do that, right?" she asks.

"What?" Then her question sinks in and I snort. "Yeah, and you know I'd never do *that*." Fuck it feels good having her in my arms again. I trace my fingers over her shoulder. "You know how much I love you, right? How much I love just being with you?"

"I do. I've missed you every day since I left."

"Same here." I swallow and try to collect my thoughts. "I don't want that to ever change."

"Neither do I."

"Good."

The apprehension that bothered me earlier finally fades.

I hold her tighter and don't let go.

CHAPTER TEN

Mallory

"I appreciate you trying to be quiet, but these walls are paper-thin," Pamela announces the next morning when I stumble into the living room.

Both the sunlight pouring into the room and her statement leave me blinking in confusion.

"I'm just messing with you!" Her gaze moves past my shoulder. "I'm jealous you're getting laid and all I got was screwed."

Chaser's hands settle on my shoulders. "Morning, Pamela," he greets with all the enthusiasm of a mall security guard making his morning rounds.

Someone pounds on our door.

Pamela's gaze darts to the bathroom. "If it's Andrew, I'm not here."

She scurries away and Chaser answers the door.

"You ready for this?" Jacob sweeps into the room without waiting for an invitation. Garrett and Alvin following behind him.

"Fuck." Chaser scrubs his hands over his face. "I totally forgot."

"How could you forget?" Alvin thumps his hand against Chaser's chest.

Chaser rolls his eyes. "Trust me. It's been a night."

The toilet flushes and a few seconds later, Pamela emerges from the bathroom.

One corner of Jacob's mouth slides up.

"Don't," Chaser warns. "You know what, fuck it." He steps back. "Have at it."

"You sly fucker," Garrett says.

I glare at him and he winks at me. "Didn't think you had it in you."

"Fuck off," Chaser growls.

"Andrew and I broke up and they let me borrow their couch. But thanks for talking about me as if I'm not even here." Pamela drops down on the couch and starts riffling through her purse, ignoring the guys.

"Pay no attention to them, darling," Jacob glides over and squats down in front of her, Prince Charming style. "Is there anything I can do for you?"

"Oh, boy," I grumble. "I'm going back to bed."

Chaser and Alvin follow me into the bedroom.

"Oh my God, can I have two seconds without someone up my butt?" I snap.

Alvin chuckles. "I'm thrilled Chaser's broadening your horizons, Mallory, but I actually need to talk to this bonehead."

"Sorry." I wave my hand toward the living room. "I wasn't expecting *that* last night."

Chaser stretches out on the bed, tucking his hands behind his head. "What time do we need to be there?"

"Eleven."

"Be where?" I ask.

"We're doing an in-store record signing at All Ears Music

store up in Union. Thom added it to our schedule last minute," Alvin explains.

"I can't believe I forgot." Chaser groans and rubs his hands over his face again. "I always wanted to do a signing there."

"Looks like you were busy." Alvin drops down on the bed and shakes Chaser's leg. "Have fun with your psycho buddy?"

Chaser sits up and in a hushed voice explains, "You have no idea the shit I had to listen to last night."

"I can guess." Alvin gestures toward the door. "I heard him screaming her name up and down the hallway. In desperation, not passion."

I giggle-snort into my hand and Alvin winks at me.

"Thanks for coming out and helping," Chaser says.

Alvin grins at him. "You seemed to have it handled. So, what happened? She find out about one of his groupies?"

Chaser's mouth twists as he fights off his laughter. "I can't..." When he finally has control, he explains the events.

Alvin falls over in a fit of giggles and promptly rolls off the bed, landing on the floor with a thud. "You're making that up."

Chaser nudges Alvin's butt with the toe of his boot. "I can't make that shit up, bro."

Like a child unhappy about being called on to provide an answer for the whole class, I raise my hand. "Unfortunately, I can confirm. It was *red* lipstick."

Alvin stops laughing. "Aw, shit. Poor Pam. That's really fucked up."

Someone knocks on the door and pushes it open. Garrett sweeps his gaze over the three of us. "Damn, thought you were having a party in here." He glances over his shoulder. "Jacob took Pamela down to his room to "console" her."

"Fucking great," Alvin mutters. "Just what we need."

"Thank fuck this tour's almost over," Chaser adds.

"Ah, Thom wants to talk to us about the possibility of another tour after we finish the album," Garrett informs us.

Another tour? More time away from Chaser?

Our gazes collide but he quickly looks away. "Headlining? Opening? What are we talking about?"

That's *so* not the question I hoped he'd ask.

CHAPTER ELEVEN

Chaser

Robbie guides our tour bus down the narrow city street toward All Ears Music. Mallory shifts in her seat and stares out the window. I'm not sure if it's hanging with the guys or finding out I might be going right back out on the road, but something in Mallory's attitude has deflated since we left the hotel.

"Damn, look at all those fuckers," Garrett peers out the window, drawing our attention. At the moment they're neatly lined up, waiting to get inside but as we pass, half the line breaks and they rush around the side of the building to follow the bus.

"Are you sure I should even be here?" Mallory asks, watching the kids trailing after us. "I'm not a member of the band."

"You're an honorary member for life." Alvin pats her leg and she smiles at him.

Robbie has to stop to make the turn for the narrow alleyway, giving the kids a chance to surround the bus, screaming and banging on the doors.

"Damn." Alvin whistles, staring out the window. "You got this, Robbie?"

"I think so." He pounds on the horn a few times and the kids back off.

Slowly, we roll down the alleyway and into the record store's parking lot. Once we're through, two guys in black and yellow polo shirts slide a massive chain link gate closed.

"Phew." Robbie roughs his palm over the back of his head. "That was intense."

As the tour progressed, the poor guy went from acting as our bodyguard to being our bus driver, security, *and* gofer. He definitely needs a pay raise if we're going back out on tour.

"Let me make sure no one's gonna mob you guys before you get off the bus," he says, hefting himself out of the driver's chair.

"Thanks," Alvin says.

"Think Jacob will make it on time?" I ask Garrett.

"When is he ever on time?"

Ever the helpful gentleman, Jacob offered to take a taxi to the airport with Pamela and then meet us at the store. Kind of hard to do a signing without our lead singer, so he better get his ass here.

Once the parking lot's clear, Robbie waves us off the bus. I help Mallory down the steps last and we follow the rest of the guys over the cracked asphalt parking lot.

"I should've skipped the heels," Mallory says.

I run my gaze over her red plaid dress—tight on top with two layers of ruffles flaring out below her hips, black lacy tights that end below her knees and shiny red spike heels. Before we left the hotel, she' added a short denim vest with little silvers studs sprinkled over the shoulders. The overall effect is a bit rock-n-roll, a little Debbie Gibson, a dash of biker chick and one-hundred percent hot as fuck.

"You can always wear whatever you want." I slip one hand behind her legs and the other around her shoulders, scooping her up into my arms and swinging her in a circle. "I gotcha."

"Chaser!" Her wild laughter dissolves in the noise of the city.

At the back door, I gently set her down.

"Thanks for the lift."

"Anytime, little dove."

The guys have already filled the small storage room in the back of the record store. The owner stops to introduce himself but keeps staring at us like we might disappear at any moment. "Holy shit! I'm so honored to have you here today." He shakes all of our hands with enthusiasm but stops dead when he reaches Mallory. "Oh my God. I never thought...I never expected you to show up too, Miss Dove. Wow. Thank you so much."

I swear he's either about to bow down to her or faint. One or the other.

Mallory beams at him and holds out her hand. "It was a last minute decision. I hope that's okay."

One of my possessive caveman arms is wrapped around Mallory like a fuckin' python, but the dude still takes her hand and pulls it toward his gaping piehole. He leans down and brushes his lips over her knuckles. "It's an honor. I'll find an extra chair for you right away."

I clear my throat and he finally drops her hand.

"Is someone still out there to open the gate?" Alvin asks. "Jacob's coming by taxi."

"Yes, yes, I'll send someone right now," he promises.

"Did Andrew know you'd be here today?" Mallory asks.

"I don't think so. Why?"

"I'm worried that we couldn't find him this morning."

Yeah, it's not a good sign but it's also really not my problem. Andrew's an adult—sort of. "Let's get through this afternoon and then I'll worry about his whereabouts."

The back door bounces open and Jacob steps through with his arms outstretched. "Your fearless singer has arrived!" he announces.

"Settle down, Rocky." Alvin rolls his eyes but slaps one of Jacob's outstretched hands.

Garrett grabs Jacob in a bear hug and bounces him up and down like a big, fat baby. Jacob grins at me over Garrett's shoulder. "Had you worried, didn't I?"

"A little bit," Mallory says.

"Nah, I knew you wouldn't miss an opportunity to have girls fawn all over you," I answer. "Pamela get to the airport?"

"Yup, on her way to L.A. now."

"Good." Since we can't get rid of Andrew, hopefully her departure alleviates some of the drama in our lives.

The owner moves us into the store where he's set up a long row of tables to form one big barrier between us and the rest of the shop. He has an impressive number of Kickstart merchandise, records, tapes, posters, and T-shirts staged at various points along the line for sale. Thom did a good job arranging this at the last minute.

I point to the first chair at the end of the table. "Jacob, you should have that spot. Let your sunny face be the first thing people see when they walk in."

He salutes me and marches toward the seat facing the front door.

Garrett takes the next chair. Mallory and I set up at the third spot, with Alvin in the chair a few feet to our left.

"Mallory." The owner drops a medium-sized, thin cardboard rectangular box on the table in front of us. "I found these in the back, if you'd like something to sign too."

He pulls the lid off, revealing a thick stack of glossy eight by eleven promo posters for 'Candy Jar' featuring Mallory in her tiny denim shorts and halter top.

For a brief second her smile falters but she pulls it together and thanks him.

"Are you ready?" he asks, glancing up and down the length of the table. "I'll have my guys open the doors and start letting them in, if that's okay."

Robbie puts his back to the wall at Jacob's end and crosses his massive arms over his chest. "Ready."

As soon as the door opens, the volume level in the building shoots up. Girls squeal Jacob's name and flock to him first. A few skip his line and move down to Garrett. Even more rush straight for me.

I'm handed a variety of items to sign. Robbie walks back and forth, keeping the line moving quickly. The owner moves to the front of the store to work the cash register.

A few hours fly by almost as quickly as time flies when we're on stage.

I'm about to ask Mallory if she needs me to get her anything to drink when another fan steps up to the table.

"Hi, Chaser." The smoky voice has a tinge of familiarity to it. I glance up and study the girl in front of us. Teased, curly blonde hair. Pretty face. Bright red lips. "Long time."

I groan before catching myself and force a bland smile. "Uh, hey."

Awkward moments are bound to pop up when you've fucked groupies from coast to coast. It's some sort of miracle this hasn't happened a lot sooner.

That Mallory's at my side jacks up the awkwardness to an almost painful degree.

"Carrie, yeah?" Fuck, I hope I'm right. I'd rather not be the asshole who forgot a one-night stand's name in addition to subjecting Mallory to this awkward moment.

"You remember!" She beams at me. "How are you? I wanted to catch you guys last time you played in Union but I couldn't get a ride."

"Bummer."

She leans over the table, all but shoving her tits in my face. I sit back and sling my arm around Mallory's stiff shoulders.

"Did you want me to sign something?" I drop my gaze to the copy of *Metal Edge* in her hands.

"Oh. Yes." Her gaze darts to Mallory and then back to me. "I didn't realize..." She shoves the magazine at me and I flip through it until I find a photo of the band. Must be from my brief cokehead era. Vacant eyes. Strained smile. Jacob looks like he nodded off in an alleyway and we carried him into the studio and propped him up for the camera. Hell, there's a good chance it actually happened that way. Fuck if I remember. I sure as hell didn't agree to the hideous hot pink background we're staged in front of. The empty bottles of Jack Daniels scattered at our feet give the photo an extra-special sleazy touch.

I scrawl my signature over my dopey face and hand the magazine back. "Thanks."

Carrie lingers for a few extra seconds.

Please don't hand me your phone number. Or anything else.

Finally, she slides over to Alvin.

"Old friend?" The tart snap to Mallory's tone bothers me more than anything else that just happened in the last thirty seconds.

"Ancient." I glance over but she's watching Carrie twirl her hair and push her boobs in Alvin's face.

Mallory shakes her head and shifts her body toward me. She runs her hand over my leg. A reassuring gesture even if she's not able to express it with words.

"Don't know how you put up with me," I mutter.

"Honestly, I'm shocked it hasn't happened sooner."

I choke and sputter but thank fuck I stop myself from agreeing.

A few more girls—none that I have intimate knowledge of, thank you, Jesus—approach. They either stone-cold ignore Mallory or give her the stink-eye the whole time they're chatting me up.

Mallory pretends not to notice, quietly handing me Sharpies or whatever else I need to keep the line moving.

When there's a break, she grasps her purse in her lap in a white-knuckled death grip. "I should've stayed at the hotel. Everyone probably thinks I'm some bitch here to monitor your every move."

"Hey." I curl my arm around her and pull her closer. "No one thinks that and if they do, they can fuck off. *I* want you here. I *need* you here with me. That's all that matters." I jerk my chin at the store owner who hasn't taken his eyes off Mallory all day. "Besides, who would old ham hands over there have to lust after if you hadn't come with us?"

"Stop. He's so nice." She taps the box of posters he miraculously found in the back room.

"Yeah, crazy how he just had these lying around." I roll my eyes.

Instead of answering, she tips her head, indicating another fan is lined up for me to talk to.

Please, not another groupie.

With a deep breath, I turn and run my gaze over the freckle-faced kid who can't be older than eleven or twelve.

"Chaser! You're my favorite guitar player ever," he gushes at warp speed while shoving several cassette tapes at me. "'Cry it Out' is the first song I learned to play."

"Yeah?" I answer, pulling out the insert and tapping it with my Sharpie. "That's really cool. Thanks."

He nods for me to sign it and fires off question after question.

"What's the first song you learned to play? Do you ride a motorcycle? I want a Harley when I can get my license. Is that what you have? Who's your favorite guitar player? How did you guys meet and start the band?"

None of the answers are things I haven't said in dozens of interviews before but I indulge his barrage of questions, charmed by his enthusiasm.

"What's your name?" I finally ask when he takes a breath.
"Reed."

I nod as I take a Sharpie to the poster he hands me next.
Reed,
Never stop rocking.
Chaser Adams.

Yeah, it's a little clichéd but I haven't come up with anything better yet.

Reed's hyper-speed mouth goes on lock down when his gaze lands on Mallory.

"Would you like me to sign one?" Mallory taps the 'Candy Jar' posters. His jaw drops and he slowly nods, tongue wagging in the breeze.

"You're so beautiful," he whispers. "You're so pretty. I, wow. You're so beautiful," he keeps repeating, his favorite guitar player completely forgotten.

Sweeter than candy, Mallory smiles and thanks him. She taps her Sharpie against the poster for a few beats before writing,

Reed,

Always follow your dreams.

Love,

Mallory

Clearly Mallory's better at this than I am. Pale-faced and slack-jawed, he stares at the message for a few seconds. Poor kid's gonna faint. Finally, a guy I'm assuming is his father nudges him down the line.

Mallory can't stop grinning. "He was *so* adorable," she whispers.

"He'd probably die of embarrassment if he heard you say that."

"Aw, hey, man. Will you sign this?" Someone tosses a piece of paper in front of me. I glance up and instantly peg the meathead in front of us for a douche. We get these types a lot. Guys itching to pick a fight. Whether it's jealousy, small dick syndrome, or pure assholery, I've never figured out. It's better not to engage.

"Sure," I answer in a bland tone. "How you doin'?"

He shrugs. "Cool." His gaze slides to Mallory and I brace myself. While I don't give a fuck if he's rude to me, disrespecting my girl is a line he better not cross.

"Mallory Dove. I'd kill to slide my hand in your candy jar."

He slowly winks as if he just uttered the most brilliant come-on ever.

Mallory flicks an indifferent glance at him.

"Take ya a while to come up with that one?" I ask, slipping an arm around Mallory's shoulders.

He shrugs. "It's a lame fuckin' song but she was hot in the video."

"Thanks for stoppin' by." I sweep my arm in front of me in a move-it-along gesture and he finally shuffles away.

Mallory scrunches her nose at his back. "What a jerk," she whispers to me.

"We get guys like that *all* the time."

She glares down the table at him where he's busy hassling Alvin. Good luck to him. Alvin has even less patience than I do for that bullshit.

"He's probably a failed musician," she says under her breath.

"Maybe. Best not to give them the reaction they're seeking. It annoys them more if they can't get a rise out of you."

"Sure. Otherwise, you hand him a great story to tell for the rest of his life. 'This one time, Chaser Adams punched me.'"

I shake with laughter and squeeze her closer. "Pretty much."

Unfortunately, he's not our last asshole of the day. No, a much bigger dickweed steps up to us next. In his preppy polo shirt, neatly tucked into a pair of pleated pants, he sticks out like a preacher at an orgy.

"Vasily. Good to see ya, buddy." I flash a big ol' grin at him. "Got something for me to autograph?"

Ignoring me, he glances down at Mallory. "You are joking, right?" He thrusts his hand in my direction. "*This* is what you chose?"

I stand and place my hands on the table, leaning in between him and Mallory. "Don't look at her. You have something to say, say it to me. Those were the terms of our arrangement, right?" I say in a lower voice, reminding him Mallory's untouchable and under my club's protection.

His ice-cold eyes meet mine and he sneers. "She would have been better off with me."

"I doubt that. Now, unless there's business you need me to bring back to my club, or you want my autograph, it's time for you to leave."

He hesitates, then pulls something out of his pocket. His asshole attitude vanishes. "Anatoly's lawyer is working on the appeal. He wants to speak with Mallory but no one knew how to reach her." He hands me the card. "We want to get him home as soon as possible." He stares at me as if he has more to say, then seems to realize we're in a record store full of people and maybe it's not the best place to discuss family business.

"I'll make sure she calls him." I hand Mallory the card and watch her tuck it away in her purse.

"Of course, I'll call," she promises.

She stands, pressing herself against my side and I slide an arm around her waist.

"Is he okay?" she asks him in a low voice.

Vasily's gaze slides over Mallory's body a little too long for my taste before answering. "You know your father. He is...making friends."

"I expect nothing less."

While I have plenty of reasons to dislike Vasily, that's not the reason I want to put an end to this reunion. The last thing Mallory needs is word spreading that her mobster father's in prison. The tabloids salivated over a non-existent love triangle when Andrew got shot. If they get wind of a scandal this juicy, they'll be wolves gnawing on a goat.

Vasily stares down at the table as if noticing the promo material for the first time. He taps one of the 'Candy Jar' posters with a perfectly manicured finger. Jesus, is that clear nail polish?

"I cannot believe this is you." It's definitely not a compliment coming from his mouth.

Ignoring his disapproving tone, Mallory flashes her camera-ready smile. "Me either."

"Your father will not approve."

She shrugs. "He'll get over it."

He keeps staring at her as if he's meeting Mallory for the first time. And I guess in a way he is. It doesn't seem like anyone in her life ever bothered to get to know the real Mallory.

Anyone until me.

CHAPTER TWELVE

Mallory

"I can't believe he had the nerve to show up there!" I stare out our hotel room window after hanging up with my father's attorney.

"What'd the lawyer say?" Chaser asks.

"Not much. I don't know what he thought I could tell him that would be helpful." I tap my lip, thinking over the conversation and Vasily's appearance. "Maybe he used it as an excuse to come see us?"

"Let us know we were on his turf?"

"Yes."

Chaser shrugs. "He left peacefully and as long as we don't see his ugly face again, I really don't care." He seems to reconsider the day's events. "I don't want you out alone while we're down here, though. You're with me anytime we're off the bus or outside. At the show, stick with Robbie, Alvin, or..." he pauses, his face twisting in annoyance, "...I hate saying it, Andrew. He's a pain in the ass but if someone tried to mess with you, he'd fuck them up."

"You think so?"

"I do."

I slide over and wrap my arms around his middle, leaning against him. "I don't plan to let you out of my sight, so it won't be a problem."

"Good." He bends down and kisses the tip of my nose. "Exactly how I like it."

"You really didn't mind having me there today?"

"Nope. Felt good having you by my side."

He says it without hesitation and that finally erases my doubts about the afternoon. Even the girl who so obviously showed up to bang my boyfriend is forgotten. "Did your father say when he's arriving?"

"Early tomorrow afternoon. Half the club's coming with him. Thom gave me all sorts of shit about finding backstage passes for everyone."

I roll my eyes. "If they can magically come up with passes for groupies every night, he can find enough for family members."

"That's basically what I told him."

Someone pounds against our hotel door. Intuition says it's Andrew. I sigh as Chaser opens the door. I don't have the energy for his crazy antics tonight.

"She left me. She really left and went home."

"I'm sorry." Chaser pats Andrew's shoulder as he barrels into our room.

"Did you take her to the airport?" Andrew asks.

"No, Jacob did."

"Did he fuck her?" Andrew's eyes widen. "Be honest."

Chaser slams the door shut. "I didn't ask to sniff his dick. Settle down."

"Sorry." He glances up and finally seems to notice I'm in the room. "Hey, Mallory. I bet she told you all about it, didn't she?"

"Just the highlights." *Please let my evasive answer be enough to escape this conversation.*

"I'm such a stupid asshole," he moans.

"Yeah," I agree.

"Hey." Chaser taps Andrew's chest with the back of his hand. "Listen up. I need you to do me a favor tomorrow."

Andrew seems to set aside his misery and straightens up. "What?"

"We had a guy show up to see Mallory today. A sort of ex. I don't want him bothering her tomorrow at the show. So, if I'm occupied, you think you can look out for her? Make sure no one's hassling my girl?"

"Yeah. I can do that." Andrew's gaze shifts between Chaser and me. "You okay, Mallory?"

Still shocked Chaser made the request, I only nod.

"My family will be there, so you can still go on about your regular business." Chaser rolls his eyes. "But just in case, look out for her, okay?"

"You got it." Andrew slaps Chaser on the back a few times. "Are you guys meeting us for dinner?"

"We'll be down in a few."

"Cool!" He waves at me before taking off, slamming the door behind him.

"Why would you do that?" I ask.

Chaser strips off his T-shirt and tosses it near our bags. "Do what?"

Trying not to get distracted by inked pecs and perfect abs, I answer, "Bring Andrew any closer to my family...*stuff* by asking him to watch over me." I follow him into the bedroom.

"Two reasons. One, I actually want as many people looking out for you as possible. Two, it'll give him something to do so he stops whining about Pamela. Make him feel useful. Half the time I think that's his problem. Not enough responsibility."

"Careful, Chaser." I bite my lip and stare as he strips out of his jeans. "Don't let his irresponsibility become your responsibility."

"Too late for that."

95

CHAPTER THIRTEEN

Mallory

Excited energy combined with a let's-get-it-over-with attitude seems to permeate the mood backstage the next afternoon. Alvin's busy picking at the buffet table set up for us, while Andrew demands my attention.

"Feels like the longest tour of my life," Andrew moans, rubbing a hand over his side.

"Does it still hurt?" I ask. "You really should've rested a few more days before getting back on the road."

"Fuck that. You know how long some of those kids probably saved to buy their tickets?"

"That's sweet but I bet they'd rather know their favorite drummer was in good health."

"Not their problem."

I can't help but be touched by his concern for his fans.

"Have you heard from Pamela?" he asks with hopeful puppy eyes.

"Not yet." I want to add we're not exactly that close, but don't see the point.

He reaches over to the large, metal tub someone placed on

the floor. It's full of ice, sodas, beer, and a few bottles of champagne. Shoving a hand into the pile of ice cubes, he pulls out a dripping can of 7-Up and hands it to me.

"Thanks." Even though I didn't ask, I am thirsty, so I pop the top and I swipe at droplets of water that landed on my leg.

"You look hot." He sweeps his gaze over me from head to toe. "Did I mention that?"

"You did. Several times." Worried I'll accidentally flash someone, I stand and tug the short leather dress down.

"Careful," Andrew murmurs, eyes glued to my chest.

"Shoot." This was a mistake. The thin little straps don't do much to keep the dress up and every time I try to pull the skirt down, I'm in danger of my boobs falling out.

"You want a T-shirt to wear over it?" he offers, picking up a black backpack and rummaging through the contents.

I glare at him. "I'm not falling for that again."

"Not that T-shirt." He tosses a grungy black shirt my way that smells like it hasn't been washed once on the whole tour. And eww, is it crusty?

"Pew!" I yelp and throw it back in his lap. "Did something die in there?"

"Oh, yeah. Whoops. A thousand potential little Andrews." He shoves his nose in it and sniffs. "Sorry. Wrong shirt."

"Gross." Vomit burns the back of my throat. "What's wrong with you?"

"I have a clean one here somewhere." He opens the backpack wider and tosses items around.

"It's fine, Andrew." Ignoring his protests, I grab the short denim vest I brought with me off the end of the couch. I slip it on, buttoning it half-way. "Does that look okay?"

He sits back and rubs his hand over his chin. "From a red-blooded male perspective, it's better without the vest in the way. But if I'm Chaser, I'd prefer it on and buttoned to the top." He touches his chin.

"Thanks," I grumble. "Very helpful."

"Are you nervous about meeting his family?"

"No, I've met them before." I doubt Stump cares what I'm wearing. On second thought, I can't seem to sit still. Maybe seeing the club explains some of my jitters.

"Are you sad the tour's over?" I ask to take the attention off me.

"Yeah." His lost puppy face returns. "Not looking forward to going home to an empty house."

"You better hope there's a house to go home *to*. Pamela was mad enough to burn it down while you're gone."

"Shit." He rubs his hands over the back of his neck. "I didn't think of that. She wouldn't...would she?"

"What you did was pretty gross."

He glances away. "Would you burn Chaser's house down?"

"No, I'd cut off his dick," I answer without thinking. "A house is a small price to pay."

He sits back and rubs his crotch. "Jesus Christ. I never knew you were so scary, Mallory."

I shrug.

"Knowing Chaser, it's just a bigger turn on," Alvin says, winking at me.

"True," I agree.

"It's kind of hot." Andrew pulls a sketchpad out of his backpack and flips it open. "How long are you and Chaser going to be gone?"

"At least a week. We can't be away too long. He has to leave and record the album."

Alvin presses his palms together prayer style. "Please, dear spirits don't let this recording go like the last one."

"Nah." Andrew waves off Alvin's concern. "Mark won't put up with any shit. Plus, Jacob's been good."

Maybe one positive thing came out of Andrew getting shot— Jacob's sobriety.

Andrew turns the sketchpad toward me. I admire his comic

book style drawings as he flips through each page. "Is there anything you're not good at?"

"Keeping my dick in my pants," he answers with a straight face.

"Well, you're self-aware." I pat the top of his head. "That's a start."

Alvin covers his face with his hands and cough-laughs.

Ignoring both of us, Andrew continues flipping through the sketchbook. "I'm thinking of starting a side project. Like a T-shirt company. Vicious Vandals-inspired. Kyle's dicking me around about using the band's name, so I might end up calling it *Kyle's-A-Cocksucker* but I think it might be fun."

I chuckle at the casual way he mentions disagreements with his bandmate.

"You think you'd be interested in modeling for me?" he asks.

"T-shirts?"

"Yeah. I mean, you've done modeling, right? Frederick's of Hollywood, Secret Nothings—"

"Wait, how do you know that?" Those jobs were before Chaser and Andrew met. I can't picture Andrew sitting around flipping through old lingerie catalogs...on second thought, yes I can.

He shrugs. "I don't know. Pamela probably mentioned it. But you have experience with regular clothes too, right? L.A. Gear, Guess—"

"Gina-Marie Johnson did the Guess campaign." I tilt my head. "Do all blondes with big boobs look the same to you?"

He scratches his head. "Not really."

"I'd let Gina-Marie ride my Johnson any day of the week," Alvin adds.

"Pipe down, over there," I say over my shoulder.

"High-five, bro." Andrew throws his palm up in the air.

The door swings open. No more time to scold the guys. Chaser enters, followed by his dad, Tally, and a few other guys I recognize from the clubhouse.

"Stump!" I rush over, happy to see him.

His usually intimidating, scary biker face softens as I approach. He opens his arms wide and scoops me up in an affectionate hug. "How you doin', princess?"

I'm too caught up in his comforting leather-and-cigarette-smoke scent to answer right away. "I'm so happy to see you," I mumble against his shoulder.

He sets me down but holds onto my hands. "You all right?"

Wow, I forgot how penetrating his stare can be when he's probing for information. "I'm good."

His gaze shifts to Chaser. "I heard you had a visitor yesterday."

"We did. It was weird, but Chaser handled it."

"Good. I had the message. Planned to let you know today. Didn't have a way to get a hold of you when you were on the road. Didn't think he'd be such an impatient asshole about it. Sorry, princess."

"Not your fault, Stump." I drop my gaze. "I'm sorry you're caught up in the middle..."

His fingers brush my chin and he tips my head back. "Don't apologize."

Chaser coughs and takes my hand. "She talked to the lawyer last night. Everything should be okay for now."

"Chipmunk!" Tally shouts.

Stump grunts and searches the room, his face lighting up when he spots Alvin. "Get over here, son."

Tally gets to Alvin first, lifting him up in a great big bear hug and bouncing him in the air a few times before setting him down. "Long time, motherfucker."

Stump shakes Alvin's hand and pulls him in for a thump on the back. "Look good, kid. Miss ya."

"Thanks, Pop." Alvin grins. "I'm so stoked you're here tonight."

Tally eyes Chaser for a few seconds before greeting me with

a, "Hey, hon." He leans over and presses a quick peck on my cheek. "Good to see you."

"You too. How was your ride down here?"

"Uneventful."

Chaser shows the guys to the buffet and introduces his father to Robbie and Thom.

Someone taps my hip and I turn to find Andrew. "You didn't tell me Chaser's dad was a biker," he whispers, his eyes darting around the room. "And his whole family."

I peer up at a him. "Was I supposed to?"

"No. I mean. That's cool. I didn't realize. The guys we met up with to go to the Palm, you know for Audrey, they were. Same club. I just didn't realize...family."

Somehow I manage to follow his word salad. Since I'm not exactly sure how to answer, I shrug. "Stump's a good man."

"Stump?" Andrew screws up his face and stares at Chaser's dad. "The guy's built more like a redwood tree."

"Please don't say that to him, Andrew," I caution.

"I mean it in a nice way."

I pat his shoulder. "I'm sure you do."

After everyone's eaten, we end up walking down the hallway to watch the roadies set up the stage for Kickstart.

"This is a far cry from those small bar stages you used to play," Stump says with a proud thump on Chaser's back.

"No kidding. Someone else gets to set up and break it all down too." To anyone else, Chaser probably seems completely at ease but I can't help noticing his jittery hands at his sides, drumming against his jeans. I wrap my fingers around his, calming his restless tapping and he smiles down at me.

"Oh, Dad." Chaser motions Andrew closer. "This is my friend, Andrew. Andrew, this is my father."

Andrew ambles forward, almost shy compared to how he normally behaves, and sticks out his hand. "Chaser always says such good things about you, Mr. Adams. Happy to finally meet you. I'm in the headlining band."

Unimpressed, Stump stares at Andrew's hand for a few seconds before shaking it.

"Your son is totally rad, Mr. Adams," Andrew continues, apparently eager to win Stump over. "We've worked together on a few pieces and he's brilliant."

"Well, I've never heard that before." Stump rumbles with laughter and elbows Chaser.

"Ha. Ha." Chaser rolls his eyes.

Stump eyes Andrew up and down. "You're the one who got him into all the trouble in Texas."

Andrew clasps his hands in front of him and meets Stump's intimidating stare. "Yes, sir. Got him out of the trouble as soon as I could too."

Stump grumbles at him.

"Wasn't Andrew's fault, Dad," Chaser says.

"They ever catch the fool who shot you?" Stump asks Andrew.

"No, sir." He scratches the side of his head. "I haven't exactly been eager to get in touch with the cops though, either."

Now, *that*, I think, Stump admires. He gives Andrew a half-smile.

"Did I pass the test?" Andrew whispers to Chaser after Stump drifts a few steps away.

"You're still breathing, so that's a good sign." Chaser slaps him on the back. "I need to go get rigged up." He nods to me. "Are you okay out here?"

"I'll be fine." I glance around the backstage area. I'm surrounded by half of Kickstart, a bunch of bikers, and Andrew. "No one will bother me."

He leans in and kisses my cheek before running off in search of his guitar tech.

"Is Chaser's dad always so friendly?" Andrew whispers to me.

"I don't know. He likes me."

"You're too sweet not to like," he teases.

I'm too wired for the show to scold Andrew for the flirty comment. It won't matter anyway.

Instead, I take a second to check on Alvin. He can't seem to stop pacing. More than his usual pre-show nerves. I stop him and pull him in for a quick good luck hug. "You're going to be amazing."

One corner of his mouth lifts. "Huge crowd tonight."

I'm not sure if he means here backstage or the audience out front already chanting Kickstart's name.

Andrew slaps him on the back, almost knocking him over. "You got this!"

"Thanks, man."

A DJ from one of the local rock stations announces Kickstart tonight. The guys line up without Jacob.

"Where is he?" I ask Chaser.

"He's coming."

"Literally," Garrett adds.

"Gross," I mutter.

"That's my boy!" Andrew cheers.

Alvin runs on stage first. The crowd's exuberant shouts shake the walls. From where I'm standing, I can't tell if their rowdy welcome calms or intensifies Alvin's nerves.

Chaser tugs me forward. "Kiss for luck," he murmurs.

Our lips meet. Pressured to get on stage or not, Chaser takes his time. Softly, gently, and thoroughly, he slides his lips against mine. I curl my hands in his T-shirt and tug. He cups my face and kisses me harder, slipping his tongue between my lips, stroking against mine. He tastes like mint gum and something sweeter.

Before we get carried away and he misses his show, I pull away, blinking up at him. "Good luck," I whisper.

"I don't need luck. I have you." He presses a quicker kiss to my forehead before strolling onto the stage, hands above his head, waving to everyone.

The audience goes wild. Many, many females screaming

declarations of their devotion can be heard above the crowd's more ordinary exuberance.

I give Garrett a quick pat on the back before he goes out.

Ignoring Thom's pleas to "hurry up and get out there," Jacob stops in front of me. "Will you be mad if I bring you out during 'Candy Jar'?" He tips his head in Stump's direction. "With your father-in-law here and all, I don't want to embarrass you."

How far we've come. A few months ago, I don't think Jacob would've given my feelings a second thought. I reach up and smooth his wayward hair into place. "If you guys want me out there tonight, I'll do it."

"You're the best," he calls over his shoulder while jogging onto the stage.

The familiar beat of Alvin's drum hushes the crowd. I move over to Stump's side. "We can watch from the front of the stage if you want a better view," I offer.

Robbie assured me earlier he'd keep an area clear for Chaser's family. Unfortunately, it's really close to the pit where fans are pressed up tight to the metal fencing corralling them away from the stage. A few people recognize me and wave. Some guy reaches over the fence, hooks his sausage fingers in my vest, and yanks, pulling me off-balance.

"Get the fuck off her!" Tally swoops in behind me and shoves the guy.

A security guard for the venue rushes over, jumping the barrier and tackling sausage fingers to the floor.

Tally glares into the crowd defiantly, daring anyone to test him.

"I'm okay," I assure Tally, yanking him away from the crowd before things get volatile.

Stump scowls at the security guards now dragging the man away. "People bother you like that every night?" he shouts.

"I usually stay backstage."

He grunts and motions for me to walk in front of him.

Robbie nods when he spots us and waves us into a darkened

space right below the stage. Chaser's on the opposite side so even craning our necks, we only get a glimpse of him every now and then.

"Can we go back and watch from where we were?" Stump shouts between songs.

"Sure."

I lead them through the darkened corridor, this time safely sandwiched between Stump and Tally. I smile up at Tally. "I could get used to this. Makes me wish you guys were with us all the time."

He chuckles. "If they get a bigger budget for their next tour, Chaser can hire some of his brothers for security."

"He'd probably prefer that. People he fully trusts. Robbie's been great but—"

"He's not a brother," Tally finishes for me.

"Right." We return to the backstage area. Andrew's busy with his usual pre-show gaggle of groupies but he waves when he sees me.

"What about you? You all right out in Hollywood?" Tally asks. "They sure print some vicious shit about you."

His gaze slides toward Andrew and shame heats my skin. Tally wouldn't bother reading stupid Hollywood gossip magazines, would he? Did he see the ridiculous articles claiming I was running around with Andrew behind Chaser's back? Does he think I'd cheat on Chaser?

"Anything to sell their shitty tabloids," I answer.

He nods but still seems troubled.

I can't worry about it now. I'd rather enjoy Chaser's last show than worry about the things I can't control back in L.A.

"Is this better?" I ask Stump.

"I remember them playing this at the clubhouse!" Stump shouts in my ear.

As cool as he pretends to be, it's obvious he's bursting with pride while he watches his son on stage.

"I'm so happy you were able to come see them. I know Chaser's happy you're here."

He shrugs. "I worried we'd make him nervous, but he seems to be in his element." A note of sadness creeps into his voice.

"We're both looking forward to coming home to spend time with you and the club."

He nods and shoves his hands in his pockets. "Good."

He wanders out a few feet in front of me, closer to the stage and leans on one of the metal supports for a better vantage point.

"How you doing, babe?" Andrew settles his hands on my shoulders.

I tip my head back and smile at him. "Not too bad. Are you nervous about your set?"

He holds his hand straight out in front of him, parallel to the floor. "Steady as a motherfuckin' rock."

"What are you doing with your hand on my son's woman?" Stump's rumbling voice holds a world of threat.

Andrew jerks his hands away, holding both up in the air. "Chaser asked me to look out for Mallory tonight."

"Looking doesn't involve touching," Stump warns. He sweeps his icy glare over me as well.

"I'm fine, Stump."

He grunts in response.

Somehow, I don't think it's me he was worried about.

CHAPTER FOURTEEN

Chaser

Maybe I'm too old for it but, there's a small part of me eager to impress my dad tonight. The crowd alone should be impressive. I almost can't look out at the sea of sweaty, happy faces without a dizzying wave of euphoria washing over me.

Pity we're at the end of the tour. The combination of a vocal coach and replacing heroin with sex has given Jacob a polished edge to his performance that I haven't seen in a long time. His steady voice leads us through each song without strain.

When it's time for my solo, Jacob flashes me a thumb's up before walking off stage. Buzzing from the energy of the crowd, I call up the notes from the song I've been calling "Salvation" in my head since Mallory and I worked on it the last time we were home. It's a slower, gentler melody and at first, I fear it might lose the crowd but when I sneak a glance, they seem transfixed. I continue, embellishing and expanding, eventually morphing the notes into another song, a riff I often play to warm up, and on and on.

Alvin's thump, thump, thump, pulls me out of the solo. A system we agreed on in case I get too carried away. Something to pull me back without jarring me. I turn and thank him with a quick salute, and he lifts his chin.

"Holy fuck!" Jacob shouts into his mic. "Did someone get that on video? That has to be Chaser's best solo yet. He must love you guys! Saved that one just for you, Union, New York!"

The crowd screams their appreciation. I duck my head and laugh.

Thinking 'Candy Jar' is our next song, I strum the first few notes.

Instead of waiting for his cue, Jacob runs off stage again and returns, dragging Mallory behind him.

Our eyes meet. She laughs and shrugs, letting me know she's fine. I'm really over the whole 'Candy Jar' dance routine. But it's the last night of the tour so I guess we should go out with a blast.

"Hey, hey!" Jacob waves his arms in the air.

My fingers slow.

"Welcome our 'Candy Jar' girl to the stage!" Jacob holds one of Mallory's hands up in the air. "Every night she's with us, she's busy watching her man play. You'd think she'd get tired of Chaser. I mean, *I'm* tired of him by now. But nope."

The crowd laughs.

I flip him off. "Tired of you too, bro," I say into my mic.

"Nah, you love me. I've grown on all of ya!"

"Like a fungus," Alvin agrees.

Laughing at their antics, Mallory takes a few steps back. Jacob pulls her forward again. "So you guys all know the story of how Chaser and Mallory met when we filmed the video for 'Candy Jar', right?"

A good portion of the audience screams back some version of *yes*. Up front, an obnoxious group of guys who've been knocking into people the whole show, slap each other. One of them cups his hands around his mouth and shouts, "Slut!"

"Fuck you, dude." Jacob points to the security guard. "Get him out of here."

"Come say that to my face later, motherfucker," I growl into the mic.

"That guy's a dick. Anyway," Jacob continues. "What you don't know is that Mallory's also our, Queen. Of. The. Road!"

He holds up his hands, waiting for us to start the song.

Okay, so I guess we're playing 'Queen of the Road' now. Thanks for the head's up, dick.

I motion for Darren to bring me my slide. Don't know what the fuck he's doing but he's not going to have it in my hands anytime soon, so when Alvin taps out his first few beats, I start the intro without it.

Mallory waves one more time and quickly scurries off stage where Andrew meets her. I eye the bottle of champagne in his hands warily. Fucker's probably planning to douse us with it since it's the last night of the tour. Tradition and all that. I guess we've gotten off lucky compared to some of the pranks I've heard of bands playing on each other at the end of a tour.

The solo for 'Queen of the Road' brings me right back to our shitty little apartment in L.A. Good memories, though. Jacob takes a seat on Alvin's riser, banging his head along until it's time for him to join in and finish the song.

With the mic at his side, Jacob yells, "Candy Jar!" at us.

Closing my eyes, I keep playing, shaping the notes from one song into the other. Two completely different pieces in my mind but the shift sounds pretty fuckin' good. I need to try that more often.

Above me, there's a whoosh. Before I can open my eyes and tilt my head back to see what the fuck it is, thousands of little Dum Dum lollipops rain down from the ceiling.

"Motherfucker!" I'm laughing too hard to sound threatening though.

Ducking my head to avoid getting poked in the eye by a wayward candy stick, I keep right on playing.

A barrage of Skittles pelts us next.

Jacob tips his head back and opens wide, filling his mouth

with the colorful little candies. I step up to my mic and finish the last few lines of the song since Jacob's mouth is occupied. Garrett reaches over to slap Jacob on the back when he coughs and chokes on his mouthful.

The entire stage is coated in lollipops and round sugary pebbles. Jacob slips, lands on his ass and raises his arms in the air.

"Good night, Union! Thanks for the treats, Vicious Vandals!"

Kicking candy out of my way, so I don't faceplant leaving the stage, I finally make it backstage.

Andrew's waiting with a lollipop hanging from his lips. "Sweet show, Chaser."

"You're a dick." I laugh. "You could've poked our damn eyes out."

He doubles over laughing and holds out his hand. I yank him closer, pulling him off his feet and he crashes into me. "Thanks, bro. Good fucking tour. Bullet wounds and arrests notwithstanding."

"We'll do it again, soon, bro," he promises. "Real soon."

I shudder at the thought. Could I survive another tour with Andrew? But tonight's a night to celebrate, so I nod and agree.

"The guys wanted to dump champagne on you but candy seemed so much better!" He nods at Mallory. "I waited until she was off stage."

"Is that why you changed the songs?" I ask Jacob.

He bounces over, grinning and shaking his head. "I had no fucking idea." He lifts his chin at Andrew. "What? No cock hammock for the last show?"

I shoot a glare at Jacob. The tour's been just fine without having to look at Andrew's dick trying to break out of its tiny leather prison every damn night.

"Nah, man." Andrew touches the side where the bullet whizzed through him. "My side is still all fucked up."

Jacob has the decency to look away. "Sorry, bro."

Garrett joins our party by punching Andrew's arm. "Ya

coulda poked my eye out with one of those damn sticks, ya fuckmuppet."

Andrew grins like a loon and points at me. "He said the same thing! You're such a bunch of pussies."

Someone bear-hugs me from behind. "Hey, sweet thang. Nice show," Vinnie shouts in my ear.

"Thanks for the candy shower, dickhead."

He roars with laughter and slaps me on the back. "You did good, kid. Fucking awesome solo tonight. Almost makes me not want to go on stage after you, ya prick."

Shit, a few months ago, I would've been freaking out to know Vinnie Price watched my performance. Now, it all seems...normal.

Andrew and Vinnie wander off to get ready for their set, leaving me with my bandmates to revel in our awesomeness.

Another set of arms try to strangle me from behind. What the fuck?

"I feel like we're real musicians or something now," Alvin says against my ear before releasing me.

"We need T-shirts printed up. 'I survived the Vicious Vandals experience, 1989'."

"Yeah!" He does a quick scan of the immediate area. "I think Tally poached some of our groupies."

"Good for him." I laugh. "Figured that was one of the reasons he came."

Mallory's standing off to the side with my father and I reach over to pull her into my arms. "Surprised you came out on stage."

"Jacob asked if I would." She shrugs. "I couldn't say no on your last night."

"Thank you." I kiss her cheek.

"You coming home with them?" my father asks Alvin.

Alvin shrugs and glances at the ground. "Not in the mood to see my parents, really."

"My dad and Mallory fixed up the house last time we were home. We have a guest room if you want to stay there," I offer.

"Nah, I don't want to be in your way."

"The house is big, Alvin. There's plenty of room," Mallory says.

I appreciate her jumping in because I suspect it's more that Alvin doesn't want to annoy Mallory that's making him hesitate.

"We'll be at the clubhouse a lot too, so you'll have it to yourself for a few days at least."

Mallory peers up at me. Staying at the clubhouse probably isn't high on her list of things to do but I can't exactly say I want to whisk her off to Niagara Falls to propose to her, now can I?

"I'll think about it."

"I had one of the prospects drive her car down, so you have a vehicle to ride home in," my father informs me.

"You couldn't trailer my bike down, old man?" I grin and nudge him with my shoulder.

"Ungrateful fucker," he grumbles.

Alvin runs his hands through his hair a few times. "I'll think it over. I might want to go down to the city for a few days. Do some exploring. Fuck a Rockette." He shrugs.

"If you change your mind, take the train and we'll come pick you up," Mallory says, ignoring the Rockette comment.

"Thanks, hon." He shakes my dad's hand and punches my shoulder before taking off.

"What'd you think of the show?" I ask my father.

He stares at me for a few seconds and just when I think he's come up with an answer, someone interrupts us.

"Chaser! Can I ask you a few questions?" A girl who can't be a day over sixteen pushes her way in front of me. "Please?" She thrusts the laminated pass around her neck toward me. "My name is Shannon Abbott. I won the KISS-99 contest and I'm a reporter for my school paper."

Shit, she's so earnest and cute, I can't say no. "Sure, Shannon. Whatcha got for me?"

Her entire face turns five different shades of red while she flips through her notebook. I tip my head at Mallory and wink.

Finally, the girl finds her list of questions. "Has there been any tension between you and Andrew since the shooting?"

Damn, cute, or not, this kid isn't fucking around.

"Not at all." I lift my chin toward the stage. "That candy raining down on us tonight was all Andrew. The two bands are closer than ever."

She diligently scribbles down my entire answer before flipping the page.

"'Candy Jar' is your most successful song to date. But it's slightly different than most of Kickstart's other body of work. Are you afraid that twenty years from now, that song will be your legacy?"

"Body of work" seems like such a serious way to describe our music but it's an interesting question. One I've never really stopped to consider before. "Honestly, if people remember our music at all in twenty years, I'll be honored."

"Are you tired of playing 'Candy Jar'?"

"Not yet. We feed off the energy of the crowd, and they still seem to enjoy it."

"What about you, Mallory?" she asks.

"Me? Uh, no." She blinks at me. "Every time I hear those opening notes, it reminds me of the day Chaser and I met."

Despite the kid reporter taking diligent notes, I have to lean down and kiss Mallory. "Same."

The girl rattles off a few more standard questions. Plans for our next tour, next album, favorite hobbies. Stuff like that. The girl has spunk for starting off with the hardest questions first, I'll give her that.

"May I take a picture with you?" she asks when she's finished.

"Sure."

Mallory offers to work the camera, but Shannon wants both of us in the photo, so my father ends up doing the honors.

"Thank you so much!" Shannon squeals before running over to Garrett and whipping out her little notepad of terror.

"Cute kid." I chuckle, wondering if she'll ask each of us the same probing questions.

"She was adorable." Mallory smiles, watching Shannon and Garrett. "I wasn't expecting those questions."

"Neither was I."

"Is it always this busy?" my father asks.

"Pretty much." I shrug and glance around. Thom's over in the corner talking to Andrew's tour manager, plotting hell only knows what. Clusters of groupies. Fans, roadies, venue security. "The mood's a bit crazier since it's the last night."

He shifts and for the first time ever, my father seems uncertain or uncomfortable. "You've got a whole life that's separate from the club."

The serious change in tone wipes the grin off my face. "What are you saying?"

"I've never been prouder than I was tonight, watching you." He shakes his head and seems to be having trouble finding the words he wants, so I stay quiet. "Really wish your mom could've seen you."

Not expecting *that* to come out of his mouth, I'm a bit off-balance. "Not like she couldn't find me if she gave a shit," I answer, harsher than I meant.

Mallory tightens her arms around my waist and I hang onto her like she's my damn life raft.

My father straightens up and adjusts his cut. "That's true." He glances out toward the stage. "Such a big crowd. It's been so damn long. She could be here and I wouldn't even recognize her."

As if that thought hasn't occurred to me every time I've stepped on a stage since I formed my first band. "I don't think 'Chaser Adams' would mean much to her. Kickstart sure as fuck wouldn't."

"Maybe." He scuffs the toe of his boot against the concrete floor a few times before glancing up at me again. "Fuck, son, I wasn't trying to ruin your night. I just wanted you to know, I want you to pursue this for as long as it makes you happy."

"Thank you."

"I won't lie. I thought you'd go out to la-la land, try this music thing out for a few months. Maybe a year. Then come home." He holds up one hand. "Not because I don't think you've got the talent. Because it's a nasty, cutthroat business."

"Yeah."

"But watching you up there." He shakes his head. "That joy on your face. That's what I want for you."

"What about—"

"Club's not going anywhere. Music industry, all that entertainment shit, can change in an instant." He snaps his fingers in front of his face. "Fickle business. Ride it out as long as you can. As long as it makes you happy."

Emotions tighten my throat. "Thank you."

The sentimental expression on his face transforms into something more familiar and casual. "You want to hire some of your Demon brothers to run security for your next tour, that might not be a bad idea either." He grins at me, working to lift the heavy tone that settled over this conversation. "You got a network of clubs around the country you can pull from."

"Really? You'd be okay with that?"

"Fuck yeah. Lot of your brothers could use the work and I don't like how close some of those crazed fans want to get to you or Mallory."

"It's only gotten worse since Andrew's shooting."

His mouth twists at the mention of Andrew's name.

I'm left wondering if his reaction is related to my brief stint in jail.

Or if something else happened while I was out on stage tonight.

CHAPTER FIFTEEN

Chaser

Damn, it feels good to be home. Clear-headed and coming off an amazing tour with the woman I want to spend my life with by my side. The five-hour drive seems to fly by with Mallory and I catching up on everything about the tour, her job, and our future plans.

At the house, we find a surprise in the driveway.

Mallory pulls up next to the truck parked in front of the garage. "Who is it?"

I recognize the battered, old truck. "Probably someone my dad sent over."

Only, it's not someone from the garage my father's part owner of. It's the man himself.

"What's this?" I ask, gesturing to the bike being rolled off the back of the truck by two prospects.

"Santa's sleigh. What the fuck's it look like?"

"So happy to see you too, Dad." I glance at the bike again. "Electra Glide, huh? Fancy."

"Shut up." He glances at Mallory and motions her over for a

hug. "How'd you two do trapped in that cage all the way out here?"

"Fine." She winks at my dad. "As long as he has control over the radio, he's a good passenger."

The two of them laugh it up and honestly, I'm loving their budding relationship so much, I don't even care if they're mocking me.

"So, you bought a new bike and came over to rub it in my nose?" I ask. "What are you doing, storing it here?"

He swivels his head between Mallory and me. "You believe this kid?" He jerks his thumb in my direction. "No, ingrate. It came into the garage. I bought it for myself but I thought you might like to use it while you're home." He slides his gaze to Mallory again. "In case you want to take some trips. See some sights." He slaps the seat. "Be more comfortable for your girl."

Gee, Dad why don't you just announce I'm planning to propose to her while we're home? Naturally, he ignores the glare I shoot his way.

He runs his hands over the handlebars. "Same feel as the FLH but it has the larger frame. Less vibration and a little roomier."

"Nice." I run my gaze over the black and gold paint. "Planning to do anything to the colors?"

"No. Strictly civilian ride." Smart choice, so wherever he plans to go, he doesn't run the risk of rolling into another club's territory with our club's colors announcing his arrival. He hands over the keys.

"You sure about this?"

"I trust you. You'll take care of her."

"Thanks, Dad. Appreciate it." I'd been fully prepared to take Mallory's car to Niagara Falls, but this will be much nicer.

Mallory grabs one of her bags out of the trunk and hurries into the house after asking my dad if he's staying for dinner.

My father stares at the front door for a few seconds after Mallory leaves. "Still planning to pop the question?"

Should I answer my father honestly? He might have changed

his mind since the last time I told him my plans to marry Mallory. "Plan to ask her before we go back to L.A."

Like last time, he absorbs the news better than I expected. "Pay off that ring, yet?"

"Need to make the final payment on it and pick it up."

"Still planning to take her to Niagara Falls?"

"Tomorrow maybe, yeah."

He nods slowly. "Things have changed a lot since I was there with your mother. Still supposed to be romantic."

Romantic? Since when does my father care about romance? "Uh, I guess." Shit, this conversation took a strange turn.

"Think you'll be back by the weekend?"

"Sounds like you need me to be." I tap the bike. "What's going on?"

"Nothing." He pauses. "Might try to have a few members of the Silver Saints over again. See if we can work on a few issues."

"You fucking kidding me? Why?"

"We both know it's in every club's best interest to work together instead of against each other."

I tap his chest and then mine. "Yeah, *we* know that. Clubs like theirs, don't."

He doesn't disagree or follow up on my statement. "We'll celebrate your engagement. That should help keep things friendly and casual."

"All right." Works for me. I'll show my face, shake some hands, then get Mallory the fuck away from those cretins. "Need me to do anything while we're in Canada?"

"No. Take your girl away. Relax. She's certainly earned a vacation after puttin' up with your antics."

"Thanks." I eye him carefully. "You sure you're all right with this?" Not that I need my father's permission to propose to my girlfriend but he's taking the news so calmly.

"It's your life." He glances down at his boots. "I know you don't feel like it, but you're both still so young. Forever's a long, long time."

"Yeah, I'm hoping we can end up one of those old couples who celebrate their seventy-fifth wedding anniversary on TV"

"Jesus Christ. Who raised you?"

I grin at him. "You did."

"Don't take this the wrong way, but..."

Ahh, here we go.

"While getting married might help keep things smooth with her father, don't do it for that reason. We're on good terms with the Russians right now."

"Don't take *this* the wrong way, but that idea never occurred to me. I love her and want to spend my life with her. Period."

His eyes widen and guilt stabs me in the gut. Active member or not, what's good for the club should *always* be the first thing on my mind.

"It's all for love then." He says it like it's a damn death sentence.

"Afraid so, Dad." Time to cut this off before it heads south. "Don't say anything to anyone before we leave. I don't want to ruin the surprise."

"I won't say anything. But I'll have to share the news before the party. Otherwise, I'm liable to get a size nine high-heel boot lodged up my ass if Doe can't throw a proper celebration together for you two."

The corners of my mouth twitch. Doe loves to mark every special occasion with a made-from-scratch cake. "That's fine."

He stares at me for a moment but doesn't say anything else.

I can't shake the feeling there's some sort of conflict brewing in his concerned-father eyes.

Whatever it is, I'd probably rather not know.

CHAPTER SIXTEEN

Mallory

"What'd you think of the bike?" Chaser asks after his father leaves.

"It's pretty. Looks comfortable."

His lips curve. "Glad you think so."

The playful gleam in his eyes suggests he has plans for the bike. "Your father said something about touring?"

"I might have mentioned that I wanted to take you on a short trip."

My heart taps a happy little dance. "Where?"

"You ever seen Niagara Falls?"

"I think my parents took me there when I was little, but I don't remember it very well." I lean back against the counter. "Why do you want to go there?"

He shrugs, but a teasing smile lingers on his lips. "Thought it would be romantic to whisk you away for a couple days."

"We're already 'away' here."

"Not the same." He clutches my hip with one hand and leans in. "Not even close."

Excitement bubbles up in me. He's right. Our visits here

haven't exactly been vacations. We tried to make the best of our trip to England, but it was still work and ended in disaster. Traveling with Chaser on tour was more grueling than enjoyable. This trip will be purely for us.

"Let's do it."

"Cool." He runs his fingers through his hair. "I can't be gone too long. I need to help my father out with some stuff this weekend, but—"

"I don't care. It'll be nice to relax, see something new. Anything as long as I'm with you."

"Thought you'd be sick of me by now."

"I don't think that's possible." I tip my head to the side. "Are you sick of me?"

"Never."

After a quick dinner, Chaser flips through the phone book and wanders into his father's downstairs office.

A few minutes later, he returns, keys in hand and jacket on. "I'm going to run out for a bit."

An uncomfortable sensation rolls over me. This feels too familiar to the last time we were here and he snuck out to get high. "I'll come with you."

"No." He leans down and kisses my cheek. "You must be tired from driving all day."

"I'm fine."

His gaze darts to the door and back to the keys in his hand. "I want to take Dad's bike for a test drive. Make sure it's safe before I take you out on it."

"Oh." While I appreciate the concern for my safety, it doesn't have the ring of truth to it. "What about you."

He knocks his fist against his skull. "You know how hard-headed I am. I'll be fine."

That's not reassuring but I'm not sure what else to say.

"I'll stop by Alice in Videoland and pick up a movie, okay?"

"*Say Anything* should be out."

"So is *Lethal Weapon 2*"

"Aww, shucks." I snap my fingers in the air and feign disappointment. "I haven't seen *Lethal Weapon 1*."

He grins and kisses my cheek. "*Lethal Weapon 1* it is."

"I walked right into that, didn't I?"

"You did."

I follow him to the door and tug on his jacket before he steps outside. "Safety check of the bike, grab a movie, and home, right?" I hate the desperate twinge to my voice but I can't help it.

"Yup." He waves at me over his shoulder.

Why am I not reassured?

Chaser

A bit of guilt follows me to the jewelry store. Obviously, Mallory fears I'm going off to score coke. Can't blame her. I kept things light and evasive. Otherwise I feared I'd confess my real mission and ruin the surprise.

This needs to be perfect. After everything she's put up with from me. I need to propose to her in the right way. Something special.

The store's about to close when I pull into a spot. I hurry inside. The jeweler's happy to see me.

"Chaser, I was just thinking about you."

"Worried I wouldn't make the final payment?"

"Not at all. I heard your tour was a success."

"A few bumps along the way but it wasn't bad."

"That's life." He bends down, unlocks a secret cabinet, and slides a blue velvet box across the glass counter.

I pop it open and check out the ring. Fuck, I can't wait to see Mallory's face when I slip it on her finger.

"Do you know how you're going to propose?" he asks as I unfold a stack of bills on the counter.

"Not quite. I'm taking her up to Niagara Falls for a few days.

Hoping for some inspiration once we get there."

He scoops up the pile of cash, and not bothering to recount it, shoves it in the register drawer. Devil Demons MC has been coming here for years for custom pieces. I wouldn't wreck that relationship by trying to short him a few bucks, and he knows it.

"Don't over think it. Spontaneous and from the heart is always best, Chaser."

"She's special, though."

He taps the top of the ring box. "It doesn't get more special than asking her to spend forever with you."

If that doesn't put things into perspective, I don't know what does.

I slip the ring box into my pocket, say goodnight, and step outside.

Tipping my head back, I stare at the darkening sky, considering his words.

Somehow, forever doesn't seem long enough.

CHAPTER SEVENTEEN

Mallory

Chaser didn't come back high, but he's in a weird mood all night and the next morning. Wired. Edgy almost. I try to chalk it up to adjusting to life now that the tour's over and excitement about our trip.

After breakfast, he follows me upstairs while I pack a few essentials in the bag he gave me to fit on the bike.

"Don't forget a sexy dress," Chaser reminds me.

I wave a slinky burgundy minidress at him. "Does this meet with your approval, Mr. Adams?"

"I like the color." He glances down at my feet. "Bring comfortable shoes, though. We might do a lot of walking."

I hold up the only pair of sneakers I brought with me—mint green L.A. Gear high-tops. "These don't go with the dress, Mr. Fashion."

"Bring jeans. Save the dress for L.A."

I set the dress on the bed and place my hand on my hip. "I *do* have a lot of wardrobe glitches when we're out and about, don't I?"

He grins and leans down to kiss my shoulder. "Yeah, but I

love helping you fix 'em." He curls one arm around my waist. "I was kidding about the dress. You're stunning no matter what you're wearing. Although, I did have this recurring fantasy of you leaning over one of the railings at the falls, hiking up your dress and—"

"Getting arrested?"

"No."

"Falling into the rapids?"

His laughter rumbles against my back. "No."

"If I bring the dress, will you promise to give me a piggyback ride?"

More rumbling laughter out of him. I'm so in love with this carefree version of Chaser.

"I'll give you any kind of ride you want, little dove."

I stuff a pair of black flats, jeans, the dress, and a few other items into the bag and hand it to Chaser.

"Bring your jacket," he reminds me on his way downstairs.

WITH THE COOLER FALL WEATHER, I'M GRATEFUL FOR THE leather jacket one of the old ladies from the clubhouse sent over with Stump. My thickest pair of jeans and black leather boots also help.

It's a shorter ride than I expected and soon we're rolling up to the Canadian border. The guard glances at our licenses and gives Chaser's bike a once-over before waving us through.

The bike thunders down the streets, turning heads. The doorman at the first hotel we stop at sniffs and informs us there are no open rooms. Chaser stares at him for a few beats before walking in anyway. We're turned away at the front desk.

The next place we try is at least nicer but they also don't have a room.

None of the hotels closest to the falls have rooms available.

"Shit, I'm so sorry." Chaser runs his hand over his head and glances up and down the street. "I thought a spontaneous trip would be fun. I should've called—"

"I don't care. I'm just excited to be here with you." I take his hand and skip ahead, dragging him along. "Let's try a little farther away from the falls."

Sure enough, we find a small motel about a ten-minute walk away with a spare room.

"This isn't what I had in mind," Chaser grumbles, glancing around at the faded, nubby brown carpet and dark wood paneling.

"It's fine." I jump onto the bed, trying not wince at the bone-jarring rattling the frame makes as I kneel in the middle. "We're not going to spend much time here anyway."

His lips curl into a smirk. "You're mistaken, little dove. I planned to have you in that bed a *lot*."

I rock back and forth, testing the mattress. Both of us burst out laughing at the predictable squeaks the ancient bed makes. Even the smallest movement elicits a metallic creak.

"The entire city will hear us in this thing," I mutter.

"Shower sex it is." He points to the bathroom. "Let's wash up, fuck, and I'll take you to dinner."

I can't help laughing at his brash orders. Or teasing him. "We should probably fuck, then wash up, and go to dinner."

"You're right." He lifts me off the bed and carries me into the bathroom, gently setting me down on the sink. "I'm gonna shoot cum all over your ass after I thoroughly fuck your pussy."

"You're so dirty."

He grins and flashes a cocky wink before stripping off his clothes. "You have no idea." He cups my cheeks and swoops in for another kiss. "We have a lot of missed time to make up for."

I promised myself I wouldn't say anything until we were back in L.A. but the words come out on their own. "And you're going right back out on the road after the album's done?"

Silence.

Slowly, I lift my gaze.

"It looks like it," he says gently. "We have three weeks off around the holidays. I'll take you anywhere you want to go."

I swallow hard and nod. "I'd be happy at home with your family."

"Yeah? You sure about that? They get pretty rowdy around the holidays."

"Maybe we can visit my dad." I bite my lip. "I hate thinking of him alone in prison for Christmas..."

"We can do that. Whenever you want." He strokes his knuckles over my cheek. "And I'm pretty sure someone has a birthday to celebrate."

"Ugh." I duck my head. "I don't want to turn twenty-one."

"What? Who doesn't want to turn twenty-one?"

"Twenty's a nice even number."

He bursts out laughing. "You can't stay twenty forever." His eyes light up. "Oh, that might make a good lyric." I'm left shaking my head while he races out to the bedroom to write down a few lines.

Chaser

The little blue velvet box I'm carrying inside the chest pocket of my jacket seems to have a pulse of its own. A dozen times while we're walking the ten minutes down to the falls, I have the urge to drop to my knees and ask her to marry me.

Especially after she came close to admitting she doesn't want me to go back out on tour. It's a good time to propose. So she knows I'm not running off on tour to get away from her.

I figure I'll pop the question during dessert? Maybe hide the ring in her cake? Fuck, that seems lame. Besides, what if she accidentally bites it or chokes on it or something?

All through dinner I keep patting my pocket. Checking to make sure the ring's still there. Contemplating if this is the right time.

Keep it simple.

Maybe tomorrow, we'll go somewhere fancier, and I'll do it then.

After dinner, we pass a booth that sells tickets for boat tours. The big boats that get up close to the majestic falls.

Fuck proposing at dinner, I have a better idea.

"Let's grab tickets for this," I suggest.

She barely glances at the brochure I hand her before agreeing. "That sounds like fun."

I hope she says yes to my proposal as easily.

They hand us thin blue plastic ponchos as we board the boat. One of the guides actually recognizes us and thoroughly shakes my hand.

"Wow. Big fan. I caught your show down in Union. It was so dope."

"No kidding. You drove all the way down there?"

"Hell yeah, Vicious Vandals with Kickstart? No question. You're my top two favorite bands of all time."

"Thank you." Sometimes, I still feel so new at this, a statement like that is hard to process.

He points to the left. "If you go to the back of the boat, you'll actually have a better view of the falls when we turn around." He nods at Mallory. "If it's too much, you can avoid the spray inside but still have a good view inside too."

"Thank you."

His gaze slides to Mallory and back to me. "So are you still friends with Andrew Lane? Like you guys hang out together and stuff?"

"Yeah. Well, we just got off tour and I went home to visit my folks but, we'll hang out back in L.A." Andrew's like lint. I can't brush him off no matter how hard I try.

"That's so cool." He bobs his head up and down. "I hope you guys tour together again."

I'm saved from answering by the guy's boss yelling at him to keep the line moving. Mallory and I duck and race for the back of the boat.

The boat hasn't left yet but a fine coating of mist sticks to us.

I help Mallory into her poncho and brush her hair off her already damp cheeks. "You don't get seasick, do you?"

Her nervous gaze studies the water. "Why? Is it that rough?"

"It might get choppier as we approach the falls."

"I'll be fine."

I slip my poncho on and hold my arms out to show it off to her. "What do you think?"

"Still a badass rock star, even in blue see-through plastic."

"Excellent." I lean down and kiss droplets of water from the tip of her nose.

The gentle rumble of the boat's engine increases and few minutes later, the whole thing lurches away from the dock. Mallory grabs the railing with both hands. I brace myself behind her body to protect her from the jerkiest movements. "I've got you."

We're instantly drenched. Water splashes up and over the railing. Mallory yelps and inhales a mouthful.

"Yuck." She sputters and spits it out, shaking her head.

Shit. There's no way I can propose out here. One of us will end up flying overboard.

"Do you want to go inside?"

She looks longingly at the indoor area and back to the water. We'll have the best view of the falls when the boat makes its turn and we head back. But we should still be able to see from inside. Hell, if not I'll just take her for another ride tomorrow.

My proposal can't wait another second.

Mallory

Soaked and shivering, Chaser leads me inside. We still have a clear view of the surrounding falls and it's easier to hear the announcer inside. I'm still worried I'm ruining the experience for Chaser.

He tugs on my hand and I turn away from the falls to find him with one knee against the ship's wet, rusty floor.

"Chaser? Are you okay? Did you slip?"

He shakes his head and fumbles a small blue, velvet box out of his inside jacket pocket.

My heart thumps. My body trembles. This can't be...

Chaser wraps his fingers around my left hand and stares up at me, so much love shining in his eyes.

"Mallory, you make me a better person."

"What are you doing?"

He answers with a half-smile. "Even when I screw up you love me and help put me back on the right path. I want to travel down every path with you by my side for the rest of my life. Every second we're apart, I want to be by your side. I love everything about you—your voice, your kindness..." He squeezes his eyes shut for a brief second before asking, "Will you marry me?"

Tears stream down my face and my throat closes, cutting off the *yes* that I want to shout at the top of my lungs. Frantically, I nod my head up and down while thrusting my hand in his face. "Yes," I whisper in an excited rush. "Yes, yes, yes!"

He fumbles with the box for a moment, then grins at me. He lifts his chin. "I wanted to do it out there when we were under the falls, but I was afraid the ring might pop out of my hand and into the water or we'd go flying overboard."

"Good call." Wild laughter spills out of me and then dies in my throat when I finally take in the ring. "Oh my God, Chaser. It's so beautiful! It's Princess Diana's ring!"

"Not exactly," he says, slipping it on my finger. "It's square, not oval." He winks. "I wanted it to be unique to *my* princess."

"It's beautiful." A halo of tiny diamonds sparkle around a large, square cut cornflower blue sapphire. "I love it so much."

Cheers and clapping explode around us and we both look around.

"Kiss her!" someone shouts.

My cheeks heat up and my gaze shoots to Chaser, who stands

and pulls me into his arms. He tips his head down, studying my face for a moment. "You gonna be my wife?"

"Only if you're my husband."

"Perfect," he murmurs, closing the distance between our lips.

The burning heat in his eyes is more than arousal. It's a vow.

"I will love, protect, and cherish you until I die, Mallory," he whispers before brushing his lips against mine.

I wrap my arms around his neck. Our slick, plastic ponchos crinkle and slide together—an obstacle to getting as close to him as possible. Finally, he pulls back.

Nervous from all the inquiring stares, I lead him to one of the benches up front.

"When did you?" I hold my hand out, wiggling my fingers in front of me. "Did you find it while you were on tour?"

"Nope. Put a deposit on it last time we were home. Picked it up the night before we left."

"Oh my God." Wild laughter spills from my lips followed by shame. "Chaser," I whisper.

"You thought I was running off to get high, didn't you?" His gentle question doesn't hold any judgment.

"Maybe a little..."

He cups my cheek and touches his forehead to mine. "I don't blame you. And I'm sorry you ever had to worry about that."

"When do you want to get married? Where?"

Instead of excitement, sadness darkens his expression. "When I get back from the next tour. It'll give you some time to plan everything the way you want it."

"I don't care about anything except you." I pause to reconsider. "Barefoot on the beach?"

"I like that idea." His mouth flattens into a serious line. "Before we return to L.A., we need to tell your father we're engaged."

The rebellious woman inside me who ran off to Hollywood shakes her fists in the air. "Why? So he can give us his blessing? I don't need or want it, Chaser."

"I'm not *asking* him anything. No one's stopping us from getting married," he declares in a defiant tone that actually puts me at ease. "But he's going to be my father-in-law for the rest of my life. I want to do my part to start off on the right foot. That means I need to show him some respect." Chaser pauses and seems to reconsider his declaration. "Even if it's not the kind of respect he demands."

As much as he jokes about being a biker-rock star-bum, Chaser has more honor and courage than any of the men who work for my father. If he can set aside his prejudice long enough to see who Chaser is, he'll be proud to have him for a son-in-law.

"He's not exactly in a position to make demands," I point out.

"No." His mouth quirks. "He's not. Lucky for me."

I snort and rest my forehead against his chest. "He should be delighted."

"The only delight I'm concerned about is yours."

"Did you tell *your* father?"

"Hell, yeah I did."

"And he was okay with it?"

Chaser takes a long, deep breath before answering. "He took it better than I expected. He was worried that we're too young for marriage." He shrugs. "I told him we want to be one of those couples on the news celebrating their seventy-fifth anniversary one day."

His voice is light and teasing but the sentiment is anything but. "I'd like that," I whisper.

CHAPTER EIGHTEEN

Chaser

Everything about our future seems possible as we leave Canada and head home. Our love is unshakable. We'll survive tours, television shows, and ornery fathers. Anything the world throws at us, we can handle.

It's late early afternoon when we pull into the clubhouse parking lot. Not a lot of action going on, which is fine. I want to enjoy our engagement without sharing the news with anyone else yet.

Except for my father. We stop by his office first.

He stands and walks around his desk to pull me in for a long, tight hug.

"Glad you're back, son."

"We have news."

He pushes me back but keeps his hands on my shoulders. The corners of his mouth twitch. "Yeah, what's that?"

I reach over and take Mallory's hand, lifting to show him her ring. "I asked her to be my wife and—"

"I couldn't say yes fast enough," Mallory finishes for me.

Dad studies the ring for a few seconds before saying

anything. Almost long enough for awkwardness to settle over us. "Congratulations."

"You getting emotional, old man?" I ask.

He waves me off. "Excuse me for being happy for my son." He drags Mallory in and gives her a fatherly hug and pat on the back. "If he ever gives you trouble, you come to me and I'll set him straight, sweetheart."

Mallory chuckles and puts her arms around him. "Done."

"And you can call me Dad or Pop now."

She stares up at him with wide eyes for a few seconds. "Okay, Dad." The endearment rolls off her tongue slowly as if she's testing it out.

He kisses her cheek. "Welcome to the family, princess."

"All right, that's enough." I slice my arm between them. "Get your hands off my fiancée."

Mallory chuckles and steps away and threads her arm through mine.

Dad gestures to the two chairs in front of his desk. "The three of us need to have a chat."

I know what's coming but Mallory's brow wrinkles in confusion. "Are we in trouble?" she whispers as we take our seats.

"No."

Dad settles in behind his desk, leans forward on his elbows, and focuses on Mallory. "Your last visit to your father went well. Things have calmed. I want to continue our respectful relationship—"

"We already talked about this, Dad."

He continues as if I hadn't interrupted him. "I need you to visit your father and tell him you two are engaged *before* you go back to California."

Mallory stares at me with wide eyes before answering my father. "Of course we will."

"Good girl."

He glances at the clock. "First thing tomorrow morning. Before the party."

THE PROCESS TO GET INSIDE THE PRISON IS JUST AS ANNOYING as it was the first time we visited.

However, on this visit, DeLova is allowed to awkwardly embrace his daughter and sit down without a pane of plexiglass in the way. I can't say the situation is an improvement.

"You came to visit again." He smiles at his daughter then casts a less enthusiastic look my way. "And brought the young Mr. Adams with you. Again."

Definitely not happy to see me.

"We have news that we wanted to share with you, Father." She holds up her left hand and proudly flashes her engagement ring at him. I'll never get tired of seeing her do that. "Chaser and I are getting married."

Damn, I still get a thrill every single time she says it out loud.

Poor old man just stares at his daughter. His expression doesn't change. Guess he's not excited about our announcement.

Mallory drops her hand into her lap. "Father, I hope you're happy for me."

His tired gaze swings my way. "Does he treat you well, Mallory? Respect you?" he asks without taking his eyes off me.

I keep my hands clasped on the table in front of me and don't move a muscle, wanting him to understand whatever comes out of Mallory's mouth is the truth and not influenced by my presence.

"Yes, Father. Chaser is good to me. He's always respectful."

"So respectful you're living in sin with this man out in the City of Angels?" He flips his wrist in a dismissive way.

Obviously, the old man is still keeping tabs on us.

Mallory inhales a deep breath. "I'm twenty years old, Father. My living arrangements are *my* business."

He snorts.

"Chaser protects me and always supports me. You will be proud to have him as your son-in-law."

"Who does my daughter need protection from?" he asks me.

A smart ass remark like "you and your thugs" flirts on the tip of my tongue but I bite it back. No reason to turn this visit into a shit show if I can avoid it. Or give the old man any ideas.

Besides, there are plenty of other things to protect Mallory from. No point in sugarcoating it. "There are a lot of sleazeballs in Hollywood, sir."

"Then why do you allow her to continue this foolish pursuit?"

What a loaded question. Where to begin?

"Your daughter's talented, sir. She wants to honor her mother's memory by pursuing this career. I support her one-hundred percent."

He winces at the mention of his wife and turns toward Mallory. "Angelina put those foolish ideas in your head, didn't she? But she never shared all the bad experiences. I kept your mother safe. I protected her from *sleazeballs*." He draws out the word in what I assume is an attempt to mock me.

"Did you protect her, sir?" I ask. "Or take something away she loved?"

He slams his fists against the table, drawing the attention of one of the guards. "She loved being a wife and mother."

"But she could have done more," Mallory whispers.

"God didn't allow her time for *more*." His cuffs scrape against the table as he reaches over and places his hands on top of Mallory's. "You're all I have left in this world."

Her bottom lip trembles ever-so-slightly, but Mallory lifts her chin and answers in a firm voice, "Then you should want me to be happy."

"I never knew you were this stubborn." He casts a murderous look my way.

"Mallory has her own mind, sir. Maybe she didn't have the courage to express it before you went inside, but I assure you her stubborn will to succeed didn't develop overnight."

"I wanted to keep you safe," he says to Mallory, ignoring my comments. "Maybe I should have explained the kind of enemies I had when you were younger..."

"You wanted to control me and treat me like a piece of property, Father." Mallory's obviously given this a lot of thought and I couldn't be prouder of the fire in her eyes and snap to her tone as she lets her father know exactly how she feels. "To you, I'm no different from your expensive paintings or your Mercedes. Find a safe place to park me and show me off when it suits you. Maybe if you and Mom had raised a different daughter that would have been okay but it's not okay for me."

Holy fuck am I glad he's chained up on the other side of that table.

DeLova works his jaw from side to side as he swallows Mallory's words down. "You're my daughter. A piece of me. I want what is best for you. Always. That is so wrong?"

"I'm my own person. Separate from *you*."

"Does she talk back to you like this?" he asks me.

Hell no, I'm not playing along with his humor-the-little-woman game. "If by *talk back* you mean expresses her thoughts and feelings honestly, then yeah. She's the smartest person I know."

He snorts and motions for Mallory to give him her hand. "Let me see this ring."

Slowly, Mallory holds out her hand. DeLova carefully inspects the sapphire and diamonds, even scratches his thumbnail against the gold band.

"You didn't ask my permission, son," he says without looking at me.

"I'm not a piece of chattel, Father." Mallory yanks her hand back. "The only permission he needed was *mine*."

Poor old-fashioned DeLova, imprisoned *and* subjected to this feisty side of his daughter he never knew existed. I barely stuff down my laughter.

He blows out a defeated breath. "Can I please walk my only

daughter down the aisle?" His blue eyes bore into me. "When you marry this man you have chosen for yourself."

That still doesn't sound like acceptance, but he's got a few more years behind bars to come to terms with me as his son-in-law.

"Well, we want to get married in California," Mallory says.

"What a vile place." Her father sighs. "I still want to be there."

"Okay," Mallory whispers. After a few beats she lifts her head and stares her father down. In a strong, no-bullshit manner she adds, "Daddy, since we're being so open and honest today, let me be crystal clear. If you *ever* try to do anything to interfere in our relationship or send anyone to harm Chaser or his family, I will disappear from your life for good. That is a fact, not a threat."

He sits back and stares at her.

Clearly Mallory knows her father better than he thought. Somewhere in his conniving, criminal brain, I'm sure he's been plotting my death from the second we made our announcement.

She leans in closer. "Vasily tried to take me once. I won't make those mistakes that led him to me again, Father. So for the sake of our relationship..." she touches the back of his hand and then her chest, "...I hope you're sincere." She glances around at the prison walls. "We're already losing enough time together. I need you to accept our engagement with an open and honest heart."

That might be difficult since what's beating in DeLova's chest is probably black and pumping acid instead of blood through his veins.

"You have my word," he promises.

"Good, because I would hate to lose you forever."

Mallory

Outside the prison, I collapse against the truck door, my head hitting the window with a thump. My heart's never pounded so fast and my knees are so weak I can barely stand.

142

Did I really say those things to my father? I've never spoken up. Talked back. Voiced an opinion to him. Not once in my life.

Chaser presses his body against mine and kisses my forehead. "I am in *awe* of you."

I lift my shaking hands between us, staring at them. "I can't believe I threatened my father."

His body quivers and when I glance up, he's laughing.

I sock him in the gut and he laughs harder. "It was *beautiful*, Mallory. Every fucking word. Priceless. Poor bastard. I almost felt bad for him."

I growl and press my hands against his chest to push him away. But he captures my wrists and pins them at my sides. "I'm serious. After the shit I've put you through the last few months, you standing up for me means everything."

"I was standing up for myself too."

"That means even more."

My gaze slips to the prison doors. "I don't trust him."

"Neither do I. But he's got no reason to come after me right now. We promised him we'd wait until he's out to get married."

"Screw that. I don't want to wait. I don't want our wedding to be a big affair that belongs to everyone except us."

He swallows hard. "What do you want, little dove?"

"Let's elope. We can do it in California without telling anyone. We'll have the big, expensive, showy party for our family and friends later. No one will know the difference."

"Mallory, I want to give you the world. Everything you desire and deserve."

"Do you know how many of those ostentatious weddings I attended growing up? I wasn't the starry-eyed little girl sitting there fantasizing about my own poofy white dress and bag full of envelopes stuffed with cash that everyone felt obligated to bring." I close my eyes and take a deep breath. "No, I dreamed of getting married barefoot on the beach and curling my toes in the sand when I said, 'I do'."

"Yeah?"

I hook my fingers in his belt loops and tug him closer. "I dreamed of a man who made me feel loved, cherished, and protected every day repeating his vows next to me. A man I chose for myself."

His eyes search my face. "That's me, little dove."

"It is," I agree, reaching up on tiptoes to kiss his jaw and whisper in his ear. "If I'd known my future husband had all these glorious muscles and beautiful ink, I would've run off to Hollywood much, much sooner."

He quirks an eyebrow. "Glorious, huh?"

I tease my fingers under his shirt, tracing my fingers over smooth skin and hard muscles. "A work of art."

"Are you sure you want to be a rock star's wife?" he teases.

"No, Chaser. I want to be *your* wife. No matter what you do. No matter where we end up in life, I want to be by your side."

I pull in a deep breath. Everyone seems to be worried that we're too young to understand the magnitude of this commitment.

And all I am is grateful we found each other now, so we can spend a long, long life together.

CHAPTER NINETEEN

Mallory

I don't know what possessed me to throw the blue leather dress in my bag before I left L.A. It wasn't because I had some sort of premonition about Chaser proposing, that's for sure. I'm still having trouble believing this is real and keep stopping to stare at my ring. Maybe I knew there wouldn't be anywhere in Kodack to buy a truly killer outfit if we attended a club party while we were here.

Tonight, it will serve as my engagement party dress.

My father would probably insist his princess wear something demure and classier for an engagement party. But demure isn't really done here at the Devil Demons MC's clubhouse.

Skintight leather dress it is.

"Fuck," Chaser groans. "You know I can't keep my hands off you in that."

I dangle the dress in front of me and wiggle my hips. "I'll require your assistance to squeeze into it."

"I swear to fuck if one of my brothers looks at you sideways, blood's gonna be spilled tonight."

"Stop." I rifle through the tiny closet in Chaser's clubhouse room. "Shoot. I wish I'd brought those silver heels with me. All I have here are black ones."

"Wear those black lace, fingerless gloves with it then," he suggests.

"Chaser Adams, are you helping me accessorize?"

He squeezes his eyes shut and holds one fist in the air. "No, I'm picturing you giving me a hand job while wearing those gloves and your engagement ring."

I fling one of my shoes at him and somehow he opens his eyes and catches it mid-air. "I got the reflexes of a cat, baby."

"And the urges of a *tom cat*."

"That too," he agrees.

The bedroom door rattles on its hinges and a few seconds later, flies open.

"Knock much, old man?" Chaser growls at his father.

"Sorry." Stump grins. "Heard you yapping, so I figured you were both decent." He jerks his thumb over his shoulder. "Can we have a word, son?"

"Sure." Chaser leans in to kiss my cheek and whispers in my ear. "I'll help you with the dress when I get back."

After they leave, I rummage through the closet, wishing I'd brought more stuff from the house with me. There's a knock at the door and I rush over to open it.

"Mallory!" Doe squeals and wraps me up in a big hug. "Stump told us the news. I'm so happy for you, darling."

"Thank you."

"You're going to be a good old lady for Chaser. I feel it." Her eyes sparkle.

I step back and must not look too sure.

"What's wrong, hon?"

"I don't think I can be his old lady if we're out in Hollywood." I meant it as a joke but it comes out so serious, Doe pushes the door closed and nudges me over to the bed to sit down.

"Sweetheart, I get that the club is...unfamiliar to you but it's in Chaser's blood. Accept who he is now or don't marry him."

My eyes must be snapping fire because she sits back and holds her hands up. "The club will be your family now too, Mallory."

"I..." I turn and take in the small bedroom. "My father's in prison. I don't want that for Chaser."

"Chaser's a smart man. Like his father. Trust him. Always have his back."

"I do." I swipe at a stray tear. "Sometimes I feel like it's us against the entire world."

"It's not, honey. I promise. The club always has your back too." She lifts her head and stares at the door for a second. "I can't tell you how many times Stump was ready to ride straight to California and kill some of those pricks who write that garbage about you two in the papers."

"What?" I moan and hang my head. "Stump's read that crap? He knows it's all lies, right?"

"Of course. We all do. Hell, honey, you two never stop eyeballing each other long enough to notice anyone else in the room. No way you're seeing anyone behind Chaser's back."

"Sheesh." I blow out a breath, mortified they've read those stories.

"The only thing stopping Stump is that he knows how much Chaser wants to keep the music thing separate from the club. It's more for the club's protection, than Chaser's."

I can see that. While news spreading about *my* father would probably kill my career, Chaser's connection to an MC would only enhance his rock-n-roll "bad boy" image. But it would also draw unwanted attention to the MC.

"I know Stump likes to tease and call you princess." She pats my back. "But you're made of strong stuff, Mallory. Let go of your fear. There's no room for it in this life. Shit gets ugly sometimes." She twists her wedding ring around a few times. "But you can't appreciate the beauty of life without the ugliness."

147

"Thank you."

"Now, let me see this ring." She reaches for my hand. "Then, it's time for a celebration."

Chaser

Dread settles in my stomach as I follow my father into his office.

"How'd the visit with DeLova go?" he asks once we're both seated.

"Even better than last time." I give him a quick rundown of our meeting. Complete with Mallory's threat if her father comes after me.

"Jesus Christ, did she wave a red flag in front of him too while she was at it?"

"I think he understood her message fine." I sit forward and knock my knuckles against the desk to gain his full attention. "He's a misguided, ruthless man, no question. But somewhere deep down in his black soul, he loves his daughter." I almost add, *just like you care about me,* but even though my father's as savage as they come, comparing him to a ruthless snake like DeLova seems wrong.

The creases in his face seem deeper than ever. "There's no reason to rush into marriage."

I knew his positive attitude about our engagement wouldn't last. "I'm not in the mood for your 'don't settle down until you're forty' bullshit, Dad."

"It's not *you* I'm worried about." He holds out his hands in a settle down gesture that has the exact opposite effect on me. "Don't lose your shit, I'm about to get blunt with you."

"Since when have you ever had any tact?"

He doesn't laugh. "Mallory doesn't strike me as the kind of girl with a lot of *experience.*"

Muscles in my neck tighten. I narrow my eyes, putting every ounce of warning into my stare. "Tread carefully, old man."

"Hear me out before you flip your shit."

He waits for a beat and when I don't say anything, continues.

"I get that it's exciting. Makes you feel like a king knowing yours is the only dick she's ridden."

"Are you motherfuckin' serious right now?"

He holds his hands up in a truce gesture but it still feels like the worst of this conversation hasn't punched me in the jaw yet.

"I'm not asking you to confirm or deny. I don't need details to see how innocent she is, son."

"Fuck off," I snarl.

He stares down at his desk and traces a pattern over the worn, scarred wood. "I met your mom when she was still in high school."

The fury boiling inside me threatens to spill over into throwing punches at my old man. "Great, so you're a class A perv."

"Maybe." He nods. "Didn't look at it that way back then. She always jumped on the back of my bike willingly."

I groan, but I can't deny there's a part of me curious to know more about their history. But not in *this* context.

He clears his throat and barrels ahead. "It was a rush to know I was the only man she'd ever been with—"

"For the love of fuck—"

"Hear me out. We were...extremely compatible and I loved teaching her everything—"

"Jesus Christ, I'm begging you to *stop*." I shift in my seat and stare at the wall over his head. "Just *stop*."

"All I'm saying is, it's fun and exciting *now*. But ten, twelve years from now she might start to regret that she had no other experience. Regret can drive even a good woman away."

That's it.

I stand and slam my fists on his desk, leaning over so I'm right in his face. "Are you really trying to say Mom wanting to sow some wild oats is what made her abandon us?" Each word drips out of me like slow, molten venom. "Is that what you want me to believe? Do you think I'm so fucking stupid I forgot that you cheated on her left and right? Do you think I don't

149

remember listening to her sob her heart out on the nights you didn't come home? You're trying to lay all the blame on *her*? Because she didn't fuck around enough before you married her? Is that the point you're trying to make?"

He works his jaw from side to side, then glances away. "I'm not saying I was perfect."

"That's an understatement."

"You're both young. But Mallory...she's really young *and* inexperienced."

"So, what do you suggest? What's your *solution* to this problem you think we have? Want me to lay her out on the pool table and offer her up to my brothers?"

"Jesus, fuck no, you little asshole."

"Then what point are you trying to make with this disgusting, shitty conversation?"

"She must have guys tripping over their balls to nail her out in California."

Thank fuck I left my hunting knife at home because I would definitely gut my father right about now.

"Maybe let her explore some." He shrugs. "If she comes back to you, great. No regrets down the road. For either of you."

"Are you going senile, old man?" I rub my fingers over my throbbing temples. "Is this dementia talking?"

"What about that lanky punk at your show?" He snaps his fingers, trying to recall the name. "Andrew. He was panting after her all fucking night."

Revulsion burns the back of my throat. "Are you suggesting I offer my future wife up to my friend? Loan her out, like she's a fucking car? Let him break her in some more and see if she still wants me when he's finished with her? Is *that* the kind of man you think I am?"

"She seemed into—"

"Do *not* finish that sentence, old man."

"I'm trying to save you some heartache later in life."

"What the fuck is wrong with you? Yesterday you were welcoming her to the family and today you're—"

"It's not just for your sake, but for whatever kids you two might have."

He did not go there. "Fuck you. Mallory would *never* abandon her children. She's not some starry-eyed teenager believing all the lies some old predator fed her."

"I never lied to your mother."

"That right? You were up front and honest about all the clubwhores you'd be fucking behind her back? You honestly believe Mom riding a few more dicks before she settled down with *you* would've made her okay with your whore harem?"

He rolls his shoulders, a sign we're dangerously close to finishing this conversation with our fists. "I know what she told me before she left."

"All your screwing around broke her damn heart, you oblivious fucking asshole!" I take a breath and calm myself. No matter how much I want to stab my father to death right now, I don't need the rest of the club to hear me yelling at our president. "I'm finished with this discussion."

He opens his mouth but I can't listen to another word. "Don't *ever* bring this up again."

"Russell..." He sounds so broken I almost want to apologize but I can't bring myself to say the words. Not after this. "I'm trying to save you some pain."

"Yeah, well, this conversation did more damage than anything Mallory could ever do to me."

I slam the door when I walk out of his office and smile with satisfaction when something crashes to the floor inside.

Tally's at the bar watching me with a bland expression.

"What?" I snap.

"Everything okay?"

I haven't quite gotten over the irritation of how close he and Mallory were while I was battling my cocaine demons. Even if he never hit on her, it still ticks me off. I glance back at my father's office. Then again, the old man *is* the one who sent Mallory out with Tally in the first place. To piss me off, no doubt. Now I wonder if he had this "experimentation" theory in mind back then?

Whatever's going on inside my demented father's head isn't Tally's fault. He's a brother. I've known him a long time and we have plenty in common.

I jerk my thumb over my shoulder. "Relationship advice from the old man wasn't high on my list of things I wanted today."

He snorts. "Neither of our fathers are qualified to advise anyone on that topic."

"Amen, brother."

Brothers stomp into the clubhouse, ready to celebrate. A few of the old ladies stop by and pat me on the shoulder or kiss my cheek to congratulate me.

Tally watches the room for a few seconds before motioning me closer to him.

"Mallory's a good girl, Chaser." His gaze shifts to the side. "What you two have is real. I respect your dad as my president. Love him like a brother. Hell, he's been like a second father to me for most of my life, but don't let him fuck up what you and Mallory have together."

"Thanks, brother." I slap his shoulder in appreciation.

"Go get your girl. It's time to celebrate." He lifts his chin toward my father's office. "Worry about it tomorrow."

Fuck that. I have no intention of letting the seed my father planted take root.

But that's the thing about intentions.

The road to hell is lined with 'em.

CHAPTER TWENTY

Mallory

Whatever Chaser and his father discussed must have been unpleasant. He returns to our room in a foul mood, slamming the door behind him and letting out a string of curses.

"What do you think?" I pose and flash my hands—partially covered in black lace gloves—at him.

His bitter expression dissolves. "I think you're beautiful and I can't wait to be your husband."

"I can't wait to be your wife."

"Come here." He holds out his arms and even though he's the one who seems to need the comforting, I take shelter against his body. "I love you so much, little dove."

The emotion in his voice sprinkles fear over our sweet moment. "What's wrong?"

"Nothing. I want to make you happy for the rest of our lives. Always."

"You already do."

"You'll tell me if I don't." It's a statement, not a question.

"Will you tell *me* if I don't make you happy?"

He kisses my forehead. "Not possible. Just breathing the same air as you makes me happy."

"Chaser, is everything okay? Did something happen because of what I said to my father?"

He steps back, brow furrowed as he considers my question. "No, I don't think so."

"Stump said he was happy for us." I bite my lip and drop my gaze. "Did he change his mind?" Not that I think it matters to Chaser, but at least one of our fathers should approve of our marriage.

A fist thumps against our door before Chaser has a chance to answer the question.

"Party's starting!" someone shouts.

"That's our cue to get out there," I whisper.

Maybe it's better if he doesn't answer my question.

Chaser brushes his knuckles under my chin. "Are you ready, future Mrs. Adams?"

I grin at him. "Absolutely, future Mr. Dove."

He pulls me in, hugging me tight. "Never happening, but I love you."

"Mr. DeLova?" I raise a teasing eyebrow.

"Fuck no. I'd take Dove before DeLova."

"Good to know. Good to know."

Shaking his head, he takes my hand and leads me into the main room of the clubhouse.

"Here's the happy couple!" Tally yells.

We stop under the archway leading into the bar area while everyone shouts congratulations and cheers for us. It's rowdy and unlike anything I've ever been a part of but I savor every second of pure, honest emotion.

I hold up my left hand and flash my ring at the room. "We're engaged!"

More cheers and a few crude words are thrown at us. Some "ball and chain" jokes and "better run while you can" comments, which Chaser ignores.

Stump embraces both of us and kisses my forehead. "Welcome to the family, princess," he whispers before turning around and pushing me forward. "My future daughter-in-law. Couldn't ask for a better woman for my son."

A beat of silence passes before everyone shouts another round of congratulations. My guess is Stump doesn't often demonstrate affection.

"Thank you, Mr. Adams—"

"Dad."

"Thank you...Dad." My eyes water and I tell myself it's only because of the heavy cloud of smoke hanging in the air. "Thank you for always making me feel like I belong here."

He stares at me and swallows hard before looking away. "You're family, Mallory. You'll always belong here."

Chaser's staring daggers at his father and brushes him off when he tries to hug him.

Well, I guess that answers my earlier question.

CHAPTER TWENTY-ONE

Chaser

The bikers who call this clubhouse home will use any excuse to party. But engagements don't happen often, so they're extra rambunctious tonight. Doe and a few other old ladies pull Mallory away to check out her ring and discuss wedding stuff. I hate to break it to Doe but I'm warming up to Mallory's "let's elope" idea every time I look at my father.

I plant my moody ass at the end of the bar where I have a good view of Mallory and the girls. Brothers stop by to shake my hand, congratulate me, and offer their advice—none as out of line as my father's, thank fuck.

I signal for the prospect behind the bar to hand me another Corona.

"You think that's a good idea?" My father's rumbling question spikes my anger right back to the red zone.

I take a long, slow guzzle before answering his question. "Come to give me more shitty guidance?"

"After your...*issue*." He nods to the beer bottle I have my fist wrapped around.

"My *issue* wasn't alcohol. This is the first beer I've touched in months." I cock my head. "What the fuck happened to you all of a sudden—get your grubby mitts on a copy of *Parenting* magazine and decide to make up for lost time?"

Instead of laughing, he hoists his big ass up on the stool next to me and orders his own beer. "I'm sorry, okay? I should've kept my mouth shut."

I peer into my bottle. Maybe the little shit behind the bar laced it with LSD. That would sure explain this hallucination. Stump Adams apologizes for nothing to anyone. Ever.

"Come again?" I cup my hand around my ear and lean closer to him.

"You heard me." He slaps me on the back with enough force to push me forward. "I ain't repeatin' myself."

I tug at my ear. "I think I heard *sorry* come out of your mouth? But that can't be right."

He mutters a few curses under his breath. "Mallory's a good girl. And I shouldn't have brought up your mother."

"Thank you." My gaze lands on Mallory again. This time she catches me staring and waves. "She's not *good*. She's *the best*. Don't forget it again, old man."

"Fine. Fine. Fuck. I wish I'd never opened my mouth."

I tap my bottle against his. "That makes two of us."

"Maybe I was worried some of my shittiness rubbed off on you. That you'll fuck things up because you need the thrill of something different once in a while."

I groan and thump my forehead against the sticky wood bar. "Really?"

"Like father, like son and all that. But you're different from me."

"You don't say," I mumble.

"In a good way."

I pick my head up and stare at him. "You ever think that growing up watching you be such an asshole helped me decide what kind of man *I* wanted to be? You taught me a lot of good things—I could always count on you to show up for me. At school, whatever I needed. Gave me your undivided attention too, even though you had a lot on your shoulders. Taught me the value of hard work. And to stand up for myself and for others. To be level-headed under pressure. When I'm ready to snap sometimes, I ask myself—would Dad handle it this way?"

He swallows hard and nods. "I tried."

"Yeah, I get that it wasn't easy for you. I know I was a little fucker sometimes—"

"Sometimes?"

"But, fuck I *hated* what you did to Mom. Hated watching her try so fucking hard to please you all the time and you not giving a shit."

"Is that what you saw?"

"Yeah, that's what I saw." I rub my hands over my face considering how to put these feelings into words. "It was hard to reconcile the two. You were a good dad. Tough on me, for sure."

"Not tough enough," he mutters.

"You were lousy to my mother, though. I couldn't comprehend why you'd treat someone you supposedly loved the way you treated her."

"I did love her."

I wave my hand toward the rest of the clubhouse. "I get that fucking without remorse is an admirable quality in a biker, but the damage caused isn't worth living up to the stereotype."

He seems to take all of that in and finally says, "I'm sorry."

"Two in one day. I should get engaged more often."

"Enjoy getting all this off your chest, Russell," he warns. "Tonight's your free pass."

"Gee, what'll you get me for our wedding?"

"A swift kick in your ass if you don't stop mouthing off."

I take another swallow of beer and consider my words. "I knew if I ever found the right girl, I'd do the opposite of whatever the fuck you did with women."

He snorts. "That must be uncomfortable."

"You know what I mean," I growl, not in the mood for his

attempt at humor. "While I was on tour, I missed the fuck out of Mallory. She wasn't out of sight, out of mind for me."

"Then you're a rare breed, son."

"Yeah, probably."

"Am I allowed to interrupt?" Mallory's soft voice eases my lingering irritation.

"Always." I curl my arm around her waist, and drag her between my knees, pressing her back to my chest. "You having fun?" I ask against her ear.

"I am." She reaches out to my dad. "Are you sure you're still happy about this?" She wiggles her fingers at him, showing off her ring.

"My father isn't giving you trouble, is he?" There's a catch in her voice. Maybe she sensed the hornet's nest Dad and I have been kicking around over here in our corner of the clubhouse. "I may have gotten carried away when I spoke to him."

"You were fantastic." I kiss her cheek again. "He needed to hear what you said."

"Yeah, princess," Dad answers slowly. "I'm happy. There's no trouble your father can throw at me, I can't handle."

"I know. Thank you," she says.

He lifts his gaze to me. "Besides, telling off fathers seems to be the theme of the day."

"Uh-oh." Mallory peers up at me. "What did you do?" she says in a teasing voice.

"You were brave today," I whisper against her ear. Louder, I add, "Figured it was time to get some things off my chest too. That's all."

"Enough of the heavy conversation." My father slaps his palm on the bar top. "My son already psycho-babbled me enough for ten years. Enjoy your party." He waves us off and turns around, smacking one of the club girls on the ass to get her attention.

Not in the mood to see *that* tonight, I turn away from them, placing Mallory between me and the bar. The dark corner and angle of my body provides enough cover that I run my hands down her sides, grazing my fingertips along the edge of her dress.

She leans back, resting her head on my chest and stares up at me.

The prospect behind the bar approaches, then steps away. Poor kid dances back and forth, trying to figure out if he should give us privacy but not wanting to neglect our drink needs. I finally end his misery by calling him over.

"Another one?" He swipes my empty bottle and tosses it in the can.

"What cocktails can you make?"

He grins. "Fuzzy Navel, Between the Sheets, Alabama Slammer...all the hard, hyper-sweet ones. Hardly ever get to serve anything except beer, though." He throws a wink at one of the club girls who walks up. "Except for the ladies."

"Easy there, prospect," I warn. "You're on duty tonight."

I wait for the girl to grab what she came for before motioning the prospect our way again.

"What interests you, little dove?" I ask against Mallory's ear.

"Me? I'm not old enough to drink."

"Doesn't really matter here."

"Oh." Her eyes light up as she studies the shelves of colorful bottles behind the bar. "I don't know. Whenever my father allowed me a sip of his drinks, they always tasted like poison."

"Something sweet then."

She finally decides on a Fuzzy Navel—peach schnapps, orange juice, and vodka.

"Easy on the vodka," I remind the kid.

"You got it."

Mallory leans over the bar to watch him mix the drink, sparking a number of dirty ideas for later tonight. I run my hand over the smooth leather clinging to the curve of her ass, up her spine, stopping between her shoulder blades

She turns, her hair tickling over the back of my hand. "What are you doing?"

"Appreciating my beautiful woman."

"Here ya go." The prospect slides a tall glass with the orange concoction Mallory's way. He even added an orange slice. Who knew fruit could be found in the clubhouse?

She takes the daintiest sip. "I don't taste any alcohol."

"It'll sneak up on ya. Go easy."

Mallory

Chaser's right. The drink sneaks up on me, a pleasant tingling sensation leaves me warm all over. "What else can I try?"

The bartender takes my glass but looks to Chaser for confirmation before offering me another drink.

"Chaser?" A soft voice to our right interrupts.

I turn and study the pretty brunette, inwardly I groan, assuming she's an ex of some sort.

"Mallory, right?" she holds out her hand to me. "I'm Alicia. I'm here with Tally."

"Oh! I've heard so much about you."

Pink spreads across her cheeks and she ducks her head. "I'm afraid to ask."

"Did we go to high school together?" Chaser asks.

"I graduated a year behind you guys." She blushes again. "Tally took me to Senior Prom. I think you were playing a club that night."

Chaser nods slowly and scans the room. "Good to see you."

"Well, I wanted to say congratulations." She nervously wiggles her fingers at us in a half-hearted wave.

"So, you're from around here?" I ask.

"No. Well, yes." She squeezes her eyes shut for a second. "I grew up here. My parents still live nearby. I'm home on break. Tally and I ran into each other and he invited me...here. Tonight."

"That's great." My overly enthusiastic shout has Chaser

peering at me sideways. Maybe I should hold off on another cocktail.

"Congratulations, Chaser." She reaches out, brushing her fingers over his arm. "On the band, I mean. It's so cool."

Underneath me, I feel him shift. Knowing how much Chaser likes to keep his music life and biker life separate, I try to think of another topic.

"So, you knew both of them in high school? Did you know Alvin too?" I ask.

She wrinkles her nose for a second. "Oh, Chipmunk! Yes. He was always a little more aloof, though."

Chaser snorts

Thankfully, Tally rescues us from the awkwardness of this encounter.

"There you are." He slips and arm around her waist.

"Good timing, Tally. I was just about to start asking her for dirt about you and Chaser in high school," I tease.

"No dirt." He peers up at the ceiling for a second and the corner of his mouth quirks. "Okay, maybe a little dirt."

Clearly enamored of Tally, Alicia giggles like a schoolgirl. He tips his beer bottle in my direction. "Mallory's on that show, *Shallow End*, have you ever seen it?"

Alicia's pretty blue eyes widen and she presses her fingers against her mouth. "I haven't, no. I don't get to watch a lot of television," she says in the most apologetic way. As if she's worried I'll be offended. Honestly, I'm relieved.

"No big deal," I assure her. "It's a small part, but a lot of fun." My standard answer when anyone asks me about *Shallow End*.

"That's so cool. I'll definitely have to watch it while I'm home."

By the way Tally keeps looking at her, TV seems to be low on activities he wants to do while she's visiting.

Eventually, they wander over to the pool table, leaving Chaser and I alone at this end of the bar.

"I'm so happy they're together," I squeal, a little louder than I meant to.

"Yeah, why's that?" Chaser brushes a lock of hair off my cheek.

I shrug. "Tally mentioned her last time we were home. That's all."

His eye-roll and the twitch at the corner of his mouth say he's less than impressed.

"Why don't you like her?" An awful thought crosses my mind and I blurt it out before thinking it through. "Did you date her?"

He huffs out a laugh. "She's not my type."

"Oh?" I arch a brow. "And what's your type?"

"You." He clamps his hands over my hips for emphasis.

"Good answer."

"The only answer," he counters. "Anyway, I couldn't place her until you asked about Chipmunk. He had a thing for her in high school too."

"Ah, so your band mate and one of your brothers liked the same girl. That's awkward."

"I'm pretty sure Chipmunk's gotten over it."

"Probably." I turn back to the bar.

Chaser's hands slide up my legs and under my dress, dragging it up a few precious centimeters. "What are you doing?" I ask over my shoulder.

"Thinking how I could easily push this up over your hips." Under my dress, he barely has room to move his big hand, but somehow he slips around my thigh and strokes down my center with his finger. "Rip these panties out of my way." His hot breath puffs over my shoulder and he nips my earlobe. "And make you come right here."

I squirm and inch my feet apart.

"You like the sound of that, don't you?"

Heat stings my cheeks and I take a quick, cautious glance around the room. "Not with so many people here." Not that it matters, half the room is engaged in much more risqué activities.

The heat of his hand disappears, and he tugs my dress into place.

"What are you doing?"

"You're right." He nods to the bar. "Do you want anything else to drink?"

I turn, leaning my elbows against the bar, so I'm facing him and arch my back. A flush of feminine pride sweeps over me as his hungry gaze travels over my body. I reach out and place a finger under his chin, redirecting his eyes to my face. "Chaser, you don't have to get me tipsy to have your way with me. I'm a sure thing."

"I don't want you tipsy." He drops his gaze again. "I need you fully engaged for what I plan to do to you."

A little tipsy, I titter at the word *engaged* and flash my ring at him.

A smile plays over his lips. "Maybe you have had enough."

The front door opens with a bang and bikers I don't recognize enter the clubhouse.

Chaser's hold on me changes from playful to downright possessive.

One biker I finally recognize. Bishop trudges over to us. The few times I've met him, he's been nice to me. Still, he's a scary guy when he's focused and coming right at you.

"Hey, Bishop." Chaser holds out his hand and the two men shake. "Thanks for coming tonight."

The older biker sweeps his gaze over us and a hint of a smile curves his lips. "I hear we're celebrating big news tonight."

"We are." I pat Chaser's arms that are wrapped around me so tight, I can barely breathe. "It's nice to see you again, Bishop."

He glances over his shoulder. "You two have a minute?"

"Sure." Chaser's mentioned more than once that his father needs the two clubs to get along, so I'm willing to do whatever I can to make that happen.

"What's on your mind, Bishop?" Chaser asks, finally loosening his hold on me.

"I need to be out of town for a few days. Got no idea where Trin's mom is at. A friend's watching her now but I don't trust her there overnight." He runs his hand over his beard and flicks a gaze toward the chapel. "She seemed to like you a whole lot and—"

My heart melts. "Absolutely. Yes. She can stay with us."

Chaser gives me a gentle squeeze. Maybe I should've checked to make sure he didn't mind but how could I say no?

"Oh." My voice falters. "We're heading back to Los Angeles next week—"

"I'll be back Tuesday night at the latest," Bishop says.

"Then, yes." I peer up at Chaser who shrugs.

"No problem, Bishop," he adds. "We're staying at my dad's house, so she won't have to hang out here at the clubhouse or anything."

"Thank you, Chaser." He glances around the room again. "I wouldn't normally ask—"

"It's really not a problem," I assure him.

"Thank you, honey. I'll bring her by here tomorrow afternoon. That all right with you?"

"Sure. That'll give me time to fix up a room for her at the house."

"You don't have to go to a lot of trouble. She's an easy-going kid." He shoves his hand in his pocket and pulls out his wallet. "I'll give you some—"

"No, no. You don't have to pay me. Really, it's fine. She's so sweet. I enjoyed hanging out with her."

He tips his head and stares me down until my mouth snaps shut. I should know better. For a man like Bishop, turning down his offer of money will probably be seen as an insult. I accept the wad of cash he hands me without counting it. Since I have no pockets and I'm not about to stuff it in my bra in front of Bishop, I hold it at my side. "Thank you. Is there anything special she likes to eat?"

His mouth curls into a softer smile—well soft for him.

"Lucky Charms, SpaghettiOs—but only with the meatballs. She's real vocal about that."

I chuckle, unable to picture it since Trinity had been so recalcitrant when I watched her the last time.

"All right then. Thank you." He nods to us and walks off, stopping to talk to Chaser's father and a few other men.

"You're not mad at me are you?" I ask, turning to face Chaser.

His lips twitch. "Mad? No. More in love with you than ever. Absolutely."

"Why?"

He wraps his arms around me, resting his hands on my butt and leans in to kiss the tip of my nose. "Because you're so fucking sweet, even a scary bastard like Bishop knows he can trust you."

"You really don't mind?"

"Nah, she's a sweet kid. Her mom…isn't the best. I feel bad for Trinity. Besides, Bishop's the SAA for his club. If he feels all warm and fuzzy toward you, that benefits *my* club in the long run."

I glance over at Bishop. He's a big man. Well over six feet, with leviathan like shoulders that barely fit through the front doors. "I don't know if warm and fuzzy is a way to describe him."

"No." He laughs. "Definitely not. Except when it comes to his daughter."

Warmth from my earlier drink still has me hot and tingly all over. "That's the kind of father you'll be, isn't it?" I rest one finger against his chest and drag it down feeling his muscles flex and contract under my touch.

"Thinking about that already?" His bland expression halts my exploration and I withdraw.

He wraps his fingers around my wrist to stop me from pulling away and brushes his lips against my knuckles. "I want that with you, Mallory," he says so low, the words almost disappear in the noise around us. "But not yet."

Mildly offended, I try to tug my hand free. "I didn't mean I wanted you to put a baby in my belly right *now*, Chaser."

He bursts out laughing. "Well, when you put it like *that*. Fuck." He presses my hand against his erection straining the metal of his zipper. Under my touch, his body jerks.

"Someone wants attention." I lean into him, cupping him through his jeans and gently squeezing. He groans against my neck.

"Hard proof how much I want you." The deep rasp of his voice melts me like butter. He tilts his head and presses his lips to my throat. "Not here."

He slides off the stool, slowly pressing our bodies together, then lifts me. Bold, possessive hands remain on my butt as he spins us away from the bar.

I loop my arms around his shoulders.

Cheers and whistles follow us out of the room. Too wrapped up in Chaser, I'm not sure if the comments are directed at us or not.

He turns the corner into the hallway that leads to his room and I open my eyes. Here, we're alone. It's dark. Shadowy. Dim overhead lights lead the way. Muted noise from the main room lingers in the air.

My back thumps against his door.

"Fuck, forgot I locked it tonight." He sets me down and I wobble in my heels for a second while he searches his pockets for the key.

"I can't wait." I reach up and kiss his neck, while my fingers dive for his belt, working it loose. "No one will see us."

His eyes close and his breath hitches.

"Can't...work...your zipper with your giant cock in my way." His eyes pop open. "All your fault."

Finally, I work it loose without nicking him in the process. His cock kicks and jerks, begging for attention. I wrap my fingers around him, slowly stroking.

"Fuck." He pins me against the door with his body and cups

168

my face, claiming a kiss. His tongue strokes mine in a slow, seductive dance. He caresses and explores, sliding his hands down my hips, over my thighs, then reverses direction, slipping under my dress and hiking it up.

I continue stroking him with both hands. Gentle but firm. His breath quickens, his need as strong as mine. Tingles race up my legs. His hips shift. He slips a hand under my thigh, lifting, lining us up.

"I like you in heels," he whispers against my mouth.

"Please, hurry."

"And so desperate for my cock, you don't care that someone from the party could walk down here and catch us at any minute."

"No." My head rolls from side to side.

"Look at me," he demands.

I flex against him, encouraging him to hurry. He groans as our eyes meet and he thrusts, hard. We shudder together and I dig my nails into his shoulders, hanging on and trying to pull him closer. Merge our bodies together. Maybe it's the alcohol or the thrill of possibly being caught but my heart pounds. He rotates his hips, slowly pushing deep inside, allowing a few seconds to adjust.

He slaps his palm against the door, next to my face, bracing himself and pulls my lower body closer with his other arm. "Hold on. Wrap your legs around me."

My heels clatter to the floor as I cross my ankles at the base of his spine and drop my forehead to his shoulder.

His body shakes with need, ruthlessly driving into me over and over. I'm overwhelmed by so many sensations. The roughness of the wood scraping against my back. The slick glide of our skin. The rasp of his stubble against my neck. His teeth nipping my earlobe. The rippling muscles in his back, straining to keep us upright.

Tingling pleasure spreads over my skin like wildfire. A sharp moan tears out of my throat with the sudden shock of my orgasm.

"Good girl," Chaser encourages. "Be as loud as you want."

I come hard and long, grinding against him, hanging on for dear life. "*Ohmygod.* That's so good."

He rolls his bottom lip, biting down, holding off until he's sure I'm satisfied. Our gazes collide and I nod frantically, dying to see him lose control. The cords in his neck strain and his muscles shake. Relentlessly he pounds into me until I fully understand the meaning of *nailed.* He groans and squeezes his eyes shut, releasing inside me. When he opens his eyes a kaleidoscope swirl of love, passion, and desire shimmer in their dark depths.

Lowering his head, he brushes his lips against mine. A long, sweet tender moment after the way we frantically went at each other.

I unwrap my legs from his body but they're too unsteady to hold me up. I slump against the door and end up sliding halfway to the floor before Chaser catches me. "Easy, little dove."

He glances down and fixes his jeans, leaving his belt undone. At some point, the key to his room fell on the floor and he leans over to scoop it up.

"Come here." He gathers me in his arms and gently sets me on the bed, stripping me out of my dress. A few minutes later he returns with a glass of water and hands me two aspirin.

"What's this?"

"I don't want you to wake up with a hangover."

I toss the pills back and chug the water before answering. "I didn't have that much to drink."

His lips quirk and he tilts his head toward the door.

I hook a finger in one of his belt loops and tug him forward. "That wasn't *alcohol.* That was my stone-cold sexy fiancé who got me all hot and bothered."

Instead of laughing, he brushes his knuckles over my cheek. "I hope when we're in our nineties, I still inspire you that much."

"I'm sure you will." I kiss the back of his hand. "I doubt you'll still be able to hold me up like that, but we'll have fun trying."

He finally chuckles, lifting whatever heaviness settled over him for a moment. "I'll prove you wrong on that one."

"I look forward to it."

"Better get some rest," he says. "Sounds like we have a big day tomorrow."

CHAPTER TWENTY-TWO

Chaser

Maybe I should've nixed this watching Bishop's daughter thing last night. Because watching Mallory get so excited about a few days of babysitting gives me a bunch of ideas I didn't expect to have for another couple of years.

"It's only a night or two," I remind her when she starts talking about tearing apart my old bedroom. "I think she'll be fine on the daybed in the guest room."

"Okay."

The kitchen's stocked with enough food to feed ten kids, and Barbies, My Little Ponies, and all sorts of girl shit the likes of which this house has never seen have landed in the living room.

"What if she doesn't like Barbie?" I tease.

"What little girl doesn't like Barbie?"

Probably should've kept my mouth shut. Now she's frowning at the dolls. "No time to go back to the store," I warn her.

I have a few errands to run with my dad, so Mallory's picking up Trinity at the clubhouse and I'll meet up with them.

"Sorry," she bites her lip, "I know this isn't how you wanted to spend your time off."

"It's a couple days max. Like I said, a favor for Bishop is good for my club."

"Are things really that bad between the two clubs?"

I hook my thumbs in my pockets and consider how to answer her question. Bikers I've known usually do one of two things with their ol' ladies. Enough disclosure to keep them safe or no disclosure at all. Anything in between just causes trouble. "Our territories are close, so we butt heads from time to time. Slights that get blown out of proportion. Issues lots of clubs get twisted up about. Dad's more concerned with some of their business activities."

"Do I want to know?"

"They run a much rougher club." I run my hand over my scruffy chin. "Don't show respect to females. Ol' ladies or not."

Sadness clouds her eyes and her bottom lip pushes out. "And that's the kind of club Trinity's being raised around."

I blow out a breath and run my hand over the back of my neck. "Not sure how much time her mother spends around their clubhouse." No, she's too busy whoring at our clubhouse. Something that's definitely gonna bring hellfire down on us one of these days. "And you've met Bishop. No one's gonna mess with his baby girl."

That seems to satisfy her. At least for now.

"You've been around my club enough now to know you're safe there, right?"

"Yes."

"Good." I lean in and kiss her cheek. "Clubhouse will still be in rough shape. Might want to meet Bishop outside. Just let Mouse or Tally know you're there so they can wait with you." I might not dislike Bishop as much as the rest of his club. Doesn't mean I want him alone with my woman. "I'll be there as soon as I can."

Mallory

CHASER TEASED ME ALL MORNING ABOUT PREPARING THE house for our little visitor. But I can't help it. I'm an only child. I don't have little nieces and nephews to spoil. And I don't want any of my own kids for at least another couple years.

The clubhouse is in a sorry state after last night's celebration. Hungover, half-naked couples entwined on every available surface, including the pool table and top of the bar. Chaser wasn't kidding about meeting Bishop outside. Looks like a couple members of the visiting club stayed over last night. I hope that's a sign they're getting along. None of what Chaser told me about the other club sounded good.

Thankfully, Tally's in the kitchen with Alicia, so I don't have to search the clubhouse for his room. Unsure of how much club stuff Alicia might know, I explain the situation without too many details.

"No problem," Tally says. "Want to walk out now?"

"Sure."

A few bodies have stirred while I was in the kitchen. Tally takes in the scene with a smirk on his face.

"I feel like I should help clean up or something since it was our engagement party."

"It'll get taken care of," he assures me.

Outside, we stand by my car waiting for Bishop to arrive. Chaser ends up there first.

"That was fast."

He leans down to kiss my cheek. "Quick and easy."

Stump joins us and gives me a brief, affectionate hug. "How's it going, princess?"

"Not too bad."

He settles his gaze on Alicia. "I remember you." He smirks at Tally. "Senior prom. Stopped by here for some photos."

Tally exhales a long breath. "Good memory, Prez."

"Always remember a pretty face. What're you doing back here? You datin' my treasurer again?"

Poor Alicia. I don't think she expected to be interrogated

175

this morning. "I, uh..." Her gaze darts from Tally, to Chaser, to me, and back to Tally. "We're hanging out while I'm home on break."

"Didn't meet anyone at college?" Stump grins. "Getting back together with your high school sweetie?"

A corner of Tally's mouth lifts. "You done, old man?"

The slightly less respectful tone he uses seems to be a warning. Chaser crosses his arms over his chest and leans on my car. "Knock it off, Dad. Alicia doesn't know you're teasing her."

"Nah, Prez enjoys fucking with us." Tally's gaze shifts to Chaser. "Sticking his nose in our personal lives."

Chaser chokes on a laugh.

"Disrespectful little shit," Stump grumbles. He pats me on the back and ambles into the clubhouse.

"Did I pass the test?" Alicia asks.

"You're fine, hon," Chaser says.

"Well, I have to go." She leans up and kisses Tally's cheek, but he grasps her hand and walks her to her car.

"Where's that going?" Chaser asks after she leaves and Tally returns.

"Where's what going?"

"She's going back to school, right?"

"What is this?" Tally rolls his shoulders. "Ambush and interrogation from the Adams family today?"

I squeeze my eyes shut and try not to laugh.

"Just lookin' out for my brother."

"Haven't stopped thinking about her since she left. Why keep fucking around when I already know what I want?"

I reach over and rub Tally's shoulder. "That's sweet."

"How do you know she's not at school datin' frat boys and livin' it up?"

A muscle in Tally's jaw twitches. "She got that out of her system freshman year. But thanks for asking."

"She plannin' to move back after college?" Chaser asks.

I can't figure out if he really wants to know, if he's messing with Tally for kicks, or he's just passing time until Bishop arrives.

"Don't know yet." He cocks his head. "You done now?"

"Yeah, just fucking with you, brother. Glad it's working out."

Before Tally can respond, a black pickup bounces down the driveway.

"That's Bishop." Chaser lifts his chin and pushes away from my car.

"Have fun with that." Tally waves at us and heads into the clubhouse.

"Why were you grilling him like that?"

He watches Bishop back in next to our car. "Just looking out for a brother," he answers without looking at me.

Like last time, Trinity's shy at first. Bishop pulls her out of the truck. She wraps her arms around his neck and presses her little face against his shoulder. He murmurs soft words to her that I can't quite catch while he carries her over.

"Thanks again, Mallory." He extends his hand to Chaser. "Appreciate it."

"Trinny, you gonna say hi to Mallory?" Bishop asks.

She picks her head up at his gruff tone and twists to see me. A flicker of a smile passes her lips. "Hi, Mal-o-wee."

My ovaries perform a little tap dance. "Hi, honey. I've got all sort of stuff for you to play with at our house."

She casts a dubious glance at the clubhouse. "Not stayin' here?"

"Nope," Chaser says.

"O-tay." She wriggles until her father sets her down.

Chaser crouches down to eye level with her and tilts his head toward her dad's truck. "When you gonna be big enough to ride on the back of your dad's bike, squirt?"

She giggles and peers up at her dad.

He leans down and runs his big hand over the top of her head. "Taken her out a couple times. Around the neighborhood."

"Yeah?" Chaser's eyes widen to cartoon size. "You like it?"

"Yes." More little giggles.

"Cool." Chaser holds out his palm and Trinity slaps him a tiny high-five.

Ovaries explosion.

The clubhouse door swings open behind us. Heavy sets of boots crunch over gravel. Chaser slowly rises and stands next to me.

"Ready to do this, Bishop?" a gruff voice I don't recognize says.

Bishop grits his teeth as the man slaps his shoulder. "Yup."

"Oh, hey, Trinity," the man says. His gaze lingers on her too long for my taste. He's shorter than both Bishop and Chaser but thick and muscled. Shoulders as wide as a Buick. His chiseled face could probably find work in Hollywood.

Trinity shuffles closer to me, shying away. I bend over and pick her up, running my hand over her back.

He gives me a long, slow eye-fondle. "Who's your new woman, Bishop?"

Bishop's expression hardens to stone. "This is Chaser's ol' lady."

Chaser slings his arm over my shoulders and stares the other man down.

"Well, shit. It was *your* engagement we were celebrating, wasn't it?" He lifts his gaze to Chaser. "Congratulations."

"Thanks, Tyler. How you been?"

"Can't complain."

"Be good for Mallory and Chaser, okay, Trinny?" Bishop leans in and kisses her cheek.

"O-tay!"

He briefly touches my arm. "Thank you for this. Didn't mean to cut into your—"

"It's really no problem, Bishop."

"You got a kiss for your Uncle Tyler, Trinity?"

She doesn't answer, just clings to me tighter. Disgusted, I move to my car and tuck her into the backseat.

Bishop hands me a bag. "Some clothes. Her favorite blankie. She won't sleep without it."

I accept the bag, setting it on the seat next to Trinity. "Thanks."

Bishop and Tyler shake hands with Chaser before leaving. I've already said goodbye to Bishop and Tyler gives me the creeps, so I slide into the front seat and start the car.

"You okay back there?" I ask Trinity.

"Uh-huh." She peers out the window, watching her father's truck drive away and the look on her face breaks my heart.

"It's okay. Your daddy will be home in a couple days."

"I know."

Chaser knocks on my window and I roll it down. "I'm gonna follow you home, okay?" He peers in the back at Trinity. "You comfy back there, squirt?"

"Yup!"

"Good." He taps the roof of the car twice. "See you at home."

Chaser

Took all my control not to punch Tyler for eyeballin' my girl. Don't know how Bishop puts up with that asshole as his president.

I'm not exactly sure how we're going to entertain a kid for the next couple days. Haven't really been around many since I was one myself.

Mallory seems to have it covered though.

"Are you hungry?" she asks once we're in the house.

Trinity found the Barbies and she's definitely a fan. She glances up from the pile and shakes her head.

"Let me know if you get hungry, okay?" Mallory wrings her hands. "Should we take her out to like a park or something?"

"She's fine. Stop worrying."

It's not a bad night. Mallory makes SpaghettiOs with Meatballs with a side of hot dogs. I pop in some Disney movie and curl up on the couch with Mallory. Trinity crawls into her lap and passes out halfway into the movie.

"She's so sweet," Mallory whispers, running her hand over Trinity's long blonde ponytail. "I want one just like her."

I think this is the point where I'm supposed run from the room but I can see us doing this in a couple years. "I don't think you can order 'em out of a catalog. Just to warn you, I was a pretty rambunctious kid."

"Surprise, surprise." She leans back and rolls her eyes at me. "Well, I was a quiet kid."

"I want our kids to be kids. Not always afraid of doing something wrong."

"I wasn't...afraid. Well, maybe a little of my father."

"You must've been so fuckin' cute."

She taps my chest. "Language."

I snort. "She's sound asleep. Besides, I'm sure she hears much worse at home."

She glances down at Trinity again. "Think we should put her to bed? I forgot to ask Bishop her bedtime and stuff."

"Yeah, probably. I hope she doesn't freak in the middle of the night or something."

"I'll leave our door open."

"How are we supposed to start on our own babies, then?"

She slaps my chest. "Help me carry her upstairs?"

THE NEXT MORNING, MY FATHER CALLS WHILE THE GIRLS ARE making pancakes.

"What's up?"

"Uh, I need you to get over here. And bring Trinity."

"Why? What's wrong?"

"Her mother's looking for her and she's pissed."

"Sweet Jesus. Are you fuckin' kidding me."

"Ooooo. Chather said a bad word," Trinity says to Mallory.

Mallory throws a scowl at me and I shrug.

"All right. We'll be there in a few. We're in the middle of breakfast."

"What's wrong?" Mallory asks.

"Her mom's looking for her."

"Oh."

"I want to stay." Trinity pouts.

Mallory's eyes shimmer with tears but she pastes on a bright smile. "It's okay. Maybe you'll get to come over and visit next time we're home."

Trinity sits at the table and picks at the plate of pancakes Mallory sets in front of her. After breakfast, Mallory packs up her stuff, tossing the dolls, coloring books, and other toys she bought in Trinity's bag.

"You're bummed too, huh?" I ask, watching her gather everything.

"A little."

It's a whole big scene at the clubhouse. As soon as Nora sees Trinity holding Mallory's hand, she kicks up a cloud of dust racing over to us.

"Are you sleeping with my husband?" she demands, getting up in Mallory's face. "You can have him, but you're not taking my daughter too."

"Whoa." I hold my arm out, pushing her back and blocking her from getting any closer. "Ease up, Nora. Bishop asked if *we* could help him out. That's all."

She squats down and yanks Trinity into her arms.

The entire situation is fucked up.

As soon as Nora burns rubber out of the parking lot, my father storms inside the clubhouse. His thunderous voice shakes the building while he yells at Trick once again for fucking around with Bishop's wife.

I squeeze Mallory to my side. "What a way to cap off our vacation, huh?"

She swipes a tear off her cheek. "Almost as crazy as L.A."

CHAPTER TWENTY-THREE

Mallory

Somehow when our plane arrives in L.A., people already know about our engagement.

The crush of reporters vying for a peek at my ring or yelling questions, leaves me shaking.

"Who did we tell?" I ask Chaser when we're finally enclosed in the car he arranged to pick us up.

"Alvin. I might have mentioned it to Thom. The whole entire club—but none of them would ever talk to the press. That's it."

He asks our driver to stop and dashes out of the car to a curbside news stand, returning a few minutes later with a handful of papers. He shows me the first page of one of the more vile tabloids.

Rock Royalty, Ready to Take the Plunge!

"Are we the 'rock royalty'?" I ask, reaching for the paper.

"Apparently."

Accompanying the headline is a photo of Chaser proposing. As far as tabloid articles go, it's tame and celebratory for a change.

"This isn't so bad." I tear out the article and fold it up,

tucking it away in my purse. "It's actually a nice memory."

Chaser growls. "Had to be the boat attendant. Hope he got paid well for it. Jackass."

I reach over and pat his leg. "It's okay."

"This better die down before I have to leave for Vancouver. I don't want you putting up with those vultures while I'm away."

"I don't plan on going anywhere except the set and home while you're gone."

"You shouldn't have to live like a shut-in. I want you to do stuff. Go where you want when you want."

"I'll be fine. I'll ask Cindy to come over or something. I'm sure Marilyn has auditions for me."

Marilyn *does* have auditions for me. In fact, while we were gone, she left about a dozen messages on our answering machine. I stare at the phone for a few minutes and Chaser must sense my reluctance.

"Honeymoon's over. Back to the real world, little dove."

"Promise me our real honeymoon will be longer." I stare down at my ring and then the stack of newspapers. "And somewhere no one can find us."

He steps closer and skims his knuckles over my cheek. "Promise."

Tears sting my eyes but I blink them away. "I hate that you're leaving again."

He swallows hard, then shrugs. "This is path we've chosen for now, Mallory. You can always come with me."

Not expecting his harsh tone, I blink and stare at him. "I can't. I have to be on set."

"And I have to be in the studio. Don't make this harder than it has to be."

Wow. I don't know how to respond, so I duck my head and pick up the phone. "I better call her back."

"I'm going to unpack and do some laundry."

"Okay," I whisper, watching him walk away. The honeymoon really is over.

A painful lump in my throat expands and settles in my chest. Maybe Chaser's tired of me being so clingy? Or maybe he really expects me to blow off work and go to Vancouver with him for the next month. Whatever the reason, it takes me a few minutes to compose myself enough to call Marilyn.

"Mallory! Are you in town? Please tell me—"

Not in the mood for her theatrics this afternoon, I cut her off. "I'm back."

"Congratulations on the engagement."

"Thanks," I mumble.

"I have good news and bad news. Which do you want first?"

I hate this game. "Bad news."

"Don't freak out. The exercise video...it's not quite what we'd hoped for."

"*We* didn't hope for anything. *You* talked me into doing it as a lucrative revenue stream."

"I know. I know. It's not awful. Not the end of the world."

"What's wrong, then?"

"It's um...a bit more salacious than I anticipated."

"Salacious, how?"

"Well," she draws out the word until I'm ready to scream. "The angles. The way it was shot. The outfit. The cheesy music. Overall, it feels more like soft core porn than an exercise video."

"What?" My voice wobbles. "I was in a leotard and tights."

"Oh, you look fabulous, honey. Killer. It's just a bit tasteless."

"That's great."

"It's fine. You've already been paid. We just won't participate in any of the promotion for it. Let it die on the vine. No biggie. We just move on."

I'm tempted to point out, yet again, that she's the one who talked me into wasting my time and energy on this project, but she's right. I was paid—well—for it. I doubt it's much worse than the 'Candy Jar' video or any of the other music videos I've shot. Lesson learned.

"What's the good news?" I ask.

"It's really good, Mallory. Really, really good. So good, you won't want to fire me for the exercise video debacle."

Wow, Marilyn was really worried. Or the video's worse than she said.

"I'm not going to fire you, Marilyn."

"Good." She takes a long, dramatic pause. "Scout Southgate is putting together a weekly primetime soap opera. And he wants *you* to audition for it."

I take a second to absorb the information. "Scout Southgate knows who I am?"

She snorts into the phone. "Apparently, his daughter will be starring on the show—don't even get me started on how that horse-faced twit can't act her way out of a paper bag—but she's a big fan of yours and told her daddy you're perfect for this role."

"Madeline Southgate knows who I am?" I'm still having trouble processing.

"Yes, Mallory. People know who you are," she says patiently. "That's the whole point of this acting thing, right?"

"Right. Okay, so when and where? And what do I do about *Shallow End*?"

"No one wants you to leave *Shallow End*. In fact, for now, I want you to keep this on the down low. Especially from Pamela Scott." She scoffs. "Not that anyone would buy her in this role, but still."

"What's the part?"

"Clueless virgin teenager from some hick town, who moves to Hollywood with the rest of her hillbilly family."

That's a lot of insults in one sentence to decipher. "Uh, okay."

"It's better than bimbo bouncing up and down in her bathing suit, right?"

"I guess."

"A little more excitement and gratitude would be nice, Mallory."

"Oh, I'm excited. Do you think I can pull off playing a

teenager, though?"

"You barely look eighteen as it is. Madeline's at least two years older than you and she's playing your best friend. Your 'brother' on the show is about thirty. You'll fit in perfectly."

"Wait, you're talking about this as if I already have the part?"

"I told you, they're extremely eager to have you audition."

"Wow. When and where?"

"Now that you're home, I'll get the audition set up. What's your schedule like?"

I give her my plans for the week and she promises to try and work in the audition so I don't have to take time off from *Shallow End*. After one more reminder to keep the audition to myself

I'm still staring at the phone after I hang up, absorbing the information.

"Sounds like a promising audition," Chaser says.

I glance over and find him in the hallway, leaning on the wall, partially hidden by mid-afternoon shadows.

"It is. I think." I relay everything Marilyn told me.

"How are you going to find the time to be on two shows?" he asks mildly.

For some reason, the question ignites my insecurities. About my career, our relationship...everything. "I'll figure it out if I get the part, I guess."

He grunts in response.

"Are you...mad at me?" I ask.

He doesn't immediately answer *no*, which unleashes more anxiety.

"I'm tired from the trip home." He yawns and stretches as if to punctuate his explanation.

"I take it that means you want to stay in tonight?"

"Why? What did you have in mind?"

"Nothing. I thought you'd want to get together with the guys...or...?"

"Fuck that. I'll see enough of them in the next couple

weeks." He holds his hand out to me. "I want to soak up as much time with my girl as possible."

That's better. "You're not tired of me? We just spent a solid week together."

He steps closer. "I'm never tired of you."

"You seem...annoyed." I don't know why I'm persisting but I can't stand the uneasiness hanging in the air. Not with Chaser.

He blows out a frustrated breath and bounces the side of his fist against the wall. "I'm pissed I have to leave. I wish we were recording the album here like we've done all the others. Figures now that I don't *want* to leave Hollywood, I have to."

"Oh." I breathe out a relieved sigh and move closer to him. "You trust Mark, though, right?"

"Don't know. I've never worked with him before."

"But it was a big deal to get him to work with Kickstart."

"It was," he agrees.

I bite my lip and glance away, worried Chaser might misinterpret my words. "Trust. You told me he's been in the business for a long time and has produced a lot of mega-successful albums, right?"

Instead of answering, he nods slowly.

"Everyone's still sober, right?"

"More or less."

"Well, the change of scenery, the new producer, everyone coming to the table with clear heads, maybe all those combined factors will spark true sonic greatness."

One corner of his mouth lifts. "Sonic greatness, huh?"

"Sonic awesomeness?"

"Why do you have to do that?" He wraps me up in his arms. "Just when I think I have a handle on how much I'm going to miss you."

"What?"

"You go ahead and come up with *sonic awesomeness* and I don't know how I'm supposed to leave you again for another four weeks."

CHAPTER TWENTY-FOUR

Mallory

"Geez, Mallory. Did you partake in a lot of home cooking while you were away on your rock star vacation?"

As nice as I've tried to be to the wardrobe girls, they still hate my guts. A few weeks off didn't mellow them out one bit. Donna's the worst, though. She makes a big show of sighing and tugging on the straps of my bathing suit. It doesn't feel snugger to *me*, but she continues grumbling about having to "go up a size."

I pat my hip as my mouth curls into a slow smile. "My man can't keep his hands off me, and that's all I care about." With a quick toss of my hair, I execute a spin and strut out of the dressing room without falling out of my flip-flops. *Yay, me!*

Heart still pounding—I hate confrontation—I make my way to the makeup room, searching for Cindy.

"What did deplorable Donna have to say today?" she asks as soon as she sees the defeat that must be etched on my face.

"Well," I answer with a dramatic flourish of my arms, "Apparently, now I'm *fat*. She needs to order me a bigger swimsuit."

Cindy gives me a critical once-over and I try not to flinch. "She's a jealous bitch. Your suit is fine." She stares at me a little longer, then smiles. "Except for that bride-to-be glow, you look the same as you did before you left."

I swear, some days, Cindy is the only reason I haven't walked off the set and quit. "Thank you."

Marilyn might have said if I get the part on the new show, I can still be on this one, but there's no way I'll sign on to take more of this crap for another season. I don't want to pin all my hopes on the new show—who knows, it could end up being worse—but I'm really looking forward to the audition.

Cindy pulls me out of my musings by waving a pan of makeup at me. "It's the nice thick, waterproof stuff. You have a shower scene."

"For fuck's sake," I say under my breath.

"Mallory!" she fake gasps. "This is a family show!"

I chuckle as I drop into my seat and wait for her to perform her magic.

EIGHT HOURS LATER, I DON'T THINK EVEN CINDY HAS ENOUGH magic to make me stay on this set another second.

"Is this going to be a problem, Mallory?" Sam asks, scowling at me so hard I want to melt into the floor.

Obviously, the director wasn't looking for any input from me about the scene. When will I learn to keep my mouth shut?

"No, it's fine." Grown women ask each other to help them shower all the time for no reason whatsoever. Totally normal.

Pamela rolls her eyes but I'm not sure if it's at me or the director. Either way, she'll have the privilege of soaping me up in the shower when we shoot the scene later in the week.

Now that I've been properly chastised in front of everyone, we're dismissed for the day.

"Total jerk-off material," Pamela whispers when the director turns his incendiary gaze on one of the show's many writers. "You know our biggest demographic is single males in the thirty-five to fifty-four years of age range, right?"

"That explains so much." I slap my hand over my mouth to keep myself from laughing.

She giggles and bumps my elbow. Except for running a few lines this morning, we haven't spoken much. Certainly, not about anything personal. I'm not sure what to say. Given that she and Andrew just broke up, and the way it happened, I don't want to rub her nose in my engagement.

"Congratulations, by the way." She nods to my ring.

"Oh." I smile down at my hand. "Thank you."

"How'd he propose?"

Since she asked, I give her the details but try not to gush too much.

"Shucks, that's sweet." Her voice lacks the usual mocking and actually seems sincere. "When you planning on tyin' the knot?"

Since I don't want to explain that we're saving the public wedding for when my father's out of prison, I go with a non-committal, "When everything settles down."

"Oh, sugar, there will never be a 'right time.' Best do it quick, so you'll be entitled to those juicy publishing royalties when you catch him in bed with the maid or somethin'."

And there it is.

I'm too tired to give her a lengthy speech about how Chaser and Andrew are nothing alike. "Thanks for the advice."

CHAPTER TWENTY-FIVE

Mallory

"Do I look like an innocent midwestern teenager?" I ask Chaser as I enter the living room.

He sets down his guitar and studies me. "Will you think I'm creepy if I say I totally would've tried to bang you in high school?" He adds an eyebrow wiggle that sets me off laughing.

"Maybe just a little."

"Mallory," he says more seriously. "You're beautiful."

"Beauty isn't the point."

He runs his gaze over me again. "Yes, I can see you playing a high school senior, no problem."

"I probably haven't worn these since I *was* a senior." I run my hands over my yellow jeans. "You want to talk about being creepy, I drove by the high school last night just to see what kids are wearing these days."

"Did you?" he chuckles.

"It was Marilyn's suggestion. At least I have some character details. Half the time, I have no idea what the casting directors are looking for." I bite my lip. "I still need to work on my Midwestern accent, though."

"I doubt they'll know the difference."

"True. Marilyn just told me to talk "flat." She seemed to assume the Midwest is one massive, uniform flatland of cornfields."

He laughs even harder. "Sort of how everyone assumes if you're from New York, you speak like a wise guy from Brooklyn?"

"Or *tawk* like you're from Long Island," I add in my best fast, hypernasal accent.

He shudders. "I've ridden through the Midwest and spent some time in a few states. Where's your character supposed to be from?"

"Nebraska."

"All right. From what I remember there's no obvious *pahk the cab* kind of accent like Boston. It's flat like she said. A more subtle merging of vowels in some words. Like cot and caught would sound the same. Stock and stalk. Dawn and Don."

I softly repeat the examples to myself, getting a feel for what he's describing.

"Honestly, though, if they're Hollywood types who only spend time on either coast, they'll never know the difference." He holds his hands in the air. "That's my totally unbiased, biker opinion."

"You're probably right."

"Come here." He holds his arms out and I happily wrap myself around him. He hugs me, slowly rocking us side to side. "You're going to be great," he assures me in a soothing rumble.

"Thank you," I mumble against his shirt. "What are you working on today?"

He takes a long, deep breath before answering, so I can already guess what he's going to say. "Andrew wants to get together and jam over at Vinnie's. Alvin's supposed to meet me there."

"Good."

"We'll see. I'm sure he's dying to pump me for information about Pamela."

I open my mouth and he presses one finger against my lips. "Nope. The less I know, the better."

"Well, she *did* warn me to get hitched quick so I can have a piece of all your publishing royalties when I catch you in bed with our maid."

He rolls his eyes. "For fuck's sake. He really breaks everything he touches, doesn't he?"

"I have a feeling she was a little messed up before Andrew. Why else would any woman date him?"

"Good point."

I poke him in the chest. "Aren't we a perfectly smug couple?"

He leans down and rubs his nose against mine. "Smug as two bugs in *luuuv*," he sings.

"Oh my God." I slap my hand against his chest and snort with laughter.

When I can finally breathe again, he's grinning at me. "I love making you laugh."

I hug him tight again and he rubs his hand over my back. "Do you want me to drop you off?"

"No, I'm going straight to work after the audition. It's at the studio. Everything is on the up and up."

He releases me and grabs a notepad by the phone, jotting down a number. "That's Vinnie's house. Call me if you have any issues. If I'm not back by the time you get home, send a search party."

"Very funny."

MY HAPPY MOOD LASTS ALL THE WAY TO THE AUDITION.

What am I doing here?

They specifically asked for me. I'm not showing up with a bunch of other random actresses vying for a part.

Once I've given myself a little pep-talk, I head inside.

The assistant to the casting director takes my headshot and resume. "We're so happy you're here, Mallory."

"Thank you. I'm excited to learn more about the show."

Settle down. Stop being a kiss-ass.

Thankfully, she doesn't seem put off by my eagerness. She hands me a thick script and asks me to follow her, stopping in front of an unmarked white door. "We'll give you some time to go over the script. Don't worry about memorizing everything perfectly. Just get comfortable with the material."

"Sure."

She opens the door to a plain room with a table, a few chairs, and a couch against one wall. I curl up on the couch and dig into the script.

First day of school:

Brittany's beat-up clunker tooling down the highway to school.

Brittany driving. Her brother Christopher in the passenger seat...

I read through the scene. Other than Brittany's brother being an annoying pompous know-it-all, she seems to have a good life. I can do this. I can be Brittany from Nebraska. I showed up to Hollywood completely clueless too and now here I am reading for a Scout Southgate show.

In the next scene, Brittany waxes on about her love of cornfields to her new super-snobby friends. Seems like a strange thing for a teenage girl to be homesick about, but Nebraska is different than where I grew up, so I accept my character's quirk and move on.

By the time I reach the end of the script, my heart's thumping. I *want* this role. I flip back through it, considering how to deliver the lines. There's limited direction in the script. What interpretation will impress the casting director?

The woman I met earlier returns. "What'd you think?"

"I love it."

She smiles at me warmly. "Good. Scout wants you to read with Colby. Follow me."

I swallow hard. I hadn't expected to read in front of the executive producer today. I thought maybe they'd film the audition and show it to him later.

Mr. Southgate approaches and holds out his hand. I'm at least a few inches taller than him and almost have the urge to bend down so we're at eye-level. "Thank you so much for coming in, Mallory."

"Thank you. I'm really happy to be here." I snap my mouth shut before I start gushing about how I've watched almost all of the shows he's produced over the years. That they were some of my mother's favorites. There's plenty of time to make a fool of myself later.

The casting director and a few other people whose names and titles I immediately forget also introduce themselves.

The actor playing my brother, shakes my hand next. "Colby Bright. Love your work on *Shallow End*," he says, and I don't even think he's mocking me.

"All right. Settle down," someone yells.

A hush falls over the set.

"Go head," Mr. Southgate says.

"Uh." I stare at my script. "Are there any—"

"Nope. Let's see how you interpret the role first, Mallory. We'll go from there."

Great.

Recalling how nervous I was my first few weeks in L.A. I don't need direction or to have the lines memorized. I *am* Brittany, the fish out of water. The hopeful girl with a world of opportunity in front of her. The words come out easily and I only have to glance at the script a few times.

"Interesting interpretation," Mr. Southgate says slowly. I can't tell if that means he's happy, impressed, or annoyed.

"Can you try the first scene with a little less of the tight-assed stiffness?" the casting agent calls out. "Looser. More sugar."

Doesn't sound like I impressed *him*.

Colby leans in closer. "He's just testing you to see how well you take direction."

We go through the scene and for some reason, I interpret "more sugar" as "southern belle" and end up doing my best Pamela impression—swaying hips, slow southern drawl, and all. And my character's supposed to be from *Nebraska*.

Mr. Southgate and the casting agent are doubled-over laughing when we finish. My cheeks flame. Marilyn handed me an almost-guaranteed role and I blew it.

"That would have been perfect on *Plantation*, Mallory," he says, naming one of his older shows. "Ignore Kurtis, darling. Your first interpretation of Brittany was divine."

Kurtis side-eyes Mr. Southgate. "We'll let you know, Mallory."

Dismissed.

CHAPTER TWENTY-SIX

Mallory

The dull throb of exhaustion beats against my forehead as I slip my key into the front door lock. The last week of filming has been one sixteen-hour day after another. I've called Marilyn to ask about the *Ocean Ave.* audition so many times, I'm pretty sure she's started dodging my calls.

Inside our house, Chaser's rushing around the living room, stuffing his wallet in his pocket and searching the coffee table for something. All I've been looking forward to tonight is a nice, quiet evening home together, but he appears to have other plans.

He stops and smiles when he sees me. "Hey, how was your day?"

"Long. Where are you going?"

My clipped answer wipes the smile off his face. "We have a gig tonight."

"What? Why? Where?" My voice rises in pitch with each question. I blow out a breath to calm myself. As we move closer to the date when Chaser has to leave to record the album, the more I resent any time we have to spend apart.

"Last minute thing Thom set up for us at the Cathouse. Supposed to be a big 'surprise' show."

"Aren't you guys too big to play the Cathouse now?"

He cocks his head. "The second I start thinking like that, is when this all goes away."

"You know what I mean." I don't know why I'm bothering to argue with him. Obviously, this is a done deal. I can't help the disappointment digging into my chest. "You just came off a huge tour. You're about to leave to record an album and go on another tour." Oh, I hate the bitter tone that crept into my voice on that last couple words.

Chaser notices it too. His face twists with annoyance. "We still need all the exposure we can get, Mallory."

"I was looking forward to spending time with you tonight," I admit. "That's all."

His face softens. "Me too. Believe me, I wasn't thrilled when Thom called."

Join the club. I'm *never* happy to hear from Thom. I keep that to myself as I walk down to the bedroom. Chaser follows and stands in the doorway, watching me undress.

"Thom also wants us to check out a band he thinks would be a good fit to open for us." He stuffs his hands in his pockets and leans against the wall.

"Why don't you sound more excited about it?"

He shrugs.

"Who's the band?"

"Iron Kiss. I don't know if you've ever heard of them."

"The name sounds familiar. Are they not a good fit? Musically, I mean?"

"They're all right. Their lead guitarist does some interesting stuff. Their image is similar enough to ours."

"You still seem hesitant."

He shrugs. "I'll sound like a massive hypocrite." His mouth twitches. "They have a big party reputation."

"Ahhh, I see. You don't want to be Shooting Fences, killing everyone's fun with their sobriety coach."

He doubles over laughing. "Jesus Christ, I hadn't even thought of it that way, but yeah, I guess so." Shaking his head, he wipes the smile off his face. "We could only be so lucky to have half the career Shooting Fences has had."

"Did you talk to Thom about it?"

"They're on our label, so they *really* want us to tour together."

"So it's a done deal?"

"Unless we really have a serious objection, it sounds like it. Thom says they're excited about the tour and will behave, but—"

"Rock stars are so untrustworthy?" I tease.

He chuckles. "Exactly."

"Did you have another band in mind?"

"Honestly, no. You know what an egomaniac I am. I'd play the whole three hours by myself."

I snort. "Egomaniac sounds so harsh. More like, passionate about your career."

"Sure, that sounds better."

"Give them a chance. Maybe they'll impress you."

"Come with me tonight."

The thought of spending the next few hours jammed into a stuffy, smoky club and then waking up at the crack of dawn is so unappealing. "I have to be on set early tomorrow."

His mouth curls into the devilish smile I can't resist as he comes closer. "Come on," he cajoles. "I'll make you breakfast, and take you to work tomorrow so you can sleep in as late as possible."

"You'll be too tired."

"I miss having you watch me play. You've missed all our rehearsals this week. I always sound better when you're there."

"That's ridiculous. You sound amazing no matter what."

"Nope. It's a fact."

"Says who?" My lips twitch. Cindy might have to dab on a lot more concealer under my eyes tomorrow—I'm seriously considering going.

"Me." He captures me by the hips and yanks me toward him. "Please?"

"Okay." I glance at my closet. The last thing I feel like doing is dressing up to go to a club.

"Throw on some jeans," he suggests, reading my mind perfectly. "Nothing fancy. We don't have a lot of time anyway."

"Give me ten minutes?" I grab a pair of skintight purple-tinted acid wash jeans and a Kickstart tank top. A skinny red, studded belt drops to the floor and I scoop it up, wrapping it around my waist twice. I glance at the neat line of pretty heels stacked in my closet and my feet cry. Can't do it. I grab a pair of black flats instead. My hair's still teased and fluffy from filming today, but I gather it into a big, poofy ponytail to keep it out of my face, slick on some gloss and hurry out to the living room.

"Sexy." Chaser runs his gaze over me and sets the phone down. "Do you mind if we take your car? I called the guys and told them they didn't need to pick me up."

"Not at all."

He lugs his equipment out to the car and loads it up. Then we're off.

The sidewalk in front of the club is clogged with people. We end up driving around the block a few times before finding a spot.

"Stay here. I'm going to grab Darren to help me unload."

I'm fiddling with the radio, not paying attention to my surroundings when someone knocks on my window. I jump so high, I smoosh my poofy ponytail against the roof.

Boobs. As I turn to roll down my window, all I see are *boobs* and long blonde hair. I recognize both. We did after all spend all day filming together. "Pamela, what are you doing? You scared the crap out of me."

She leans down until her face finally takes the place of her boobs. "Why didn't you tell me Kickstart was playing tonight?"

"I didn't know until I got home."

"Oh." She sinks her perfect white teeth into her plump, glossy bottom lip. "Well, I kind of—"

I unlock the passenger side. "Get in before someone runs you over."

She sashays her way around the front of my car. Damn, for a last-minute outfit, she didn't hold back. Her skintight black vinyl minidress and spike heels put my hastily thrown together outfit to shame. She executes a ladylike sit-and-turn into my car and slams the door shut.

"I needed to get *out*. Since Andrew...I haven't been anywhere. Or had any fun at all."

"I'm glad you're here, then."

"Then I thought." She stares straight ahead and gnaws on her bottom lip again. "I don't want stories to get back to Andrew that I was out all by myself like some pathetic loser."

"So," I shrug, "hang out with us tonight."

"Are you sure?"

"Of course." We haven't spoken much about what went down in New York. It didn't seem polite to bring it up unless she wanted to discuss the situation.

"Have you seen him?"

"Who? Andrew? I haven't. Things have been too hectic. Chaser's getting ready to head up to Vancouver to record their album."

"Has Chaser seen him?"

"I think they've hung out and played a few times. Why?"

"Is he," she takes a long, dramatic inhale and exhale, "seeing anyone?"

"I don't know."

She keeps drilling me with her big blue eyes and I finally hold up my hands in surrender. "I swear, I don't know. Chaser hasn't mentioned it if he is."

"Good." She folds her arms over her chest. "I hope his balls explode."

I burst out laughing and she joins in. We're interrupted by the hatch lifting. "Hey, Pamela," Chaser calls out. "What're you doing here?"

She twists and wiggles her fingers at him. "I came to see my favorite band play, of course."

I barely hold back a gag and an eye-roll.

He chuckles for a second, then he and Darren start moving the equipment out.

"Guess it's time to go inside." I grab my keys from the ignition, stuffing them in my pocket and we follow the guys to the backstage loading area.

"Wait." She grabs my arm and stops me before we enter the club. "Andrew's not coming tonight, is he?"

Somehow, I get the impression, she's hoping he *will* show up. I take in her outfit again—definitely an eat-your-heart-out ensemble. "I really don't know. Like I said, Chaser sprung it on me when I got home."

"Well, I'll stick with you just in case." She pulls away. "Although, you are like an Andrew magnet sometimes."

"He likes hanging out and playing with Chaser. That doesn't have anything to do with me."

She stares at me for a few seconds, then shrugs. "If you say so."

"Babe," Chaser holds out his hand. "You coming?"

"Yup." He pulls me to his side, and I lean up to whisper in his ear, "She's worried Andrew might show up tonight. You didn't tell him about the show, did you?"

"Never had a chance to. Doesn't mean he won't hear about it from someone else and decide to show up." He turns to Pamela. "Come hang with us in the green room. Jacob will be ecstatic to see you."

I appreciate his attempt to ease her worries and make her feel included.

He wraps one arm around my waist and slings the other over

Pamela's shoulders—*all right, Chaser, no reason to make her feel that included*—and steers us down the hallway.

It's almost comical how quick Jacob jumps up when he sees her. "Am I dead? I'm seeing angels. This must be heaven." He clutches his hands over his chest.

Pamela squeals and rushes over to say hi.

Alvin catches me gagging and winks at me. "Glad you came."

"Chaser made me an offer I couldn't refuse."

Pamela nestles on the couch right in between Garrett and Jacob.

"G, you gonna come watch the first band with us?" Alvin asks.

"No, I trust you," he answers without looking away from Pamela.

Jacob's also not interested in leaving.

I don't even bother asking Pamela if she wants to join us. She looks way too content being the ham in the Jacob/Garrett sandwich. After what Andrew did to her, I'm happy they can cheer her up. Then again, I don't trust them not to do something even worse.

Chaser

I wasn't kidding about playing better when Mallory's here. Maybe it's all in my head and no one else can tell the difference. I still prefer it when she comes to our shows. Unfair, since I know she has to be up early.

The disappointment on her face when I told her I had a show tonight stirred up my knee-jerk, asshole reaction. I hate disappointing her so much. Thank fuck I reined it in long enough to convince her to come to the show with me.

"I'm so glad you're here." I squeeze Mallory to me and kiss her temple.

She wraps her arms around me and tips her head toward the couch. "Sorry about that."

"Why? He's been asking about her constantly. Maybe they'll be good for each other."

Mallory wrinkles her nose.

"I know. I heard it when it came out of my mouth." I tap my lip. "Sounded more reasonable in my head."

Next to us, Alvin snickers. "Can we please stop worrying about who's sticking their dick where and go watch this band that we might have to be on the road with for a couple of months?"

Outside our dressing room, we run into Thom. At least he showed up tonight. After springing this on us last minute, it would've been a dick move not to be here.

I scan the crowd of people clustered backstage. Looks like someone from our record label also made an appearance. I can't decide if that's good or bad.

"Is he from the label?" I ask, nudging Thom's arm.

"Yes. He wanted to get a feel for the chemistry between the bands tonight."

"We barely know each other."

He shrugs. "Then make a good impression."

Make a good impression. I'm about five seconds away from making an impression of Thom's skull in the drywall.

Alvin must not appreciate the remark either. He snarls at Thom as he marches by. We both ignore the suit and find our way to the entrance of the stage. Three members of Iron Kiss are clustered around, fretting like little chickens. Their nervous behavior pulls at whatever remaining sympathy strings I still possess after all this time in Hollywood.

I stick my hand out to their lead singer. "Sergio, right?"

His eyes go wide and he grabs my hand with both of his, shaking vigorously. "Shit, Chaser Adams. So stoked to finally meet you in person."

The guitar player butts in, pushing Sergio out of the way. "Fuck, you're such an inspiration, Chaser. Thanks so much for this opportunity. I'm Hector. We're really looking forward to touring with you."

Taken aback by their enthusiasm, I simply nod and introduce them to Alvin. They greet him with the same fervor.

I lean down and whisper in Mallory's ear, "Was I that—"

"Yes," Mallory answers before I even squeeze out the question.

My eyebrows knit together in a skeptical frown and she chuckles softly.

"Andrew Lane, I saw you at the Troubadour the second I moved out here. You're my favorite drummer ever!" she teases in a whisper not meant for anyone else.

"You're exaggerating."

She pinches two fingers together. "Maybe a little."

I tune back into the conversation in front of us. "We're excited to see you play."

Poor Nick rocks back on his heels like he's going to keel over at any moment.

Thom slithers over and rests one arm on my shoulder and one on Alvin's. "How's everyone doing over here?"

"Easy breezy," Alvin says.

"We'll let you get ready," Thom says, steering us away.

"We're cool, Thom. What's the problem?" Alvin asks.

"Nothing, I want to talk to you for a second. Short set tonight. Just want to give people a taste. Work out some of the new stuff you're planning to record."

"Uh, yeah. We know how this works," I answer.

He pushes open our dressing room door. Pamela and Jacob are busy talking. Huh, didn't realize he knew *how* to talk to women. Garrett's moved over to a table by himself and appears to be using his Walkman to tune them out.

"Mallory, will you go with me to the ladies' room?" Pamela asks, standing and fixing her dress.

"Sure."

I lean down and kiss Mallory's cheek. "Don't let anyone hassle you."

"We'll be fine."

Jacob watches them leave, then scrubs his hands over his face. "She is the hottest fucking chick I've ever laid eyes on."

"God help us," Alvin mutters.

"She's so sweet once you get past all that fake Barbie bullshit, too." Jacob waves his hand at the door.

"Can you all discuss your love lives some other time?" Thom snaps his fingers in front of Jacob's face. "Business mode, please."

"This *is* his business mode." Garrett slips off his headphones. "All the blood rushing to his cock, helps him think better."

"It's true," Jacob confirms.

Thom groans.

Normally, I would've told Jacob and Garrett to knock it off by now, but I fully support them in antagonizing our manager, so I kick back and laugh while Jacob mimes jerking off and ejaculating all over the place.

"How the fuck you guys manage to accomplish anything is beyond me," Thom fumes.

"This is our process." Garrett blows him a kiss. "Deal with it."

Jacob finally settles down and focuses his attention on me. "How do you feel about working some of the new song—'In Your Hands' into the middle of 'Queen of the Road'?" Jacob asks.

"Yeah, that was dope when you tried it at practice the other day," Garrett chimes in.

"I was just messing around but I can make it work."

"Is that new stuff?" Thom asks.

"Yeah," Jacob answers. "Thought it might be fun to slip it in there. Shake things up a bit."

"I like that," Thom says, as if we asked for his blessing. I slide a look Alvin's way and he lifts his gaze to the ceiling.

"How do you feel about Iron Kiss opening for you?" Thom asks, getting down to business whether we're ready to or not.

"They seem cool," Alvin says. "Still like to see them play before we make a final decision."

"Do they reel in the fine, young snappers?" Jacob asks. "If so, they get my vote." He waves his hand at me. "Chaser settling down with Mallory seems to be scaring all our hot groupies away."

Garrett and Alvin both frown at him.

"Were you *not* just trying to dip your wick in Pamela's inkwell?" Garrett asks.

"Dip my what, where?" Jacob grabs his crotch. "I'm at least a jumbo-size Sharpie."

Alvin picks up a black marker from the table and studies it for a second before throwing it at Jacob. "I wouldn't brag about that, bro."

Thom's face isn't getting any less beet-red. "How have you not seen them play live yet?"

Kudos to Thom for side-stepping that whole dick-size detour. "In case you haven't noticed, we've been a little busy on the road and writing material for the new album."

"I don't see the fire lately, guys." Thom presses his fist against his gut. "I was always impressed with how hungry you were. You need that recapture that raw, gutter-punk edge that got you here."

"Told ya." Jacob points at me.

"There's nothing wrong with growing artistically," Alvin says.

"I'm talking about knowing your competition too." Thom points to the door. "You knew every band on the strip back in the day. I know you did."

"You've been managing us for ten minutes. Don't lecture us on how we got here," Garrett growls.

"It's a big deal for us to headline, Thom," I say as diplomatically as possible, since I'd rather punch him a few times instead. "We want to make a thoughtful decision."

Alvin ducks his head and laughs.

I look over each of the guys. "We've worked hard to get to

where we are right now—artistically, physically, and mentally. I'm not willing to jeopardize that by taking some random punks out on the road with us."

"I'm glad everyone's kicked their bad...*habits*." Thom might as well be a hippo in a tutu dancing through a mind field while he tries to tiptoe around the word heroin. "But your...*health* is your responsibility. Every band...*parties* to some degree."

Garrett lifts his arms and slow claps. "Ten points for not calling us drug addicts. Bravo, Thom."

"Why are you guys busting my balls about this?"

I slap Thom's shoulder. "We can't afford any slip-ups. We're being cautious."

I catch Jacob's eye and he stares back. While he's stayed clean since Texas, I keep getting the impression he feels sobriety is a diet he can go off of once he hits a magic number, instead of a permanent lifestyle change. To say I'm worried about what the next few months will bring is a massive understatement.

Our worst nightmare would be him diving back into the junk while we're on the road. I'll do whatever I can to stop that from happening.

CHAPTER TWENTY-SEVEN

Mallory

The day I've been dreading is finally here.

"I'm going to miss you so much." Chaser leans in and kisses my forehead. "Can't wait for you to come visit."

"Me too."

"I'll try to scope out a few places so we can do some sight-seeing. Eat some good food."

"As long as I'm with you, I don't care."

"Thom says the house they rented for us is pretty big."

"You sure you can tolerate living with the guys again?" I tease.

"No."

Alvin comes up behind Chaser and jumps on his back, hugging him around the neck. "You're excited. I can tell."

"You miss us. Admit it, ya fucker!" Garrett shouts.

Chaser coughs and pulls Alvin off him. "I really don't."

"We miss you," I whisper and wink at Alvin.

He walks over and gives me a gentler hug. "I'll take good care of him, Mallory."

"Take care of each other." I tap his chest. "I expect sonic awesomeness from you guys."

"Yes, ma'am." Alvin salutes me and walks off.

"Still stuck on that sonic awesomeness, huh?" Chaser's lips twitch in amusement.

"Yup, so if you use it in a song, I want credit."

"Fuck, I'm going to miss you." He picks me up and spins me around in a brief circle before setting me down in the grass. "Nail your auditions. Don't take any shit from anyone. And if you get that callback from *Ocean Ave.* I want to know right away."

"I will." I swallow hard and force a smile on my face. This is it. They're leaving. We decided last night I wouldn't go to the airport with them. Chaser didn't want to risk any paparazzi bothering me when he couldn't be there to keep them away.

He cups my face and tips my head back. "I'll call you every night at eleven, okay? I'll get you the numbers for the studio and the house. Call me whenever you need to. For any reason."

"I will." I reach up and squeeze him tight one last time. "Sonic awesomeness, Chaser."

CHAPTER TWENTY-EIGHT

Chaser

Adapt or die. My dad tosses that saying around the clubhouse when brothers bitch about trying something new. Such as "the government's coming down hard on drug selling of any kind, maybe it's time the club look into selling weapons." Adapt or *die in prison*, in that case.

My situation is less dire. Turns out, when everyone told us Mark Cutter was a demanding producer, I should've listened.

Talk about regimented. We're not in the studio for a few hours a day and then left to run wild through the streets of Vancouver like Jacob had hoped. No, Mark puts us on a schedule that includes bed times and wake times.

Jacob didn't take it well. Hell, none of us were thrilled. But Mark wasn't cheap and we've produced some quality material the last couple weeks, so we adapted.

Adapt or languish in obscurity. We need to get this album out before people forget who we are.

The shower spray I'm currently under suddenly turns ice-cold. "What the fuck!" I yell, slapping the water off.

What I *haven't* adapted to yet—living with these three clowns again.

Yup. Mark Cutter insisted we all rent a house together. It's a big house, plenty of room to get away from each other but close enough for Jacob to wander into my room at all hours every single time a lyric pops into his head.

I snap a towel off the hook, wrap it around my waist, and storm out of the bathroom in search of someone to strangle. At least when the hot water runs out at home, it's because Mallory and I were busy fucking in the shower. "Why the fuck is there no hot water?"

"Sorry, bro!" I only get a glimpse of Jacob's naked ass scampering up the steps with two equally wet and naked females, but it's enough to put the pieces together.

"Fucker," I grumble.

ALVIN KNOCKS ON MY DOOR AS I'M FINISHING GETTING dressed. "Mark wants to see you."

"What? Why?" I'm really not in the mood to be scolded or lectured today. Or any other day.

"I think he's sitting down with each of us individually," Alvin says. "He held me after our session yesterday, remember?"

I'd been so drained, I hadn't thought much about Alvin staying to talk to Mark. He must've felt the same because he didn't come find me when he got back to the house.

I'm annoyed, but like a dutiful musician, I hoof it down the few blocks to the studio. Mark's waiting in the suite reserved for us and I knock on the door as I push it open. "You wanted to see me early?"

He waves his hand. "Come on in. How are you?"

"Fine." I take one of the seats and pull it around so we're facing each other. "What's up?"

A relaxed smile spreads over his face and he kicks back,

throwing his sneakered feet up on the table next to him. "Nothing bad. You can wipe that nervous look off your face. I'm checking in with each of you individually."

I scratch my chin. "Thanks?"

"How do you think things are going?"

"Great."

"You're okay with the schedule?"

It's annoying to admit it, but his grueling schedule is exactly what a bunch of unfocused punks need to stay on track. "I think it's working for us."

"Good. I don't want to squash your creativity, but sometimes we also need to rein it in to produce results. Inspiration is important. But if we waste too much time waiting around for you to be 'inspired' you might never write another lick. We want to get new music out there while you're still relevant. It's a delicate balance."

I understand the wisdom in what he's saying. "If I want to be a professional musician, I need to work at it every day. Treat it like a job. If I were a mechanic in my dad's garage, I wouldn't have the luxury of saying 'I'm not inspired to change those brake pads today, Dad. Maybe tomorrow.' Is that what you're getting at?"

"Exactly!" He slaps his leg. "Hell's fucking bells, you're the first musician I've worked with who's nailed it so eloquently."

"It's not quite the same thing—"

He holds up his hand to stop me. "I understand. I absolutely do. And I respect that. You *are* an artist." He taps his temple. "You're creating something out of nothing. Creating from your very soul. It's an incredible gift to be able to do that, Chaser. It's *not* the same as brake pads." He holds out his hands palms up. "But I want to help you strike the balance between naval-gazing artist wallowing in his perfectionist vision of the perfect sound and musician who gets to eat and keep a roof over his head."

"It feels a bit like selling out."

"Is it though? If you spend two, three years dicking around,

215

then what? No one hears your greatness. Kids move on. Find other bands to listen to and forget about you. The real fans will be back but how many do you lose? How much patience does the label have? I want to help you produce the absolute *best* album Kickstart is capable of producing, *right now*. Not a perfect, musical masterpiece five years from now."

I can't decide if we're lucky to be working with Mark or he's a lunatic who's way overstepping his job description. "I do enjoy eating and sleeping indoors."

"Good. I'm not saying you have to be one or the other. I want to help you figure out where *you* want to be and help guide you there."

"Thanks." I cock my head and study him for a second. "You having this same conversation with all of us?"

One corner of his mouth twitches. "That's confidential."

"I should warn you, then. Jacob's all about the naval-gazing artistry."

"I've noticed. You guys all balance each other out well."

What a diplomatic answer. Kind of makes me like him even more. "We try."

"How often do you practice, Chaser?"

"Every day."

"Are you focused or playing whatever comes to you?"

"A little of both. I try to spend the first few hours on technique." I wiggle my fingers at him. "Get them where I want to go. Then I'll work on a current song we're writing. I'll wind down with something experimental and play around a little." When I'm in L.A., I'm usually getting to that last part about the time Mallory comes home from work. Damn, I miss her. I've been all out of sorts since we got here.

"That's a solid approach. I like that. Do you practice with other people?"

"Yeah, when we lived together, we'd always jam during the day. Now we're a little more spread out but we still get together every couple days and play for a few hours."

"How about outside the band?"

"When I can, yeah. I've played with Vinnie and Andrew quite a bit."

"It's good to expand your circle. Learn new things and ways to create. As long as you're not always the one contributing to the creative flow. You need to get back some of what you put in."

I definitely understand what he means. The first band Alvin and I started had tons of negative energy. We couldn't put a label on it at the time. All I knew was that playing with them drained the life energy straight out of me after every session.

"I've been there."

"Avoid those people like the plague." He leans forward and slaps my leg. "What inspires you? Nature? Cars? Sunrises? Your girlfriend?"

My lips quirk. "All of the above. But I'm definitely more inspired since I've been with my fiancée."

"It's one thing to write about what you think love is," He holds up his right hand, palm up, "And another to write about what it truly is once you've experienced it, isn't it?" He holds his left palm up higher than the right.

"Fuck." I sit back and nod. "Yeah. That's exactly it."

"Heartbreak's an even better motivator."

"I'd rather not go there."

"What's your best moment in music been, Chaser? One thing that defined for you why you're doing this?"

I sit back and consider his question carefully. Getting our first advance—people actually paying us for the music we created was pretty fucking awesome. Meeting Mallory? That's the best damn thing that's ever happened in my life, period. We were destined to be together one way or another, so I don't think that counts. And I wouldn't consider 'Candy Jar' a musical high point in my career—even if the label says otherwise. Winning the "Guitar God" award was cool but also sort of embarrassing. I'm twenty-two, hardly a god.

Suddenly, I know *exactly* which moment stands out the most.

"I met these two fans while we were in England." I give him the story behind the song 'Cry it Out' and how the girls explained what the song meant to them. "It was a low point on that tour." Real low point. Mallory had to leave the tour and go home by herself. There was a good chance I was going to kill Davey Revolver if he kept fucking with the band. "But something about their story made all the other shit worth it, you know?"

His eyes light up. Maybe his artists usually say, "free cocaine and all-you-can-fuck pussy."

"That's it, Chaser! *That's* why you do this. Not the fame, money, or girls. That stuff fades. But if you touch someone with your music." He rests his hand over his heart. "You can make an impact on their entire life."

Someone knocks on the door.

Guess our music therapy session is over.

Garrett and Alvin push open the door and join us. A few seconds later, Jacob enters, closing the door behind him.

"I have so much stuff, it's insane." He tosses his lyric book at me. "Whatever that was you kept playing over and over last night must have seeped into my brain."

"The entire hot water tank of water you went through this morning didn't help?"

"Oh, that too." He cracks up and slaps my shoulder.

Mark steeples his fingers under his chin and looks us over "I'm glad you're all here. I want to talk to you about something."

We all lean in during his dramatic pause. Even me. It's like with one conversation, Mark managed to anesthetize my inner cynic.

When he's positive he's captured our attention, Mark continues, "Have you ever considered contributing a song to a movie soundtrack?"

"Hell yeah," Jacob pumps his fist in the air, "That'd be cool. Well, depending on the movie."

"No sappy love songs," Garrett adds.

Alvin casts a dubious look Jacob's way. "No porno

soundtracks, either."

"Hey," Jacob protests. He jumps up, thrusting his hips and screaming "bow-chicka-bang-*bang*" at the top of his lungs. "We would rock the fuck out of that."

Mark slides his gaze my way and smirks. "Anyway, an offer like that would usually go through your label or manager but I have a friend who's in a bit of a bind."

"What kind of bind?" I ask.

"The band who was going to do the key song for this film flaked out at the last minute. Movie's coming out soon, so they need a replacement like yesterday. The director's a fan of Kickstart and a friend of mine. When he heard I was working with you, he asked if you'd be interested."

"What about our album?" Garrett asks.

"Well, that's just it. I figure we're already here. We're working on the album anyway. Let's maybe see if we can come up with something. We can record it and send it on. You'll get paid. Win-win. The timing and publicity from the movie will be great. Most likely right before your album releases."

"What kind of movie?" Garrett asks.

"Big action flick. They want a strong, heart-pounding, adrenaline-pumping rock song. No love ballads or sappy ballads. This movie's all car chases, flashy explosions, fight scenes, and special effects."

I've heard enough. "I don't see a downside here."

"I'm in," Alvin agrees.

"What's our theme?" Jacob asks.

My mouth twitches but I bite back my laughter. Now I understand why Mark chose today to have his conversation with me.

"Well, it's an action flick. But there's a central love story too."

Jacob groans but I'm even more intrigued. And once he names the director and lead actor, we're all sold.

This could be huge.

I can't wait to call Mallory and tell her about it.

CHAPTER TWENTY-NINE

Mallory

After the night out at the Cathouse, Pamela and I seem to have called some sort of truce. We're almost like...*friends.*

"Goodness gracious, it's like the writers have no respect for normal plot rules." She bumps my shoulder and giggles on our way out of the studio. "Demonic possession? Poor Billie. They're going to make her spew pea soup."

"Eww." I glance over my shoulder to make sure no one's within earshot. The coast is clear, but I still keep my voice low. "I can't decide if we're on *Gilligan's Island* or *Tales from the Darkside* lately."

"Dang right," she agrees.

Our camaraderie lasts all the way out to the parking lot.

As we approach our vehicles, my gaze lands on a big black and red Harley parked beside my car and my heart skips. It doesn't even look that much like Chaser's bike but it's another reminder of how much I miss him.

"What the heck?" Pamela mutters. "Why is Andrew here?"

I glance around, then realize *he's* on the bike, helmet tucked under his arm. He waves to us.

Well, this is awkward. He's parked so close to my car, it's impossible to quietly turn invisible and give them privacy.

"Why are you here, Andrew?" Pamela stops by the front wheel and crosses her arms over her chest. The hopeful note in her voice pricks my heart.

Oh, Pamela, he's not worth the heartache.

Andrew's gaze lingers on her breasts for a few beats before swinging my way. "I'm not here to bug you, Pamela. I need to talk to Mallory for a second."

Wait, what?

Pamela shoots a glare my way.

Buh-bye, budding friendship.

My shoulders jerk up in a helpless shrug. I didn't ask Andrew to stop by. And I sure as hell wouldn't ask him to visit me at work.

"You could *call*, Andrew. Not come to my job." The confusion in my voice seems to satisfy Pamela. She focuses her scary face on Andrew again. My bewilderment quickly morphs into annoyance. I'm not in the mood to be used as a way to make Pamela jealous.

"I need to go." I give Pamela a quick one-armed hug. "See you tomorrow."

I unlock my door and try to open it without tapping Andrew's bike. I'm about to squeeze myself inside when Andrew calls out, "Wait, wait, I really did need to talk to you, Mallory."

Pamela flips him off and storms away. A few seconds later, her tires chirp over the pavement as she blasts out of the parking lot.

I slam my door and glare at Andrew. "Why are you here? I have to work with her. Now she's going to be pissed with me."

He shrugs. "She's just jealous of you."

I scoff. "Hardly."

"She is. You're a way better actress and she knows it."

"Don't do this." I turn back to my car. "Please, don't put me in the middle of whatever you're doing."

"We're over. This has nothing to do with her." He pats the back of the bike. "Let me give you a ride home."

"Andrew," I say as patiently as possible. "You're parked *right next* to my car."

"Ride to the beach?" he asks with hopefully raised eyebrows. "No."

"With Chaser gone, I thought you might miss riding." His voice wavers with an enticing lilt that I'm sure works wonders on other women, but is only making me angrier.

"That's...a weird thing for you to be concerned about." I can't picture any scenario where Chaser would be thrilled about me going for a ride on the back of Andrew's bike. "I can't."

"Why?"

"Don't you know it's bad biker etiquette to try to get another man's woman on your bike?" I snap.

"You're not *allowed?*" he says as if he's a kid dying to break the rules just for the sake of breaking the rules.

"I don't *want* to."

"Well, that's different."

"Andrew." I draw out his name in an effort to capture his hummingbird-quick attention span. "This is my *job*. If you're trying to make Pamela jealous, please do it somewhere else. And *with* someone else."

He sighs, and straps on his helmet. "Believe it or not, this had nothing to do with her. I wanted to take you to dinner or something in case you were lonely with Chaser being gone."

I wish I could believe his visit is as innocent as he's trying to make it sound. But even if it is, I don't think I'd accept his invitation. It's too...uncomfortable. "Thank you. That was sweet."

"And, I didn't want to mention this in front of Pamela because it *would* make her jealous—"

"What?" A suspicious note creeps back into my voice.

"Those samples of the T-shirts I'm designing arrived. You still cool with modeling them for me?"

"Do you promise that none of them are of the 'I fucked Andrew Lane Club' variety?"

He holds up one hand and with a straight face, promises, "Swear to God."

I completely forgot that I'd agreed to do it weeks ago. And now I feel bad for turning down his invitation to dinner. "Okay," I answer hesitantly. "I'll do it."

"Cool. Thank you."

"Do you have a hair and makeup person?"

Confusion draws his brows down. "You always look fine. Can't you do that yourself?"

"Not if you want it to look professional." I glance toward the building. Cindy could use the extra work. Maybe if Andrew's shirt business takes off, he'll hire her to do all his shoots. "I know someone who's really good. If I bring her, will you pay her daily rate?"

He hesitates for a second. "Yeah. Whatever you want."

"Thank you."

"Cool, stop by tomorrow after work. I'll show you the shirts. We can do a few test shots. You can help me scout out a few locations on my property—"

"You're doing this all...yourself?"

"Well, yeah. I want to test the waters before I jump in, you know?"

"I guess."

"It gives me a different creative outlet while we're between recording and touring."

That sort of makes sense.

"Anyway, you're off Saturday, right? I'll get my other models together—"

"Wait, I'm not the only model?"

His mouth curls into a sly smile. "No, but you're the star."

At least I won't be alone with Andrew at his house.

"You think Chaser would be interested? When he gets back, I mean. For the men's line."

224

I can't picture Chaser wanting to add "model" to his resume but who knows. "Maybe."

"Cool. I want it to be sort of edgy and punk rock but also super classy."

"That's a lot of expectations."

He half-shrugs. "I have faith in you, Mallory." He starts the bike up. The deafening rumble shakes the ground, vibrating straight through me. "Sure I can't interest you in a ride?" he shouts.

"I'm sure." I shake my head for some *no way* emphasis.

He waits until I'm in my car before taking off, handling the big machine with the grace of a panther.

It's late and I'm starving. I put Andrew's visit out of my mind and head home.

CHAPTER THIRTY

Mallory

The pain of missing Chaser wraps tighter and tighter around my ribs with each day he's away. I'm so excited for his eleven o'clock call, I practically pounce on the phone as soon as it rings.

"How's my girl?" he asks.

I swear hearing his voice makes my eyes water. "Missing you."

"I miss you too." He pauses and my heart skips. "I have good news though."

"You finished the album and you're coming home sooner than you thought?"

He lets out a soft huff of laughter. "No, little dove. We're making progress though."

"What else?"

"Mark worked out a deal for us to contribute a song to the *Elimination Date* soundtrack."

"Seriously? That's wonderful!" I stop and consider the irony. "I auditioned for a bit part in that."

"What happened?"

I shrug even though he can't see me. "I never got a callback."

"Fuck them," he growls. "Maybe I should've said no."

Now I wish I hadn't told him. "Don't be crazy! This is huge for you guys! They probably heard I won't flash my boobs and wouldn't have hired me anyway."

He chuckles.

"Wait, does this mean you're going to be up there even longer?" Dammit that sounded more selfish than celebratory. Thankfully, Chaser doesn't hold it against me.

"I don't think so. We'll work it into our normal schedule. Mark says we'll be invited to the premiere. You'll need a killer dress so they know what they missed."

He tells me about the ideas they kicked around in the studio. I share how embarrassed I was when I flubbed my lines today.

Basically, we talk about everything that's happened in our lives since we spoke yesterday.

Well, almost everything.

It's on the tip of my tongue to spill all the details of Andrew's visit, but for some reason, I don't.

Whenever Chaser's away, he encourages me to share every little mundane detail of my life. Why don't I want to tell him about Andrew's visit to the set?

Part of it is my excitement over the soundtrack. The next best thing to seeing *myself* on the silver screen would be hearing one of Chaser's songs in a film.

My eyelids grow heavy and our pauses extend for longer periods of time. Chaser and I frequently fall asleep on the phone together. I'm dreading the day our phone bill shows up in the mail, yet we always have trouble saying goodbye.

"Time for bed, little dove," he says.

"I wish you were here."

"Me too. You're coming to visit soon. I wish I could say I'll show you around but honestly, I haven't done much exploring myself."

"Cutter really cracks the whip, huh?"

"Yup. It's working, though. Except for the random chicks

Jacob keeps finding and bringing back to the house, he's on the straight and narrow."

"Well, he needs at least one vice so don't be too hard on him," I tease.

We finally say good night.

I lay in our bed, staring at the ceiling for a long time after we hang up.

The nagging thought that I should've told him about Andrew's visit won't go away.

Then again, I never mentioned Andrew's offer to model the T-shirts, either. I guess, I figured it was another one of Andrew's big ideas that would never come to fruition.

Besides, after the tour, Chaser and I went home. Got engaged. Who cares about some stupid T-shirts when your boyfriend takes you on a romantic getaway to propose?

Maybe deep down I'm being selfish. I don't *want* to tell Chaser. He'll be pissed. And I don't want to do anything that delays him finishing the album and coming home to me as soon as possible.

Even if he has to go right back out on the road.

I toss and turn for most of the night.

CHAPTER THIRTY-ONE

Mallory

Pamela's still cool to me the next morning. I can't decide if I should apologize for Andrew showing up yesterday or let it go and hope she forgets all about it.

At least Cindy's cheerful and happy to see me. As she spreads foundation over my forehead, I peek up at her. "Are you doing anything after work tonight?"

"Does drinking a bottle of wine alone in my apartment count?"

"You can always come visit me. Or we can go out to a movie, grab dinner, or something?"

"You don't see enough of me here?"

My shoulders jerk up. Maybe Cindy has enough friends and isn't interested in socializing with me outside of work. Whatever. *Please let her be free to go to Andrew's with me tonight.* After all my tossing and turning, I decided I can't go there by myself.

"So, I have a friend who's putting together an ad campaign for some T-shirts he designed. Are you interested in doing the hair and makeup?"

"Are you serious? God, Mallory, yes!" she squeals in my face. In a quieter voice she adds, "I could use the extra cash."

"Awesome. Thank you."

"No, thank you. I appreciate it."

"Do you mind going with me tonight? He wants to check out a few spots on his property for the photos."

In the mirror I catch her frown. "Is your friend doing this at his house?"

"Yeah, it's all very low budget. But he said he'll pay you your regular daily rate," I hurry to add.

"Who is it?"

"Uh, one of Chaser's friends."

"Oh, okay. Sure. I can stop by for a little bit. That way I can get an idea of what look he wants. When's the full shoot?"

"Saturday."

"Perfect." She bends down in front of me. "Close your eyes. Don't blink," she whispers as she sweeps shadow over my lids. I don't blink, but I sneeze in her face which is worse.

"I'm sorry!"

She waves off my apology. "I've had worse. Maybe you're allergic to this, let me go find something else."

As she steps away to rifle through her makeup kit, I catch a glimpse of Pamela in the doorway. "Hey!" I wave to her. "Are you coming or going?"

Her frosty glare should send a shiver down my spine but I think I've built up an immunity to them. "Waiting for the chair."

"I'll be done in a sec," Cindy says without looking up.

I lean forward and pick up my script, waving it at Pamela. "Do you want to run lines?"

"Sure. I'll be right back."

Phew. It'll be nice if we can go back to being friends again. Although, will that be possible when she finds out I'm modeling Andrew's shirts?

Or will it drive another wedge between us?

CHAPTER THIRTY-TWO

Mallory

I'm a mess of nerves as I leave the set.

"I'll follow you up, okay?" Cindy says.

I'd feel better if we were going to Andrew's together. That way she can't leave me. But that's a horrible thing to think, right? If I'm so damn nervous, why am I doing this in the first place?

Andrew's a friend. He's Chaser's friend. I'm doing Chaser's friend a favor. There's no harm in that. Everything's fine.

"Are you sure you don't want to ride together?" I ask.

"I can't. I need to be home by seven."

Shit, shit, shit.

"Okay. Follow me."

I move through traffic at a snail's pace earning a few honks and middle fingers from my fellow drivers. Cindy stays right behind me. We pass the turn for my road and I glance at it longingly.

We continue up the short, narrow maze of tiny streets leading up to Andrew's much plusher home near the top of the Hollywood Hills. Cindy leaves her car on the street in the perfect spot for a quick getaway.

She pulls a small makeup trunk out of her car and joins me. "Are you nervous?"

"No. Just tired. It was a long day. I should've rescheduled or something."

We pass Andrew's Ferrari, his black Chevy Blazer, his Harley, and a few other motorized toys before reaching the side entrance. I take a deep breath before knocking.

The door swings open. Andrew's lean, shirtless body fills the space. Without permission, my gaze travels down his inked torso to the dips at his hips, disappearing under his tight, low-slung jeans, all the way to his bare feet.

"Hey, girl. Feel like I haven't seen you in forever." At first, he seems happy to see me. The welcoming smile fades as I shift and his gaze lands on Cindy. "Mallory, who's your friend?"

"This is Cindy." I wrap my arm around her shoulders, pulling her forward. "The makeup artist I told you about."

"Oh. Right. You didn't need to bring her today."

I shrug. "I thought she could help us with the location and lighting or whatever."

Cindy holds up her makeup trunk. "I brought a few things to get an idea of the look you want."

"Cool. Cool. Thank you." He stands back and opens the door wider. "Come in."

The place is neater and tidier than I expected now that Pamela's gone. Although the furniture has been replaced and rearranged.

"You were right," Andrew says over his shoulder as we follow him through the house. "Pamela barbequed all my furniture after New York."

I snort and choke on my laughter.

Cindy taps my shoulder. "*That's* Pamela's ex?" she whispers.

"Yup."

"Jesus, he's hot. And I don't even like rockers."

"He's a serial cheater," I warn.

"And that's why I don't date rockers." Her mouth twists down. "Sorry."

I'm not offended. Chaser's nothing like Andrew. "Nope. I hear you."

Andrew stops at the sliding glass door that leads to a patio of sand-colored slate leading to a kidney-shaped deep blue pool the size of a small lake. The property curves to the right with lush trees and shrubbery providing the allusion of a private, island oasis.

"This is beautiful, Andrew," Cindy says, staring at everything.

He stands by the pool and throws his arms out wide. "This is my Zen. My peaceful, happy place, you know?"

Cindy's intrigued and keeps studying the pool and trees. "What's your vision?"

Andrew stares at one of the elegant black, iron lounge chairs scattered around the pool deck. "Maybe some old Hollywood glam with a punk rock vibe?"

Even with his eyes hidden by dark sunglasses, when he turns my way, my skin sizzles. "Can you make her hair all wavy." He flips his hands around his face. "Like Cleo Moore? Mallory always reminded me of that actress."

That's news to me, but okay.

"Definitely." Cindy pulls me closer and pushes me into the lounge chair. "Mallory's hair is longer, but I can curl it away from her face. Give her some sophisticated loose waves. Here." She brushes my hair back from the side of my face. "And here."

"Yeah, that's good." While Andrew seems excited, I'm more and more weirded out with every passing second.

"Who are your other models?" I ask.

"A couple girls from the clubs and um, this kid from another band." He turns to Cindy. "You mind working on some other people too?"

"Not at all. I can handle all of it."

They end up walking over the grounds, talking about which spots might work best. My inner matchmaker thinks they'd make a cute couple but then my practical side says Cindy doesn't need the heartache.

"Oh shoot!" Cindy stares at her watch. "I'm so sorry. I have to go."

"That's all right. You've been a huge help, Cindy." Andrew pulls out his wallet and hands her some cash. They speak in low tones for a few minutes while my gaze lingers on the gate leading to the driveway. I plan to make my escape with Cindy.

Andrew walks us out front with a hand at each of our backs. Cindy breaks away from us and jogs down to her car. "See you Saturday, Andrew. See you tomorrow, Mallory." She waves before taking off.

I grab my car door handle, but Andrew presses his palm against the glass. "Hey, can you come back inside for a second? I have something I want to show you."

"Uh... sure." I follow him back into the house. "Do you feel better about the shoot now?"

"Yeah, I meant to take some test shots of you but we can do that Saturday."

Inside the house, I'm not sure where to go. He bounds up the stairs. Instead of following, I perch on the edge of the couch.

Andrew returns a few minutes later and holds up a navy blue T-shirt about ten sizes too small for him to his chest. "What do you think?"

"Oh! Is that one of your shirts? It's cute." I stand and move closer so I can study the fairy-tale-like scene depicted on the material. Except, on closer inspection, it's kind of gory. The busty, blonde, barely dressed princess wields a bloody knife and wears a deranged smile. "Wow, that's...something." I stare at it a little longer. "It's so...detailed. You drew that?"

He shrugs. "I like drawing crazy stuff. Always have."

"It's incredible." I return to leaning against the couch, my gaze straying toward the door. "Maybe you should publish comic books, instead of T-shirts?"

"Maybe." He slings the shirt over his shoulder and

approaches. "Thanks for being so cool about my art. Pamela always told me how lame it was."

"It's not lame at all. You're really talented." My eyes return to the door. "I should probably..."

"Come here, girl." He envelopes me in a friendly enough hug, patting my back a few times. "I've missed you guys. How's Chaser doing locked up with Mark?"

"Good, I think." I pull away and hold up my hand between us, flashing my ring. "He proposed when we were home visiting his family."

He rolls his lip and stares at the ring for a second. "I heard about that. That's great. Congratulations," he says with all the enthusiasm of someone just given a week to live.

Huh. Maybe his breakup soured him on all relationships.

He lights up a cigarette. My eyes water and my nose twitches. I step away and run my hand over the back of the new couch. "This looks nice."

He snorts a stream of smoke through his nose and casts a sad glance at the new furniture. "It's been hell without her."

My heart twitches but I can't muster up any sympathy after what he did. So, I say nothing.

"Do you want something to drink?" He bangs his palm against the side of his head. "Fuck, I should've asked you sooner. Sorry."

"It's fine." He seems so forlorn or anxious. As much as I'm dying to leave, I can be polite and stay for a simple glass of water, right? "Water would be good."

"Have a seat." He sweeps his arm in the general direction of the couch.

I set my purse on the coffee table—noting the absence of the giant cocaine-filled Tupperware containers—and perch on the edge of one stiff couch cushion.

A few seconds later, something instrumental that I strongly suspect is Andrew playing the piano drifts from the speakers. "This is pretty," I call out. "Is that you?"

"Pretty." He returns to the living room with two wineglasses and a green glass bottle. The cigarette in his mouth bounces. "It's something I was fucking around with since I have all this time on my hands."

He sets the wine and glasses on the coffee table in front of me. "I'm all out of water."

"Seriously?" The last thing I need to do is get tipsy when I'm alone with Andrew. "I'm not a fancy girl. Tap water is fine."

He drops down next to me, so close his body heat simmers over my skin. I shift away but he follows.

"I can't believe you two are engaged." He takes my hand and stares at my ring. "Where'd Chaser get this from? A gumball machine? It's not even a diamond."

Stunned by the bitterness in his voice, I yank my hand out of his grasp. "It's a sapphire. Like Lady Di's ring."

"I expected him to be more original than that." Andrew shrugs.

"Well, I love it and he knew I'd love it."

He turns his big puppy eyes my way. "How'd he do it?"

"In Niagara Falls." My heart flutters at the memory and I can almost feel the mist from the falls over my skin.

"What a sap," he grouches, wiping the smile off my face.

Maybe he's just being a jerk because he's upset about his own breakup. Had he planned to propose to Pamela eventually? "I'm sorry about you and Pamela."

He shrugs like it's no big deal. "It's my own fault."

"Can't argue with you there."

He twists, tucking his leg under him so he's facing me. "So, what's next? Going to settle down and pop out some babies?"

"Sheesh. Why does everyone keep asking me that?"

"It's a natural question" His gaze drops to my left hand. "Why bother getting married otherwise?"

"Because we love each other."

He reaches over and brushes his knuckle over my cheek, pushing a few strands of hair off my face. "You're so pretty. I only watch *Shallow End* to see you every week. Did I ever tell you that?"

"Uh, no." I scoot back a few inches. Nervous laughter bubbles out of me as I try to subtly shake off his touch. "Why wouldn't you watch for Pamela? She has way more lines."

"That's only 'cause her tits are bigger. You're a better actress."

I blink, and stare down at my chest, unsure of what to say. An icky sensation rolls over me from talking about Pamela this way with him.

As I'm trying to come up with something to break the silence, Andrew cups the back of my head and drags me toward him.

"Whoa. Stop." I slap my hand on his chest and shake out of his hold. "What are you doing?"

His gaze drops to my lips. "Kissing you."

"Hold up. What?" My eyes bug out. "No. No way. You and I are friends, Andrew. That's it. I'm with Chaser. We're *engaged*."

"Jesus Christ, Mallory." He throws his hands in the air and swivels away from me. "I don't want to be your *friend*."

"W...What?"

When he turns my way again, sweet fun-loving Andrew has left the building. I barely recognize the wicked sex fiend in front of me. "I want to *fuck* you." Each word oozes from his mouth with deliberate ease.

"You and me would be fire together," he continues. His gaze drops to my chest. "I've been motherfucking *obsessed* with you since the first time I saw your picture in *L.A. Weekly*." He licks his top lip and meets my eyes. "But I'm not interested in being your *friend*."

"Oh." Mortification heats my skin from chest to toes. I'm such an idiot.

"Trust and believe me when I say, I have *never* put so much effort into fucking a woman, Mallory."

"What are you talking about?"

"It feels like every move I've made for months now—"

"Wait a second." The double-sting of humiliation and betrayal ignite my anger. "All this...time...collaborating with Chaser, defending Audrey, taking Kickstart on tour...asking me to model for your —"

His face screws up as if he can't believe he did all those nice things. But he shakes off the confusion quickly. "No. Chaser's a talented musician. I like hanging out with him. Love working with him. Kickstart was a business decision. They're a solid band that complements my band. Our audiences overlap. They work hard and they puts asses in the seats."

"Then, it's all business?"

"Not at all. I would've loved it if I could've gotten Chaser to bang some groupies. And if it worked out that you caught him and fell onto my dick to ease your pain, that would've been a fantastic bonus."

My head hurts from trying to make sense of his explanations. "So...when you brought those girls on Chaser's bus? You weren't kidding around?"

"Fuck no." He clenches his teeth, emphasizing his angular jawline. "Jesus Christ, I found blondes, brunettes, redheads, fat chicks, skinny chicks, Big tits, small tits. *Nothing* made him bite."

The pain in my chest expands. I honestly thought Andrew's antics were silly and harmless. Just him goofing off. Playing pranks. Chaser was right to be so angry. "You would've hurt me like that?"

He rubs the back of his neck and stares at the ceiling for a few seconds. Obviously, my feelings were never a concern. "You should thank me. He was a fucking monk on the road." He snort-laughs and looks away. "I gotta be honest, it just made me even more obsessed with you."

"Okay. Wow." I blink and sit back. That's a whole lot of honesty.

I'm a mix of emotions as I take in everything he laid out. Disgusted, hurt, offended, guilty, and furious. I've met so many shitty, disgusting men in Hollywood. Despite his obnoxious antics, I thought Andrew was different. I thought he was my friend—something I don't have many of out here. I'm such an idiot.

"Is there anything about me that you actually *like*, Andrew?" I ask quietly. "As a person, I mean."

He rakes his fingers over his jaw as he considers the question. "You're not as annoying to talk to as most chicks."

"But I'm nothing more than another disposable girl you'd like to add your list of conquests?"

He grabs my hand again, yanking me forward. "What do you want me to say, Mallory? That I'd put a ring on your finger and swear I'd never look at another woman again?" He runs his gaze over me. "I don't think I could make that promise to *any* woman if it makes you feel better."

I pull my hand back. "So, your interest in me...it's nothing more than some sort of compulsion?"

"Why all the questions?" He brushes his knuckles against my cheek. "If you're so committed to Chaser, why do you care?"

My body trembles as I shrug. "I don't know."

A giddy, wide-eyed expression transforms his face. "Are you *attracted* to me, Mallory?"

My throat tightens and I drop my gaze, shaking my head.

His fingers graze my chin and he forces my head up. "You are. A little bit, aren't you?"

"No."

"Mallory." My name passes his lips like a scolding. "Don't lie when I've been totally honest with you."

I shake my head, scared to admit how repulsed I am by his confession. How disappointed I am that he's no different than every other sleaze I've met in Hollywood. I have no words to express the hurt and betrayal digging into my ribs that he'd disrespect the man I love with all my heart by saying these things to me.

He inches closer and slides his hand to the back of my head, holding me still. My eyes widen as he swoops in. Too shocked to move, my body remains rigid—a rabbit caught in psychedelic headlights. His lips slide against mine for the briefest second.

Wrong. Andrew's so wrong about us. The fire inside me isn't passion, it's fury.

Tears sting my eyes as I pull away, breaking the brief, tentative kiss. I swipe my hand over my mouth, wishing I could erase the feel of Andrew's lips. "I love Chaser."

He releases me. "Love has nothing to do with this."

"He's your friend. How can you do this to him?"

A tiny bit of remorse pinches his brows together. "I feel shitty for wanting to fuck you so bad. He saved my life. I have mad respect for him."

"Just not enough respect not to hit on me."

"I'm way past hitting on you, Mallory. If I didn't respect him, I would've told you this a long time ago."

"Your restraint is admirable." I lean over and reach for my purse.

Ignoring my sarcasm, he blocks my hand. "One time." His pleading eyes beg me to reconsider. "It's just sex."

"Maybe to you it is."

He snort-laughs and slaps his thighs. "Fuck, you know Kyle boned Pamela the first time we broke up?"

"She mentioned it."

His eyebrows shoot up. "See? It wasn't a big deal."

Maybe that's how it works in his dysfunctional brain but this visit to crazy land has been more than enough for me.

"Shit." He draws out the word in disbelief. "Pammy told me once Chaser's the only man you've ever slept with. I didn't believe her until now."

That bitch. I never should've opened up to her. I bet they had a good laugh about poor prudish Mallory.

"Is it like a religious reason?" he asks.

"What? No."

"Do you need to be in love or something?"

My heart races. I'm a confused mouse being batted around by Andrew's paws of crazy.

"You like me a little, at least. Right?" he persists.

"I used to." In a stronger voice, I add, "But not in the way you seem to think."

He rests one of his big hands on my thigh. "How can you marry him when you've never been with another man? Aren't you curious what it's like with someone else?"

Acid burns the back of my throat at the thought. "Not even a little."

"*Fuuuuuck,*" he groans and covers his face with his hands, scrubbing hard. "I just want you out of my fucking head."

"Words every woman longs to hear." I force a laugh.

He gives me a crooked smile in return. "Do you need me to say *I love you*? I can say it if that will change your mind."

"You wouldn't mean it. And I'll *never* change my mind. So what's the point?"

His fierce expression sends shivers down my spine. "I think about you all the time, Mallory. First thought that pops in my head every morning: 'I wonder what Mallory's doing? Does she sleep naked? Does she like to wake up with a long, slow, morning fuck?'"

"Stop it! What's wrong with you?"

"You know Chaser wouldn't even give up simple details like that?" he continues like a petulant child who's been denied a trip to the most magical kingdom. "I'm an open book. Tell you anything you want to know. Not Chaser. Locked down tight when it comes to *you*."

Thank God for that.

"Last time I was inside Pamela all I thought about was *you*." He closes his eyes and thrusts his hips. "Is Mallory's pussy—"

"Stop!" I jump up but he grabs my hand tugging and almost knocking me off balance. "Let me go, Andrew."

"Even your voice." He groans. "I can't get it out of my head. It drives me crazy when you say my name. Jacob told me you make all these wild sex noises when Chaser fucks you. I had to lock myself in the bathroom and jerk off for like an hour."

The heat of embarrassment crawls up to my forehead. Why am I surprised, though? Jacob asked me to orgasm on their album for God's sake.

Am I really that loud?

It doesn't matter. I'm not the one who should be embarrassed. "Let me go."

"I'm sorry, okay?" he pleads. "I didn't mean to be an asshole. You asked and I've been dealing with this for a while."

And I'll need a lifetime of therapy to deal with this conversation. "Don't apologize. It's good to know how you really feel." I jerk away from him and scoop up my purse.

"Don't leave mad," he pleads.

"I'm not mad." Completely disoriented, I spin in a circle before marching toward the door. "I'm informed. It's all good," I say over my shoulder.

"Mallory." He catches up to me and slaps his hand against the door, holding it closed.

"Please let me leave."

"I'm sorry." His voice breaks and he pushes my hair out of my eyes. "I get nasty when I feel like I'm being rejected."

I duck away from his touch. "I think you were being honest."

"I've got no impulse control, Mallory. I can't tell you how many times I wanted to grab you and kiss the fuck out of you. Taste you...but I didn't." He stares at my lips for a few beats. Slowly, his eyes widen and he lifts his gaze. "Fuck, maybe I *am* in love with you."

"I don't think *this* is love."

He shakes his head but not in a dismissive way. More like he's considering all the reasons that support his crazy new theory. "It makes sense. I *knew* how pissed Chaser would be so I kept my mouth shut. I've never let friendship stop me before—"

"Maybe you're in love with *Chaser*," I suggest.

He gasps and staggers to the side, giving me room to wrap

my hand around the doorknob but not enough to open the door. At least sweet escape seems closer.

Andrew still seems to be considering my off-the-cuff retort. "No. I can't be gay. Or even bi. I love pussy *way* too much."

I groan.

"Like right now, I'm wondering if your—"

"Don't say it."

He frowns. "You don't even know what I was going to say."

"I'm sure it will elevate this conversation to a new level of disgusting and awkward, so do us both a favor. Don't."

"No, I mean, everyone else is fair game. I don't think Chaser would react well to a three-way though. And honestly, I'm not into the two dudes, one chick thing. If it's a multiple person situation, I prefer three females and *me*."

I blink rapidly, trying to follow his chaotic line of thought. "Andrew!" I snap. "It's never happening. Please stop making this worse."

"Promise you'll be here Saturday for the shoot?"

"No way in hell." I should have listened to my gut and never come over here today.

"Please? I need you. I promise I'll be a perfect gentleman. I have the other models. And Cindy will be here. Strictly professional. I promise."

"Why? You could call any agency, hell, you could walk into any club on any night and pick half a dozen pretty girls to wear your shirts."

"Yeah, but they wouldn't be you." His softer pleading tone returns. "Please."

"No, Andrew."

"Please?" He puts his hands under his chin and pulls that sad puppy dog face that usually makes me laugh. The one I thought was an innocent prankster. Now I know better.

"I'll consider it." *As in, nope!*

He stares at me for so long and so hard, my heart thumps with the fear that he'll try to kiss me again. His unfathomable dark eyes plead with me. There's pain hidden somewhere in those depths. Pain that isn't my problem or responsibility.

Finally, he slides his hand down the door and twists the knob, yanking it open.

"Ten a.m. I'll be waiting for you."

Afraid he'll change his mind and try to cut off my escape again, I slip out the door instead of answering.

CHAPTER THIRTY-THREE

Chaser

We don't get a lot of calls at the studio. Mark seriously scowls at anything not music-related happening during studio hours.

We're on a break, munching on sub sandwiches one of the assistants brought us when the phone rings. I'm closest, so I pick it up. "Yeah?"

"Chaser? Is that you?"

The smile fades from my face and I sit up. "Pamela?" Why the fuck is she calling here?

Jacob holds out his hand. "It's for me."

I jerk my shoulder away from him. "What's going on? Is Mallory okay?"

Her sweet, soft southern belle voice vanishes, taking on a sharper edge. "Mallory's perfectly fine. She's slutting around with Andrew. Did you know that?"

"Excuse me?" My ice-filled voice stops Jacob's grabby hand act and he backs away from the phone. "What are you talking about?"

"You know he's been trying to fuck her all along, right?"

"What are you doing, Pamela?" I ask in a bored tone. Mallory would never cheat on me. "There's no way that's true."

"Oh no? Then why'd he stop by the set the other night to take her for a ride on the back of his bike, hmmm?" she purrs.

An icy bucket of dread pours over me, choking off my air supply. Things were a little rocky between us when I left, but Mallory and I have spoken on the phone every single night. Everything's fine between us. She would've told me if she'd gone out with Andrew. No, scratch that, I *know* Mallory. She wouldn't go out with Andrew at all. She sure as fuck wouldn't get on the back of his bike.

"Bullshit. I don't have time for whatever game you're playing, Pamela." Yet, for some reason, I don't hang up the phone.

"It's true. He came to visit her on set. I can put you in touch with a dozen people who saw them together. And I heard her making plans to go over to his house tonight."

No. No fucking way. Pamela's always had some weird, petty jealousy thing going with Mallory. For fuck's sake, she's eyeballed *me* like a black widow spider stalking her next sperm donor too many times to count. I don't trust a word out of her mouth.

"You're full of shit, Pamela." Part of me can't stop wondering why Pamela's doing this. Why today? Why now? She and Andrew broke up weeks ago. She should be over it.

"Okay," she sings. "Don't believe me." Her voice lowers to a pouty, mocking tone. "Mallory's such an, innocent, inexperienced little lamb. And you know what kind of guy Andrew is. Even if I'm wrong, do you really want them spending time alone together?"

I slam the phone down and stare at it, considering Pamela's words. *Innocent* and *inexperienced* keep repeating over and over. Same words my father used.

It doesn't mean anything.

"What's going on? Why didn't you let me talk to her?" Jacob whines.

"She called for me." I push myself out of the chair and pace to the other side of the room.

Alvin frowns and sits up. "Everything okay, Chaser?"

"Yeah. Everything's fine."

"Let's get back to work!" Mark claps his hands like the world's most annoying kindergarten teacher as he enters the room. "Chaser. You give any more thought to that riff you were working on for 'In Your Hands'?"

"What? No."

He scowls at me and I scowl right back.

We get back to work but that phone call keeps playing in my head on an endless loop.

I don't believe a word Pamela said.

Do I?

CHAPTER THIRTY-FOUR

Chaser

We managed to finish one more song this afternoon. I'm too distracted to enjoy it and don't even want to celebrate with the guys.

"Innocent, inexperienced little lamb." Pamela's stupid words echoed in my head all afternoon.

I'm edgy, eager to get back to the house after we leave the studio.

"You're not gonna grab dinner with us?" Alvin asks.

"Nah, I want to work on a few things and get to bed early."

He glances over at Garrett and Jacob. "You sure you're okay?" he asks in a lower voice. "You've been weird since Pamela called." He cocks his head. "Why *did* she call you, anyway?"

"Who the fuck knows."

"Look, she's a nice girl. It was a real shitty thing Andrew did to her—"

"But?"

"She and Andrew have that whole dysfunctional, swirl of chaotic energy around them. Don't let her suck you into their vortex of crazy."

Wise advice.

"She's been cozying up to Jacob for weeks," he continues. "Calling you when you're with Mallory. It's not right."

Should I confess what Pamela said? Let him tell me what I already know—that it's garbage? No, because then I'd probably end up blabbing about my father's warning after Mallory and I got engaged. I don't want to say any of it out loud to anyone. It's bullshit.

I force a laugh. "I'm going home to call Mallory right now, bro. Just didn't feel like listening to everyone bust my balls for being pussy-whipped."

He frowns. "When have you ever given a shit what anyone thinks of you?"

"Never." I pat his shoulder. "Don't stay out too late. I have a feeling Mark plans to push us hard tomorrow."

There's more he wants to say, his dissatisfaction with my answers is clear. But Garrett and Jacob start whining for him to hurry up. I use the distraction as my opportunity to escape.

Mallory and I usually wait until eleven—when long-distance rates are cheaper—for our nightly call. But there have been plenty of nights where one of us called earlier.

I dial the house and wait.

My voice on the answering machine greets me. "You've reached Chaser and Mallory—"

"Fuck." I slam the phone down.

I prowl through the house, convincing myself everything's fine. She works late on the set all the time.

I try her again.

And again.

Finally, at ten she answers.

"Where've you been?" I try to force my voice into something casual, but the question comes out harsher than I intended.

"Did you call earlier?"

"A few times."

"Oh." Her sigh of relief stabs me with guilt. "I would've

picked up if I'd known it was you. I didn't expect you to call until later."

Great, so I scared the shit out of her with my constant calls and hang-ups. "Sorry. I was eager to talk to you tonight."

"Everything go okay with Mark today? Did he sit you down for more career-counseling?" Normally the question would be teasing but her voice sounds too heavy. I wish I could see her face.

"We finished up the track I told you about last night."

"Are you happy with it?"

"It's all right." I need to steer this back to her. Music's the last thing I want to talk about. "Anything exciting happening to my favorite lifeguard?"

She snorts softly. "Just showers and jogging on the beach with a splash of demonic possession. Speaking of, I'm really tired and I need to be on set early."

"Yeah, I'll let you go." So what if we usually stay on the phone until we're both almost asleep? Some nights we have stuff to do and say goodnight earlier. "I love you."

My heart trips when she doesn't answer right away. "Love you too, Chaser. I miss you. A lot."

More conflicted than ever, I stare at the phone for a long time after we hang up.

"CHASER, WHAT'S GOING ON?" MARK ASKS THE NEXT morning. "Things were moving along great yesterday. Then the rest of the afternoon...your spark's gone. Talk to me."

"Just some stuff." Stuff like, I slept like shit. The more I thought about our brief phone call, the more worry gnawed at my gut. Mallory didn't sound right. Was it guilt because she'd been out with Andrew and didn't want to tell me? Or simple exhaustion and an early-morning call time like she said? Or something else I hadn't thought of yet? Why didn't I just point-blank ask her if what Pamela said was true?

Am I afraid of the answer? Or do I need to see her face when I ask?

Maybe I should've called Andrew to feel him out. But no, he can't lie for shit and if I detect a hint that Andrew's been sniffing around Mallory, I'll need to beat the shit out of him. And I can't do that over the phone.

That's why I'm headed home this afternoon.

Mark blows out a breath and taps his fingers against the desk. "You guys have accomplished a lot in the short time you've been here. Truly. I'm impressed." He circles his fingers in front of my face. If anyone else did that, I'd slap their fucking hand into next week. "But this whole attitude of despair you have going on, isn't good for the process."

"I don't have an attitude of despair." No, what I have is a plane ticket to L.A. waiting for me.

We're both quiet for a few seconds, staring each other down. Finally, he relents. "I've been working the four of you really hard. Let's get a rough cut of 'Always Be Mine' finished today and I'll let you guys have a three-day weekend off to recharge your creative batteries. Sound fair?"

One way or another I'll be on a plane to L.A. later today, but I pretend to graciously accept his "offer." "Thanks, Mark. I think that's exactly what I need. Some time to recharge."

Recharge. Beat the shit out of Andrew. One or the other.

Mark's wrong. I'm not in despair. I'm *pissed*.

Anger is a much more useful emotion than despair.

Problem is, I can't figure out who I'm angry with. Pamela? Andrew? Mallory?

Or myself?

Doesn't matter. The only thing I know for sure is I'm headed home to get some answers.

I'm not losing my girl without a fight.

CHAPTER THIRTY-FIVE

Chaser

My flight home's easy. I call a cab, and I'm at our house by six o'clock. Mallory's car isn't in the driveway. Nothing suspicious about that. She's at the studio late plenty of times.

I drop my bag in the bedroom and wander through the house. Nothing out of place. No sign anyone's been here except Mallory.

What am I doing?

Did I really fly all the way down here based on some fairytale my friend's ex concocted?

What's my plan? Pounce on my fiancée when she walks in the door? Accuse her of fucking around with Andrew? All because *Pamela* said so?

That makes zero sense.

Irritated with myself, I run my hands through my hair. We can't go this long without seeing each other. Missing Mallory so much has fucked with my head.

There's my answer.

That's why I'm here. I missed Mallory and wanted to surprise her with a visit. Mark gave us the weekend off. The fact that I already planned to come down here to do...I don't know what isn't important.

Dinner. I'll make her dinner. Set up some candles. Music. The whole romantic bit, so she'll be surprised instead of suspicious when she comes home.

Now that I've got a plan, I roll my bike out of the garage and ride down to the store for a few groceries.

She's still not home when I return—again, not unusual. I kick off my shoes and start working on dinner. Fish tacos—the first meal we ever shared together.

The doorbell rings. Motherfuck, if it's a reporter, I'm spilling blood.

I fling the door open and find an enormous vase of plump pink roses in my face. "Mallory?" The person holding them asks.

"No," I snap.

The delivery guy cranes his neck around the flowers. "Does she live here?"

"Yeah." The knot in my gut tightens to a painful degree. I accept the vase from the guy with both hands. "I'll make sure she gets them."

Without giving him a chance to answer, I kick the door shut. "You've got to be motherfucking kidding me."

I don't even have to read the card to know who they're from. Same fucking arrangement Andrew bought for Pamela. For such a creative genius, he sure sucks in the flower department.

Since he sent the flowers to *my* fiancée, I feel entitled to pluck the card out of the envelope.

Dear Mallory,

Thank you for being such a beautiful person inside and out. Looking forward to Saturday's shoot.

Your friend,

Andrew

Red. Motherfucking red stains my vision. Christ, I probably popped a blood vessel. Mallory will come home and find me bleeding out on the floor.

Breathe.

In and out.

Deep breaths. One after the other.

Roses don't mean shit.

Innocent.

Inexperienced.

Regrets.

My father's words weren't a warning—they were a motherfucking hex.

Friend? Andrew isn't friends with women. He fucks, uses, and discards them. Friendship isn't part of the equation.

Beautiful person inside and out. What the fuck is that supposed to mean? Did they—? Am I too late?

The rage monster beating against my skull wants to smash the vase against the wall.

After several deep breaths, I calmly set the vase down on the entryway table, and pad into the kitchen to turn off the stove. I move through the house in a fog, flicking off every light, except for a small lamp next to the roses.

Finally, I drop my ass into the chair that gives me the best view of the front door.

And I wait.

CHAPTER THIRTY-SIX

Mallory

This has been the worst day. The director yelled at me more times than I care to remember. Pamela kept shooting me smug little smiles that I couldn't decipher. We filmed some scenes at the beach and I swear there's still sand in my underwear. I'm damp, shivering, and longing to change into something warm and cozy.

At least my shitty day helped me forget about the catastrophe at Andrew's last night.

I trudge into the house and drop my bags by the door. Coming home to an empty house is wearing on me. I usually leave more lights on so it doesn't seem so gloomy. But there's only one lamp lit by the door, illuminating a giant bouquet of pink roses.

My heart stutters.

Where did they come from? Someone was in my house?

Recognizing Andrew's handwriting on the outside of the envelope, stalls my freak-out. I pick up the card. My nervous gaze darts around the dark and shadowy room, afraid he'll jump out at any moment. I eye the long umbrella in the corner. I am *so* jamming the pointy end into his crotch if he broke into my house.

Dear Mallory,

Thank you for being such a beautiful person inside and out.

Beautiful *person.* Bullshit. He should've written 'thanks for being three holes I'd like to stick my dick in.' At least it would've been more honest.

Looking forward to Saturday's shoot.

Too bad for you. I told Cindy today I had to cancel but stressed she should go ahead with it since I know she needs the money.

Your friend,

Andrew

Your friend? *Friend.* What the hell? Is that some signal? After he so bluntly explained he didn't see me as a friend? Is his apology sincere?

I toss the card on the table. It's a lie. Another attempt to get me into bed.

"Nice flowers from your *friend.*"

I jump five feet in the air. "Oh my God!"

A light snaps on, revealing Chaser in one of the chairs across the room.

Heart pounding, chest heaving, I gasp. "What are you doing home?"

His fierce expression doesn't change, nor does he move a muscle. "What's wrong, baby? Thought you'd be happy to see me."

I rub my hand over my breastbone, willing my chaotic heart to settle down. "I am. But you scared me to death."

He sits forward, casually resting his elbows on his thighs and spears me with an anything-but-casual look. "Why is Andrew Lane sending my fiancée flowers?" he asks with lethal calm.

"I—I don't know."

"What shoot is he talking about?"

"Huh?" I step closer, then stop. Chaser's brimming with

anger. He didn't greet me at the door with a kiss... Something's really, really wrong here.

"Answer my question. What shoot is he talking about?"

"You read the card?" Oh, shit. I'm going to have to tell him everything that happened a whole lot sooner than I planned. Good Lord, Chaser wanted to put a bullet in Andrew for bringing girls on his bus. Trying to get me into bed? He'll kill Andrew for sure. This time, he'll go to prison and stay there.

His face twists with fury and he jumps out of the chair, charging half-way across the living room. "Who the fuck do you think accepted the delivery? The flowers-for-other-men's-fiancée's fairy?"

"What?"

"Why is *your friend* Andrew Lane sending you a big ol' bunch of 'let's get buck naked and fuck' flowers?"

Holy hell, this is bad. So, so bad. "He asked me to model for the T-shirt line he's creating." My shoulders lift in what I hope looks like a casual shrug.

"Are you fucking serious?"

Heat races over my cheeks. As the words came out of my mouth, I realized how stupid they sounded. Too late.

"Were you at his place today?"

"No, yesterday." I glance down at the flowers. "The shoot's supposed to be tomorrow, but—"

"Like fuck you are."

"Excuse me?"

"Pamela's been calling Jacob. Offering to come up to Vancouver and visit." Chaser's low tone sets my nerves on edge. "But yesterday, she called *me*."

Pamela called him? "Why?"

"To let me know Andrew's been showing up on set, asking you out, having you over for dinner—"

"That's not even true." I back up until my butt hits the table and brace myself against it. The roses rustle against each other. One lone petal drifts down, tickling the back of my hand.

"So, he didn't show up on set?" He steps forward.

"Yes, but—"

Anger and maybe fear glitter in his eyes with his next question. "And you weren't at his house?"

"I was but—"

"Mallory." Disappointment wrecks his voice.

"He asked me to model some shirts for him," I hurry to explain. "Back in New York. I never said anything because I didn't think anything of it. Then he brought it up again. I thought he was trying to make Pamela jealous," I finish babbling out all that jumbled nonsense and take a breath. "I brought Cindy with me. Did Pamela bother to tell you that?"

He pauses. Obviously, Pamela *didn't* mention that part.

Of course, I haven't yet confessed how Cindy left early and Andrew told me in great, disgusting detail how much he wants to fuck me.

"Even if that's true, you're way past modeling some shitty line of vanity T-shirts."

"What do you mean, 'even if that's true?'" I swallow hard and avert my eyes, staring at the rose petal next to my fingers. "When have I ever lied to you, Chaser?"

"You're not telling me everything. I can see it all over your face, Mallory. You talk to me about every single job offer and audition that comes your way. Why hide this one?"

"I didn't *hide* anything. Andrew yaps about stupid projects all the time." I flap my hands in the air, completely frustrated. "Like his funk-country-rock music idea. Some dumb T-shirts weren't important enough for me to remember."

"You spending time alone with a man who's been out to fuck you since the get-go is fucking important!" he shouts as he stalks closer. "You like him, don't you?"

"No!"

A cruel smile curves his lips. "You need a one-off, Mal? I get that our score cards are uneven. Andrew Lane's beneath you, in my opinion—"

"What?" The high, shrill tone of my voice makes me wince. He can't possibly— "What does that even mean?"

"Do you want more *experience?*" With the anguish on his face and the raw rasp of his voice, I can't understand why he'd ever suggest something so awful. "Feel like you need to experiment more?"

At my blank look he forces another harsh smile.

"Do you need to *ride a few more dicks* before I tie you down for good?"

"No! Gross." Shock keeps my voice several octaves higher than normal. "Why would you even suggest that?"

Wait a second. Is he projecting his desires onto me?

Pain encircles my throat. "Is that what *you* want?" I ask with more calm than I actually possess. "Is that why you've been talking to Pamela? Do *you* want to experiment?" I swallow hard. "With her?"

"No." His face twists into a frown. "Jesus Christ. No."

"Then why are you picking a fight over nothing?"

"Is it nothing?" He gestures toward the vase. "I thought Pamela was full of shit but I come home and—"

"You don't trust me?"

"I don't trust *him.*"

His crude, insulting suggestion unfurls in my head, elevating my anger to a whole new level. "But you think your former-virgin-fiancée is so desperate for new dick that if Andrew whips his out, I'll jump on it? *That's* what you think of me?"

"Is that what happened?" he roars.

"No!"

He stares at me for a long time. "I hate this."

"What? Us?"

"No."

I wait for him to continue.

"Andrew's clearly been into you since the night we all met," he says slowly.

"So what? Jerks have been hitting on me since day one. You usually *protect* me from them not get mad at *me*."

He closes his eyes and pinches the bridge of his nose. "He's the first one you seem to like back."

"That's not true," I whisper. I stupidly thought Andrew was a friend. Until he explained in lengthy detail how I'm nothing more than a few holes he wants to explore. "I like Alvin, you don't get mad about that."

Chaser glares at me. "Alvin's not trying to fuck you."

I swallow hard and glance away. "Neither is Andrew."

"Who are you trying to fool? Me or yourself? Men don't send roses to women they don't want to fuck, Mallory. Especially Andrew."

"Can you stop being so disgusting?"

"This is who I am, baby." He holds his arms out wide. "You don't like it, maybe *your friend* Andrew is more of a gentleman. Although, we both know that's not true."

"Chaser, I love you." As the words come out of my mouth, my heart cracks with the weight of guilt. "Please stop this. I won't do the shoot. I already told Cindy I'm not going tomorrow."

"Hell no. I won't let you turn it down so you can be pissed at me later."

This is ridiculous. We're going in circles. "I won't be pissed at you later, but I'm damn sure pissed at you now." I spin around and swipe my leather jacket off the hook by the door.

"Where are you going?" he demands. "Gonna go say hi to Andrew?"

"No!" I scream. "I want to get away from you!" In my fury, the heavy sleeve of my jacket whacks into the vase, sending the roses crashing to the floor.

Glass, water, and rose petals shatter and splash over the hardwood floor, leaving a mess.

Just like us.

CHAPTER THIRTY-SEVEN

Chaser

Mallory's gone. Out the door. Running like the devil's on her tail.

Can't let her get to her car.

That's the only thought pounding through my head.

I trample over the broken vase, and crooked roses. Slivers of glass and sharp thorns pierce the bottom of my foot but I'm too focused on Mallory to feel the pain.

Don't let her get away.

"Mallory!" Her name tears from my throat.

I'm vaguely aware that I'm bleeding. Christ, I hope no photographers are hanging around the house today. All I need to make this shitastic day complete is a picture of me shirtless, barefoot, and limping after my girlfriend splashed all over *L.A. Weekly.*

"Mallory, don't."

She stops at her car, resting her hand on the hood. Her head falls down, all her beautiful hair hiding her face.

Afraid she'll somehow slip out of my grasp, I tackle her around the waist, burying my face against her hair.

"I'm sorry," I whisper. "Please don't go. I love you so much."

The sobs that shake her body wreck me.

"I love you too," she whispers. In a stronger voice, she adds, "But I think I'm going to stay at a hotel tonight."

"Please don't."

Why couldn't I keep my mouth shut?

I let my father's idiotic warning smolder in my brain until Pamela's phone call lit the fuse and now we're paying the price.

The fucking roses sure as shit didn't help.

"I don't trust you."

"What?" Slowly, still scared she'll run, I turn her to face me but keep my hands around her waist. "Why?"

"Why would you believe anything Pamela said about me?"

I shake my head, not having any good reason except a gut feeling. Saying that will only make her want to leave me more. "I didn't mean to upset you."

She snorts. "What? You thought accusing me of...whatever you were implying back there would make me happy?"

"I'm sorry."

She gasps and pulls away. "Chaser! What did you do? You're bleeding."

Her gaze skips over my shoulder and I turn, surprised at the bloody trail staining the concrete. I stare down at my feet. That's when the ribbons of pain slicing through my tender flesh hit me.

"Fuck," I breathe out.

"Oh my God." She chants the words over and over. "Let me see. Oh my God, I'm going to throw up."

"It's nothing." I pick up my left foot and yank out a jagged chunk of glass. "Fuck, that's bad." I pluck a few thorns out of my heel and smaller shards of glass lodged between my toes.

She reaches for me with shaky hands. "Chaser, we should go to the hospital."

"No thanks."

"We need to clean that gash. It *is* bad. You probably need stitches."

"I'll wash it and take another look."

"Let me grab your shoes so you don't get more cuts."

"I'm fine." As much as I try to stay off my injured foot on the walk up to the house, waves of pain jar my body with every step. Even so, when we reach the door, I sweep Mallory into my arms.

"Chaser, put me down. You can't carry me."

"I don't need you getting sliced up too."

"I'm wearing shoes." She zips her lips. Arguing is pointless since I'm already past the mess. I set her down outside the bathroom and limp my way over to the tub.

"Shit." I twist the taps and nearly scream when I stick my foot under the running water.

"Chaser, it looks bad." Her voice quivers. When I glance back she's wide-eyed and pale.

"Call Thom. He knows someone who'll come to the house."

"Okay," she whispers, turning and running away.

After a few minutes, I ease my foot into the water and slowly start washing dirt and blood away. Over the rush of water, I catch snippets of Mallory's anxiety-laced voice speaking on the phone. I hiss out a pained breath and twist off the tap.

Glass tinkles from the living room. "Leave it, Mallory! I'll clean it up. I don't want you cutting your hands."

"I'm fine," she yells back.

God fucking dammit. I wrap a towel around my foot, trying not to notice the huge circle of red seeping through. "Mal, leave it."

The only answer I get is the vacuum humming to life. I hobble out and find her finishing the cleanup.

"You should've let me do it," I say when she shuts off the vacuum.

"I'm fine. Doctor West should be here within the hour."

"Thanks."

We stare at each other from across the room. The space isn't that big but the distance between us might as well be an ocean.

CHAPTER THIRTY-EIGHT

Mallory

"Please sit down." My voice breaks. "I don't want to think about all the damage you're doing to your foot."

"I'm fine." The grimace slashing across his face says otherwise. At least he finally drops his heavy frame into a chair.

Nervous, I can't sit still. All my fury from our fight has twisted into shame and fear.

But maybe a little bit of anger still lingers. I can't seem to find the words to apologize.

"Do you want something to drink?" I ask.

"Do we have a bottle of whiskey or two laying around?"

"No." I jump up and scurry into the kitchen. My nose wrinkles as a fishy scent wafts over from the stove. "Were you...cooking?"

"I was making us dinner." He pauses and adds in a much more sarcastic tone, "Until your *special delivery* showed up."

I toss the fish in the trash, pour two glasses of water, and return to the living room.

"Can you grab my shirt?" He points to the arm of the couch.

The soft pile of worn cotton smells like Chaser. I have the

urge to bury my nose in the fabric until it washes all this ugliness away.

"Tell me nothing happened," he rasps.

I drop the shirt in his lap. "Please, can we take care of your foot, right now?"

"Mallory—"

Finally, a knock at the front door rescues us from this misery. I run for the door like my ass is on fire and there's a bucket of water waiting for me on the other side.

"Hi! Doctor West. Thank you so much for stopping by." The doctor's older, with gray hair and beard. Distinguished and professional. I'd been worried about what type of doctor made house calls at this hour but he's sharp and quick to let me know what he needs as soon as I explain the situation.

"Bring another lamp over here." He points to the floor next to Chaser's chair. "Hurry."

I gag and almost faint when I get a glimpse of the gash on Chaser's foot.

"Bring me a bowl. You have a big bowl? Hot water." He barks a bunch of orders at me and I run to find the items requested.

"I already washed it," Chaser argues.

The doctor grumbles at him and gets to work.

Except for a few hisses of pain and a wince here and there, Chaser's stoic. Unable to take it, I reach down and curl my fingers around his. He tips his head back and peers up at me with an unreadable expression.

"You need stitches," the doctor warns.

Chaser grits his teeth. "Do what you gotta do. I'm fine."

"I'll give you an injection to numb the area but it's not going to feel good."

Chaser pulls me down so I'm sitting on the edge of the chair and curls his arm around my waist, resting his head against my side. "Do it. Sew me up, Doc."

He squeezes his eyes shut as the first needle slides into his foot.

A soft sob escapes me. My punishment should be to watch every excruciating second of the doctor's handiwork, but I'm too squeamish. Instead, I wrap my arms around Chaser, wishing I could absorb his pain.

We stay that way—awkwardly clinging to each other, until the doctor declares he's finished. He wraps thick gauze around Chaser's foot and gives him a list of instructions to follow. "I brought a cane. It's in my car. I'll go grab it."

"I don't need it."

The doctor ignores Chaser.

After the front door shuts, Chaser gestures toward the bedroom. "Go grab my wallet, babe. He give you any idea what he charges?"

"No, Thom said he'd take care of it."

"What'd you tell *him*?"

"That you had an accident and hurt your foot. He wanted to know why you weren't in Vancouver."

"And?"

I hang my head. "I told him you wanted to surprise me. I didn't know what else to say."

"Well, it's true."

Something about his glib answer reignites my anger. "You wanted to *ambush* and accuse me. Don't pretend it was some romantic gesture that brought you home."

His jaw locks but the door swings open and the doctor rushes in before we can say anything else.

He sets a bottle of pills on the table and rests the cane against the wall behind Chaser's chair. "Thom's handling the bill. If you need anything or you see any signs of infection, call me. I understand you'll be up in Vancouver. Make sure you go to a hospital if you have any issues."

"I will. Thanks, Doc."

He eyes both of us with a hint of suspicion before nodding. I walk him to the door and say good night.

"Do you want something to eat?" I ask, suddenly nervous

271

now that we're alone again. "I'm starving. I had an awful day at work."

"And a shit night at home?"

I slide my gaze his way. "Do you really want to do this right now? Can I at least eat something before you accuse me of wanting to fuck other men again?"

He squeezes his eyes shut. "I'm sorry." Finally, he opens them and points toward the kitchen. "I bought shrimp too. They're in the fridge."

I follow the simple directions he gives me to cook the shrimp and prepare everything else to go along with the tacos. When I finally call him to the table, I can't help wincing at the awkward way he limps over.

"I'm fine. Stop acting like I'm gonna die. I've had worse injuries."

"Such as?"

He regales me with stories of flipping over an ATV when he was a kid, losing control of his first motorcycle and crashing it into a tree, along with dozens of other terrifying tales.

"That's it." I point my fork at him. "Our sons will *not* be allowed to ride or drive any motorized vehicles until they're at least thirty."

He sets his fork down with a soft clink. "Just the boys?"

"Girls are more responsible. *I* never did any of those things."

He huffs out a laugh. "That mean you still wanna have babies with me?"

I'm still not in the mood to laugh. "Not today."

"Fair enough."

CHAPTER THIRTY-NINE

Chaser

Mallory's tough girl attitude dissolves when she has to help me to the bedroom.

"You're in the middle of recording. How are you going to play like this?" A tear runs down her cheek, damn near breaking me. "I'm so sorry."

"I'll be fine, Mal." I hop my way to the bed and drop down on the edge.

"It's my fault—" She leans against the doorway and won't meet my eyes.

"Come here." I hold out my hand to her and after a few beats, she comes closer and takes it. "It was an accident. It's not like you threw the fucking vase at me."

She sniffles. "You had me so angry, I *wanted* to throw the damn thing at you. And in my hurry to leave, I broke it."

She's so fierce and sad all at the same time, but I hate that she feels so guilty.

"It's my own fault for making you so mad." I cock my head. "You still wanna go stay at a hotel?"

"No." She lifts her chin. "How am I supposed to leave you limping around?"

Not exactly a declaration of love. "Don't stay out of pity. I can take care of myself."

"Do you *want* me to leave?" She drops down on the bed next to me.

"Christ, Mallory. I tore up my foot trying to *stop* you from leaving. No."

Her lashes flutter and she twists her fingers in her lap. "Then why would you ask me if I want to...to sleep with someone else? The way you asked was humiliating."

In addition to the pain in my foot, my head throbs. I'd do anything to erase those words from her memory.

"Maybe I don't have as much experience," she continues, "But I love you. Why would you say those things?"

I blow out a breath and turn away. "Just stuff I've been thinking about since we got engaged."

Stupid bullshit my father put in my head for no damn good reason.

"You don't want to get married anymore?" Her voice falls to a whisper. "We don't have to." She stares at her ring and slowly twists it around her finger. "We can wait if that's what you want."

Hell-fucking-no, I want to go down to City Hall this weekend and tie the knot before I return to Vancouver. "It's not that."

"Then what?"

I strip off my shirt and toss it toward the closet before falling back against the pillows. "I don't want to talk about it right now."

"Well." She shifts and kneels up next to me so she can look me in the eyes. "You're a captive audience at the moment. What are you going to do, get up and hobble away if I want an explanation?"

"I can hobble if I need to." I reach over and swipe the bottle of pills the doc left and rattle it at her. "He gave me some damn good pain killers."

"Chaser, I'm serious. What's going on?"

She's not going to drop it and I owe her an explanation. I scrub my hands over my face a few times to help get the words moving. "My father said some shit while we were home. That, combined with the way Andrew's so obviously been after you. Being away from you again. It's been bugging me." *Why didn't I tell her all of this sooner?*

"So your father *isn't* happy about us?"

"We talked it out. He apologized—which he doesn't do often."

"This was at our engagement party wasn't it?"

"Right before." I rest my hands on her shoulders and squeeze. "It doesn't matter what he thinks or what he said. It changed nothing for me."

"But he told you I'm too...inexperienced to be your wife? I don't understand."

My lips twitch in disgust as I recall my father's crude words, then shame when I realize in the heat of the moment, I said even worse to Mallory. "It was stupid stuff. Things that had more to do with him and my mother than you and me. Believe me, I had it out with him." I drop my gaze and shake my head. "But I don't know. Some of it must have clung to me."

"Your father's a forceful man. Whether you accept it or not, his opinion matters to you." She briefly touches the back of my hand, drawing my attention up again. "Still, you could have told me. I wouldn't have been mad at you."

I snort out a laugh. "I like that you two have your budding father-daughter relationship thing going on. I didn't want to ruin that. I made it clear his 'advice' wasn't welcome."

"Huh." She bites her lip. "Do you think it's possible my father threatened him after our visit?"

Well, fuck. I'd gotten so riled up at the *details* he shared about my mother, I'd never given a lot of thought to *what* prompted the conversation. Maybe that was his goal. "I guess it's possible." Even for my dad, who's about as vulgar as they come, the whole thing *was* pretty disgusting and seemed to come out of nowhere.

"Could we be in danger?"

"No," I answer quickly. "If we were in true danger, he wouldn't have let us come back to L.A." I consider the situation more thoroughly. "Your father wants access to Canada. Something he can't get without my club. Besides, he knows there are two Demon charters in this state that will rain down hellfire if anyone comes near us."

"What about Vancouver? Are you safe up there?"

"I don't see them wasting time tracking me down." I tuck her hair behind her ear. "Even if I'm not here, I'll always make sure you're protected."

"I know you will." She licks her lips and glances down. "You were right."

I don't like the shift in her voice. "About what?"

"About Andrew." She twists and rubs her fingers together. "Yesterday, after Cindy left. He...told me he's...interested."

"I knew it." There's no satisfaction that comes from being right. "And?"

"He admitted to trying to break us up by bringing girls on your bus. Claimed that he's been obsessed with me for a long time." She shrugs.

"Motherfucker." I roll over and pull my nightstand drawer open.

Her soft fingers close over mine. "What are you doing?"

The weight of the revolver feels good in my hand. I've been itching to shoot this motherfucker for months.

I shake her off and straighten up. "I'm going to stop by Andrew's place and blow a hole through his skull," I answer with matter-of-fact calm.

"Chaser! That's not funny."

"Oh, I'm not joking, baby."

"Chaser," she protests again.

"Should've done it months ago. Already sat in a jail cell for it. Might as well get the satisfaction of actually putting a bullet in that disloyal asshole."

"He's your friend."

My jaw drops and I stare at her. "Friends don't tell my fiancée they want...whatever the fuck he told you."

"True." She hangs her head. "I don't think he meant any of it."

"Don't make excuses for that piece of shit." The fact that she's even trying to excuse his behavior pisses me off even more. Sometimes she really is too sweet for her own damn good.

"I'm not," she protests.

"Tell me everything."

Fear enters her eyes. That bad, I guess.

"You kiss him?"

"No," she whispers.

"But he tried to kiss you? Touch you?"

Silence.

"Are you fucking kidding me right now?" I roar, throwing the covers back and jumping out of the bed. I choke down a scream when my bandaged foot hits the ground.

"It was nothing." She kneels up in the center of the bed and reaches for me. "Please."

I drop the gun in the drawer and slam it shut.

My foot protests the weight I place on it as I hop to the bed and rest my knee on the mattress. "Nothing?"

She nods and bites her lip.

I grab her hips and drag her closer. "Nothing?"

Tears shine in her eyes. If nothing else, I'm going to strangle Andrew for the emotional roller coaster he's put her through.

"You are not *nothing*. You're *my* girl. My fiancée. Soon, you'll be my wife. The mother of my children. You're my whole world. My *everything*. No one touches what's mine. No one hurts you."

Her lips part but I cut her off before she makes a sound by

pressing a finger against her lips. "Don't make another excuse for that motherfucker."

I slide my finger along her bottom lip. "Mine to kiss." I swoop down and press my lips against hers hard enough to erase memories of anyone else. She moans into my mouth and drags her fingers through my hair. I grasp her hand, pinning it to her side.

"Chaser?" she whispers when I draw back.

Without answering, I slide my hand from her hip, between her legs, and cup her center. "Mine. To touch. Mine to lick. Mine to pleasure. Only mine."

She rocks against my hand and I grab her hip, keeping her still. "Is that clear?"

"Show me," she whispers.

I draw back and study her face. "Excuse me?"

Slowly, she lifts her gaze to mine. Challenge glitters in her eyes. "Prove it."

"You chose a bad time to dare me, little dove." I press my mouth against hers and use my weight to push her down to the mattress.

Mallory

One minute Chaser has me so frustrated I want to strangle him, and the next he has me pinned to the mattress. His arms resting on either side of my head, caging me in.

"Did you hear what I said?" he rasps.

"I heard everything you said tonight," I whisper.

He closes his eyes for a brief moment.

I reach up and brush my fingertips over his cheek. "I've never...not for a minute have I felt that you're not enough for me."

"You think you'll still feel that way, ten, twenty, thirty years from now?"

It would be so easy to blurt out a *yes*. But Chaser doesn't want easy answers. He wants the honest one.

I blink, trying to stretch my imagination that far into the future. What will it look like? Where will we be?

We.

"Every vision of my future includes you. No matter where I go, I want you by my side. I want to come home and find you practicing guitar in the living room. Go on tour with you. Accept awards with you. Travel everywhere together." I run my finger over his furrowed brow. "Have a family with you—"

He slams his mouth over mine, cutting me off, claiming my lips and my heart.

Hot, undeniable sparks fire through my veins. An electrical current of energy running between our bodies. A whimper of need and desperation tears from my throat. He answers with his own needy rumble.

I slip my fingers over his hot skin and hard muscles. Stroking over firm abs, his sides, to his back.

He groans again. Leaning on one arm, he runs his hand down my side, and tugs my shirt up. I lift up to help untangle it from my arms and stop to undo my bra.

The corners of his mouth lift with approval. His dark eyes glitter with desire. Our lips meet again. My lips part and his tongue strokes against mine.

"My girl," he whispers against my lips.

I nod slowly.

He dives lower, kissing along my jaw, down to my neck. His scruff setting fire to my sensitive skin where he stops to suck and nip. I angle my head back, offering my neck as a canvas to leave his mark.

Little cries of pleasure escape my lips as he continues kissing and claiming every inch of me.

He slips one hand between our bodies. I gasp as he brushes his fingers over my inner thigh, up under my shorts. His teeth scrape my nipple as his fingers stroke the edge of my panties.

I gasp and try to sit up but he keeps me pinned. Desire turns me inside out and I struggle under the weight of his body.

"What's wrong, little dove?" His wicked smile even more of a turn-on as he slowly slides his fingers under my panties. His thumb brushes over my clit and my body jerks.

"Mmm, I like that." He strokes in firmer circles until I squeeze my eyes shut, trying so hard to concentrate on the delicious sensations. My thigh muscles quiver in anticipation but he leaves me on the edge, never pressing hard enough to set me off.

"Chaser," I whine and try desperately to grind myself against his hand.

I blink up at him. His dark eyes are heavy-lidded with desire. "I love watching you," he whispers. Still watching me, he dips his head and tugs at the button of my shorts with his teeth.

A pathetic whimper leaves me as he eases his hand away from my center and works my shorts loose. "Get these off," he growls.

I lift my hips and he shimmies my shorts and underwear down my legs, stopping to press a kiss to my bellybutton.

"That tickles." My belly quivers with held back laughter as her runs his scruff over my skin.

He slides his body off the mattress, kneeling at the foot of the bed.

"Come here." His low, guttural demand has me scooting down the bed. Not fast enough, apparently. He slips his arms under my legs, and yanks me to the edge. Using his wide shoulders, he presses my legs open. The scratch of his stubble against my inner thigh sends more tingles of anticipation through me. He kisses and nibbles. When I think I can't take another second of torment, he places his wicked mouth where I need it most.

"Oh!"

He groans and uses his tongue to flick my clit. My thighs clench, squeezing his head, until he pries me open again. Breathless, ragged noises escape my throat. I reach down, tangling my fingers through his hair.

He tastes and teases, lapping and swirling his tongue in the most provocative ways, always leaving me teetering on the edge.

He returns all his focus to my clit, sucking gently. My legs shake. My toes curl against the sheets. He twines his fingers with mine and I finally break. Waves of pleasure pulse through me, leaving me breathless and dizzy.

When I can't take any more, I buck my hips, shaking him loose. He sits back and chuckles, pressing a slippery kiss to my thigh.

I curl my finger at him. Pressing his fists into the mattress, he rises. A flash of pain creases his face and I bolt up. "I'm sorry."

"Shh." He presses a finger to my lips. He gestures to his jeans. "Take my cock out."

Eager to return the favor and make his knees quiver, I free him, shoving his jeans over his hips. His abs tighten and he sways as I slide my hand up and down his cock. I circle the tip with my thumb and he hisses.

"Lie back."

"But—"

His dark expression cuts off my protest. I scoot a few inches up the bed. Resting on my elbows, I dig my heels into the mattress and spread my knees wide. "Like this?" I ask in an innocent whisper.

He growls and falls down over me. He reaches between us, positioning himself at my center. Rubbing up and down for a long moment while staring down into my eyes.

"Give me—"

He cuts me off, sliding into me, hard, in one smooth motion.

"Oh, fuck." My teeth sink into my bottom lip as I struggle to adjust.

He presses his lips to my forehead and stills his movements. "You still with me, little dove?" His raw voice expresses his need more than his words.

With him in this moment? With him for life?

All of the above.

I blink up at him. His intense eyes wait for an answer.

I squeeze my inner muscles around him and he shudders.

"Yes," I whisper.

That's the answer he needed. He clutches my hips and pulls back, slamming back in a second later. Not fast. Slow and hard, so I feel every inch.

My greedy body aches with the demand for another release. Chaser's controlled but relentless. Another orgasm builds, almost painful in its intensity.

"I can't—"

"Yes, you can." He slows his pace, leaning down to kiss me again. "Please."

His gentle plea after all our harsh words tonight unlocks my body. He comes with me, burying his face against my neck, whispering words of love in my ear.

No one—no matter how hard they try—will ever tear us apart.

CHAPTER FORTY

Mallory

"You're going to that photo shoot tomorrow," Chaser says later as I'm falling asleep.

His words are jolt of caffeine that pushes me upright. "No. I'm not."

He sits up and clicks the lamp on. "Yes. And I'm going with you."

"Why? To confront him?"

"I can't let him get away with what he did, Mallory. You know that. Tell me exactly how it happened this time," he demands.

I swallow hard. The pain and guilt almost make it impossible to say the words. I feel so stupid as I go over the events in my head. But I finally convey enough of the story to satisfy Chaser but not push him into hunting Andrew down and killing him.

"What a fucking asshole."

"I'm not trying to make an excuse. I really don't think he's dealing with the breakup well. He didn't seem like himself."

"Did he hurt you?"

"No." I duck my head. "Not really."

"Mallory," he warns.

"He hurt my feelings, okay? But I handled it. The whole thing was so bizarre and crazy," I lift my chin, "but I handled it."

"Hurt your feelings, how?"

Oh boy. This is never going to end. "When I told him not to kiss me, that we were just friends, he made it clear he *didn't* consider me a friend and that he only wanted to fuck me."

Chaser growls low in his throat. "That fucking card makes more sense now."

"Yes." I shrug. "He really didn't seem to see the harm. He told me how Pamela and Kyle hooked up and he took her back—"

"Fuck." Chaser runs his fingers through his hair. "A long time ago, he kept pressing me about whether or not I'd be mad if you fucked a director or something for a part. Kept trying to tell me it was just sex and no big deal."

"Yes! That's what he said. 'It's just sex.'" I glance down and scratch my nails over the comforter. "He sort of said something similar to what you said. How could I marry you without ever being with anyone else? I think that's why it hurt so much when you said it."

"I'm sorry." He rests his hand over mine and squeezes. "Why does he even know—"

"Pamela. So much for girl talk." I roll my eyes.

He chuckles and tugs me closer.

"Oh, Jacob must've told him how um, loud, I am too, because—"

"Jesus Christ," he groans. "Why do we know so many obnoxious assholes?"

"Am I really that loud?" My lips twitch. "You know, since you're vastly more *experienced* than I am and all."

"Mal—" He stops and glances over at me. "I can't believe you're making a joke about this."

"Would you rather I cry?"

"Never." His expression turns more serious. "I can't joke

about it. You're my whole life. Nothing that happened before we met matters or compares."

"Chaser." How do I respond to such a sweet sentiment? Void of words, I sigh and cuddle closer, resting my head on his chest. He wraps his arms around me and I soak up his warmth.

"For the record, I love all the little noises you make." He strokes his fingers over my shoulder. "I'm the one who makes you lose control. Forget where you are. It's a huge rush. Excellent for my already giant ego."

I bury my face against his chest, shaking with laughter. "You're nuts." I pull back and slap my hand over my mouth. "Oh my God."

He raises an eyebrow. "What?"

"I told Andrew he might be in love with *you*. I think he actually considered the idea."

"You, *what?*"

I give him the general gist of that part of our conversation. Chaser doesn't seem to find it as funny as I do.

"Mallory, I want to give you all the experiences you desire but I couldn't watch another man touch you and not beat him to death. Seriously." He stops for a second and stares at the ceiling. "Nope. Couldn't even do it with another female."

"I thought that was every guy's fantasy?"

"Maybe," his fists clench, "but even thinking about it is pissing me off."

"Besides hurting my feelings, I was really angry that he betrayed *you* that way, Chaser."

"I'm not as shocked as I should be. He's not wired right."

"So we agree, no photoshoot? I'm not even calling him to say I'm not coming. Cindy can tell him."

"No, we're going."

"We? No. This is...there will be other models there. A photographer. Cindy...You can't."

He rolls his lip. "Then he shouldn't mind if I tag along. You said it yourself, Andrew and I are friends. It won't seem weird."

"He's going to ask why you're home when you're supposed to be in Vancouver."

"Yeah, interesting timing, huh? He just *had* to photograph those shirts while he knows I'm tied up in Vancouver."

Damn, why hadn't I looked at it the same way? "I'm such an idiot. He said the shirts just came in and I believed him."

"You're not an idiot. You're a good person who doesn't immediately assume others are being dishonest. But yeah, I bet he thought he'd talk you into bed and you'd spend the weekend with him." He's quiet for a second, considering his words. "Don't take this the wrong way, but I have a feeling when you show up tomorrow, no one else will be there."

"I doubt that."

"We'll see."

"No, he's really excited about the shirts." But even as I protest, I have a feeling Chaser's right.

CHAPTER FORTY-ONE

Chaser

Irritation that Mallory talked me out of bringing my gun with me this morning still ripples down my spine as she parks her car in Andrew's driveway.

We step out of the car and start walking up to the front door.

"Huh. Would you look at that?" I stop and do a slow exaggerated scan of the area. "We must be early. Not another vehicle in sight."

"Smug's an ugly color on you, Chaser," she scolds.

I sweep my hand in front of me. "I'll let you go in first."

"Great," she mutters, hesitating with her raised fist, about to knock. "You promise you're not going to kill him?"

"I'll do my best."

"Why is that not comforting?" she grumbles as she raps her knuckles against the wood.

"Mallory!" Andrew's goofy fucking voice reaches me in my tucked-out-of-view spot. "I didn't think you were coming after... well, you know." Is that a note of shame I detect in his voice? Doubtful.

"I wasn't planning to," she admits.

"Did you get the flowers?"

"Oh, *yes*." She draws out the word with dramatic flair. "Biggest part of my night."

"Look, I really am sorry. I'm so happy you're here."

I bet you are. Knowing Andrew, he probably assumes Mallory showing up today means she's ready to hop into his bed. Just the thought is enough to propel me out of the shadows.

The happy expression slides off Andrew's face as I step into view.

I flash a cocky motherfuckin' grin at him. "How ya doin', *friend?*"

"Chaser, what're you doing here?" His gaze pings between Mallory and me for a few beats. "When did you get home?"

"Last night."

"We had an eventful reunion," Mallory adds, leaving it to up to Andrew to interpret anyway he wants.

I'm still thoroughly pissed that this asshole's actions prompted such an ugly fight between Mallory and me. But at the same time, it was the push we needed to air out a few things I'd been avoiding.

Andrew opens the door wider, motioning me to come in. I limp my way across the threshold—those fucking painkillers have *not* been as effective as I'd anticipated. But I sure as fuck wasn't bringing that cane with me.

"What's up, bro?" The nervous wobble in Andrew's voice almost makes me laugh. "You limping?"

"Cut up my foot. I'm fine."

"Why aren't you in Vancouver? Mark usually keeps that leash tight when you're in the studio."

"Yeah, I bet you were counting on that."

Mallory may have talked me out of blowing Andrew's brains out, but I never agreed not to be a dick.

"Where is everyone else?" Mallory asks, covering up the awkward silence.

Funny thing about Andrew—he's honest to a fault. Something I once appreciated about him.

He's also a terrible liar.

His shoulders jerk and his arms twitch. "Fucking flakes canceled on me. That's cool, though. Glad you're here, Chaser. You mind throwing on a few T's for me?"

"Sure thing." I glare at him, and he has the decency to look away. "Anything for my *friend*."

"Cindy's not here either?" Mallory persists.

"Well, I, uh, when everyone else said they weren't coming..." he gestures wildly in Mallory's direction, "...and I assumed you weren't coming, I called her and canceled."

"Oh." Mallory's gaze darts to me. I try to stop the told-you-so grin from forming but fail miserably. She rolls her eyes and shakes her head.

I jerk my thumb toward the kitchen. "You mind if I grab a glass of water?"

"Yeah, sure. Go ahead." Andrew waves his hands in the air. "Whatever you need."

My foot's throbbing from all the activity. I'm dying to pop another pill. Plus, I'm curious. What will Andrew say to Mallory if I leave them alone together for a few seconds?

How much rope does he need to hang himself?

Mallory

Andrew watches Chaser limp into the kitchen.

As soon as the swinging door stops moving, he turns to me. "Did you tell him?" he whispers in a low, urgent voice. "What I said? Jesus fuck, what are you trying to do to me?"

I give him a cool look. "What am I trying to do to *you*? Don't blame me for your impulse control issues."

"Why is he home?" He runs his hands through his hair. "He knows doesn't he? You told him?"

"I can't lie to him, Andrew. Look on the bright side. At least I talked him out of killing you for trying to kiss me."

"Jesus fucking Christ, *why* would you tell him *that*?" He rakes his hands through his hair again and tugs on the ends. "He's going to hate me now."

"Did you honestly think if you broke us up, you two would remain buddies?"

"I didn't want to break you up. I wanted to—"

"Fuck me. I remember."

He leans down, so we're eye to eye. "Why are you so insulted?" His desperate question pulls no sympathy from me. "You know how many girls beg to jump on my cock?"

"Andrew, I don't know what kind of damage is in your past, but you really need to seek therapy."

He scratches his head. "I see someone once a week."

"Well, start going more often or find a new therapist."

"I told her all about you." He straightens up. "Fuck, I had to have an emergency session with her after you left yesterday."

Fantastic.

"She thinks I'm a sex addict." A dark chuckle spills out of him. "She said it like it's a bad thing."

"You're out of your mind."

"Maybe. I also told you I'm *in love* with you," he whispers. "Or did you forget that?"

If only I could fry him with the power of my eyes. "You're *not* in love with me."

"Trying to kiss my girl again, Andrew?" Chaser's grim voice sends a shiver down my spine.

Andrew's face pales. "Just talking," he answers without turning around.

"Whatever you have to say, you can say in front of me. No need for secrets, buddy."

"You going to shoot me now?" Andrew puts his arms in the air and turns around.

"That *was* my preference." Chaser leans over and sets a glass of water on the coffee table. "Mallory talked me out of it for some reason." He straightens up and points an imaginary finger gun Andrew's way. "I'm always willing to reconsider."

"Bro, not funny." Andrew's fingers brush against his bullet wound.

Chaser's controlled his anger for an admirable amount of time, I have to admit. But he finally snaps.

Faster than his injured foot should allow, he rushes Andrew. His fist flies through the air. The punch slams into Andrew's cheek. He's knocked sideways, landing on the hard tile with a *smack*.

I gasp but don't say a word or try to stop Chaser.

"Don't fuckin' *bro* me ever again, motherfucker," Chaser snarls. He cocks his fist back and punches Andrew in the face again. "You went after my girl behind my back." *Punch.* "Lied to my face." *Punch. Punch.*

"I can't help it, Chaser." Andrew holds up his hands, blocking the blows and scoots backwards. "I've got a problem."

Chaser burrows one hand in Andrew's hair and yanks his head back. "How many times did I tell you she was off-limits?"

"A lot."

Without turning around, Chaser motions toward the door. "Go, Mallory."

"What? No way."

"I'm not going to kill him."

"That's not reassuring."

Andrew lifts one hand in the air. "I'm not feeling reassured either."

"Shut up." Chaser releases Andrew and limps over to me. As furious as he is, he's gentle as he takes my elbow and guides me to the front door. "Go wait in the car so Andrew and I can talk for a minute. Please?"

CHAPTER FORTY-TWO

Chaser

"Are we good now?" Andrew asks after Mallory leaves.

He picks himself up off the floor and warily circles me.

Not trusting his intentions, I track his every movement. "You're joking, right? You hit on my fiancée and you think we're cool?"

He touches his jaw. "You punched me. Several times."

"That doesn't come *close* to making us even."

"You know I've got a problem." He leans his hip against the back of his couch and gives me that pathetic sheepish shrug that's probably gotten him out of trouble his entire life. "She couldn't reject me fast enough, so—"

"If you're waiting for me to say *thanks*, you can fuck off."

Shame seems to transform him. His shoulders slump forward and he hangs his head. "I'm really sorry."

"You don't understand the meaning of sorry."

He rubs his fingers over his chest. "No, for the first time, I think I really do. It aches." He squints as he seems to search for the right words. "It feels *heavy* in here. I don't like it."

"That's *guilt*."

"This is different. Usually I have some momentary disappointment when I don't get my way. Or, I'll be mad I got caught. But this...this is so much worse." He rubs his chest again. "I can't get rid of the hurt."

"Save your breakthroughs for therapy."

"I'm sorry," he repeats.

Christ, he's pathetic. "Do you even understand the damage all your shitty behavior causes?"

"I didn't want to hurt you. I didn't think—"

"Yeah, you never think. That's the problem. You let your inner child run loose and create havoc for everyone else to deal with."

"That's fair."

"Fuck you and fair."

"This is another rock-bottom for me, Chaser. The shooting got me off drugs. And this... You're one of my only true friends and I don't want to lose you."

Some fucking friend. "I don't think you understand friendship. I've put up with a lot of shit, Andrew. A lot."

"I know."

"You have some good qualities. I appreciate all the help you've given the band, but messing with Mallory and me, you crossed a line—"

"I'm sorry."

"I believe you."

"What can I do to make it right?"

"Nothing right now."

"Will we get through it?"

I stare long and hard at his desperate hound dog face. "Give it time."

The spark of hope lighting up his childish eyes kicks me in the gut. I'm never getting this lunatic out of my life, am I?

"Tell me what to do, Chaser. And I'll do it." He watches me, waiting expectantly for an answer.

I blow out a long breath. "You're *never* alone with Mallory again."

He holds his hands up in the air. "Done. Swear." Slowly, he lowers his hands. "That's probably for the best, anyway."

I growl.

"No, no, I mean, she's gotta be pretty pissed at me."

"Her feelings aren't your concern."

He taps his chest. "Yeah, but that's part of what feels so bad in here." He jerks his shoulders up and down like he's trying to will the bad feelings away. "Can I at least apologize? I was a real dick to her. I knew I was being an asshole but I couldn't stop myself."

"Send it in a letter," I spit out. Fuck, I knew Mallory held back some of the story, probably figuring I'd kill Andrew if she told me every ugly detail.

"I accept that." He holds out his arms.

I stare at him in disbelief. "Are you shitting me, right now? I'm not *hugging* you. I'm not done *punching* you yet."

His eyes widen just in time to see my fist flying at his face again.

"Oh, fuck."

CHAPTER FORTY-THREE

Chaser

"Quit being such a baby. You'll live."

Andrew jams a tissue up his nose to stop the bleeding. I don't even feel remotely sorry for fucking up his face.

"Now..." I grab his elbow and steer him out into the living room, "...walk outside with me and wave, so Mallory knows I didn't kill you."

He glances down at my foot. "Seriously, what'd you do to your foot? Is that why you came home?"

"Don't worry about why I came home." I have no plans to toss Pamela into this theater of absurdity by admitting to Andrew that she called me. She'd probably be thrilled to know she caused so much turmoil. And he'd probably take it as a sign that she wants him back.

"Mark let you leave?" he asks.

"He gave us the weekend off."

"Damn. You must be doing good work. He never cuts us any slack."

I hate the part of me that wants to discuss the recording sessions and ask for Andrew's opinion on a few of the things we're trying out for this album. Out of all the musicians in Hollywood, why the fuck did I have to pick this chaos-addicted man-child to be my mentor?

"Did he let you go because you hurt your foot?"

I stop walking and give him a quick shove. "Jesus Christ, you nosy prick. Mallory broke your giant gaudy vase and I cut up my foot on the glass. Ya happy now?"

"Fuck," he breathes out. "Oh, fuck."

"Yeah. Exactly."

"She broke it?"

"You're kinda focused on the wrong thing for someone who's sorry."

"No, no, it's not that. I really was trying to apologize to her. I didn't mean to piss her off even more."

"It was an accident." I give him a sideways glance. "She wasn't going to change her mind and jump into bed with you, though. Roses or not."

He has the nerve to act insulted. "That's not why I sent them."

"Sure it's not."

"So, are you headed back to Vancouver now?" he asks.

"Don't worry about where I'm headed or when."

"I didn't ask...because...She's not why I asked."

"Yeah, but see, I don't *trust* you anymore."

"I'm sorry," he whines.

"No more visiting Mallory at work."

"She told you about that too, huh?"

I ignore his question. "I'm not fucking around. If you're sincere, really sorry, still want to be friends or ever work together again—"

"I am, Chaser. I swear."

"We'll see."

I finally step out of his madhouse and he follows me, stopping to wave at Mallory.

She hesitantly lifts her hand and wiggles her fingers at us but doesn't get out of her car.

Andrew twitches and bounces from foot to foot. I sense he's planning to attempt another hug, so I back away.

"We'll talk?" he asks.

"Give it time."

"Good luck with the album."

"Thanks."

I limp my way over to the car. Mallory starts the engine before I reach her. Guess she's as eager to get the hell out of here as I am.

"Nice touch having him come outside with you, so I'd know you didn't kill him," she says without glancing over.

"Liked that, huh?"

She snorts as she reverses out of his driveway but doesn't answer.

"He's seriously fucked up."

She flicks a no-kidding glance at me before putting the car in drive. "I hadn't noticed."

I blow out a long breath. Why the fuck do I feel compelled to tell her this? "He wanted to apologize to you. I guess he realized whatever he said to you was pretty shitty and he's worried he hurt your feelings."

Her mouth twists from side to side. "I'm done talking about this, Chaser."

"Are you sure? You still sound pissed."

She's silent while she pulls into our driveway and turns off the ignition. Before answering, she unsnaps her seatbelt and turns to face me. "I hate that you trusted Pamela more than me."

"That's not true." I stare out the window, not sure circling back to last night is the best idea when we should be moving forward. "It wasn't Pamela."

"But you said she called you."

"She did. That's why I came home." I tap my knuckles against the window and stare at the shrubs lining the driveway.

"When I got here, I realized how stupid that was. I do trust you, Mallory, I swear."

"But?"

"Those flowers were delivered. He used to joke about giving pink roses to the girl he's—"

"Ohh," she breathes out. "You know I don't care about stuff like that, right?"

"I know."

"I don't even like roses."

I pick up her hand and kiss the back of it. "What do you like?"

"Sunflowers, daisies, irises, tulips...but I don't *need* flowers, I need *you*."

Should I really keep picking at every last thread? I think we need to if we're going to move on. "You have to trust me too. When I called, you should've told me what happened."

She fiddles with the radio knob. "You know why I didn't?"

"You were afraid I'd be mad at you."

"No." She squeezes her eyes shut and I can't help reaching over to skim my knuckles over her cheek. My heart practically jumps out of my chest when she leans into my touch. Finally, she opens her eyes, staring into mine. "I didn't want to do anything to mess with the recording of the album." She touches her temple. "To take you out of your creative headspace."

"Mallory, I appreciate that, but—"

"You don't understand. I didn't want anything to delay you finishing the album and coming *home*." Tears shine in her eyes and she glances down. "I didn't want you to be away from me any longer than you had to be."

I wish we weren't in the car so I could pull her into my lap right now. "I hate being away from you too, you know that, right?"

"I do."

She sniffles and a hint of a smile flickers over her lips.

"Except for making up with you last night. I want to forget that the last forty-eight hours even happened."

"Couldn't agree more." I rest my hand on her leg. "Come back to Vancouver with me."

"What? I can't. I have to be on-set Tuesday."

"So? That gives us two days. I can't keep going these long stretches without seeing you. It's making me crazy."

"I hate it too."

I reach over and capture her hand, tugging on it until she looks at me. "I love talking to you every night. But it's not the same. I need to see you. Touch you. Otherwise, I'm miserable and can't think straight."

"Chaser." She cups my cheek, rubbing her thumb over my ever-present scruff. "I'm always a little lost without you."

"Let's make a pact."

"What kind of pact?"

"No more than...two weeks without seeing each other. No matter what."

"That's so long."

"We've been through worse."

"Ten days?" she counters.

My chest squeezes—she's as into this idea as I am. "It won't be easy."

I lean in, pressing my lips to hers to seal our deal. "Ten days."

CHAPTER FORTY-FOUR

Mallory

Tuesday morning, I arrive at the studio early. Pamela slides up next to me in the parking lot, flashing a fake smile. "How was your weekend, Mallory?"

God, I want to strangle her.

Instead, I smile sweetly. "Lovely. Chaser came home and surprised me. We had an amazing time together. Truly electric." *Well, that's one way to put it.* "Then I went back to Vancouver with him." I yawn, and hold up my arms, in a long, lazy stretch. "I got back late last night and I'm exhausted."

She blinks rapidly and purses her lips together.

"Well, we're going to be late. Come on!" I pull my script out of my bag and flip to my one short scene for this week's show. It's going to be a boring couple of days of sitting around doing nothing most of the time.

"Can you believe this?" Billie, one of my fellow "lifeguards" wags her marked-up script at me. "One week I'm possessed by demons. Now, I'm supposed to break up a fight between two rival gangs with the power of my boobs? Who writes this shit?"

I cast a furtive glance around before joining in on her

laughter. Good grief, it's like we're all begging to be fired from this crazy show.

"Now, Billie." I adopt the haughty tone of a movie critic. "It shows true artistic creativity that two historically chauvinistic criminal organizations were willing to listen to the heartfelt advice of a five-foot-two inch blonde-haired pixie," I say with a straight face. "That would *totally* happen in real life."

"Holy!" Her eyes bug out and she explodes with laughter. "You should be writing the scripts, Mallory."

I bet she wouldn't find it as funny if she knew how much experience I actually have with such criminal organizations. It was part of why the script seemed more over-the-top idiotic to me than usual.

Will I mention it at our table read today? Nope.

"Hey," Cindy greets me with downcast eyes. "Uh, your friend canceled this weekend. I hope I didn't do something to—"

"Oh my God, no." I squeeze her shoulder and she finally looks up at me. "It had nothing to do with you. Honest. I'm sorry I even roped you into it."

"Okay. Cool. I was worried."

I open my mouth, then close it. I don't want to talk about the weekend here. Where *certain* people might overhear. "Everything is fine," I promise her.

Chaser

The drama of the weekend's firmly behind me when I limp my way into the studio Tuesday morning.

"Have a nice trip?" Jacob sneers at me from across the room.

"I did. Thanks for asking, dick. Where were you?"

"Checking out the sights." He scowls at my foot. "What the fuck's wrong with you?"

"Cut my foot on some glass. I'll be fine."

Mark sits forward, concern etched in his face. "Are you all right to play? You were planning to experiment a little with a distortion pedal on 'Lush Mountain'."

"I can make it work."

"Mallory get home okay?" Alvin asks.

"Yeah, she called me when she got in."

"She was here?" Jacob asks.

"Yeah, bro. She came back with me. Where the fuck were you?"

He shrugs. "Recharging my batteries like Mark suggested."

Garrett stretches, arching his back. "That's code for *fucking strippers*."

Jacob snickers and waves his lyric book at me. "They weren't strippers, they were *muses*."

"Fantastic," I mutter.

"What'd you bring back?" Jacob asks, peering over at my own notebook.

I'd scribbled out a whole lot of rage-filled lyrics after the fight with Andrew. Worked on an aggressive new sound I've been trying to capture. After that, a whole lot of sappy shit flowed from my fingertips. "Came up with a few heavy riffs. I think I finished 'In Your Hands'.

Jacob raises his eyebrows. "Yeah? Still wicked sappy?"

"Yup."

"Panty melter." Garrett points at me. "The song, not you. Girls love that sappy shit."

That's not why I wrote it but as long as they're not going to fight me about putting it on the album, I don't care.

"I think we all know Chaser's a panty melter as well," Jacob says.

"I'm flattered."

"All right." Mark stands and waves his hands in a settle down gesture. "Time to focus. Redirect our energy toward finishing this album."

"Right-o!" Jacob shouts.

"We've recorded some solid stuff. All killer, no filler." Mark goes through the list of songs we want to include on the album. It's long and it's time to start narrowing them down.

"'Always Be Mine' is the one that fits the *Elimination Date* soundtrack the best. It's a killer song. Represents Kickstart's sound really well. Great way to introduce you to a new audience. How do you feel about letting them have that one?" he asks.

We take a vote and it's unanimous. My chest pumps with excitement. It's really happening. One of our songs on a soundtrack. For a major motion picture.

"'Misery Pangs'...I'm not loving that one as much. It's not as strong as the others. Feels more like a B side." Mark glances up to gauge our reaction.

So much for 'all killer, no filler.' That song's kind of Garrett's baby. We all worked on it but he brought it to the table. It's a solid, quick rock song. But there's no emotional pull that really grabs me one way or another. I'm not about to shit all over Garrett's contribution, though.

"Eh." Garrett scuffs the toe of his sneaker against the carpet. "I'm not super attached. If you don't think it fits, let's set it aside for now."

"We'll circle back to it," I say and everyone agrees.

"The label still wants 'Cry It Out' on here," Mark says. "Non-negotiable. But I thought maybe we could do something really different with it."

"Like?" Jacob prompts.

Mark's gaze lands on me. "You should sing it."

"What?" My eyes widen and I glance at each one of my band mates. Did they put Mark up to this to fuck with me? "No. I'm not a singer."

"It's a personal song." Mark taps his chest. "Your vocals will give it more depth. Maybe not the whole thing but the first verse." He glances at Jacob. "You cool with that?"

Jacob, predictably is *not* down with this plan. "How are we going to work that out live?"

"Race the clock to get a blow job." Alvin rolls his eyes. "It's a solid idea. It will help set us apart from everyone else."

"It's also an old song," Garrett points out. "We need to make it as fresh as possible, otherwise fans are going to be annoyed."

"Yeah, cool. Whatever." Jacob waves his hand in the air.

I shoot a glare at Mark. Head's up might have been nice.

"We'll go over some vocal techniques this week but I want it to have that raw, unpolished edge to it." Mark squeezes his fist in the air. Guess he's given this lots of thought.

Mallory

"You know how you always say you like my voice?" Chaser asks after sharing the news about which song they picked for the soundtrack.

Keeping the phone to my ear, I flop onto the bed and roll over on my stomach, kicking my feet in the air. "I really do."

"Mark wants me to record the vocals for 'Cry It Out'."

"No way! Really?" My nose scrunches up. "How'd Jacob take that?"

He huffs a laugh. "Not well."

"You don't think it's going to make him start using again, do you?"

"Jesus, I hope not. I wouldn't do it if I thought it would fuck him up that much."

Chaser has more faith in Jacob than I do. And I'm worried about Chaser when they go back on the road. "Just...be careful."

"You know I will. I still haven't decided how I feel about it or if I'm going to even do it yet."

"I think you should. The song's personal to you."

"Tell me what crazy shit happened on *Shallow End* this week."

"Then I'll spoil the show for you!"

"Trust me, your version and what's shown on screen are entirely different things."

I snort-laugh into the phone. "Well, Billie's recovered from her demonic possession."

"Naturally."

"And she gives a stern lecture to two rival gangs that helps them end their feud."

He roars with laughter. "Priceless."

"I thought so too."

"Sounds like Billie's getting a lot of attention, is that driving Pamela nuts?"

I frown but instead of brushing it aside, say exactly what's on my mind. "Why do you care about Pamela's feelings?"

"I don't. I'm worried that if she's not the center of attention, she'll try to stir up trouble for *you*."

"Oh." I pick at a loose thread in the comforter. "I didn't tell her anything about what happened."

"Good, I never told Andrew about her phone call."

"Has she called up there again?"

"Not that I know of."

"Good."

"Mallory?"

"What?"

"I don't want to talk about Pamela. We just wasted at least thirty cents on her, and that's way too much."

"Agreed." I yawn and roll over. "What do you want to talk about?"

"How the first morning I'm home, I plan to wake you up with my tongue in your pussy."

"Ooo..." I laugh softly. "I'm listening."

CHAPTER FORTY-FIVE

Mallory

The call to film the pilot for *Ocean Ave.* finally comes from Marilyn a few days later.

"I got it! I really got the part?" I shriek.

"Easy, Mallory. It's just the test pilot. Network still has to decide if they're going to pick it up." She pauses. "But Southgate rarely has anything turned down. Everything he touches is gold. He really liked you too."

"He's so nice. Everyone there was."

She snorts. "Don't get used to it."

"What do I do about *Shallow End?*"

"I'll smooth that over. You say nothing. I don't want you ending up on *no* shows. Loose lips sink ships. Are we clear?"

"Crystal."

THE MORNING I LEAVE TO FILM THE PILOT, I FIND A BRIGHT arrangement of sunflowers, and irises sitting on the doorstep. Grinning from ear to ear, I pick them up and bring them inside.

M-

Knock 'em dead.

C

He remembered.

The bouquet is so pretty, I hate leaving it. I check the water and set the vase on the kitchen counter before leaving.

The guard at the gate remembers me from the audition and congratulates me. "Your co-stars are already arriving." He points to the left. "You can park along that wall. Any spot that isn't marked 'reserved.'"

"Thank you!"

Nervous, excited energy bubbles up inside me. I might actually be on another television show.

Overwhelmed, once I find a parking spot, I take a deep breath and tip my head down. "You're always on my mind and in my heart, Mom. I don't think I could do this without you watching over me. I hope I make you proud." How I wish I could share this news with her. She'd be so excited for me and want every little detail. "I miss you," I whisper.

A knock on my window startles me out of my reverie.

An extremely thin blonde woman peers in through the glass and waves. "Mallory! Right?" she shouts.

I motion that I'm going to open the door and she jumps back.

"I'm Madeline Southgate." She wraps her arms around me. Strong hugger for such a bony girl.

I awkwardly hug this person I've never met before back. "Uh, Mallory Dove."

"I'm so happy you're here," she gushes. "You're going to *love* working with my dad. Everyone does."

Remembering Marilyn's words about how Madeline only has her part because her father's the producer, I almost roll my eyes. But, really, who am I to judge? If my father were a famous Hollywood producer—instead of a mob boss parked in federal prison at the moment—I'd probably ask to be cast in his shows too. She's certainly not trying to hide their relationship, and I actually respect that.

"I know you met Colby at the audition and Joan and Kurtis," she rattles off a bunch of other names as she loops her arm through mine and leads me into the studio.

"Don't worry about the show. It'll get picked up. In thirty years, my father's only had two shows get turned down," she assures me.

"Well, I hope we're not the unlucky third." I laugh nervously.

"Shh." Her gaze darts around the cavernous room. "Don't even joke about that." She points to the ceiling. "The T.V. gods are always listening and very fickle."

I blink and stare. Great, another crazy person.

She breaks into wild laughter and slaps my shoulder. "I'm fucking with you, Mallory. Although, yeah, half of Hollywood is crazy superstitious. Come on, let's go find your dressing room."

By the end of the day, I'm exhausted, but hopeful.

CHAPTER FORTY-SIX

Chaser

Maybe Mark got wind of Jacob's attempt to talk my fiancée into orgasming on *Lies and Other Promises*. Music industry folks love to gossip and I'm sure after working with us, the sound engineer we used needed to seek therapy.

Whatever the reason, Mark calls in a guy to mix the album before we leave Vancouver. No fucking around this time. Mark stays with us throughout the process, cutting off any attempts by Jacob to start navel-gazing. If the urge to stab Andrew wasn't still lingering in my gut, I'd call and ask him if this is Cutter's usual process.

"You did good, kid." Mark shakes my hand and gives me a fatherly pat on the back when the album's finally finished.

He glances around the sound room, but we're alone for now. "You ever record those tracks with Mitchell?"

Not all that surprised he knows about it, I nod. "I think he only used one of them, though." I hesitate, wanting to choose my words carefully. Last thing I need is gossip floating around that I trashed America's beloved pop music superstar. "It was a... strange process."

"Mitchell's a strange guy." He glances at the doorway again. "Are you interested in working with any other mainstream acts? As a featured guitarist? Or even contributing some lyrics."

"I'd have to consider the project. Do you have someone specific in mind?"

"A few artists, but I wanted to know if you were open to the idea, first."

Not expecting this, I run my hand over the back of my neck a few times. "I need to be home for a few weeks before we go back out on the road. I can't—"

"No, no. We'll schedule it in L.A. for you. This..." he sweeps his hand over the soundboard in front of us, "...was to get your album done in a reasonable amount of time so the label didn't drop Kickstart."

My stomach plummets into my boots. "What? Was that a possibility?"

He arches a brow. "You didn't hear that from me. But after the EP took so long...the rumors of Jacob's drug habits, Andrew's shooting, your arrest for the shooting... Let's just say, the suits have had some reservations about Kickstart's long-term viability."

"Fuck." I stab my fingers through my hair and stare up at the ceiling. "Thom never said anything."

"I doubt they were that blunt with him."

"Shit."

"Every label's signing metal bands now. There's a race to produce as many albums as possible and cash in on the trend before the bubble pops. Half of them are garbage. Hell, more than half. Kickstart's got staying power, Chaser. *You* have staying power. Real talent. You're more than a trend. I'm glad you have an open mind."

Of course, I do. If I can keep publishing rights to just one hit song, it could set Mallory and I up for years to come. "I'm always willing to listen, Mark. And I'm open to all different genres."

314

He grins. "Andrew talk to you about his rock-rap-blues fusion project?"

I snort. "Yeah, I think I talked him into adding a little country into that mix."

"Holy smokes. I don't know if I'm going to touch that one." He chuckles. "If anyone could make it happen, though, the two of you could."

Sorry to disappoint, but I'm not working with Andrew any time soon.

I don't bother saying that to Mark. As close as we've gotten while working together these last few weeks, it's still better to keep that whole goatfuck of a weekend to myself. In musical matters I trust him, personal stuff, not so much.

"We'll see."

Alvin slaps his palm against the open door and pops his head into the room. "Pizza's here."

I turn to leave, but Mark stops me. "Keep this between us for now."

As much as I hate hiding shit from Alvin, he won't hold it against me. Garrett won't give a shit either. Jacob, on the other hand, he'll pout like a baby. "No problem."

Someone added champagne to our pizza order. I almost question whether that's a good idea for Jacob, then remember how annoyed I was when my dad questioned me having a fucking beer at the clubhouse. Jacob's worked hard. Hasn't slipped up once. We finished an album for fuck's sake. We *should* celebrate.

"To us!" Jacob cheers. "We actually fucking did it!" He slams his glass into mine, spilling liquid everywhere.

"You did good, Jacob." Mark slaps him on the back. "You each brought your A game. I'm incredibly proud. I think this album's going to be *huge*."

"I'll toast to that!" Garrett raises his glass.

"Mmm. Pizza and champagne. Almost feels like the early days." Alvin nudges me. "Well, pizza and cheap beer."

"What do you mean *old* days? That's still your go-to dinner," Garrett says.

"True." Alvin grins. "No shame."

We finish up in the studio and head back to the house.

"You all packed and ready to go?" Alvin asks.

"Fuck yeah."

"Sweet, let's grab our shit and haul ass to the airport."

Jacob and Garrett planned to stay and bum around the city for a while.

Not me. I've been away from my girl long enough.

Mallory

"Chaser!" I jump and wave, hoping he can see me over the crush of people.

He scans the crowd and I wave again.

Suddenly he's pushing and weaving past bodies. I say a quick prayer of thanks that he's not still limping from his injured foot. Behind him, Alvin raises his arm in hello.

I squeal and laugh when Chaser scoops me up in his arms. "Oh, fuck I missed you," he says before slanting his mouth over mine.

I throw my arms around his neck and pull him down for a deeper kiss, welcoming him home with everything I have. Breathless, we part and stare at each other. "We cut it close on the ten-day mark this time."

"We did." He hugs me again and lifts me for another quick kiss. "But I'm all yours now."

Alvin's patiently waiting behind Chaser and once I'm on my feet, I give him a quick hello hug. "Welcome home."

"Thanks, Mallory. It's nice to have someone happy to see me."

Chaser slaps his friend's shoulder. "Quit whining. I just spent weeks holed up with you and *I'm* still happy you're here."

Alvin cracks a smile, then his expression darkens. "Fuck, I forgot. I don't have anywhere to go home *to*."

"You'll come home with us," I answer quickly. "We have plenty of room."

"Nah, I'll go stay at a hotel."

"Bro, come on," Chaser says. "You're always welcome at our place."

"Are you sure?"

"Yes," I insist. "Come on. I want to hear *everything* about the album."

Chaser curls his arm around me and kisses my cheek again. "What are you even doing here? I didn't want you to have to come pick me up."

"I wanted to surprise you."

We hit traffic at the worst possible time of the day but finally arrive at the house.

Thankfully, when I planned Chaser's welcome home dinner, I bought extra steaks in case any of the guys ended up joining us.

Chaser eyes the platter of meat with a smile twitching at the corner of his mouth. "Are you putting me to work already?"

"Yup." I wave at the patio. "I don't know how to use the grill. Doug will probably be mad if I set the house on fire."

"I'll supervise," Alvin promises.

I'm busy chopping vegetables for the pasta salad I'm throwing together when Chaser joins me a few minutes later, wrapping his arms around my waist, molding himself to my back. "Thank you for this."

"What?"

"A nice quiet night home." He kisses my neck. "Feeding us. Letting Alvin stay here. Just generally being awesome."

I set my knife down and lean into him. "You don't have to thank me. I'm so happy you're home." I turn and loop my arms around his neck, tipping my head to meet his eyes. "I'm excited for you guys. I can't wait to hear the new album."

His gaze darts to the side for a second. "I'm not supposed to say anything to the guys," he says in a low voice. "But Cutter asked if I'd be interested in contributing more riffs to other artists. Like I did for Mitchell Howard. Maybe doing some songwriting with other people too."

"Wow." I pull back, considering what that means for Chaser. "That's huge."

"It is," he agrees. "I hate not talking to Alvin about it."

Damn, it sucks that Cutter put Chaser in such an awkward position. "I understand. But what if nothing comes of it? You'll make things uncomfortable for no reason."

"True." He cocks his head. "Good point. Seventy-five percent of this business is talk that never comes through."

I hate even bringing this up but can't seem to help myself. "Does that mean you'll have to—"

"Nope. First thing I asked. He says he'll set it up somewhere in L.A." He leans down and presses a brief kiss to my cheek. "I don't want to be away from you any more than I have to."

"I don't mean to be selfish..."

He brushes his knuckles under my chin and tips my head back. "You know how happy it makes me that you *want* me around as much as I want to be around you?"

After a few seconds, he backs up and glances out the sliding glass door. Alvin's busy clearing off the wrought-iron patio furniture we've only used a handful of times since we moved into the house. Chaser returns his gaze to me. "Cutter also let it slip that the reason he was so adamant about all of us staying in Vancouver through the mixing was that the label was considering dropping us if the album wasn't finished in a timely fashion."

"Oh my God. Really?"

"Yeah, the shooting, the amount of time it took us to finish the EP, rumors of Jacob's drug habits, my arrest...none of it made them happy."

"What about...They don't know about your...?"

"No. Thank fuck I kicked my problem before it got back to the suits. If they caught wind that both of us were addicts, they might've gone ahead and cut us loose." He squeezes me tighter, resting his hands on my butt. "I have *you* to thank for that."

"Me? I didn't do anything special, Chaser."

"Yes, you did. You stuck with me. Believed in me. Didn't take any shit from me. I've never properly thanked you for all of it."

"Yes, you did." I poke his chest and smile up at him. "In front of the whole world when you accepted your Guitar God award."

"Right." He releases me and lifts his chin toward the counter. "What're we doing here?"

"Pasta salad." I point to the bowls set up along the counter. "Just chopping those up."

He boosts me onto the counter. "I've done enough yapping. I want to hear more about the pilot. I'll do the chopping while you give me all the details you didn't over the phone."

"Hmm." I swipe a carrot off the cutting board and munch on it while I think over the few days of filming. "Everyone's so nice. They've all worked together on different shows or movies over the years. I guess Mr. Southgate tends to hire and re-hire the same people if he likes them. He's very loyal."

"Unusual in Hollywood."

"Right? No one made me feel like an outsider or anything. Madeline's really sweet. Super bubbly and talkative but *so*...nice. I never realized I had this negative impression of her because of all the crap written in the scandal papers. But she's nothing like they say."

Chaser grunts. "We've learned the hard way that most of what they print is outright lies."

"True." I grab another carrot. "The outfits are hilariously ridiculous. Like, huge shoulder pads and wild prints—stuff I don't think anyone, let alone teenagers, would wear in real life. But the wardrobe people are so much nicer. And no crotch rub from skimpy bathing suits."

A teasing smile flickers over his lips. "The only crotch-rubbing you should be getting is from me."

I snort. "I hate to break it to you, but I'm looking forward to not having to wax my entire undercarriage every couple of weeks."

He sets the knife down, squeezes his eyes shut, and shakes with laughter. "Jesus, Mallory." He steps between my knees and rests his hands on my hips. "Shave it, wax it, shape it into a bonsai tree, let it grow into a little jungle if it makes you happy. Nothing's going to keep me away from your *undercarriage*."

"Christ, is that what passes for sweet talk these days?" Alvin says from behind us. "No wonder I'm still single."

Thoroughly embarrassed, I drop my gaze to my sandals and shake my head.

"That's what you get for being a creeper." Chaser picks up a celery stalk and flings it in Alvin's direction.

Alvin catches it and takes a big, crunchy bite. "Steaks are done," he mumbles around the mouthful. "Come on, Tarzan, grab Jane and let's eat."

Chaser pelts Alvin with the remaining carrots.

"Stop wasting my vegetables," I scold, but I'm laughing so hard, neither of them seem to understand me. They keep flinging little orange and green missiles at each other instead.

When we're finally situated at the table, Alvin leans over and pulls a slice of celery out of my hair. "Sorry about that, Mallory."

"I'm just happy to see you guys laughing. You both looked so serious when you got off the plane."

Alvin nervously glances across the table at Chaser. "I'm not supposed to say anything but, I hate keeping shit from you, bro."

Chaser sets his fork down. "What are you talking about?"

"Before we left, Cutter asked if I'd mind doing a 'guest appearance' in a Penny Driver video."

I glance down at my plate and bite my lip.

Chaser blows out a breath. "Thank fuck you said that. He asked *me* if I'm open to another featured solo. He didn't give me a name though."

Alvin cracks up. "What an asshole. I've been flipping out with no one to talk to about it." He hesitates. "You think it's a dumb idea? Think associating with Penny Driver will kill our 'street cred'?"

Instead of answering with a quick, no, Chaser pauses, and seems to seriously consider the question. "Some people might bitch and call it selling out, but they're not our true fans anyway, you know? She's got a huge audience. It could be good exposure for the band."

"That's what I thought too." He stabs his fork into a big chunk of steak and stuffs it in his mouth. "Garrett's had a crush on her forever. He's going to be jealous."

Chaser snorts. "Who knows what secret project Cutter has lined up for Garrett. Sounds as if he had something up his sleeve for each of us."

"Probably a guest-starring role on a porno for Jacob," Alvin mutters.

Chaser raises his glass. "Talk about exposing us to a new audience."

CHAPTER FORTY-SEVEN

Chaser

Since we were such good boys and finished the album on time, the label throws a party for its release. Based on the guest list, they're not planning to drop us any time soon. Everyone important in the industry came to celebrate the release of the album we ended up naming *In Your Hands*. Not that I notice any of them. The short, skintight gold dress Mallory picked out for the event has my full and undivided attention

I curl my arm around her waist and tug her closer, bending down to whisper in her ear, "We're dropping everyone else off first on the way home."

She tips her head back. Wide blue eyes staring up at me. Pink spreading over her cheeks. "Why?"

"Because I can't stop thinking about peeling this dress up, and making you ride my cock in the back of the limo." Fuck. I bite my lip hard enough to draw blood, willing my erection to settle down. Mallory doesn't help the situation when she leans in close enough to graze my dick with her body.

"Oh my," she breathes out, a teasing smile playing over her glossy pink lips. "It feels like you might need *immediate* attention."

I squeeze her hip, wordlessly begging her to stop. "Don't make me come in my pants in front of all these people."

She chuckles softly and slides her arm around my waist, leaning in and staring up at me. "Chaser, we both know you have more self-control than that."

"Not tonight, I don't." I flick my gaze up and around the room, landing on someone who definitely ruins the fun moment I'm having with my girl.

Fucking Andrew.

I glare at him across the room and he sends me a half-hearted wave.

"What's wrong?" She frowns and tries to turn but I block her, shifting us to the side. "Chaser, what—"

Jacob stumbles over to us, double-fisting two glasses of champagne with Garrett by his side keeping him upright.

"What the fuck happened with you and Andrew?" Jacob slurs, jerking his head in Andrew's direction.

Mallory stares down into her own champagne glass.

I shrug. "Nothing. We're cool."

"He looks scared to death of ya," Garrett says.

As he should be.

"Hasn't even come over to say anything or creep on Mallory," Garrett continues. "It's fuckin' weird."

My foot's mostly healed. The fury in my gut still lingers, so I'm not about to wave Andrew over and pretend nothing happened.

Alvin's the only one I told about the incident and he agreed I should close the door on Andrew's world of mayhem.

"Who knows what's going on in his head." I shrug and search the room for Alvin. He spots me and waves, working his way over to us. Halfway across the room, he stops, cocks his head, and points up.

I shake my head and he laughs.

It's our party. They've been playing the new album in a loop all night. I've been trying to block it out but still cringe every time 'Cry It Out' comes on.

"You sound amazing." Mallory closes her eyes and sways from side to side for a second. She smiles at Jacob. "Both of you. You complement each other really well."

Jacob flashes a thin smile. "Pretty soon, Chaser can take over the whole thing by himself." He slaps my shoulder and takes off before anyone can respond.

"Can't wait to go out on the road with his moody ass." Alvin watches Jacob stumble over to the bar.

Mallory sips her champagne. "I shouldn't have said anything."

"Don't worry about it." I lift my chin at Garrett. "Watch him. He can't get trashed in front of everyone tonight."

Garrett rolls his eyes but goes after Jacob. Maybe he's tired of playing babysitter, but fuck knows, Jacob doesn't listen to a word I have to say these days.

"Jacob better get his shit together. I'm not in the mood for his sulking every night for the next couple months."

"Are you planning to play it every night on tour?" Mallory asks.

"We'll see how the crowd reacts." Alvin swivels his head, checking out the party goers. "If it's bumming 'em out, we'll pull it from the set."

Something crashes over by the bar, and everyone turns to stare. Jacob holds up a broken bottle of Jack Daniels and yells, "Oops!"

A few people laugh. Most ignore him. A few flashbulbs go off. Fucking great.

Obviously, Mark never had the "you came this close to having the label drop your druggie ass" speech with Jacob. Or maybe he did, and Jacob doesn't give a fuck.

Garrett puts his arm around Jacob and leads him out a side door.

"Fuck," I mutter. I catch Alvin's eye. "What are we going to do if he goes off the rails while we're on the road?"

He shrugs. "Pray like fuck he doesn't take us all down with him?"

CHAPTER FORTY-EIGHT

Chaser

The next morning, we wake up to the news that *In Your Hands* debuted at number two on the Hot 100 charts. A huge deal for a heavy metal album.

"We did it!" The paper rustles in my shaking hands. "Holy shit."

Tears glitter in Mallory's eyes and she squeezes her fists together under her chin. "I am *so* proud of you guys. You've worked so hard."

"Come here." I wrap her up in my arms, resting my chin on top of her head. "Thank you."

"Call your dad." She pats my chest.

I track him down at the clubhouse. "I have news," I say as soon as he answers the phone.

"So do I. Hang on a minute."

I roll my eyes at Mallory.

Papers crinkle in the background. "Are you listening?" my dad asks.

"Yeah, I kind of have something important to tell you, though."

"*In Your Hands*, the third full-length studio album by American heavy metal band *Kickstart* displays a harsher, more aggressive sound than their previous work. Yet, it's a thought-provoking collection of songs that avoids the hard rock clichés they became known for with their previous hit, 'Candy Jar'."

I'm speechless. "What is that from?"

"Local paper."

I snort out a laugh. "No kidding?"

"Proud of you, kid."

"Well, I have better news than the blessing of the *County Freeman Journal*."

He snickers. "What's that?"

"The new album debuted at number *two* on the Hot 100 chart."

"Yeah? Who's number one?"

I grind my teeth. "Penny Driver."

"Never heard of her."

"Of course not."

"I'm proud of you, Russell," he adds in a more serious tone.

"Thank you."

"Getting ready to go out on the road?"

"We're leaving this week."

We talk a little longer before saying goodbye. I find Mallory in the kitchen fixing breakfast.

"Was he excited?"

"I think he was more excited about the local paper's validation than the Hot 100 chart." I snag a piece of bacon and pop it in my mouth.

She waves a spatula at me. "Go sit down."

I groan as I plop down into one of the chairs at the kitchen table. "I'm going to miss having breakfast with you every morning."

"Me too," she says softly without looking over. "I'm worried you're not going to eat enough out on the road."

I flex my arms and puff out my chest for her. "You calling me scrawny?"

Without answering, she sets a plate of scrambled eggs, bacon, and toast on the table. My gaze drops to the tiny sleep shorts she's still wearing. I reach out, catch her around the thigh and drag her closer.

"Chaser!" she yelps.

"You didn't answer, so now I have to prove my strength. Come here." I pull her into my lap.

"The last thing I'd ever call you is scrawny." She curls one arm around my neck and plucks a piece of bacon off the plate, bringing it to my lips. "Eat."

I take a bite of salty, fatty goodness. Mallory cooks it perfectly every time.

"I'm out of my damn mind for leaving." I hug her tighter. "My beautiful goddess who feeds me bacon."

She laughs softly. "I hope I do more for you than *that*."

"You know you do." I can't stop touching her, running my hand up under her shirt, over her back, her shoulders, under her hair. Like my fingers need to map and memorize every curve and contour of her body.

"Chaser?"

I sit back, spreading my legs wide, pulling her against my chest.

"What are you doing?" she whispers.

"Shh." I nip her earlobe and kiss her neck. "This has to go." I yank her white cut off T-shirt with red hearts scattered all over it off and toss it aside.

"Now I'm topless."

"Observant. I like that." I slip my hands behind her knees and lift her legs, draping them over mine. "You're so pretty all spread out for me." I cup one breast, gently massaging, and rubbing my thumb over her nipple.

She squirms, throwing her head back to rest on my shoulder.

"Fuck, yes." I kiss her exposed neck while shoving my free hand down her shorts.

"Oh." She gasps as I gently stroke between her legs. "Mmm."

"Think you can come on my fingers?"

"If you want me to."

I pull away and gently slap her pussy. She jumps but only moans louder. "What do *you* want?"

She curls one arm up and around my neck, runs her fingers through my hair and kisses my cheek. "This." She gasps when I push a finger inside her. "You. Oh my God. Touching me. Like that."

It's not at quite the right angle but I'm a creative guy and know how to get my fingers into tight places. I tease and stroke until she's shaking in my lap, so close to the edge. I dip down and kiss her cheek. "I love you like this. All wet and needy." I pump my fingers inside her one, two more times. "Hear that?"

She moans louder. Squirms harder, grinding her ass against my dick.

"Answer me."

"Y-yes."

"Clamp that pretty little cunt around my fingers for me."

"I'm trying," she gasps and bucks her hips.

I band my arm tighter around her waist, pinning her to me. "Don't try. Feel." I keep strumming my thumb over her clit in a soft, steady rhythm.

"Feels...so good," she whispers. "Please don't stop."

"We've got all morning. I'm not stopping until you come nice and hard for me."

"Oh!" Her back bows. She squeezes her eyes shut, her head rolls from side to side. "There. Oh, fuck."

Her eyes are still closed, and she's barely finished when I lift her up and set her on the edge of the table.

"Chaser, what are you—?"

I answer by ripping her shorts off the rest of the way and

sweeping the plate of eggs and bacon to the other end of the table.

She reaches for my shorts, but I grab her hands and pin them to her chest. "No." I lick her cheek and she squirms. "Tongue. I need you to come on my tongue next."

She squints at me. "Well, licking my *face* isn't the way to do it."

Choking on my laughter, I release her wrists and grab her by her ankles, lifting her up enough to swat each butt cheek. "Smartass."

"You're getting warmer," she teases.

I lean in and bite her thigh. "Get those feet on my shoulders, sassy girl."

Ah, fuck. I sit back and for a second can't even breathe she's so beautiful. "You're so fucking wet and pretty. This is better than breakfast."

I scoop my hands under her thighs, spreading her wider and shove my face between her legs.

"Fuck, Chaser," she gasps as I trace her wetness with my tongue. She slides one hand through my hair, lightly tugging.

I spend a few minutes licking and teasing her before getting down to business. Her little clit's hard and waiting for me. Her body jerks and shudders as I suck on it.

"Again. More." She moans, arches her back, and yanks my hair.

I drag my tongue down, savoring all her sweetness. Over and over until she's rocking against me and comes moaning, thrashing, and panting on the table. Her wild breathing and heaving chest works me up to an unbearable degree.

She hasn't even come down from the high before I stand, shove my shorts down, yank her to the edge of the table and thrust inside her. "Time to come on my cock, little dove. And I'm not going to last long, so I'd hurry if I were you."

She slowly opens her eyes only to narrow them. "So ambitious this morning."

331

"You calling me a slacker?" I drive into her again.

She laughs softly and reaches up to trace her fingers over my chest. "That's one thing I'd *never* call you." Her eyes roll back. "Oh, God. Right there, Chaser."

"That's better." I slide out, inch by inch, then rock back inside. "Fuck."

I rub circles over her clit and her body trembles.

"Oh," she chants over and over, chasing her bliss.

I'm right there with her. White-hot satisfaction practically blinds me. The orgasm seizes my body. How can every time be better than the last?

I'm still groaning in pleasure when she pulls me down for soft, sweet kisses.

"I love making you come," I murmur against her lips.

"I love when you make me come," she whispers. "And I love watching you." She slides one finger between my eyebrows and down my nose. "You concentrate so hard. It's sexy. Just like when you're on stage, except this performance is *all mine*."

I frown down at her. "I make my orgasm face on stage?"

She jiggles with laughter. "No."

I groan as I stand and pull her up with me. "Come on. Let's clean up. I'll reheat breakfast, then we're going back to bed to do this again."

CHAPTER FORTY-NINE

Mallory

Our ten-day rule hasn't been easy to stick to. Not with Chaser on tour. Between *Shallow End* and a few other projects, most of the time, I'm working six days a week. So I can't hold up my end of the bargain as easily.

I'm sitting in my car, flipping through my calendar, searching for a free day this month or even the next, when pain spears my lower back, stealing my breath.

I scoot forward, resting my head on the steering wheel and clutch the spot, rubbing as if it will help slow down the intensity.

I'm going to be late if I don't get moving.

Finally, the spasm ebbs but only for a second. My jaw locks as a vicious cramp ripples through my front. I don't need this today.

I frantically flip through my little calendar. My period isn't due for a week.

I flip back to the previous month. *Huh.*

Another cramp brings on a wave of nausea and I close the book.

Please go away. This isn't something I relish discussing with the wardrobe department. I dig through my purse and pop a few tablets of Advil, hoping they'll do the trick.

The pain finally subsides enough that I step out of the car. My legs wobble and I rest my butt against the door, closing my eyes and soaking in the sunshine.

"You look like shit, Mallory. What's wrong?" Pamela says as soon as she sees me.

"Good morning to you too."

"Sorry. Seriously, though. Are you okay?"

I'm surprised she cares. We haven't spoken much since the weekend she tried to cause trouble. I didn't want to let her know how much pain and chaos her phone call caused. And hell will freeze over before I tell her about Andrew's 'let's fuck' offer. Still, with the way we've avoided each other, even though we work so closely together, she must have an inkling *something* happened between the three of us.

"Why do you care?"

Her full lips twitch into a pout. "I'm sorry, okay?" She blows out a frustrated breath. "When things ended so badly with Andrew, it really hurt." She spears me with a pointed look. "I know you know I called Chaser and told him you were running around with Andrew."

"Which I wasn't, by the way."

She sighs. "I don't care who Andrew dates but for some reason the thought of you and him...bugged me. And that he would ask *you* to model his stupid shirts after I helped him with those designs really pisses me off."

"But I'm engaged to Chaser. I have no interest in Andrew. Never have."

"I know that now." She clasps her hands together. "Forgive me. Please?"

It will sure make life on set easier if we get along. "I'm sorry I ever agreed to model anything for him." I regret it for lots of reasons but if I really want to be friends with Pamela, favors for her ex isn't the way.

"Pshh." She waves off my apology. "I know you're still going to hang out with him because of Chaser."

I highly doubt that. Chaser still hasn't spoken to Andrew as far as I know. "Not likely."

"How's Kickstart's tour?"

Another cramp seizes my insides and I double over, squeezing my eyes shut.

"Shucks, Mallory." She touches my shoulder. "Are you okay?"

"It's just cramps," I breathe out. "I haven't had them this bad since high school."

"Jesus." She squats down on the ground and digs through her massive purse. "Let me find some Midol for you."

"I already took some. It hasn't done a damn thing."

"Maybe you should see a doctor?"

I glance over at the studio. We're going to be late if we don't haul ass inside soon. "I don't have time. It's not like they give us sick days."

"You can't film if you're in this much pain."

"It'll go away." My cheeks heat up from the mere thought of asking the director for the day off because of cramps. No way.

"Here." She hands me a pink box. "I'll call my doctor and try to get you in." She stares up at me. "You don't think you're pregnant, do you?"

"I'm on the pill." Growing up without a mother or any female relatives I felt comfortable talking to makes it hard for me to engage in such personal conversations. "Although, I forgot it a few times when I went to visit Chaser."

"Oh, shit, Mallory." She bites her lip.

"I can't be pregnant." I snatch a tampon out of my purse and wave it at her. "I've gone through like five of these this morning."

"That can't be good."

"Maybe my womb misses Chaser." My attempt at a joke sounds ridiculous.

She wrinkles her nose. "Womb? Really, Mallory," she teases.

"Come on." She links her arm through mine and drags me across the parking lot.

I suffer through wardrobe more than usual. The suits don't exactly leave room for the imagination as it is.

"Mallory, you should let us know when it's your time of the month," Donna hisses at me.

Heat blasts my cheeks. I just want to go home and crawl into bed.

I pop two more Midol and waddle out to the set. They're not ready for me, so I pretend to study my script, waiting for the painkillers to kick in so I can function.

"Mallory! You're up!" the assistant director shouts. From his tone, I gather he's called me more than once.

I take a step.

An angry fist from the depths of hell hammers into me and I double over in agony.

Pamela was right.

This can't be normal.

CHAPTER FIFTY

Chaser

Tucson.

Phoenix.

El Paso.

Mobile

Thousands of screaming faces show up for Kickstart. Dozens of backstage interviews. Lines of fans waiting to meet us after every show.

We rock them all.

Huntsville—Jacob shows up late. We barely make it to the stage on time.

Lafayette.

Jackson.

Somewhere around Birmingham it all starts to fall apart.

I should've gone home to see Mallory on the band's one day

off. Even if she's working and I only get to see her for a couple hours. It would've been better than *this*.

Who are all these people hanging out in Jacob's room? How'd they find their way here? Two of the guys from Iron Kiss, a few groupies, roadies, and then a whole bunch of seedier folks I've never seen before.

My gaze drops to the lines of coke Jacob's busy laying out on the table, then back to his new buddies.

Which one is responsible for the party favors?

As I watch Jacob chop up those pristine white lines, the ghost memory of a burning rush haunts my nasal passages.

I haven't touched coke or even thought about it much since I kicked my habit in New York. Yet, here I am again, thinking I'm different from other addicts who struggle every day. What an arrogant miscalculation.

Jacob peers up and catches me watching him. He gives me a slow, sly smile. "Come on, golden boy. You've been *so* good. You deserve a reward."

The fact that I'm craving it so intensely, *and* actually considering leaning over and inhaling the contents of the entire table jolts me out of my trance.

Ignoring him, I jump up and pace a few feet away.

Across the room, the phone rings.

"Chaser, it's for you!" Brian bellows across the room.

"Who is it?" I shout back.

He shrugs and mouths something I can't quite catch.

"Take a message!"

He leans over and scribbles something down on a pad. I glance over, watching Jacob hoover up a line as long as the table.

I swear I can taste it on my tongue.

One time. I gave it up before easily enough.

Forget those sweaty coke demon nightmares so soon, asshole?

The angel and devil taking up residence on my shoulders this afternoon are clearly in a bickering mood.

I close my eyes for a second, picturing Mallory. How

disappointed she'd be if she knew where I was right now and what I was contemplating.

She never has to know.

Sure, after all the stuff we've been through, doing some blow behind her back seems totally reasonable.

Fuck this.

I turn away and slide open the door to the balcony. The cool air brushes over my skin and I finally take a breath.

"Chaser?"

"What?" I snap, turning around to face an about-to-piss-himself Brian.

"Here." He hands me a folded piece of paper. "It was some chick named Pamela? Sounded important."

Fuck that. I'm not letting that crazy bitch suck me into her drama vortex again. I fell for it once and it blew up in my face.

I crumple the paper in my hand, then pause. Pamela and Mallory were working together today. What if something happened to Mallory?

The paper crinkles as I unfold it. *Cedar Hospital.*

"What the fuck is this?"

Brian shrugs. "I couldn't understand her over all the noise. She said she was headed to Cedar Hospital? Or *see the* hospital? I don't know."

"Did she say why? Or leave a fucking phone number?"

"No, man." He holds up his hands and slowly backs away.

"Motherfucker." I stare at the note, then jam it in my pocket.

High or not, people move the fuck out of my way when I storm back into the room.

"Chaser, where are you—"

Jacob doesn't even finish his question before I slam open the door and jog down to my own room—where I should've been in the first place.

Sure enough, the red message light on my phone is lit up like the devil's own beacon of misery.

I swear to fuck if this is some stunt by Pamela to get between Mallory and me again, I'm gonna ring her skinny little neck.

I snatch up the receiver and jab the button to get my messages played back.

"Chaser, shit, where are you?" Pamela's anxious voice rips me in two. "Something happened with Mallory on the set. She... passed out. They took her to Cedar Hill Hospital. I know you're on tour but if you—"

I slam the phone down before the message finishes.

Bag. Throw in some clothes. Wallet. Got some cash. Good, I'll need it. Credit card. Need that too.

I'll try calling the hospital from the airport.

In the hallway, I run into Alvin and a tall, leggy redhead I vaguely remember from last night's show.

He stops and stares at my bag. "Where are you going?"

"Home. Something happened. Mallory's in the hospital? I don't know."

"Fuck." He drops the redhead's hand. "You need me to go with you?"

"No." I glance back at my room, then hand him the key. "Will you pack up the rest of my shit and throw it on the bus for me, though? I'll meet you guys at the next—"

"Don't worry about it. I'll take care of everything."

I slap him on the shoulder and he pulls me in for a quick hug. "Call and let me know if she's okay," he says, pulling back.

"Thank you."

Should I let Thom or the other guys know I'm leaving the tour? Maybe. But there's time for that later. Right now, I need to find out what's going on with my girl.

CHAPTER FIFTY-ONE

Chaser

I could've rented a car and driven to L.A. faster.

My flight finally lands and I fight my way off the plane. Thankfully, I find a taxi to take me straight to the hospital.

Outside, I find Pamela. She jumps up off the bench she'd been sitting on and runs over. "I'm so glad you're finally here!"

I grab her shoulders and hold her at arm's length. "What the fuck happened?"

"I don't know. She didn't feel well this morning. Said it was her period but she was bleeding heavily and she...passed out."

"Jesus. Is she okay?"

She bites her lip and whispers, "I think she had a miscarriage, Chaser."

The word slaps me in the face. "Where is she?"

"They won't tell me anything but you're her emergency contact, so they should talk to you."

Panic, frustration, and rage, all follow me inside. Pamela directs me to the front desk where I'm given Mallory's room number.

"Thank you." I don't even say anything to Pamela before running down the unfamiliar hallways.

Finally, I spot my girl in a darkened room all by herself.

"Mallory. Thank fuck," I mutter. My feet pound so hard over the hospital tiles, they can probably hear me in the basement.

Her eyes widen and she tries to sit up, then winces.

"Baby, what happened?"

"Chaser." The raw devastation on her face cuts me deep. Tears run down her cheeks as she reaches for me. She opens her mouth but no more words come out.

One of her hands is a road map of IV needles, hospital tape, and bruises, so I grasp her other hand.

"What happened? Are you okay?"

She shakes her head. "No. Chaser, I—"

I don't think I'm ready to hear this. And I can't help thinking this is somehow my fault. "I should've been here sooner. I'm sorry it took so long." I slide my hand over hers, twining our fingers together and press my forehead to her knuckles, my subtle ask for forgiveness. "I'm so sorry, little dove," I whisper.

"I'm just happy you're here now." She squeezes my hand.

None of this seems real. Inside, I'm coming apart, but I need to hold it together and take care of my girl

Above me, she sniffles, and the sound shatters me.

"I was so scared," she whispers through her tears. "I thought I was dying. It hurt so bad." She stops and shines sad, watery blue eyes my way. "Chaser, I lost our baby."

I stand and gather her in my arms the best I can with the hospital bed in our way.

All I want to do is take her home and curl up in the dark and let the crushing grief envelop us.

"I'm sorry I wasn't here with you." I'm sick knowing that while she was suffering through this alone, I was hanging out with a bunch of degenerates, considering blowing my sobriety.

"I didn't know," she whispers. "Why didn't I know? How can it hurt so much when I didn't even know?"

In a way, I'm glad we *didn't* know. It would have made this loss so much harder to endure. I don't dare say that, though. It's time to shut up and listen to whatever she needs to say.

"Why?" she sobs.

"I don't know." I kiss her temple and run my hands over her hair and down her back. "I don't know."

I hold her the best I can, promising her we'll make it through this, and everything will be sunshine again.

But will it ever be okay?

Finally, she falls asleep. Slow, so I don't wake her, I slide my arms from underneath her body and drop into the chair by her bed.

A doctor who doesn't look a hell of a lot older than Mallory wanders into the room head down, studying a clipboard. Worried she'll wake Mallory; I stand and quietly approach her. She picks up her head and jumps back.

"She just fell asleep," I explain in a hushed voice.

"Are you Mr. Adams?" she whispers.

"Yeah, I just got here."

"Good. Good. She kept asking for you."

A few more bricks of guilt land in the emotional knapsack strapped to my back.

"Let me check a few things, then we can go out in the hallway and talk." Obviously, I can't stop her from doing what she came in here to do, so I hover, probably closer than appropriate. Even though she's the doctor, I can't stand anyone near Mallory. Waking her up, bothering her, poking at her when she needs to rest.

When the doctor finally finishes, I'm able let out a long breath and follow her into the hallway.

"All her vitals are good." She scribbles something on her clipboard.

"When she wakes up, I'll start her discharge—"

"She can go home already?"

"Yes. She might have some bleeding for a few days but she should be fine."

"Do you know what caused it?" I ask.

"There's no way to know for sure. Miscarriages are exceedingly common." She hurries to add, "It's not her fault or anything she did—"

"I didn't think it was." What kind of jerk do I look like? "Will she be okay?" I swallow hard. "Can we still have another baby?"

Her tense expression softens. "Whenever you're ready, it shouldn't be an issue. Most women will go on to have a healthy, full term pregnancy."

I blow out a breath. "Good. That's good. She really wants kids. She's so great with them... Jesus we didn't even know."

"I understand. That's not uncommon, either."

"What do I need to do for her?"

"Keep an eye on her. If the bleeding gets worse or doesn't stop after a week or so, she needs to see her doctor. She might be sad. Emotional. That's normal. Be patient with her. But if she's not moving past it, have her talk to someone."

"Okay."

What else should I ask? There has to be something. I've never been so at a loss for words.

"Go and sit with her." She pats my shoulder. "She shouldn't be alone."

Alone. What would have happened to Mallory if she'd been at home instead of on set? I wouldn't have known anything was wrong until I tried to call her and even then, I might have assumed she'd gone to bed early.

I return to her bedside, drop into my chair, hold her hand, and watch her until my eyelids start to droop.

CHAPTER FIFTY-TWO

Chaser

A shadow falls over the doorway, pulling me out of my half-sleep.

I glance up. "Are you fucking serious?" I growl and jump out of my chair.

Andrew steps back into the hallway, hiding his face between the over-sized bouquet of assorted white flowers in his hands. "Easy. I heard what happened. I just wanted to make sure she was okay. To make sure you're both okay."

I grab his elbow and lead him away from the door in case this conversation gets loud. "What the fuck are you doing here?"

The flowers rustle against his side. "Is she okay?"

An enormous part of me wants to tell him to fuck off. Mallory's not his problem or his business. But fuck if anyone else has shown up to check on us. Not that anyone even knows where we are or what happened.

"Yeah, the doctor said she's going to be fine."

"Pam said..."

"She lost our baby." I grind out the foreign words, not sure the impact of them has even hit me yet.

"Fuck, brother. I'm so sorry." He reaches out and awkwardly squeezes my shoulder. "Are you going to try again?"

I narrow my eyes. Why does he always have to be such a nosy bastard? "We weren't...we weren't *trying*. We didn't even know."

"Doesn't matter." He shrugs. "Still your kid. I'm really sorry, Chaser."

Andrew's somber demeanor knocks me off-balance. He's the kind of person I'd expect to make a "get out of jail free card" joke in this situation, not offer compassionate words. "Thanks."

"Do you need anything? Want me to bring you some stuff? Food?"

My stomach growls at the mention of food, but I refuse to eat until Mallory's able to. "Nah, we shouldn't be here much longer. They said they'll discharge her tonight."

"That seems soon?" He scrubs his hand over his cheek. "Do you need a ride home?"

Fuck, actually we do. But no matter how nice he's being right now, I sure as shit am not accepting a ride from Andrew.

"I'll send Benny over to pick you guys up," he says, as if he'd read my mind. "Have him bring some clothes for Mallory or whatever."

I try to hide my shock that he understands with a simple, "Thanks."

"I get why you still don't want me around her. But I want to help."

Exhaustion and too many emotions tug at me to argue. "Thanks."

We stare at each other for a few seconds, then stare at the walls, the ceiling, the floor. It's awkward as fuck. A somber Andrew is unnerving and let's face it, I still don't trust him as far as I can throw him.

"Here." He thrusts the flowers at me. "Tell her they're from you. I don't care. I wanted to do...something for her. That was the only thing I could think of."

"I'll tell her you stopped by," I promise.

346

"If you need something, call me. I'll send Benny over now, so when they let her go, you don't have to wait around."

"Thanks." I lift my chin. "Appreciate it."

Mallory's blinking and trying to sit up when I return.

"What's wrong? Are you okay?" I set the flowers down on the table by her bed and hurry to her side.

"No, I feel like a cement truck backed up over my lower half." Her gaze lands on the flowers. "You didn't have to do that."

Could I lie and never tell her about Andrew's visit? Sure. Is that the kind of man I am? Will I feel good about lying? No and no.

"They're from Andrew. He stopped by to check on you."

"Really?" Her tone's neutral, or maybe wary. "You didn't get into another fight?"

"No."

"God." She covers her face with her hands. "Pamela probably told him and everyone else."

"I doubt it. Well, maybe Andrew, I don't know. She was pretty shaken up." I pry her hands loose. "She's the one who called me so I could get my ass here."

"Oh." A quick smile flickers over her lips. "Well, we had a brief heart-to-heart this morning before..." Her jaw drops and her eyes water. "I passed out on set, Chaser. Bled everywhere. That's so..."

"Awful. Thank fuck they got you to the hospital so fast."

"I vaguely remember...something." She shakes her head. "I've never been in so much pain before. Or so embarrassed."

Christ, I'd do anything to have taken that pain on for her. "Try not to worry about anything right now. There's nothing to be embarrassed about. You need rest."

"I need to be on set tomorrow."

"No. You don't." I press my finger to her lips when she opens her mouth to protest. "You need to rest and recover. It's not optional."

She dozes again for a while. A nurse comes in to check on

her, assuring me everything's fine and they'll be discharging us soon.

Someone raps their knuckles on the open door and clears their throat. "Chaser?"

I turn to find Benny filling up the doorway and walk over to shake his hand. "Hey. Thanks for this."

"No problem." He jerks his thumb to the left. "I'll park myself in the waiting room. When you're ready to go, say the word." He holds up a plain, brown paper bag. "Brought some sweats for her."

"Thanks."

He peers around me. "Hey, Mallory. You doing all right?"

She blinks at him, then me before finally answering. "Getting there."

"See you in a bit." He waves at us and turns away.

"What's Benny doing here?" Mallory whispers.

"Andrew sent him. Knew we'd need a ride."

"Oh." She yawns. "That was nice of him. I guess."

I set the bag on the bedside table and pick through the contents. Nothing fancy. Plain gray sweatpants. Sweatshirt. White canvas shoes and socks. Benny probably stopped at the first store he saw and grabbed stuff off the racks. Still, I'm grateful I don't have to leave Mallory's side to search for clothes.

My mouth twists into a grin when I reach the bottom of the bag. Benny even tossed in a cheap, over-sized pair of sunglasses and a black baseball cap. I hold them up. "Benny's got you covered."

"Aw, that was so sweet."

"Knock. Knock." A soft voice draws our attention to the door. The woman holds up Mallory's purse and another bag of stuff. "I'm sorry I couldn't get here sooner."

"That's okay, Cindy." Mallory waves her inside.

"Are you all right?" She leans over and pulls Mallory in for a gentle hug. "I was so worried about you. And Sean was a total dick. Wouldn't tell us anything. He was livid that Pamela took off with you. I should've gone too. But he wouldn't let anyone else leave the set. I'm so sorry." Her quick, bumbling rush of words is way more information than Mallory needs right now. I gently touch her shoulder and she quiets down. "Sorry. How are you feeling?"

"Better than I was." Mallory's face twists into a grimace. "But still in a lot of pain."

"Well, Sean said they're going to shoot around your parts, so don't worry about doing anything but getting better for the rest of the week."

Week. Fuck that. She'll take as long as she needs and Sean or whoever *Shallow End's* director-of-the-week is can fuck the hell off if he thinks Mallory's coming back a minute sooner.

After Cindy leaves, a different doctor examines Mallory and declares she's ready to go home.

While I'm helping Mallory get dressed, an orderly wheels in a chair and promises to return in a few minutes.

"Wait here." I set Mallory on the edge of the bed and help her put on her sneakers. "I'm going to let Benny know we're ready to leave so he can get the car."

She winces. "I'm not going anywhere. Trust me."

Benny tosses the magazine in his hands to the side when I pop into the waiting room. "We're ready to leave. Orderly's got a wheelchair for her."

"Cool." He jumps up and I walk him over to the elevator. "Uh, look," he mumbles, "There were some paparazzi waiting out front when I got here. I'm going to pull the car to the back entrance. Orderly should know where to take you. They're used to this—"

"Wait a minute. Used to what? Paparazzi? For us?"

"Yeah, I think so." He glances away.

"Shit." That's the last thing Mallory needs. "Okay. I'll meet you around back. Thanks." I slap his shoulder and return to

Mallory's room. She's waiting in the wheelchair, her purse, and a few other plastic bags gathered in her lap while she finishes signing a clipboard full of forms.

She glances up with tired eyes and gives me a half-smile. "I already need a nap."

"Let's go." I nod to the orderly. "We're getting picked up out back. You know where to go?"

"Yup. That's probably best, sir. Follow me."

The day's long gone. It's dark. The mild air feels good after being in the stale hospital all afternoon. At the end of the long, curving sidewalk, Benny's bright, red Toyota 4Runner shimmers under the parking lot lights. He jumps out and hurries to open the back door. The truck's lifted so I have to give Mallory a boost. She's stoic and doesn't make a sound until she's situated. No one bothers us.

The vehicle's awkwardly quiet. What the hell are we supposed to talk about? I know Benny from the tour but it's not like we're best buds. I end up turning around to check on Mallory about a hundred times.

I'm still facing her when we turn onto our little street.

"Fuck," Benny mumbles and slaps his palm over the horn. "Move, asshole."

"What's going on?" I peer out the window at the small crowd of reporters covering our front lawn. "What the fuck are they doing?"

He shrugs but it's more of a nervous jiggle. "I, uh, they were all over Andrew's place earlier too. Guess they found their way down here."

"Why? What's their problem?"

He keeps staring straight ahead. "I don't know."

A sick feeling settles in my gut.

Benny nudges his truck into our driveway. "Stay there. I'm going to walk you up to the door," he promises.

"Why are there so many people on our lawn?" Mallory's sleepy whisper is barely audible over all the noise from outside.

"I don't know. Stupid tabloid assholes."

"Because of me? That's sick. Who does that?" At least she sounds more angry than sad, although I'd prefer neither.

Benny opens my door and then the back door, shielding us from anyone who tries to get too close. "Back the fuck off," he growls. "You're trespassing."

Ignoring everything around us, I reach in and slip my arms under Mallory. "Hang on to me." I press a quick kiss to her cheek and lift her out of the truck.

"Mallory! Are you okay? Do you want to tell us what happened?" a woman shouts.

"Get the fuck out of our way," Benny barks.

Mallory wraps her arms tight around my neck and buries her head against my shoulder. "Why are they doing this?" she whispers.

"I don't know."

Benny shoves photographers right and left, clearing a path for me to follow behind him. Flashbulbs go off. Lawsuits are threatened. A camera cracks and shatters against the sidewalk. Finally, we make it inside the house.

Benny casts a nervous glance at the door. "You need me to stay, Chaser?"

"No, I think we'll be fine." I set Mallory down on the couch and she drops her bags on the floor.

"You really might want to think about hiring someone until this dies down," Benny says. "I know a guy."

"We'll be okay. Thanks, though." I can always call on my MC brothers if this continues.

He slips a card in my hand. "If you need something, call me. Don't worry about what time it is, okay?"

"I will. Thank you, man. Tell Andrew I said thanks, too. Okay?"

"You know it."

The noise and questions start up again when we open the

door. Benny slips out into the crowd. I slam the door shut, throwing all the locks into place.

Mallory slumps against the couch and closes her eyes.

"Let's put you to bed," I offer, picking her up off the couch.

CHAPTER FIFTY-THREE

Mallory

Zapped of energy, I can barely move. I'm uncomfortable, though. Need to visit the bathroom and change the stupid pads the hospital gave me. Chaser carrying me around everywhere isn't helping.

"I need to do a few things, first." I push at his arm, hoping he'll take a hint and set me down.

But Chaser's not a take-the-hint man. He's all direct words and actions.

"What do you need, little dove? Tell me."

Heat burns my cheeks. "Female stuff." I point to one of the bags on the floor I'd brought home from the hospital. "I need some...things. Don't worry about it."

He leans in and kisses my forehead. "I'm sorry to tell you but I'm not one of those men who runs screaming from the room at the words 'female stuff' and I worry about everything when it comes to you."

Of course that's his answer. "Can't you leave me to wallow in my misery and shame alone?"

"No." He dips down and scoops up the bag.

Thankfully, he does drop me off at the bathroom and give me privacy. I take care of myself and give the shower a longing stare but there's no way I can stand up for that long.

Chaser knocks on the door. "Ready for bed?"

"Yes." I open the door and he hands me a glass of water.

"You need to eat something before you take those pain meds."

I drop my gaze to the cup of yogurt and spoon in his other hand. "Okay."

I wobble my way into the bedroom on my own and perch on the edge of the bed to spoon down some of the yogurt before accepting the pain pills. "Thank you."

He tucks me in and as soon as my head hits the pillow, I'm drifting away.

Sometime later, the bed dips and shifts behind me.

"Chaser?"

"Right here." He gently curls himself around my body and kisses my shoulder.

"Thank you."

"You never have to thank me." He nuzzles against my neck. "I'm so sorry, I wasn't here, Mallory."

I turn so we're facing each other and rest my forehead against his chin. "I'm happy you're here now."

The day's events or maybe the pain pills must be making me slow. I tip my head back. "Oh my God, you're missing shows, aren't you? I didn't—"

"Shhh." He places one finger over my lips. "Today was an off day. It doesn't matter, anyway. Nick will fill in for me tomorrow night."

I scowl and pull back. "He's not half the guitar player you are."

He chuckles and leans in again, pressing his lips to my forehead. "Nothing in the world is more important than being with my girl, right now."

PAIN WAKES ME THE NEXT MORNING.

I lurch my way into the bathroom, take care of myself and open the door to find Chaser waiting for me. "This is a little creepy, Chaser."

"What? That I'm worried about you?"

"I'm too big to fall in the toilet and drown," I mutter as I shuffle back to bed.

Behind me, he chuckles and follows. "Do you need anything?"

"Sleep. More pain meds."

I must drift off because a few minutes later, he's nudging something cool into my hand and asking me to sit up. My stomach lurches at the yogurt. "Ugh, I can't eat any more of that."

"I don't know what else to give you. You can't take those pills on an empty stomach."

My head's pounding. I sip some water and eat as much of the yogurt as I can tolerate, then swallow the pills.

Chaser crawls back into bed with me.

I peer over at him. Usually, he's up and practicing guitar by now. "What are you doing?"

"It's still early. I'm going back to sleep." He holds out his arms. "Come here."

I scoot over, snuggling up against his warm body. "Sorry, I'm so cranky," I whisper.

"You can be as cranky as you need to be." He runs his hand over my hair. "Don't ever apologize to me."

Tears sting my eyes and my nose twitches. "I'm sorry."

"Shhh. Why?"

"I screwed up. I wasn't supposed to get pregnant. How could I not even know? I feel awful. I shouldn't be so upset but I'm so...*sad*."

"You're allowed to feel however you need to feel." He squeezes me tighter.

I run my hand over my side. "The one thing my body's designed to do, I can't even do right. I'm so...*embarrassed* that I screwed it up."

His eyes narrow and he cups my head pulling me closer until our foreheads touch. "You didn't screw up anything. That's not your only purpose in life."

"But I want to have a baby someday. I want to be a mother. What if I can't?"

It doesn't seem to matter to Chaser that my rambling complaints all contradict each other. He has a gentle, patient answer for everything.

"We're going to be fine. The doctor said most women go on to have totally normal pregnancies."

"Really?" I peer up at him. "You asked the doctor about that?"

"Yes."

"Oh." I don't understand why I can't let this go. "What if I hadn't...what if today hadn't happened?"

"What do you mean?"

"What would we have done? I'm on set for twelve, fifteen hours a day some days. You're away on tour. I don't want other people raising our children, Chaser. I had that and I hated it."

He blows out a long breath, ruffling my hair. "I don't know."

"Would you have been angry with me?"

"Fuck no," he growls. "Mistakes happen. You need two people to make a baby, so how could I be mad at you?"

I shrug, thinking over something his father once said to me. "I wouldn't want you to think I tried to trap you."

"Trap *me*? We're engaged." He laughs so hard, the bed shakes. "Mallory, you're so embedded in my soul, you'll never shake me loose. My heart's been in your hands since the day we met."

The intensity and passion behind his words melts my remaining fears.

356

"I want to marry you. Spend the rest of my life with you." He sighs and reaches down, twining our fingers together. "You're right, though. A baby right now would be tough. I hate leaving you so much. I can't imagine leaving you *and* our child to go off on tour." He wiggles his eyebrows. "I'll need to start selling a hell of a lot more albums so I can afford an extra tour bus for my family."

My lips twitch into a smile and I rest my forehead on his chest. "You'd do that? It's not very rock-n-roll."

"Rock-n-roll is whatever the fuck I say it is."

"Now, *that's* a very rock-n-roll answer."

"Anything else bothering you?"

"Everything's bothering me."

"Anything you want to talk to me about?" He shifts, reaching over me to pick up the discharge papers off my nightstand. "Anything you need me to run out and grab?"

"Give me that." I snatch the papers away, folding them up and tossing them behind me. "No. They sent me home with...stuff."

Instead of answering he frowns at his hand, twisting and wiggling his fingers. "So, many, paper cuts. What's the big deal?"

"This whole experience has been humiliating enough. I've never been asked so many personal questions and felt so invaded."

"I hate to break this to you, Mallory." He tickles his fingers over my arm. "But from what I've heard, if you *really* want to have a baby, the stork doesn't deliver them. You're going to have lots of people up in your business. It's not the neat and clean process shown on television. It's messy."

"How do you have so much knowledge about the subject?"

He shrugs. "I paid attention in biology class."

"I bet you did." I poke his side. "I didn't learn about that until seventh grade. And even then, it was a bizarre, secret that we were never supposed to talk about."

"Your mother—" He stops himself and shakes his head. "I'm sorry."

Just the mention of my mother brings me right back to that scared thirteen-year-old girl, desperately wishing someone would explain what was happening to my body. "My father wasn't as evolved as you seem to be."

He smirks. "No kidding."

"And my aunt told me it was a shameful secret I should never, ever discuss with anyone."

"That's really fucked up. You shouldn't be embarrassed about something that's just...nature."

"I guess."

"Didn't your father take you to the doctor?"

"Yeah, but my regular, eighty-year-old pediatrician. He gave me a book once about my changing body but it was all about how to cover up weird body smells and stuff. Nothing helpful. I didn't see a...you know, *girl doctor*, until I came out here."

"I hope you understand I'm not like that. If we have girls, I don't ever want them to be ashamed of anything." He pauses and seems to consider a few scenarios. "Although, you should definitely still have that talk with them."

"You'd want daughters?"

"Hell, yeah, I'd love a couple little girls who look just like you."

"A couple? No sons?"

He shrugs. "I don't think we can really pick and choose. One of each sounds nice, though."

"I like the sound of that."

Chaser

Our talk seemed to wear Mallory out. I hate leaving her side but I can't delay calling the band any longer. I stop to watch her sleeping peacefully for a few seconds before ducking out of the bedroom.

It takes a several phone calls to track down the band's hotel. I'd left my itinerary along with everything else in my room.

Finally, I get Alvin on the line and explain what happened as plainly as possible.

"Is Mallory okay?"

"We're getting there. I'm going to be a few more days, though."

He's silent. Alvin's not one to thoughtlessly run his mouth, but I expected him to say something. "Bro, have you watched any of the tabloid shows?"

"Fuck no. Why would I watch that shit?"

"I think you should have a look tonight. *Dirty Headlines* is running a piece about you guys at seven."

"About my fiancée's miscarriage? Why?"

"It's not quite about that." There's a muffled rustling sound in the background. Alvin yelps.

"Alvin?"

He comes back on the line. "Jacob wants to talk to you."

Just what I need.

"Chaser! Where are you?" Jacob shouts. "You've gotta get here for tonight's show."

I glance at the clock. Even if I left right now, there's no way I'd make it on time. "Can't. I'm sorry. I don't know if Alvin told you, but—"

"Alvin didn't need to tell us anything. Why the fuck were you even trying to have a kid right now?" His vile outburst shouldn't surprise me but I pull the phone away from my ear and stare at it for a few seconds. He's still ranting when I return. "We're on tour for the next few months! Not the time to be trying to spit out a damn kid!"

"We weren't 'trying', you asshole. And it's—"

"Then what's the fucking problem? Get your god damn ass—"

"Fuck you." Blind with rage, I slam the phone down and yank the plug out of the wall.

"What's wrong?" Mallory's soft voice extinguishes my fury.

I toss the phone and cord aside. "Nothing. Why are you up? Come on, let's go back to bed."

She holds out her hands, stopping me in my tracks. "I can't. I hurt all over and feel gross. I need a shower."

"All right. Let's get you showered up."

The corners of her mouth tilt up a fraction, then her gaze lands on the massacred phone. "Was that the band? Are they upset? Do you need to go?"

"It was Jacob. He's an asshole. And I'm not going anywhere."

"Chaser." Her gentle, reasonable tone triggers my fight response.

"No. Not up for discussion. I can't right now." I take a few breaths. "I need to be with you."

The doorbell rings and without thinking, I open the door. "Chaser! Can I ask you a few questions?" a reporter shouts. "Did Mallory have—"

"Get the fuck off my property." I slam the door shut.

"What's going on?"

"Apparently our tragedy is newsworthy."

"What's wrong with people? Why?"

"I don't know." I stare at the door and the walls around us. The doorbell rings again.

Mallory bites her lip. Her scared, tired eyes dart around the room. Jesus, after everything she just went through, she doesn't need this extra stress.

"We can't stay here."

"Where should we go?" she asks.

"Home. Let's go home."

CHAPTER FIFTY-FOUR

Chaser

Not a trace of guilt follows me to the airport. There's a flight that would take me within hours of where we're playing tonight. If there are no delays, I could probably get there in time to go on stage.

I book two flights home instead.

Am I destroying everything I've worked so hard for? A couple years ago, if you'd told me I'd leave in the middle of a headlining tour, I would've laughed. Now, other things just seem more important. I can't explain it and I won't defend it.

Mallory sleeps on the long flight to New York. I have to gently shake her awake when we land.

My father meets us at the gate and envelopes her in a gentle hug.

I hadn't given him a lot of details when I called him and asked him to pick us up at the airport. Maybe he saw the news and understood my need to come home. No one should know how to find us here.

"Welcome home." He pulls back and stares down at her. "Everything's gonna be okay, princess."

She gives him a weak smile and nods.

"You okay?" he asks, clasping my shoulder.

Am I?

The whirlwind of emotions I've been through the last few days hasn't begun to settle. My biggest concern is Mallory's health. The doctors assured us that physically, she was fine to travel.

Emotionally, I'm not so sure. Not after all the reporters clogging up our driveway, shouting obnoxious questions at us.

The ride to the house is quiet. Mallory rests her head on my shoulder and closes her eyes.

"House is all ready for you," my father says. "Her car's there. If you need to get anything."

I snort. "You know I can barely drive that thing. My knees are too far up in the dash to work the clutch."

"I'll get someone to come pick me up and leave the truck."

"You don't have to. We'll be fine."

"Doe brought groceries but you might need other things." He glances over at Mallory. "I don't know."

"I'll worry about it later."

At the house, Mallory sways on her feet. I get her to drink a glass of water before taking her upstairs and tucking her into bed. "I'll be right downstairs."

My father's pacing in the kitchen when I return.

"She okay?"

"She seemed to be doing better until the circus of reporters wouldn't leave us alone."

"Then you better keep her away from the television," he warns. "And grocery store magazine racks."

"Seriously? All the way out here?"

He tosses a thin, glossy entertainment rag at me. One of those an-alien-ate-my-baby sort of papers. It's wrinkled from being rolled up and shoved in someone's pocket but not enough to obscure the picture on the front.

Mallory standing in between Andrew and me. Backstage at

one of our shows. Her bright, beautiful smile obscene against the ugly headline.

Whose baby was she carrying?

"Motherfuckers." I squeeze my eyes shut, wishing we hadn't been so quick to leave L.A. Seems there are a few reporters I'd like to have a word with.

My father's staring at me when I open my eyes. As if he's waiting for some sort of answer. Maybe it's exhaustion or misdirected fury but I grab a handful of his shirt and shove him. Hard.

His back hits the wall with a thud and his eyes widen.

"Don't you fucking *dare* question her," I snarl. "The baby was *mine*."

He drops his gaze to where his shirt's in my clenched fist and after a moment I release him.

"I can't imagine the grief you're going through right now, son, so I'll let that slide." He adjusts his cut. "Someone planted that article. You got any idea who would do something like that?"

I flick the magazine across the table. "Could be anyone. A reporter. Andrew's ex. Take your pick."

"Andrew?"

He's a first-class motherfucker for sure but we came to an understanding. Besides, as big of an asshole as he is, deep down in his twisted soul, he cares about Mallory. I can't picture him showing up to the hospital with flowers and offers to help us out, then turning around and hurting her on purpose.

"He'd be at the bottom of my list of suspects."

"Well, last thing I need is her father getting wind of it."

Laughter bursts from my lungs at the absurdity of his concern. "I don't think they allow tabloids in prison, Dad."

He doesn't join in on my merriment. "Don't fool yourself."

"Fuck." I run my fingers through my hair. "He's the least of my worries right now. I left in the middle of a tour. The band's going to kill me. Jacob's a fucking mess. And I'm out of fucks for anything besides Mallory right now."

"You need me to call anyone for you?"

I'm too old to have my daddy making phone calls for me, but I still give him Thom's number.

"Tell him I'll try to make Atlanta on Friday. If Nick can fill in for me, I'm fine with it."

"All right." He pats my shoulder. "Go take care of your girl."

After he leaves, I prowl through the house, checking the doors and windows. Locking everything up tight. I leave one lamp on in the living room, then make my way upstairs.

Mallory's curled on her side but stirs as I crawl into bed. "Is your dad okay?" she whispers.

"Shh, he's fine. Don't worry about him." I kiss her shoulder. "Are you okay? Need anything?"

"Will you hold me until I fall back asleep?"

We're going to be okay. We'll make it through this no matter what.

I wrap my arm around her, pulling her close. "I'll hold onto you forever."

CHAPTER FIFTY-FIVE

Chaser

Maybe my father's worried I'm brooding too much or need to get out of the house. The next afternoon, he invites me to sit down at the table with the club for church. And by "invites" I mean "orders."

"All right." He holds his hands up, halting the conversation going around the table. "Our last two visits with the Lost Kings went well. Now it's time we extend the same courtesy—"

"Brother, I gotta object here," Mouse interrupts. "No matter how much titty-fuckin' we all did down at Crystal Ball, I don't fuckin' trust their current president."

Well, I guess I didn't miss anything on the club's last run to Empire. Every time my club visits Crystal Ball, the brothers come home and start bugging my dad to open up our own strip club.

"Good, 'cause Ruger ain't coming. His SAA is the one making the trip."

"That's even worse," Tally says. "Their prez wants to do business here but can't drag his lazy ass out and show us some respect."

"Let's see what Grinder has to say before we blow off the Lost Kings. Bishop's stopping by too." My father shrugs a little too casually. "Maybe our three clubs can work out something that benefits everyone."

"Great, Bishop and Grinder will probably kill each other. Problem solved." Mouse slaps his hands together. "Saints and Kings don't mix well."

My father snorts. "They're two obstinate fuckers, aren't they?" He points down the table at Trick. "Stay the fuck away from Bishop's ol' lady this weekend. I don't need more bullshit in this clubhouse over that fuckin' whore."

"Nora isn't a whore," Trick grumbles.

My father's expression doesn't change.

"Fine." Trick throws his hands in the air. "I won't tell her about the party. Nothing I can do if Bishop tells her."

I roll my eyes to the ceiling. Hell help that fucking woman if she comes near Mallory again.

My father asks me to stick around after the meeting. "I know you're headed to Atlanta for your show. Think you'll be back for the weekend?"

"Sounds like you need me to." I tap the table again. "Since so many different clubs are stopping by."

"We'll try to keep things friendly and casual."

"Mallory's staying here. You think you or Doe can check up on her?"

"You really need to ask?"

CHAPTER FIFTY-SIX

Chaser

I was only gone for a couple of days, yet the atmosphere's turned sour when I catch up with the tour.

"Are they really that pissed at me?" I ask Alvin.

"You know how Jacob and Garrett are. They don't get normal, human emotions and shit."

"Who am I kidding, things were starting to go off the rails before I left."

"True." He pats my back. "Mallory doing okay?"

"Yeah, she seemed to be feeling better when I left." Getting her out of L.A. was the smart decision. "Kept her away from papers and tabloid shows."

He shakes his head. "Those stories were so bogus. No one believes them. You know that, right?"

"I don't give a fuck what anyone believes. I know the truth."

"Andrew's a dick for not stepping forward and squashing the rumors immediately."

"Nah, that would've made it worse." I snort out a humorless laugh. "Besides, now that he doesn't need me to collaborate with

367

and he's not trying to worm his way into Mallory's pants, he's got no reason to battle the press on our behalf."

"Yeah, but this was really ugly." Alvin shoves his hands in his pockets.

"He came to visit in the hospital."

"Seriously? Surprised you didn't tear off his head and use it as a bowling ball."

So am I. "He helped us out. Seemed sincere. I didn't have any extra fucks to give at the time, you know?"

"Good. Doubt we'll be touring with them anytime soon."

"Amen to that."

"No, I mean, rumor is Vicious Vandals are breaking up. Andrew and Vinnie are fighting Kyle and Boner over rights to the band's name and everything. It'll probably go to court and be a huge mess from what Thom says."

"Holy shit, really?"

"Yup." He lifts his chin. "Be real with me, you think it'll come to that for us one day?"

Jesus, this conversation took a sharp detour. A year ago, I wouldn't have hesitated to say no. "What makes you ask that?"

"Ah, the old answer a question with a question. That's not a good sign, Chaser."

"That's not an answer, Alvin."

He stares down at the ground. "You and I have known each other a long time. I don't want to play with anyone else."

I lightly punch his shoulder. "Same, brother."

"This isn't me trying to guilt you." He tips his head up and the serious expression he's wearing seems so foreign. "It was disorienting having Nick take your place. We're supposed to be family. The shows should've been cancelled so we could support you guys."

"Aw, fuck, brother." I pull him in for a quick hug and pat his back. "Thanks for saying that."

"I mean it," he mumbles.

"I know you do." I draw back, still holding onto his shoulders. "We've always said the show has to go on. It's okay."

He nods and a hint of his usual playful grin returns. "Nick's been shitting bricks that you wouldn't get here tonight."

"Poor kid. How'd he do?"

Alvin shrugs. "He's not you. But he did all right. First night he played everything straight like a perfect rendition of our studio album."

"Yeah?" I chuckle at that, impressed he knows our material that well.

"Next night he added his own flair." Alvin holds up his hands. "Nothing crazy."

"Cool." I'm surprised how much I'm *not* bothered by it. I can't decide if it's a sign of maturity or impending doom.

Before the show, I find Nick backstage and thank him for filling in for me.

"No problem, Chaser. I didn't do your sound justice. But I tried."

"I'm sure you were great. I really appreciate it."

"Hey." He reaches out and steps closer. "I'm sorry about what happened."

"Thanks."

Jacob and Garrett roll into the arena close to the time we're supposed to go on stage. After skipping out on the last couple shows, I feel like I've lost the moral high ground so, I keep my mouth shut about it.

Jacob wraps his fingers around my arm and drags me into a semi-quiet corner backstage.

"What's going on?" I shake him off, still pissed about his shitty attitude last time we spoke on the phone.

He laces his fingers behind his head and stares up at the ceiling for a few beats.

"Jacob?" I prompt.

"I'm sorry."

My shoulders drop and I blow out a breath.

"I'm not gonna make excuses," he continues. "I felt like shit after we hung up but I didn't want to make things worse."

"Thanks. I'm sorry it seemed like I took off in the middle of our tour. But I wouldn't have been any good to the band."

"Is Mallory..." He shrugs. "Is she all right?"

"She'll be fine. I'm flying home tomorrow morning since we had the day off anyway. But I'll meet up with you in Vegas and we'll get back to normal after that."

"Cool." A devilish smile curls his lips. "Not like you want to party with us anymore, anyway."

Shit. As soon as he says it, I flash back to what was going down when I took off. "About that, what happened? You were doing so well."

"Christ, Chaser. You come back to lecture me? I'm fine."

We need to be on stage in about five seconds, so we'll have to argue about this another time. "No lecture, bro. Just worried about you."

"Worry about the show." He flashes a crooked grin. "You don't want us to replace you with Nick permanently, do you?"

"Fuck off."

He chuckles and strolls away.

Maybe I'm tired or still numb from everything, but an air of indifference clings to me all night. My own playing lacks any "flair" as Alvin put it.

Afterward, Jacob's twitchy and eager to leave the arena. I climb onto the tour bus weary and ready to crawl into my bunk and pass out.

A short time later, the bus rolls to a stop. I pull back the curtain. "Why are we stopped?"

Robbie shrugs at me helplessly. "Jacob said he needed something."

"Jesus Christ." I slam my fist against the bottom of Alvin's bunk.

"What?" he groans.

"Get up."

I throw on some clothes and toss Garrett's curtain open. Empty. "Motherfuck."

Alvin and I peer out the window at the seedy gas station. Place doesn't look like it's been open for business in years. "Why here?" I ask Robbie.

"I don't know. He gave me the address earlier."

"Fuck." I grab my small flashlight.

Alvin and I step off the bus and stare at the building until our eyes adjust to the darkness.

"Too fucking creepy to be a whorehouse," Alvin quips.

"Yeah, but perfect for a shooting gallery."

"Ah, fuck. He hasn't touched smack in months."

We walk over the cracked blacktop, glancing at the half-assed cars thrown into random spots. An orange glow lights up the inside of one car and I stop to check if Jacob or Garrett are inside.

"Get the fuck out of here." A scraggly blonde girl rolls up the car window. A puff of burning chemical stench hangs in the air.

"Shit." Alvin grabs my arm, tugging me away from the car and toward the building. "People going in the side door."

Place must've operated as a garage at some point. Inside, people are spread out over the broken concrete floor, stained and sticky with motor oil and years of accumulated filth.

Jacob's off to the side, sitting cross-legged on a pile of raggedy blankets with Garrett pacing behind him.

Ignoring the scene around us, I march over to Jacob and kick his booted foot. "What the fuck are you doing here?"

"Piss off," Jacob says in a weak imitation of Garrett's accent. He giggles and stares up at Garrett. "How'd I do?"

"Shitty, come on. Let's go, fucker." Garrett grips Jacob's arms and attempts to lift him.

"No way," Jacob argues.

I shoot a glare at Garrett. "Why are we here?"

He gives me a helpless shrug. "I don't know. He was gettin'

off the bus one way or another." He glances around the space. "I didn't want him going alone."

"Fuck. Okay." I scrub my hands over my face. "You should've woken me up."

"Number two. On the Hot 100." Jacob thrusts two fingers near my face. "And we never properly celebrated."

"Seriously?" Alvin kicks Jacob's other foot. "We had a party thrown for us. How much more do you need?"

"Jacob, come on, let's go." The vibes in this place are beyond bad. I'm convinced that if I can get him back on the bus, he'll be fine. Everything will be okay. We can forget this happened.

"Fuck that. I'm not going anywhere." He puts a pipe to his lips and inhales with suicidal urgency.

"When did this start?" I ask Garrett.

"Don't know. The Iron Kiss guys brought some to our room one night. He's been on about it ever since."

"That's great." So much for all the assurances Thom gave us.

"They know how to party." Jacob raises one fist in the air.

I glance around the filthy old garage. "Yeah, some party."

His high must be fading. He looks at our surroundings and holds out his hand for Garrett to pull him up off the floor.

"Can we go now?" Garrett begs. "Please."

"Let me pick up another rock." Jacob shoves Garrett and stumbles away.

"Don't lose sight of him," I warn Garrett. I slap Alvin's chest. "Stay here. I'm gonna grab Robbie."

Some skinny guy's prowling around our tour bus, testing the door. Just what we need—to get jacked in the middle of cracktown.

"Get the fuck out of here!" I shout and the guy skitters away. I pound my fist on the door and Robbie opens it. "You need to go get Jacob. I don't care if you have to knock him out and sling him over your fucking shoulder."

"Chaser, I don't want to leave the bus here."

"All set!" Jacob hollers across the parking lot. He holds up a handful of clear plastic baggies. Great. Our very own pied piper about to lure all the crackheads to our bus.

Completely stupefied about the wrong turn our night took, I just watch Jacob trip up the stairs onto the bus like it's no big deal.

I promised my dad and Mallory I'd be back tomorrow but now I'm afraid to leave.

CHAPTER FIFTY-SEVEN

Mallory

Cool air hits my back. The bed dips. "I'm home, little dove."

"Chaser?" Groggy and somewhere between asleep and awake, I turn over, praying I'm not dreaming.

"Oh!" I sit up and glance at the clock. "Wow. I only meant to take a quick nap."

"You need the rest." He sits with his back against the headboard and holds out his arms. "Come here."

I snuggle up to him, resting my head on his chest. "When did you get here?"

"Dad just dropped me off. Told him I'll be by the clubhouse in a little while. Needed to see you first."

"How was the show?"

"The show itself was fine." He groans and runs his hand over his face. "Afterward was a bad mash-up of a horror flick and an after school special."

"Good grief." I bite my fist after Chaser finishes his story. "What are you going to do?"

"I don't know." He cuddles me closer. "We still have a couple of months left. I don't see how we finish the tour with him dragging us off to every trap house some random crackhead tells him about."

I squeeze his arm and run my hand up and down, hoping he won't be offended. "Were you okay?"

"Fuck," he groans. "Last night was so...seedy and bizarre, partaking in any of it was the last thing on my mind."

"Well, I guess one good thing came out of your adventure."

"The *only* good thing. I was really torn leaving this morning. Two days off? I don't even want to know what kind of trouble Jacob will drag them into."

"I wish Alvin had come home with you."

"I offered." He blows out a breath. "Fuck, we have the *Elimination Date* premiere coming up. He's gotta get himself in check before then."

"Everything's going so good for you guys. Finally. I don't understand—"

"Put it out of your head." He runs his fingers through my hair. "You have enough to worry about right now. Are you sure you're up for this party tonight?"

"I've actually been looking forward to it. I went over and helped Doe last night."

"You didn't have to do that."

"I wanted to." I glance over at the closet. "I'm not wearing anything fancy though."

"It's just a mixer. Nothing fancy required."

"That creep Tyler isn't coming, is he?"

He chuckles and presses a finger to my lips. "No, and don't say that to anyone besides me."

I flick my gaze up. "I'm not stupid. You said another club was coming too."

"The Lost Kings MC. We're on better terms with them. Probably because their territory's about four hours away."

"Good buffer."

"Still, be careful. I'll be with you most of the night. But just in case, watch who you talk to and how much information you divulge. Even innocuous conversation with their old ladies—if they bring any."

WHILE THINGS MIGHT GET ROWDY TONIGHT, THE CLUBHOUSE is fairly quiet when we arrive a few hours later. The visiting club only showed up with a few members. Chaser makes a few introductions before his father calls him away to help with something.

I wander over to the bar, observing the clubhouse in its pre-party state.

The youngest member of the visiting club ambles my way.

"You're the chick from the 'Candy Jar' video, right?" He looks me up and down in a salacious manner. The kid can't be more than sixteen, but he already seems to be quite the sweet talker.

"How old are you?" I ask, placing a hand on my hip.

His mouth curls into a way-too-sure-of-himself smirk. "However old you need me to be, sweetness."

"You barely look old enough to drive." It's fun to humor him, and it certainly lifts some of the dark cloud I've been living under recently. But I probably shouldn't encourage his behavior. Chaser won't care about the kid's age. If he finds him flirting with me, he'll probably knock his teeth down his throat. "Either way, kid. I'm not available."

He runs his hand over his chin and looks me up and down again. "That's a shame—"

"Rock," an older biker snaps. "What the fuck you doing, hittin' on the future VP's ol' lady?" He glances down at me. "Sorry, sweetheart. I need to put a leash on this one."

I smile, recognizing him as the enforcer for the Lost Kings. "Hey, Grinder, right?" I jerk my chin toward the kid. "So, how old is little Romeo here?" I tease.

"*Rock*," the kid reminds me, as if I could forget. He gets

cuffed on the side of the head by Grinder and a warning to be respectful.

"What's up?" Chaser asks, slipping an arm around me.

I force a bright smile and pat his chest, making sure to flash my engagement ring. "Grinder was just introducing me to his...son?"

"My club sponsor," Rock corrects. Behind him, Grinder shakes his head and glances at the ceiling.

"When you patching in, kid?" Chaser asks.

"Few years," Grinder says. "Boy's still got a lot to learn."

I duck my head and chuckle. Chaser seems to pick up what was going down. He rumbles with laughter and reaches out to rough his hand over Rock's head, drawing a scowl from the kid. Chaser leans in closer. "Seems you got lots of stuff to learn. Like, at least be old enough to shave before you hit on another man's fiancée. Don't you think?"

Rock holds up his hands. "Don't have a cow, man."

Grinder smacks the kid on the back of the head and Rock has the decency to blush. "Didn't notice the ring," he mutters. "No disrespect intended."

Chaser

This kid probably deserves an ass-kicking. I'm too amused with his brashness to dish it out, though. Grown ass men hitting on her or being disrespectful absolutely require a beating. But Mallory seemed more amused than uncomfortable by the kid's attention. Besides, what kind of pussy does it make me if I'm intimidated by some kid flirting with my ol' lady?

Mallory reaches up and kisses my cheek. "I'm going to say hi to Alicia." She smiles at Grinder and Rock. "I'll catch you two later."

"Sweet girl you got there, Chaser. Where'd you two meet?" Grinder asks. The words have the flavor of fatherly curiosity more than lechery, so I don't take offense.

"In L.A." I doubt Grinder knows or cares about my band, so I don't bother explaining how we met.

Rock glances up at his mentor. "She's the chick from the video where they turn the fire hose on—"

I bust out laughing. "That's her. We met on the set of that video. No one warned her we'd be hosing her down with freezing cold water. Thought she was gonna cry." I shrug and try to act casual about the day that changed my life for the better. "Tried to make it up to her by taking her for a ride."

Grinder rocks back on his heels. "Back of the bike will do it every time."

"Aren't you on a tour right now?" Rock asks.

The question stops me cold. What a shit week. "Yeah. We had a little time off. Mallory wanted to visit. My dad needed some help around here." I shrug.

"That's cool." Rock squints at me. "How you gonna be traveling with your band and be VP here?"

Grinder elbows the kid. "Mind your business."

It's a good question. One I can't answer right now, even if I wanted to. The band's had fun. Achieved some of what we set out to do.

I glance around the clubhouse. This will always be home. But I'm not sure if it's where we're meant to be right now.

My father opens the doors and motions for us to come inside the chapel. Grinder grips Rock's shoulders and steers him toward the bar. "Don't move," he orders.

I'm holding in my laughter when Grinder returns. "He's a bold little shit. What is he, fifteen? Sixteen?"

Grinder shakes his head. "Almost fourteen. Big for his age, so no one questions me 'bout having him 'round the club. Trying to keep him out of trouble. Thinks he's Don-fucking-Juan ever since he nailed his babysitter."

I burst out laughing. "Shit, are you sure the ol' ladies are safe with him on the prowl?" I joke.

"Yeah," he grumbles. "He'll behave. He recognized Mallory from that video, so I think he was a little star struck."

"He's not the first." I clap him on the back. "You're a good guy for looking out for the kid."

He glances back at the bar where the kid's staring straight ahead, sipping on a bottle of soda. "He'll be an asset to the club. A good leader one day. *If* he learns to keep his damn dick in his pants."

"Won't we all," I mutter, making Grinder laugh.

Even though we're laughing it up, I wonder what Grinder has in mind for the future of his club. Their current president, Ruger, keeps pushing them into riskier business deals and I imagine it's causing a lot of friction with their members. Ruger sent his SAA out here with only a few of his men. While our clubs get along, it sends a lukewarm message at a time we've been working to bring most of the outlaw clubs in the area together.

With the way law enforcement's been cracking down on motorcycle clubs lately, it's in all our interests to stay under the radar. A message not every outlaw accepts. Tonight's a test of sorts and I guess we'll see who passes.

CHAPTER FIFTY-EIGHT

Mallory

I emerge from the kitchen and find the chapel doors firmly closed and the clubhouse mostly empty. My gaze lands on the flirty young biker sitting at the bar all by himself.

"So, Rock." I sneak up behind him.

Either he heard me coming or he doesn't startle easily. He turns and stares at me with a raised eyebrow, patiently waiting for me to continue.

"You said you recognized me from 'Candy Jar'. How'd you *not* know I was with Chaser? Stories about us have been on MTV, in every music magazine, and tabloid for months now."

He snorts and shakes his head. "You think going to school and working for the club leaves me time for shit like sittin' around watching MTV and flipping through gossip rags? Please. I caught the video while I was manning the door at our strip club."

Feeling foolish, I blurt out the only question that comes to mind. "Aren't you a little young to be hanging out at a strip club?"

He shrugs and takes a swig of soda.

I tilt my head toward the chapel. "Why'd you get kicked out?"

"Never got invited in." He taps his plain black leather cut. "Not a patched member." He nods to one of the other prospects who came with the Lost Kings. "Not even a prospect yet. Grinder lets me be involved more than a regular prospect, but not today," he says, pride coloring his words. From the information I've gathered about the MC world, unless his father's a member, allowing him to be so involved at such a young age is unusual.

"Is your dad a member of the club too?"

"Nah, he's a useless drunk since my mom died."

My heart breaks at the matter-of-fact way he states such a tragic situation. While he came on strong at first, he doesn't seem to hold a grudge over me shutting him down. Now that he's not trying to impress me, he's actually kind and easy to talk to. "My mom died when I was a kid too," I say softly.

"Sorry." He stares at me with calm gray eyes for a few seconds. "Your father treat you okay?"

"More or less." I snort out a laugh. "He's in prison at the moment."

He doesn't even blink. "Got any other family?"

"Just Chaser. And the family he's given me."

"Sometimes it's not about the blood you share. It's about finding the ones willing to bleed *for* you."

Wow, such a painful lesson to have already learned at his age.

For a moment I'm speechless. "Some days I barely even remember what my mother looked like."

He nods slowly like he understands how hard it is to hold on to precious memories. He slides his hand in his pocket and pulls out his wallet. It takes a few seconds to find what he wants—a small picture of a beautiful young woman with long, shiny brown hair holding a little boy while they both smile at the camera.

"Is that you and your mom?"

The corners of his mouth lift. "Yeah." He slips the photo back in his wallet and tucks it away. "I like to keep her with me."

"I don't blame you. I managed to keep some photos of my mom too." When I stole money from my dad and ran away to California but that's hardly a story to share. "They're at our house in L.A., though."

He peers over at me. "L.A.'s a long way from here. You like it?"

I reach over the bar and grab a bottle of soda from one of the buckets of ice while considering his question. "Yes and no. California itself is beautiful. Vastly different from the East Coast."

"First thing I want to do when I can ride is take a cross-country trip."

"Chaser and I did it once. I don't remember much of it though."

My fingers slip on the bottle cap and I search for something to open it with. Rock takes it from me, pulling an opener from his pocket and popping the top before handing it back.

"Thanks."

"Go on." He circles his fingers in a continue-the-story-gesture. "California."

"Well, L.A. Hollywood. It's an ugly business."

"Sounds like you're successful, though."

Am I? And at what cost?

I glance away, uncomfortable talking about my success or lack thereof. "I'm like one, single speck of glitter in a bucketful that gets tossed around every week out there. For every successful big name actor you could name right now, there are probably two thousand struggling to make it."

"Shitty odds."

"It brought Chaser into my life, so I can't complain."

My soul searching is halted by the front door to the clubhouse slamming open.

Rock jumps off his stool, placing himself between me and the man who storms inside.

Before he gets himself into more trouble, I tap Rock's shoulder. "It's okay. I recognize him."

I wave. "Hi, Bishop. How are you?"

He gives me a quick chin lift. "The old man here?"

"They're in the chapel." Shit, what am I supposed to do? Stump's made it crystal clear I'm not supposed to disturb the men when they're at the table. Bishop's from another club, is he even allowed at the table? Lost Kings are there, so maybe? I bite my lip unsure of what to do.

Thankfully, Tally solves the problem for me. He pushes the door open and waves Bishop inside. Rock watches the men carefully until the chapel doors close.

"The Saints' SAA hang here frequently?" he asks in an almost too casual way.

"Once or twice," I answer vaguely. For some reason, I have a feeling that information falls under club business I shouldn't discuss with outsiders. Not even a horny thirteen-year-old who's a hell of a lot smarter than he looks.

I look him over once more. Maybe that was his purpose for coming today. Chat up Chaser's old lady and see what information he can bring back to the club?

He catches me studying him and a half-smile tugs at his lips.

Too bad the only stories he'll have to bring back to his club are about my dead mom and the perils of Hollywood.

CHAPTER FIFTY-NINE

Mallory

Our L.A. bungalow is dark and quiet when we return. Not a reporter in sight.

"Thank fuck," Chaser mutters as he opens the door.

There's a script for *Shallow End* waiting for me but I don't have the energy to look at it yet.

I press play on the answering machine and Marilyn's frustrated voice grates my nerves. "*Ocean Ave.* was picked up! You'll start filming after New Year's." There's a pause. "I have something else to discuss with you but I'd rather do it in person than over your machine. Call me when you're back."

"I only caught the last part, but it sounded ominous," Chaser says.

"Well, I'm too tired to call her now." I clap my hands together and let out a happy squee. "The part you missed is that *Ocean Ave.* got picked up for a full season."

"That's awesome." He hugs me tight and my body perks up from the closeness. "So proud of you."

Maybe I rub myself against him a little too long. He grasps my hands and pushes me back. For a second we stare at each other. He bites his lip. "I'm gonna go pack a bag for tomorrow."

I follow him into the bedroom. "I'm going to tell Marilyn I don't want to renew the contract for *Shallow End*."

He quirks an eyebrow. "Yeah?"

"I really hate it." I kneel on the bed next to the bag he's packing. "Chaser? Are you sure you still want me?"

He stops moving and stares at me. "Are you out of your damn mind? You're my girl. You'll always be my girl, no matter what." He drops the T-shirt in his hand and clutches my hip. "How could you ever question that?"

"After..."

He tips my head back. "Baby, I can't keep my damn eyes or hands off you. I'm hanging on by a thread over here." He runs his knuckles over my cheek. "I've been trying to give you space and time. That's all."

"Oh."

He leans in and presses a soft kiss against my lips. "I hate leaving again too."

While I'm sad he's leaving, Chaser's been my anchor in a tumultuous sea these past few days. I won't do anything to make him feel worse. "Vegas will probably be a fun show. I've never been. I wish I could go with you."

"But then I'd drag you off to the first chapel I find to get hitched and we wouldn't have your dream beach wedding."

"I'd be okay with that," I whisper.

"I wouldn't. You deserve to have everything the way you want it." He pauses. "And Vegas would probably be the worst place to have a secret wedding. Word would get back to your father in no time."

"I definitely don't want that."

He holds up two T-shirts. "Help me decide. Black or dark black?"

"What, no light black?" I tease. Leaning up, I run my hands over his chest. "What are you planning to wear to the *Elimination Date* premiere?"

"I'm not *planning* anything." He kisses the tip of my nose.

"That's a girl thing. I'll throw on the first clean items I find. Are you looking forward to it?"

"Yes. It'll be fun. I'll have you home for a few days. Get to hear your song in a movie."

"I'm not sure I'll believe it until I actually hear it. Still convinced we'll get a phone call saying it's been cut."

"They better not," I growl.

"So feisty." He kisses my cheek again and then returns to packing.

I SLAP MY ALARM OFF THE NEXT MORNING. NEXT TO ME, Chaser groans.

The script I tossed on my nightstand last night catches my attention. I never even flipped it open. I sit up and pluck it out of the envelope, flipping through pages for the scenes I'm in.

"You're cute when you're so focused," Chaser whispers.

I glance down and find him staring up at me. "Creep." I whap him with my script.

He curls his hand around my leg and pulls me closer. "What's happening this week on *Shallow End?*" He gasps and widens his eyes. "Will someone confront their stalker?"

I fall over laughing. "We've only had three stalker story lines."

"I love making you laugh." He tickles his fingers over my ribs and sits up, pulling me into his lap.

"Stop! I need to finish this." I frown, flipping through the pages. "I think they're bringing in sharks?"

"Isn't it set at a pool?"

"Yeah, but they let us go to the beach sometimes."

He starts humming the theme from *Jaws* and nibbles on my arm.

"You're..." I'm laughing too hard to finish my sentence.

"What, little dove?"

"Dangerous!" I slap his chest and try to wriggle out of his lap.

His eyes spark with the fire that excites me every time it blazes and his arm clamps around my waist, holding me tight. "Yeah, but I'm the *best* kind of dangerous."

"How's that?" I gasp, rubbing myself against him.

He runs his fingers under the edge of my underwear, slowly peeling the material out of his way. "Because all I want to do is make you happy."

I gasp as his knuckles brush against my skin. My whole world shrinks to where his thumb rubs over my clit. "Oh," I moan, "That's making me *very* happy right now." Heat slides down my spine, intensifying the ache between my legs.

He leans forward, kissing the column of my throat. "Do you want me to make you come?"

"God, yes. More than anything."

"How?"

My heart pounds with nervous anticipation. I reach down and move the sheet out of my way. Slowly, I slide my hand up and down his erection. "On your cock."

Tension has his muscles locked tight. "My pleasure." The desire coiled in his hoarse voice and the heat of his skin drives my need higher. He squeezes my hip. "Come here," he whispers.

I straddle his lap, positioning myself over him. He slides my underwear to the side and continues stroking me. Slowly, I lower myself over him, gasping with excited pleasure when he nudges my entrance.

A flash of pain crosses his face. "Easy. You don't have to—"

"No, you feel so good."

His muscles shake with the effort of holding back. While I slowly rock my hips, taking him inside. I pant and shudder as he spreads me open. "I feel you everywhere," I whisper.

"Don't be upset if I don't last long."

I wrap my arms around his neck. Our foreheads meet and I roll my hips with more urgency while staring into his eyes.

"You're my whole world." He strokes his fingertips up and

down my spine. "My everything." His feather-light touches push me toward the edge. I buck harder, my eyes rolling back in my head. I'm swept away.

His breathing's hard and choppy, holding back. "Come, come with me," I urge. He's tried so hard to be gentle, but now his fingers dig into my hip. He dips his head and scrapes his teeth over my nipple.

Finally, he throws his head back, a raw sound rumbling from his throat. I can't stop touching him. Running my fingers over his neck and shoulders, down his stomach. His body jerks and twitches. "You're tickling me, little dove."

"Tickling." I tease my fingers, feeling his cock jerk inside of me. Little aftershocks. "I think we're doing it wrong if it *tickles*."

He grabs my hips and lifts me off him, rolling us so he's on top, staring down at me. "There was nothing wrong about that."

I wrap my arms around his neck and pull myself up to kiss him over and over. "Thank you."

"Come on." He presses a quick kiss to my lips. "Let's get you showered and ready for work."

I don't want to leave our little love island. I want to spend every second I can with him while he's here. "Do you want me to drop you off at the airport?"

"Nah, I'll call for a car."

"Are you sure?"

He leans down and kisses my cheek. "If you take me to the airport, there's a good chance I don't get on the plane."

At least I know we're both feeling the strain of him leaving.

MY BEAUTIFUL, PERFECT, LOVE-SOAKED MORNING TAKES A dark, confusing twist as soon as I park my car at the studio. A swarm of people rush me as I try to cross the parking lot to get into the building.

Swept up in a sea of strangers, flashbulbs, and question, my body locks up. I freeze, unsure of how to respond.

"Mallory, do you want to share your side of the story?"

"W-what story?"

"Your miscarriage."

"It's no one's business." I hate the trembling indignance in my voice. How dare they ask me such an invasive question. "Chaser and I would appreciate some privacy and respect." I elbow my way through and refuse to say anything else.

"What about the rumors that you were carrying Andrew Lane's child? Do you want to address those?"

The question stops me cold. Why would *anyone* assume that? "I have no need to address vicious lies," I answer tartly, tossing my hair back.

I knew my first day back on set would be awkward.

A soft, cool hand lands on my shoulder, pulling me to the side. "That's enough. Go away and leave her alone," Pamela scolds the throng of reporters.

"Ms. Scott, do you want to address the rumors of Mallory and your ex?"

"No, and you shouldn't waste your time with that hogwash either." She leans down and whispers in my ear, "Come on, let's go inside."

"Thank you."

Tucking me close to her body, she strong-arms our way through the wild crowd. "Get them out of here," she snaps at the security guard.

Inside the studio, she releases me. "Are you okay?"

"I was better until that." I jerk my thumb over my shoulder. "Why would anyone even think..." I shake my head. "Whatever. Nothing should shock me anymore."

"It was a big story while you were...gone."

Chaser must have worked hard to intercept those stories while I was recovering. I knew reporters were camped out at our house, I'm so used to the lies tabloids tell, I've learned to ignore them. It never occurred to me to pick up a paper and see what their angle was on this story.

"Did you see the script?" I wave my copy at her. "What's going on in that last scene?"

She bites her full bottom lip and looks away. "You'll have to ask Sean."

"I GET EATEN BY A *SHARK*?"

I set my script down on the table in front of me. We've finished the read-through with the entire cast. Now I understand why my final scene trailed off into nothing.

My character—a lifeguard—gets swept out to sea while surfing.

And eaten by a shark.

None of the other actors have the courage to look me in the eye. I suppose being written off the show is akin to catching a disease. They're worried it's contagious.

The worst part is working all week, knowing the end is coming.

"I'm sorry," Cindy says, when I stop by for her to go through hair and makeup for the few scenes I'm in...you know, before I'm eaten by a shark.

"It's fine."

At lunch, I call Marilyn. "Shit, Mallory. Are you on the set right now?"

"Did you know I was being written off the show?" I glance over my shoulder to check that no one's listening.

Her heavy sigh comes through. "Yes. Apparently, the "bad publicity" from your miscarriage was in conflict with the "family values" of the show."

"Bad publicity?" I take a second to let that sink in. "You mean the made-up bullshit?"

"I'm sorry."

"Isn't that some sort of discrimination? What about the "bad publicity" of firing someone who just lost a baby? Talk about conflicting with family values."

"It's unconscionable, Mallory. I agree. But in the long run, you're better off."

I blow out a breath.

"This show was doing nothing for you. *Ocean Ave.* will be much more successful. And you won't have to be half-naked all day long."

"Or eaten by sharks."

CHAPTER SIXTY

Chaser

We missed our ten-day mark for a visit. But we both agreed since I'd be home for almost a whole week to attend the premiere of *Elimination Date*, and handle some other business, it would be okay.

I still wish I'd been here to comfort Mallory after her last day of filming *Shallow End*. As much as she wanted off the show, I don't think she's taking the whole "eaten by a shark" thing well. Even though she insists she's fine.

She's been banging around in the kitchen all morning and I decided it was best to leave her be.

The scent of chocolate chip cookies finally pulls me away from guitar practice.

"Hey, shark bait." I kiss Mallory's cheek. "What'cha baking?"

"It's not funny," she grumbles.

Nope. Still too soon for jokes. "Do they ever find your character's body?"

"No, thank God."

"That means they left it open for you to make a big surprise comeback." I hold my arms out in front of me, "Thriller"-style, and shuffle forward. "Zombie lifeguard. Eat brains."

She skewers me with a stare while I do my best to maintain my zombie pose.

"I wouldn't go back if it was the *last* acting job in Hollywood," she huffs.

"Never say never." I drop my arms and grin at her.

"Out of my kitchen." She jabs her spatula in the direction of the living room.

I grab one of the cookies she just took out of the oven. Oozing chocolate sears my skin and I fling it down on the tray. "Fuck!"

"Duh, they just came out of the oven," she teases.

At least she's laughing a little now. Even if it took a zombie shuffle and burning my fingers to coax it out of her.

"Pout all you want today, little dove. But when we hit that red carpet tomorrow night, you're my takes-shit-from-no-one girl. Chin up. Own that shark-death like it's the highlight of your acting career. Feel me?"

Her bottom lip juts out and she comes closer, wrapping her arms around my waist and burying her face against my chest. "Thank you."

I push her hair off her cheek. "You're Mallory fucking Dove. Starring in the new Scott Southgate show."

"Scout."

"Don't interrupt."

She giggles and rubs her cheek against my shirt. "We're there to celebrate the new movie and Kickstart's song in the movie. Not my fledging television career."

"Fuck that. You're there to network too."

"I'm going to support my man." She runs her hands over my ass and squeezes.

"Good, support me by doing some networking."

"Ugh. Marilyn already gave me a *list* of people she wants me to try to meet."

I grin down at her. "Excellent."

"I don't like using my fiancé—"

"You're not *using* me. We help each other out."

"How exactly do I help you?"

I lean down and kiss her. "By being you."

THE NEXT NIGHT, I'M PACING THE LIVING ROOM WAITING FOR Mallory to emerge from the bedroom. Cindy came over to help her get ready and we're cutting it close to when the limo's supposed to arrive.

"What do you think?"

Finally.

I turn around.

And stone-cold stop breathing for a second. "You look incredible."

Whatever that shiny, satin, skintight pale-pink material is, Mallory needs a *lot* more dresses made out of it.

"The skirt's a little tight." She pinches at the material glued to her hips. "I'll have to mince my way down the red carpet."

I hold out my arm as I walk over to her. "I'm always ready to assist with any wardrobe glitch you might have, Ms. Dove."

"Thank you."

I lean down and kiss her. "You take my breath away, woman."

"Well, don't think less of me, but," she lifts her dress a few inches, revealing shiny silver Reebok high-top sneakers, "They asked if I'd wear them to an event after I did that ad campaign and I couldn't say yes fast enough."

"I think you're brilliant." I wiggle my eyebrows at her. "And can't wait to see you wearing those and nothing else, later."

"I thought you might say that." Her expression turns more serious. "I'm so proud of you."

"Proud of you too," I rest my forehead against hers. "It's hard to believe things are actually...coming together for both of us."

"Believe it." She reaches up and rakes her nails through my hair. I close my eyes as the pleasurable shivery sensation ripples down my spine. "I'm always in your corner, Chaser. No matter what."

My chest expands and fills with love. The music accolades are great, but it means so much more that I have this woman to share everything with. She never judges me, and cares about each success and failure as much as I do.

Outside, a horn honks, pulling us apart. I glance over at the door, growling low in my throat.

Mallory pats my cheek. "Easy there, junkyard dog."

I growl even louder and nip at her fingers until she's shaking with laughter. "Stop. I can barely breathe as it is in this dress."

"Mallory!" Cindy hurries down the hallway, dragging her giant makeup case behind her.

"Cindy, let me take that." I grab the handle before she has a chance to protest. "Thanks for coming over and helping Mallory."

She blushes and glances at her feet. "No problem, Chaser." Her eyes widen. "Oh! I almost forgot. Take this." She hands Mallory a small pouch. "Will it fit inside your bag?"

"Shoot. My bag." Mallory hurries down the hallway, leaving Cindy and I to awkwardly stare at each other.

Someone bangs on the front door and I lean over to open it.

"What's taking so long, fucker?" Garrett says. Alvin shoves him from behind and Garrett stumbles inside.

"We're coming. Settle down." I glance at Garrett's dark red velvet sport coat and black jeans. "Spiffy. Aren't you worried you're going to sweat your ass off?"

"Just wait'll you see Jacob's get-up." Alvin smirks while he adjusts the cuffs of his simple black-and-white-striped button-up shirt.

Mallory talked me into a loose, black button-up shirt with silver threads running through it to go with my black jeans and Chucks. I don't hate it.

"Well, hello." Garrett finally notices Cindy and glides over to her with his hand extended and perv face working overtime.

Alvin rolls his eyes at me.

"Garrett, this is Mallory's friend, Cindy, please don't be a creep to her," I introduce. He ignores me, of course. But Cindy doesn't seem to mind the attention, so I leave them alone.

"Ready!" Mallory re-enters and beams when she sees Alvin. "Looking good, kid."

"You too." He jerks his thumb at me. "I see you got this clown into a grown-up shirt."

She gives me a sly smile as she approaches and gently rests her palms against my chest. "Doesn't he look handsome?"

"He looks...*something*." Alvin grins and I flip him off.

I glance down at Mallory's fingers, busy unbuttoning my shirt practically to my navel. "Uh, what're you doing?"

"There." She pats my chest. "Much better. Show off more of that sexy ink."

The guys—dicks that they are—howl with laughter.

"I better get going." Cindy gives Mallory a quick hug. "Have the best time tonight."

"I'll walk you out," Garrett offers.

Since he's suddenly such a gentleman, I shove Cindy's makeup case into his arms.

Mallory bites her lip as she watches them leave. "They'd make a cute couple," she whispers.

Alvin rolls his eyes. "You wanna play matchmaker, find *me* someone."

"Aw, Alvin, why didn't you say something?"

"I'm kidding."

"You got everything?" I ask Mallory.

She holds up a silver drawstring bag. "Change of clothes." She twists and turns, checking out the back of her dress. "I'm a little scared if I move wrong, I'll split this thing down the middle."

"Don't give him any ideas, Mallory," Alvin jokes.

Mallory

"About time." Jacob tugs on his frilly white sleeves and readjusts his shiny, metallic-blue lamé jacket. "We're going to be late."

Chaser climbs into the limo behind me and immediately starts laughing when his gaze lands on Jacob's outfit.

"What look were you trying to achieve?" Alvin flicks his fingers against Jacob's shoulder. "Glamorous pirate? Prince Charming meets Optimus Prime? What's happening here?"

Garrett snaps his fingers. "The love child of Rainbow Bright and the Village People?"

My gaze drops to Jacob's leather pants and royal blue cowboy boots. "Space Cowboy?" I blurt out.

Chaser chokes on his laughter.

Ignoring the guys, Jacob slides his gaze over my dress. "What look were *you* going for, Mallory? Cotton Candy Barbie?"

I lift my chin and run my hands over my hips. "Yes, actually."

That seems to break the budding tension. Jacob grins. "Come on! I was going for twentieth century Shakespeare. Lead singer. Rock star. Poet? Don't you get it?"

"One," Chaser says, "It's a movie premiere, not Halloween. Two—"

"Fuck off." Jacob thrusts his hand in Chaser's face and Chaser slaps it away.

Jacob tugs on the lapels of his jacket. "The designer said this was one of a kind."

"Individually, they're all interesting pieces," I concede, taking in the whole outfit again. "Together, it's a bit much."

"Just like me." Jacob grins.

"A-fucking-men to that," Chaser agrees. "Can we continue this episode of *wardrobe tips for the insane* later, please?"

"Sorry," I mouth.

Chaser shrugs.

Jacob seems to be over it and our teasing hasn't dimmed his enthusiasm for the night. Without a concern for his fancy leather pants, he crawls over the limo's red carpet to the bar, pops open a bottle of champagne, and passes over-flowing plastic cups full of bubbly to each of us. "May this be the first of many soundtracks!"

We all raise our glasses and cheer.

CROWDS OF PHOTOGRAPHERS LINE THE SIDEWALK AS WE PULL up to the theater. I run my hands down the sides of my dress, smoothing out a few wrinkles.

"Stop fussing." Chaser captures my hand. "You look beautiful."

"Everyone'll be photographing Sandra Felton," Jacob says. "No one's gonna notice you, Mallory."

"Thanks," I mutter. He has a point. The photographers *should* be more interested in one of the stars of the film more than me, but still. At least I don't feel bad for making fun of his outfit anymore.

"Go." Chaser shoos the guys out of the limo when our door finally opens. "You okay?" he asks once we're alone.

My heart squeezes. This is his night and once again, he's stopping to check in with me. "I'm great." I rub my palm against his cheek. "Are you?"

"It's not that big a deal. But what if people hate the song or say it ruins the film or something?"

I flick my gaze out the window, staring at one of the tall movie posters featuring a half-robot man, with a scantily clad woman draped over his shoulder and a futuristic gun in his hand. "Or, what if people say the *movie* ruins your song?"

His tense expression melts and he swoops in to kiss me. "I love you."

While the guys didn't have any trouble moving up the red carpet, reporters, and photographers swarm around us when we step out of the limo.

"Mallory! Why aren't you in the film?"

"Chaser, did you write this song with Andrew Lane?"

"Mallory, were you written off of Shallow End *because of your affair with Andrew Lane?"*

I scowl at that question. For some reason, I expected a higher caliber of reporter at a film premiere.

As we move closer to the entrance, the questions even out to more normal ones focused on music, entertainment, and our engagement. We stop to answer a few of those.

"Have you set a date for your wedding yet?"

"As soon as our schedules line up and are families are able to attend," Chaser answers.

"Will you be writing a song for the next Bixby Arrowood film?"

"We'd love to," Chaser answers. "Anytime."

We meet up with the guys at a small area set up for photos and interviews. I step inside the theater and off to the side to get out of the sun while the guys pose together for a band picture and answer more questions.

"I misjudged you," a deep voice says behind me.

Startled, I turn, searching for the source.

Davey Revolver.

I should've known I'd run into this jackass again eventually.

"Hiding behind the potted plants is awfully creepy. Even for you," I say, turning away to peer through the doors so I can catch a glimpse of Chaser.

"Didn't realize you were into gutter trash like Andrew Lane."

I guess he can't take a hint. Turning to face him, I glare up. "Don't worry, Davey. You're still the sleaziest man I've had the bad luck to encounter."

Yup, when I consider the long, long list of creeps—Andrew included—Davey still sits near the top.

This business is *exhausting.*

"Besides," I add, "You should know better than anyone how easy it is to plant *fake* stories in the tabloids."

He sneers. "Enjoy it now. You won't last here long."

I rub my left hand over my chin, showing off my engagement ring, not that he cares. "Gee, I'm pretty sure it's more than six months later, and I *still* don't regret turning down your charming offer." I flick my wrist at him like he's a fly I'm trying to shoo out a window. "Now, run along before my fiancé kicks your ass again."

"Whore," he spits out before turning on his heel and stalking away.

"Very original," I mutter.

"What did he say to you?" Chaser growls behind me.

I whirl around. The guys are still over by the interview station. Chaser must have ditched them when he saw Davey. He's snorting like a bull about to charge. "Nothing," I assure him in a low voice since people are starting to take notice. "Calm down. I don't want the headlines tomorrow to be about that jackass."

His shoulders relax and he drops his gaze to me. "Are you okay?"

"I'm fine. Got some things off my chest. It felt good."

He curls his arm around my waist and guides me back outside. "I got worried when I lost sight of you, then I saw him talking to you and almost lost my shit."

"I'm fine."

Someone more famous must pull up to the curb next because the throng of reporters rushes away, forgetting all about us.

"That was fun." Jacob adjusts the ruffled, frilly collar of his shirt and ends up tangling his fingers in the ties.

"Come here," I motion him closer.

He flicks his fingers against the lace jabot. "It's detachable."

"Do you want to take it off?"

He glances down and grins. "Nah, it looks too cool."

"It really doesn't," Garrett says.

I untangle the strings that theoretically tie the collar together. "Why don't we leave this open, so it looks a little more rock star and a little less Mr. Darcy."

"Thank you, Mallory." He flashes a goofy-kid grin at me.

"All right. Enough of that." Chaser takes my hand and whispers in my ear. "You know he's more Wickham than Darcy, right?"

"Chaser Adams, you surprise me every day."

We're ushered into the theater and directed to a cluster of seats in the middle. It's an engrossing film. Lots of action and explosions. I recognize Kickstart's song immediately in the opening scene and reach over to squeeze his hand. During Sandra Felton's topless scenes, I pick up nervous giggles from the back of the theater.

After the screening, everyone circulates through the lobby, shaking hands, sipping drinks, talking about the film.

"Mallory, thank you for coming." A man who looks vaguely familiar holds out his hand. "Rex Hewson."

"Oh! Yes, Mr. Hewson." The director was definitely on my list of people Marilyn wanted me to talk to tonight.

Chaser steps to the side but keeps his arm around my waist and a hand on my hip.

"You read for Sandra's part, right?" he asks. "It was a close call if I remember."

"I'm flattered to hear that. Sandra was terrific, though. You made the right choice."

He inclines his head, studying me until I'm ready to fidget. "What are you working on right now?"

"Um, a new show Scout Southgate's putting together. We start shooting in January."

"But you're still interested in film?"

"Absolutely."

"Great." He nods to Chaser. "Perfect song. Thanks for coming tonight."

After he wanders away, Chaser gives me a wide-eyed look. "See, you made an impression."

Inside, I'm bursting but try to remain calm on the outside. "I know!" I whisper.

As things wind down, people start leaving for exclusive after parties.

"Atlas Gates invited us to Creeping Vine for a private after-party," Garrett says. "We *have* to go."

"Cool," Chaser says, but by his tone, he's not as enthusiastic about hanging out with the star of the film. "You want to go?" he asks me.

I wait until the others are ahead of us. "Will you be disappointed in me if I say no?"

"Fuck no." He breathes a sigh of relief.

Jacob's wild-eyed and twitchy when we catch up to the guys outside. Obviously, he's had more than alcohol tonight.

"Come on, let's go!" he shouts.

"Will you watch out for him?" Chaser asks Alvin.

"You're not coming?"

"Nah, we're beat."

Alvin glances over his shoulder. "Sandra Felton gave me her number. I'm gonna try to meet up with her at Creeping Vine." Like two teenagers, they high-five each other.

I pat Alvin's arm and wish him luck.

Alvin, Garrett, and Jacob end up taking a limo with a group of other people.

"Seems we have our limo to ourselves," Chaser says as it pulls up to the curb.

My lips twitch. "Whatever shall we do with it?"

Once we're safely tucked inside the car, Chaser tugs at the zipper of my dress. "First, I want you out of this," he murmurs. "Hold your hair up."

Laughing, I lift my heavy pile of long spiral curls. "What are you doing?"

I peer out the window. The limo hasn't started moving yet.

We're inches way from dozens of people still lingering from the premiere. "No one can see us, right?"

"No and I told the driver to take his time getting us home," he rasps.

Cool air soothes my heated back as he tugs the zipper all the way down. For the first time tonight, I can finally breathe.

Chaser lets out a low whistle. "Good thing I didn't see what you were wearing under the dress before we left. Turn around."

It's not easy. I crouch and twist my way out of the dress, trying to avoid bopping my head on the ceiling.

He runs his fingers under my garters, straight up to the beige lace thong barely covering me. "Very pretty."

"Thank you." I kneel down in front of him and he captures my hands as I reach for his belt.

"What are you doing?"

I stare up at him and slowly lick my lips. "If you take your cock out, I'll show you."

His intense expression doesn't change. "I don't want you on the *floor*." He slides his hands under my arms, pulling me up until I'm straddling his lap. "Goddesses deserve to be worshipped."

I reach between us, working his belt loose. "I need you, Chaser."

He cups my face, dragging me down for a kiss. I work the buttons of his jeans and he slides down a few inches to make room. "That's better," I whisper.

When I finally free him, he's heavy in my palms. Hot, hard as stone. I slide my fist up his length and he groans. "This isn't what I planned, but fuck if I'm gonna stop you," he murmurs, eyes half-closed.

"Good boy."

His lips quirk.

He slides his thumb beneath the edge of my thong, slowly stroking. "So slick." His dark eyes glitter with heat in the shadowy confines. He pushes two fingers inside me and flicks his thumb over my clit.

"Oh," I gasp and throw my head back. "Shit."

"Mallory, we just started," he teases.

I rest one hand on his shoulder and lift myself enough to hover over him.

"That's it." He clutches my hips, guiding me down. "All the way."

We're so close, enclosed in the tiny space, our own little world. I rest my forehead against his, staring into his eyes as I take all of him.

"Good girl." He slides his hand under the tiny bits of lace, covering not much at the moment and rubs the pad of his thumb over my clit in slow, soft circles.

"God you know I love that."

He hums an encouraging noise of agreement and keeps up the rhythmic movement. Sweat mists over my forehead and chest. I reach back and undo my strapless bra, tossing it aside.

"Even better." He sits forward, capturing my nipple with his mouth and sucking hard.

"Oh!" I slap my hand against his shoulder at first pushing him away, then drawing him closer.

He moves to my other breast, lashing his tongue over my nipple.

"Slower," he warns.

But I'm too wild and far gone. I rock my hips faster, ready to burst into a million pieces. "So close," I whisper.

He applies more pressure to my clit and my body jerks and pulses with pleasure. "Yes." I slam my palm against the roof to keep my balance and keep wildly bucking my hips.

"Fuck, yes." Chaser curls his hands over my shoulders, pinning me down while he pounds his hips up. His entire body shakes as he finds his release. "Fuck."

I keep moving my hips, slowing my movements until he finally opens his eyes again. "Come here." He wraps his arms around me, crushing me against his sweaty chest, kissing the curve of my neck.

When our breathing returns to semi-normal, he helps me dress in the jeans and T-shirt, I'd brought to change into. He brushes my damp curls off my forehead. "It's still early if you want to go somewhere else."

"Nope. I want to go home with you."

CHAPTER SIXTY-ONE

Chaser

The next morning, I stretch, reaching for Mallory before I'm even fully awake. Soft laughter greets me. Little fingers tickle over my ribs and up my chest.

"Morning." Her husky morning greeting finally peels my eyes open.

"I had the most amazing dream."

She rolls to her side, resting her head against her hand. "About?"

"I was at this party and the most beautiful woman in the room went home with me." I reach over and trace my fingers over her neck and down her chest, flicking the sheet out of my way. "She was wild and begged to ride my cock in the backseat of the limo."

"Sounds pretty hot."

"Come here." I hold out my arms and she snuggles closer.

"Mmm. You're nice and warm," she mumbles.

I restlessly stroke my fingers up and down her back. "Hey, Mallory?"

"Hmm?"

"Now that you have time off until the next show starts shooting, come out on the road with me. Tour ends in Portland. We can hop a flight to Hawaii and have our secret beach wedding."

She pulls back and stares at me with wide eyes. "You want to? So soon?"

"Yeah. We keep talking about it. Saying we'll do it when this is over or that's done. We'll have our beach wedding. Spend a few weeks just relaxing with each other. It'll be perfect."

"You won't be upset if your father's not there?" she asks. "And the club?"

"No, we'll do a big showy spectacle for our families when your dad gets out." I roll her on top of me. "But I can't wait that long for you to be my wife."

She cups my face with her hands and leans down for a kiss. "I love that idea."

I hold up my left hand, showing off my ring finger. "Every fucking tabloid will seize on it if I start wearing a wedding band. I'm thinking of getting your name tattooed here instead."

"Ouch. Won't that hurt?"

"Nah." I brush my fingertips over my arms and chest. "No worse than any of these did."

"You sure...you want something...so permanent?"

I squint at her. "You really need to ask?"

She presses her lips over my heart and peers up at me. "I think it's kinda sexy."

The shrill ring of the phone next to the bed jars us out of our love bubble.

"Yes, I'll come with you," she answers before I roll over to scoop up the phone.

"Hello, Adams-Dove Loveshack, Chaser speaking."

Mallory presses her forehead to my chest and giggles.

"Chaser." Alvin's shaky voice wipes the smile off my face.

"What's wrong?" I sit up so fast, Mallory spins onto the mattress with a soft thump.

"Chaser." He breaks down. Bawling so hard I can barely understand him.

Chills race down my spine. "Alvin. Talk to me. What happened?"

Mallory kneels next to me. "What's going on?" she mouths.

I shrug, waiting for Alvin to calm down.

"Jacob overdosed. They found him this morning. Outside Creeping Vine."

"Oh shit. What hospital?" I jump out of bed, swiping my jeans off the floor and shaking them out. "I'll be there as soon as I can."

"No." Alvin sniffles and in that brief pause, the truth barrels down on me. "He's dead, Chaser."

Still holding onto the phone, I fall against the edge of the bed, sliding down until my ass hits the floor. "Are you sure?"

He lets out a humorless laugh. "Yes."

"Fuck. Oh my God." A thousand waves of guilt crash over my head. I should have gone to the after party with the guys.

The buzz of the rarely used television we keep in the bedroom pulls my attention. Mallory turns the volume all the way down but a picture of Jacob's smiling face next to the stony-faced VJ delivering the news drives the truth home.

Jacob Whitfield, lead singer of Kickstart, found dead at age twenty-three.

Sobbing, Mallory drops down on the foot of the bed and covers her face with her hands.

"What the hell happened?" I shout into the phone.

"I don't know." He cries even harder. "He was drunk but fine when I left."

"Where's Garrett?"

"I don't know. He took off as soon as he heard about Jacob."

"Did he stay with Jacob after you left?"

"I don't know!" Alvin yells.

"Okay. I'm sorry. What do you need me to do?"

"Nothing. There's nothing *to* do. We're done. Over. Our singer's dead. We can't replace him. The band's finished."

I hadn't gotten that far in my thought process yet.

This isn't real. It can't be happening. I open my mouth to refute one of those statements, but nothing comes out.

"Thom said he'll take care of the funeral arrangements if his parents won't—" He starts crying again and I feel so fucking useless, sitting there holding a phone listening to my friend break down with no way to comfort him.

CHAPTER SIXTY-TWO

Mallory

It's a blustery, cold day for California the day of Jacob's funeral.

"Are you ready?" I ask Chaser.

He steps away from the mirror, adjusting his tie. "Jacob would laugh his ass off if he saw me wearing this thing."

The humorless joke is better than the days Chaser spent riddled with guilt and drowning in despair.

"He probably would." I reach up and smooth a few runaway spikes of hair off his forehead. A sob catches in my throat. "I feel so bad for teasing him about his outfit the night...the last time..."

He presses his finger against my lips. "Shh. He loved clowning around with everyone." He takes my hands and steps back. "You look pretty."

I kept it simple—a black dress with elbow-length sleeves, modest neckline, and a flared skirt that falls below my knees. "Thank you."

We stop at Alvin's house and pick him up first. The guys are silent for most of the time as I drive the hour north to where Jacob's parents live.

Chaser casts a hesitant look at the cemetery. Reporters are held back by wooden barricades, but plenty have cameras at the ready.

"Vultures," Alvin grumbles.

They chase after my car for a bit but are finally stopped by security.

A large crowd dressed mostly in black announces where we're supposed to go.

Chaser grabs my hand. Alvin looks so bereft, I slip my other hand into his and pull him along. He gives me a brief, sad smile.

Garrett's standing with a young woman who looks an awful lot like Jacob. He lifts his chin when he spots us.

"Hey, Janey." Chaser leans in and hugs her. "I'm so sorry, sweetheart."

She sniffles and accepts the brief embrace but doesn't seem to be able to respond.

Alvin hugs her too and she ends up clinging to him until an older couple joins us.

"Hello, Mr. Whitfield," Chaser greets.

"I don't want to speak to you." He glares at Alvin and Garrett. "Any of you. Stay for the service and then leave."

"I'm sorry," Jane mouths as her father pulls her away.

"Wow," Alvin mutters.

"What'd we expect?" Garrett glares at the man's retreating back. "He did fuck-all for Jacob. Why would it be any different now?"

"Let's just get through this," Alvin says. "We can deal with them later."

Unfortunately for Jacob's parents, they're outnumbered by the very people they want to avoid. Musicians, models, actors, Jacob was more loved than I think he ever realized.

Thom tries speaking to the Whitfields, but their conversation looks brief and tense from where we're standing. He finally retreats and joins us.

He gives Garrett and Alvin a fatherly hug and pat on the

back before nodding at Chaser and me. "We're going to have a gathering at The Palace afterwards. I tried inviting them, but ..."

"It's okay," Chaser says. "Thanks for trying."

"We're not going to The Palace to fucking celebrate," Garrett spits out.

"No, no," Thom says quickly. "A memorial. Rich is shutting the whole place down. It's only open to friends and family."

"We were his family." Garrett glares at Chaser. "And we treated him like shit."

"You really want to do this now?" Chaser asks in a tired voice.

"Guys, settle down," Thom urges. "This isn't the time or place."

Across the cemetery I spot a familiar figure. I whisper to Chaser that I'll be right back and walk over to meet her.

"Hi, Val."

"Mallory," she sobs, pulling me into a tight embrace. "What happened?"

Practically choking on her heavy floral perfume, I draw back. "We're not sure about all the details." And the ones we *do* know are too gruesome to spill where anyone could overhear.

"Poor Jacob." She pulls a tissue out of her pocket and swipes it over her nose.

"Hey, Val." Chaser joins us, hands in his pockets. "Fair warning, his parents aren't speaking to any of us."

She snorts. "They never forgave him for dropping out of school when I signed you guys."

"Nope." He shrugs.

"Are you okay?"

"No, Valerie. I'm not."

Alvin joins us next, hugging Valerie tight. "I can't believe you'd show up after how we—"

"Not now, honey," she says gently. "Of course, I'd be here."

Chairs have been set up around the gravesite for the service. I spot a number of familiar faces—Vickie, and Dorothy, Holly sitting with Jacob's sister, the two girls clinging to each other and weeping. I nod to Pamela and Vinnie but ignore Andrew. More faces that I vaguely remember from the nights they played shows on the strip. The owners of bars, members from rival bands, roadies, and bouncers.

The first row on the left side seems to have been reserved for us. Chaser and I take the last two chairs. Maybe he wants to be able to make a quick escape. He's so blank, expressionless, showing no emotion other than squeezing my hand every now and then.

A priest reads all the usual funeral passages. After that, Jacob's father stands. I brace myself for whatever he's about to say.

"Today we join thousands of families who lay their loved ones to rest due to addiction. Our hearts are broken. We tried for years to save him and couldn't." He breaks down and finally returns to his seat.

Garrett stands up.

"Fuck," Chaser mutters under his breath.

"Jacob's my best friend." Garrett's voice cracks. "He was my only friend when I first moved to this country." His mouth twitches and he scuffs the toe of his boot against the grass. "Forced me to play bass when I wanted to be the singer. He was a forceful little wanker when he wanted to be." Garrett sweeps his arm Alvin and Chaser's way. "We struggled with how to help Jacob. Our hearts are broken too. Jacob was only twenty-three. He accomplished so much in such a short time and he wanted to do so much more. He lived his life to the fullest and touched thousands of lives." His voice breaks again. He hangs his head and finally sits without another word.

Chaser stands, clearing his throat. He reaches over and squeezes Garrett's shoulder. "Jacob could be as stubborn as he was passionate. He worked hard and cared deeply. The pages of his book will never be closed. We will always remember him through the music he wrote and the lives he touched." He slowly turns his head toward the shiny black casket. "You will never be forgotten." Chaser drops into his seat resting his elbows on his knees and head in his hands. Someone else stands to speak and I tune them out, focusing on Chaser.

I run my hand over his back and lean close. "That was sweet."

"It was the best I could do without outright lying." His fists clench. "I wanted to wring his neck more often than not lately."

"You had a long, complex relationship."

While one person after another walks up to leave a rose on Jacob's casket, I study the people around us. Who was a true friend to him and who used him? How many of them helped him buy drugs, gave him drugs, or watched him shoot up?

Which one was with him in those last moments before they left him on the sidewalk to die?

CHAPTER SIXTY-THREE

Chaser

Grief's a complicated emotion all on its own. When the person who died could be a real shithead sometimes, the grief comes tinged with guilt, resentment, and a whole lot of anger.

But how can you be mad at someone who's dead? And am I really mad a Jacob or myself? I should've stuck with him that night. I knew he was on a downward slide. But I left him and now he's gone.

Once we're alone in the car together, I reach over and rest my hand on Mallory's leg. "Thank you."

"For?"

"Being here today." I open and close my fists. "He was really awful to you at times, and—"

"He was your friend for a long time and now he's gone. It's normal to be shocked and sad, even angry."

I turn her words over for a few miles before responding. "I'm definitely angry."

"Just don't let it eat you alive." She gives me a sad smile. "I know you're a big, strong man, but give yourself permission to feel what you feel instead of holding it all back."

"What I *feel* is guilty for being mad at him."

She sighs again. "Death doesn't erase the effect someone had on other people. Good and bad. It's okay to be angry about some of the things he did while sad that your friend is gone."

Her words finally loosen some of the knots in my chest. "We don't have to go to this," I say as she pulls into the parking lot behind The Palace.

"I think we should."

Alvin grabbed a ride with Garrett, and we meet up with them at the back entrance. "You two okay?"

"No." Garrett tosses his cigarette on the ground and stamps it out. "But Jacob would be insulted if we didn't get shitfaced at his memorial."

The club's somber. Low music, soft lighting, food, and drinks. Rich, the owner, welcomes us and gives us our favorite round booth in the back. On stage, a single light shines down on a life-size photo of Jacob.

Alvin and I side-eye each other.

Rich leaves a bottle of Jack Daniels at our table. Garrett and Alvin immediately start pouring shots for all of us. A few minutes later, Thom slides into the seat opposite me and leans forward. "I know you don't want to talk about this now—"

If he mentions the tour, an album, or anything business-related, I'm going to strangle this motherfucker.

"Don't fucking do it," Alvin warns. "Not today, Thom."

"We need to—"

I slam my glass on the table, making everyone jump. "Go, Thom. Now."

Grieving or not, my scary biker scowl still works. He hauls his ass out of our booth, fading into the growing crowd.

Garrett slides out of the booth and Alvin scoots closer to Mallory and me. "Are we planning to sit here all night and pretend Jacob wasn't an addict who almost got us all killed more than once?"

I snort and reach for the bottle, pouring myself another shot. Under the table, I pat Mallory's leg. "Tell him what you told me on the way over."

She hesitates before repeating her earlier advice.

"Fuck." He thumps his back against the booth and stares at the ceiling. "That's profound, Mallory."

"I think you're a little drunk," she says. "There is no right response to death. Allow yourself to feel the cocktail of emotions without blaming yourself, okay?"

He rolls his head our way and smirks. "You said cocktail. In a bar."

"I did." She pushes her shot glass away. "Maybe I should ask for some water."

"Hey, guys," a deep voice tinged with sadness pulls our attention up.

"The fuck you doing here?" Alvin sits up straight, glaring at Andrew.

"I just wanted to come over and say I'm sorry." He shifts from foot to foot and glances at the empty space next to me.

I point to the opposite side of the booth. "Sit. Over there."

"You have fucking nerve," Alvin says.

Ignoring Alvin, Andrew leans forward, clasping his hands on the table in front of him. "Listen, I wanted to tell you this in person. They caught the guy who shot me. I had to fly down to Texas to testify." He hesitates and briefly closes his eyes. "Just like when I made my original statement, I left Jacob out of it." He glances down at the table. "What happened to him was bad enough. No need to drag his name through the mud more than it has been."

Alvin finally settles down. "Thanks."

Andrew squirms. "Uh, can we talk..." He shifts his gaze to Alvin. "Just the three of us?"

"Alvin knows all about it, so speak freely." I smirk at him.

Mallory scowls at me and I shrug.

"Fine." He shoots another look at Alvin. "I took Mallory's advice and found another therapist. I wanted to apologize." The whole time he hasn't looked at Mallory once, but his gaze finally lands on her. "I'm sorry. Truly."

"Thank you."

"What do you want, Andrew?" I sit up, leaning over the table. "You wanna come over and play Scrabble? Hold hands? Go fishin' together? Ride bitch on the back of my bike? What?"

Whiskey shoots out of Alvin's nose, spraying the table. "Aw, fuck! That burns." He lays his head down, laughing and pounding his fist against the table. "Jesus Christ, Chaser."

Andrew doesn't seem to find it as amusing. "None of that. We're still in the same business. I'm trying to..." he waves his arms in the air, "...extend like, an olive branch, or whatever."

"Business." I scoff. "In case you haven't noticed, our band's done."

Andrew's mouth turns down. "I know, man. I'm sorry."

Alvin picks his head up off the table. "Vandals are done too, right?"

"Uh," Andrew's crazy eyes dart around the room. "Looks like it. I can't talk about it, though." He lifts his chin at me. "What're you going to do? Go back to New York?"

Fuck, what *am* I going to do? I guess now would be a good time to head home. My father could use the help with the club. But how can I ask Mallory to leave when she just landed a part on a new show?

Mallory turns her questioning eyes my way. Guess she had the same thought.

"Mallory starts filming a new show soon." I curl my arm around her shoulders, and she leans into me. "We're not done with Hollywood yet."

CHAPTER SIXTY-FOUR

Chaser

Months ago, I promised Mallory we'd run away to have our private beach wedding. But after Jacob's death, taking off to celebrate our marriage felt fifty kinds of wrong.

By the time I pulled myself out of my spiral of grief and remorse, she was already busy filming *Ocean Ave*. Six days a week. Not exactly the time for a honeymoon. So, I didn't bring it up. And neither did she.

Alvin's renting a house not too far from us and I spend most of my days hanging out with him. Not really talking or even working on new music. Sometimes we ride up the coast and reminisce about when we first moved out here. How different it is from where we grew up.

Garrett teamed up with Vinnie Price to form a new band. They asked us to be a part of it, but it was too...strange. What were we going to call it? Vicious Kickstart? Three-fourths Kickstart and a Vandal? Who would we find to front such a project?

Alvin and I both declined. There were no hard feelings. I'll be first in line at Tower Records to pick up a copy of their album —if they ever record one.

Slowly, I started returning phone calls, beginning with Mark Cutter. He sets me up with several artists. Writing songs. Contributing guitar solos. It's lucrative. I don't have to go out on the road and be away from Mallory for extended periods of time. And I'm finally having fun creating music again.

By the time the last week of filming for *Ocean Ave* starts, it's time to set new plans in motion. The show's been picked up for another season, so I only have a few months to work with. It hasn't escaped my notice that Mallory's turned down all offers to work over her summer break.

Maybe she knows what I have planned.

Mallory

"Bye." Madeline hugs me in front of my car. "I'm going to miss you! We have to get together and have lunch or something, okay?"

"Sure. You have my number."

"I'm filming up in Canada, but I'll definitely call you when I get back."

She hugs me again before taking off. I'd been offered a small part in the made-for-television woman-in-peril movie Madeline was starring in but turned it down. I can't shake the feeling that I somehow abandoned Chaser when he needed me by starting filming so soon after Jacob's death. He's never hinted that he feels the same.

It seems like Madeline stars in one of these low-budget films every couple of months, so I'm sure I'll have another opportunity. If not, that's okay too.

Some things are just more important.

Chaser's bike is in the driveway. A grin the size of California stretches across my lips. I shove the car door open and jump out.

He steps outside to meet me, grinning from ear to ear.

"What's that look on your face?" I call out, running up the sidewalk so fast, my feet barely touch the concrete.

Without answering, he sweeps me into his arms, smashing his lips against mine. "Missed you today," he murmurs. "How'd it go?"

"Great." I open my mouth and fake a wide-eyed, shocked expression. "We left it on a cliffhanger. Will they or won't they leave sunny San Diego and move back to Nebraska?" I gasp and pretend to bite my nails.

Chaser's rumbling laughter warms me all over.

"I kind of feel bad for our fake dad," I continue. "He has this great job opportunity back home and all my 'brother' and I did was nag him about staying in L.A. to work on our tan lines." I scrunch my nose. "It was shameful."

"Can't wait to see it."

He's vibrating with an electric energy I haven't seen in months. Once we're inside the house, he can't contain himself any longer. "Pack your bags."

"Why? Where are we going?"

"You're done filming, right? Today was the last day?" Concern creeps into his questions.

"Yes."

"Good." He picks up an envelope off the entryway table and hands it to me.

Slowly, unsure of what's happening here, I pull open the envelop and slide two tickets out. My heart pitter-patters. "Kapalua?"

"White sand beaches, sparkling blue water, exceedingly private." He hands me a brochure featuring stunning photos of everything he described. "Will you run away with me? Vow to love, honor, and fuck me until the day I die?"

"Yes!" I give his rock-hard shoulder a little shove and the corners of his mouth twitch.

"I'm sorry to spring it on you, but I couldn't wait. We can pick up a bathing suit and whatever you need when we get there."

It's time for my own sly smile. Disengaging from our

embrace, I hurry into the bedroom. Quickly, because Chaser's bound to follow me in here, I pull out the pink satin pouch tucked at the back of my top dresser drawer and peek inside. The fanciest swimwear I've ever seen, let alone owned is neatly folded inside. I've been saving it in anticipation of our beach wedding. Hopefully, I'll be able to figure out how to get myself into it without Chaser's assistance.

"Ready?" Chaser asks from outside the doorway.

I jump and shove the pink pouch into my suitcase.

Curiosity piqued, he strolls into the bedroom. "Whatcha hiding?"

"Nothing."

I stop him with a hand against his chest as he reaches for my suitcase. "It's rude to go through your wife's clothes, Chaser. Let there be some mystery."

A smirk flirts with the corners of his mouth. How I've missed his playful, teasing expressions. He curls one hand over my hip and tugs me closer. "No mystery. No secrets between us."

"I want you to be surprised. When I walk down the aisle, I want your jaw to drop so hard, you'll have a mouthful of sand."

He chuckles. "Doesn't matter what you're wearing. I'm always in awe of you." He tilts his head. "Wait, you already have your wedding...whatever?"

"Yup. I've been ready whenever you were."

His expression softens. "I'm sorry it's taken so long."

I loop my arms around his neck and reach up to kiss him. "This is better. We have the whole summer together. How long are we staying in Hawaii?"

He shrugs. "We have the resort for the week. We can go island hopping. Whatever you want."

WHEN WE ARRIVE, WE'RE WHISKED INTO A CAR AND DRIVEN about an hour from the airport. "Everything's so beautiful."

"We're not doing the spend the night before our wedding apart thing, are we?" he asks.

"Seems kind of pointless." I narrow my eyes at him. "You can't see me before the wedding, though. You'll have to get dressed somewhere else."

His lips twitch. "Fair enough."

"You're sure..." I glance at our driver who doesn't seem to be paying any attention to us. "No one will find out?"

"I was assured absolute discretion. They're not even going to be fully staffed to minimize the risk. But they do this sort of thing for celebrities all the time they told me and never had an issue."

"Chaser, it must have cost a fortune."

"Nothing's too good for my girl."

The tang of sea-salt greets us at the resort. We're shown to our room. Soft, white curtains billowing in the breeze frame a picturesque ocean view.

"I love this."

"I thought you might." He nods to our suitcases. "You want to unpack? Day after tomorrow's the big day." He slaps his hand over his eyes. "I promise I won't peek."

"It's bad luck, so you better not."

The playful expression vanishes. "We've had enough of that."

CHAPTER SIXTY-FIVE

Chaser

The morning of our wedding, I slip out of bed early to check on everything. Lush flowers decorate the bannister of the staircase. Mallory said she wanted pink and purple flowers and that's what they are.

"Perfect," I mutter.

"Are you trying to escape?" Alvin greets me downstairs.

"Fuck, when did you get in?" I give him a quick hug. "I was worried you weren't going to make it."

"Just now." He cocks his head toward the door. "Audrey and Doug just got here too."

"Great. Mallory will be so excited." I slap his chest. "Come check the wedding site out with me?"

The officiant with the hotel is a kind man with a genuine smile. He shakes my hand and gives me a few encouraging words as I inspect the area.

"Do you have a ring?" Alvin asks.

I pat my pocket. "Yup."

"You want me to hang onto it?"

"Nope."

"If you're keeping this a secret, aren't people going to notice a wedding ring?"

"Nah." I pull out the small blue velvet box and show him the slim diamond band. "It should fit right under her engagement ring. I'll buy her a matching one to stack on top when we do the big, public thing."

Since we've spent so much time together over the last few months, Alvin knows all the details about Mallory's father and why this secret wedding is so important to us. Mallory and I trust him not to share that knowledge with anyone.

A path down to the beach has been marked off by large green palm fronds, seashells, and pink flowers. No chairs. The ceremony won't be long and the guest list is short.

On the way back, we run into Doug and Audrey.

"Thank you for coming." I hold out my hand to Doug and give Audrey a quick embrace.

"Where's the bride?" she asks.

"Still sleeping." I nod to the beach. "I wanted to check on all the stuff I asked for."

"You planned this?" Audrey searches my face. "By yourself?"

"I didn't plan much. I paid them a lot of money and told them what we wanted." I shrug. *Thank you, Mitchell Howard, for asking me to play on three more songs for your new album.* Even if he never uses them, at least the checks cleared.

"Mallory finished filming, so I whisked her away."

"Wow, Chaser. I never would've pegged you as such a romantic when we first met."

I shrug again, uncomfortable with the turn our conversation's taken. "Had no reason to be before Mallory."

Mallory

Waking up alone isn't how I thought I'd start my wedding day.

There's a note on the pillow next to me.

428

Beautiful Bride,

"No bad luck today. Everything will be sent to your room. I'll meet you at the altar.

Love,

The Groom

"Chaser," I whisper.

First, breakfast is brought to my room.

While I'm finishing that, someone knocks and opens the door. "Hey, Bride!"

I blink and almost explode with happiness when Audrey walks in. "Oh my God! What are you doing here?"

"We happened to be at the resort next door." She squeezes me tight. "What do you think? We're here for your wedding!"

"Thank you." Tears sting my eyes. "When did you get here?"

"This morning. Don't worry. We're not crashing your private honeymoon. Doug's taking me to Lanai tomorrow to look at a property he's thinking of buying."

"I'm not worried about that. I'm just so happy to see you."

Chaser

Alvin, Audrey, Doug, the officiant, a discreet photographer, and I are the only ones on the beach.

The crashing ocean and my pounding heart provide the only soundtrack I need. The setting sun turns the sky vibrant shades of pink and purple, the perfect backdrop.

No one needs to nudge me when Mallory arrives. Her magnetic pull is enough to turn my head as she glides down the simple sandy path lined with big green palm fronds and plump red flowers. She's an image from my dreams. Simple white two-piece bathing suit, with straps crisscrossing under her breasts and pink ribbons tied into little bows at her hips. Pink and purple flowers at her ankles, wrists, and tucked behind her ear. A small bouquet of matching island flowers is clutched in her hands. Pure love curves her lips and shines in her blue eyes when

429

she reaches me. I extend my hand and she twines her fingers in mine. Together, we face the officiant.

"Welcome, friends. We're here today to celebrate the marriage of Mallory and Russell. Marriage is one of the greatest blessings and challenges of human relationships. Only through love, patience, dedication, and perseverance can two people create a marriage. I am here to help you affirm the choice you have both made to spend your lives together as husband and wife."

"Thank you," Mallory whispers.

He nods to her. "I understand you both have personal vows you'd like to recite."

"We do." I pull the slip of paper from my pocket although, I probably have the words branded into my soul, I've gone over them so many times.

"Mallory, you're the strength I didn't know I needed in my life and the happiness I didn't realize I was missing. No matter what challenges life throws at us, I promise to always protect you, cherish you, and to love you for the woman you are today and the woman you'll become." I take a breath. My body's coiled tight, my voice hoarse with emotion and the most important parts are still to come. "I pledge to always nurture your dreams and help you reach them. My whole heart, my body, and soul are yours. My love for you is never-ending. I am honored to be your husband. To be by your side for the rest of my life."

Mallory

I'm a blubbering mess by the time Chaser finishes his beautiful pledges. His dark eyes reflect nothing but honesty and devotion when I peer up at him. He takes a deep breath and releases it slowly, gently rubbing the pads of his thumbs over my hands.

"Mallory? Do you have vows you've written as well?" the officiant asks.

"Oh! Yes." I slip the piece of paper out from under the ribbon holding my bouquet together.

I'm so overcome with emotion, I have to blink and silently read my vows several times. It's not like I memorize lines for a living or anything. But these words are the most important I'll ever speak. I need the extra second to compose myself.

"Chaser, you love me and complete me in ways I never imagined were possible. You have held my hand through my biggest challenges, encouraging me to grow, and believe in myself. For as long as I live, I pledge to always support you, inspire you, and love you. I will celebrate your successes and mourn your failures as if they were my own. Together, anything is possible. I am so proud to choose you to be my husband, my one and only, today and for the rest of my life."

"Thank you," he whispers, pulling me just a bit closer.

"Russell Everett Adams, do you take Mallory Angelina DeLova to be your wife?"

He doesn't take his eyes off me as he answers, "I do."

"Do you promise to love, honor, cherish, and protect her, forsaking all others, until death parts you?"

"I do."

"And, Mallory, do you take Russell to be your husband?"

"I do."

"Do you promise to love, honor, cherish, and support him, forsaking all others, until death do you part?"

"Yes, I do."

"Do you have rings to exchange?"

"I do!" I carefully work the knot holding Chaser's ting to my bouquet loose. He raises his eyebrow when I hold out the ring. "I know you wanted..." I trace my fingers over his knuckles. "But I had to give you something today," I whisper.

He stares down at the polished platinum band. "When did you...?"

"A while ago."

The officiant clears his throat. I guess we've gone rogue.

"Mallory and Chaser will now exchange rings as a symbol of their love and commitment to one another."

Chaser pulls a small blue velvet box out of his pocket, leaving it closed. He's probably as worried about dropping it in the sand as I am.

"Your rings are a circle—a symbol of your never-ending love for one another."

"Chaser, please place your ring on Mallory's left hand and repeat after me."

I don't process the few short lines Chaser repeats. I'm too dazzled by the slender, sparkling diamond band Chaser slides down my bare left ring finger.

Then, it's my turn. I hold out the ring I fell in love with the first time I visited Cartier and slip it on Chaser's finger.

He's all mine.

I'm so happy, laughter and tears flow together. A pleasant buzzing in my ears almost drowns out the last lines of the ceremony.

"Love will make your relationship work. Trust that you always want what's best for each other. Remember to learn and grow together. Remain loyal to one another in times of uncertainty. And now by the power vested in me by the state of Hawaii, it is my honor to declare you husband and wife. Go forth and hold true to your journey together." He winks at Chaser. "You may kiss your bride."

"Finally." Chaser swoops in, coiling his arms around me, and sealing his mouth against mine.

I curl my toes in the soft, warm sand, still trying to convince myself this is real and not a dream. "I love you so much," I whisper against his lips. "Thank you."

"You've made me the happiest man in the world."

CHAPTER SIXTY-SIX

Chaser

After a simple island dinner on the beach with our friends, I finally have my bride all to myself.

"You know I've been dying to peel that suit off you all day?"

After the ceremony, she tossed on some sort of see-through beach cover-up over the suit. It just made me want to rip off everything even more.

Inside our room, I don't bother flicking on the lamp. Mallory leads me onto the patio leading to our private piece of beach. Together, we dance under the light of the moon. The humidity and sea breeze coating our skin.

"You feel good in my arms, Mrs. Adams," I whisper.

She answers with a happy noise. My hands slip on her slick skin, brushing against the ties holding her top together. I tug at the knot. "Let's go inside."

I stop her on the patio, eyeing the wicker chair-swing dangling in the corner. A perfect egg-shaped nest for my little dove. It instantly inspires a dozen dirty ideas. "Come here."

I leave her standing there for a second, while I duck into our room to grab a towel to spread over the cushion.

AUTUMN JONES LAKE

"Come sit." I hold the swinging chair steady while she lifts herself into the seat, then release it to gently sway side to side.

"I think it's big enough for two." She reaches out her hand to me.

"Not for what I have planned."

I kneel down in front of her and finally get my fingers on the pink ribbons at her hips. "These have been fucking with me since you walked down the aisle," I mutter, working the left one loose and then the right.

Her soft laughter floats away on the ocean breeze.

"Spread your legs."

Almost shyly, she parts her thighs. Not enough. I grasp one foot, lifting and bracing it against the outer edge of the swing. Getting the idea, she lifts her other leg, leaving her wide open and bare to my hungry gaze.

I sit back on my heels. "Fuck, that's nice. We need one of these at home."

Slow enough to drive me insane, she brings her fingers to her mouth and licks, then slides them over her perfect, pink pussy. "Mmm. We could hang it facing the front door and I could greet you like this every night when you come home," she purrs.

"We should've added *that* to our vows." I'm hypnotized, watching as she lazily keeps sliding two fingers through her wetness.

"Chaser?"

"Huh?"

"Are you planning to help me out here?"

I flick my gaze up to her teasing smile. "I'm enjoying the show."

She reaches for me with her free hand, curling one finger to beckon me closer. I grab the bottom edge of the swing, pushing it away. A surprised hiss of breath escapes her soft pink lips as the chair sways back and forth. I could listen to her make that little noise all night.

434

Each time she swings forward, I plant a kiss—on her inner thigh, behind her knee, whatever part comes closest. I finally stop the chair's movement and drag it closer. I take her hand and suck her fingers into my mouth.

"My wife tastes like heaven."

"Your wife wants her husband to fuck her."

"What a filthy mouth you have." I slide the pad of my middle finger against her entrance, slicking her wetness up to her clit and slowly circling it.

She leans forward, watching as I lick and kiss her pussy.

"Oh, right there." She twists her fingers into my hair and yanks.

There's nothing hotter than my woman—now my wife—this wild for me. I keep kissing and licking, relentlessly devouring her. I suck her clit into my mouth and she jumps. The chair lurches away. Growling, I pull it toward me, lick, and let her swing away. Lick and swing.

"Chaser! Stop."

Her pussy glistens with arousal. I hold her still and trail my tongue over her throbbing clit. She's writhing, breathing hard, chanting part of my name—she can't seem to get the second syllable out.

My dick's begging to escape my shorts. I try working the button loose with one hand, not wanting to let go and have her swing away again. Her head's thrown back, eyes closed, but maybe she senses my dilemma. She locks her legs around my head, anchoring herself, giving me time to shove my shorts down.

"Chaser. Don't stop," she gasps.

I want to assure her I won't stop but that would mean taking my mouth off her. Little earthquakes rock her body as she comes all over my lips and chin, screaming my name. I bring her down slowly, kissing her inner thighs, rubbing my hand over her belly up to her chest.

She lowers her legs but they're still trembling, dangling off the edge of the swing. I give her a lazy push backwards and she lets out the sweetest, contented sigh.

"We're not done," I warn her as I straighten up, wiping my hand over my mouth.

She blinks open her eyes and smiles.

I pull her to the edge of the swing, lining myself up, rubbing the head of my cock against her wetness as she comes closer.

She lets out a whimper as she swings away. I planned to play with her like this for a while, but that'll have to happen tomorrow. The next time she swings close enough, I hold her steady and shove myself inside.

"Oh, fuck," I groan. "You're so fucking wet."

"You're harder than ever." She wiggles her hips, and my eyes roll back in my fucking head.

"I think it's the angle," I grit out between clenched teeth.

I pull back and drive deep inside. So fucking good. She moans every time I roll my hips. Within minutes, she's close again. She wraps her fingers around my forearms, digging in her nails. "Oh my God."

Her screams push me toward the peak as I keep fucking her through another orgasm. The second I think she's finished, I move my hands to her hips, holding her in place. My body burns hot, sweat coats my skin. Pure, carnal pleasure rocks through me. "Fuck. I'm coming. Hard."

She shudders beneath me. "Yes, yes."

I collapse on top of her and the swing lets out a loud, squeaky groan. Too spent to move, I mumble "That can't be good," against her stomach.

She murmurs soft, sweet noises, while running her fingers through my hair.

The swing protests again and this time I sit up, taking her with me.

I stare at her in amazement. "How do you still have your top on?"

"You got carried away." She reaches between us and strokes my spent cock. "We have all night."

I brush a kiss over her cheek. "Give me a minute."

CHAPTER SIXTY-SEVEN

Mallory

Sometime in the middle of the night, I stretch, twisting in a tangle of crisp white sheets, scented with marital bliss. A sea-salt breeze drifts through the open door leading outside.

"Wake up, Mrs. Adams," Chaser rasps against my ear. "I need you."

His strong arms curl around me, sliding me closer until our bodies mold together. "Say that again," I whisper.

"What?" He strokes his fingers down my neck and over my collarbones. "Mrs. Adams?" He trails his lips over my neck, nuzzling against my shoulder. The fingers caressing my throat drop to the bodice of the brief nightgown I'd thrown on before we passed out.

"This is sexy as fuck," he murmurs while working the laces loose. He slides his other hand up my thigh and over my bare butt, stopping to clutch my hip. "Do you enjoy teasing your husband?"

I shift arching my back, pressing against him. "Teasing how?" I ask innocently.

He thrusts his hips, and I reach behind me, wrapping my fingers around his hard length and stroking.

"Fuck." He kisses my neck. "Like that."

Chaser

I swear, I meant to be all soft and honeymoon sweet but the second Mallory wrapped her hand around my dick, I lost it. Good thing we have a lifetime ahead of us to work on my self-control.

"Oh." She moans and arches against me, pressing her breasts in my hands. At least I think so. One arm's gone numb from her using it as a pillow. Totally worth it.

I clutch her hip, rocking her back and forth. Can't get deep enough at this angle. "Get on top of me." I roll to my back, shaking out my arm as I go.

Apparently, she's as eager as I am. She scrambles to her knees and wastes no time throwing her leg over me and sinking down on my cock. I groan as she closes her eyes and tips her head back. "You're so beautiful." I hook my fingers in the skinny little straps hanging off her shoulders and work her skimpy nightie below her tits. "Much better."

"Oh my God. I love you inside me," she gasps, grinding down harder.

"Fuck." I squeeze my eyes shut. Maybe I'm *too* deep now. After last night, I shouldn't be on the edge of exploding this soon. "I love being inside you."

"Chaser." Her body trembles. Thank fuck, she's close. I wet my thumb and bring it to her clit, rubbing gently until she comes apart.

She lets loose with a string of high-pitched little noises, pussy clamping around me so fucking tight, I'm letting out my own curses a few seconds later.

Maybe mid-afternoon, we stop to take a break and rehydrate.

"Think I should call downstairs and see if they have any Gatorade?"

She chuckles and accepts the glass of water I hand her. While she sips it, I flop down onto the bed and roll to face her.

"So, who do you think your father will send to kill me if he finds out we got hitched without telling him? Vasily?" I lazily trace my fingers over her shoulder and down her arm. "Someone else? Or do you think he'll wait and do the deed himself?"

She presses her palm against my chest, pushing me away. "Is this your version of sexy talk? Because I'm not feeling it."

"Nah, I was just thinking."

"I thought you said you trusted this place?"

"I do. I was kidding."

"Do you think your dad will be upset he wasn't here?"

"Disappointed, maybe. But he'll understand." He's not big on weddings and probably would've thought our whole simple, beach thing was a stupid waste of money.

Her mouth twists down as she considers the scenario more thoroughly. "For something that personal, he'd do it himself."

I'd love to see him try. "Well, I guess I'm safe until he gets out of prison, then."

CHAPTER SIXTY-EIGHT

15 Years later
Kodack, NY

Chaser

I pull the Manila envelope out of our mailbox and stuff it inside my cut before continuing down our long, secluded driveway.

Angelina greets me at the door by jumping up and wrapping her arms around my neck. "I'm so happy you're home, Daddy!"

"Were you good? You didn't shoot your brother in the ass again, did you?"

"Jeez." She steps back and scowls at me. "One time. It was an accident."

Still funny as shit too. Poor Dylan hasn't lived it down yet.

"Where's Grandpa?" She peers around me to stare at the front window. "Isn't he with you?"

"He stopped at the clubhouse. He'll be over for dinner later."

"Oh, goodie! I'm making a chocolate marshmallow cream pie for dessert."

"Yeah? You trying to give him another heart attack?" Her

face falls. I probably shouldn't tease my daughter about that. "I'm kidding. Sounds delicious. Where's your mother?"

"Out back." She drops her gaze to the envelope in my hand. "Who's sending stuff here to you and Mallory *Dove*?"

I wave the envelope in front of her. "It's from Uncle Alvin." "What is it?"

I hold it out of reach. "It's private. For your mom and me." "*Eww*."

Who knew our "famous" pasts would be so embarrassing to our pre-teen daughter? Anytime she catches a snippet of 'Candy Jar' on VH1 or an old episode of *Ocean Ave.*, she cringes, covers her ears, and starts singing at the top of her lungs.

"I have a test to study for." She waves at me before bounding up the stairs.

I wander through the house and out the back door leading to the patio and pool.

Even after all these years and everything we've been through, my breath catches the second my gaze lands on Mallory. Still as beautiful as the day we met.

Red toenails, long legs, red and white polka dot bikini. My brain catalogs every detail as I creep up next to her. I lean over and tug her headphones off. "You still take my breath away, woman."

"Jesus!" She jumps about a mile and presses her hand to her chest.

"Chaser, you scared the shit out of me."

Laughter rumbles out of me and I drop down on the edge of her chair, running my hand up one smooth, bare leg. "I hope you're wearing sunscreen."

She curls her fingers in my cut, pulling me down for a kiss.

"Missed you, little dove," I murmur against her lips.

"I'm so happy you're home."

"How happy?" I wiggle my eyebrows at her and tip my head toward the pool house.

She takes my hand and lets me pull her up out of the chair. Together, we race over the patio.

"Do you miss when we didn't have to hide from the kids?" she asks.

"Nah, it's more fun this way." I close the door and slip the lock into place—learned the hard way on that one. "Besides, they'll both be leaving for college soon enough and we won't know where to fuck first."

When we bought the place, we thought we'd offer the little cottage out back to her father when he wanted to visit. He usually chooses to stay somewhere else, which hasn't hurt my feelings one bit.

She fiddles with the collar of my cut. "How'd it go?"

"Good. They seem to have control of things up in Toronto now."

"For how long?"

"Don't know." I boost her up onto the small counter and keep my hands on her hips. "I'd like having you on more runs with me."

"I'd like that too." She cups my cheeks and rubs her thumb over my lips. "Make sure girls in every clubhouse know you're taken."

I flex my left hand in the narrow space between us. "If the ring doesn't let them know. Your name does." The tattoo around my finger kept fading so I'd had her name inked on the inside of my wrist in thick, bold script. I brush my fingers under her chin, tipping her head back. "You're still the only woman who sets me on fire with one look."

She curls her arms around my neck and leans forward, pressing her forehead to mine. "Prove it."

MUCH LATER, WHEN FAMILY DINNER NIGHT WITH MY DAD IS over, the kids are in bed and we're tucked away upstairs, catching up on the last few days, Mallory reaches over and picks up the envelope from Alvin.

"What's this?" She smiles when she sees Alvin's name on the return address label. "Aw, I miss him."

"He'll be here for the summer run." I lift my chin. "Open it."

"Do you already know what's inside?"

"Nope."

"Hmmm." She peels the envelope open and slides out a magazine. "*Rolling Stone*. Top One Hundred Rock Albums," she reads the headline splashed over the front.

The photo's a collage of cover art. She peers at it closely. "Oh! I see Kickstart!" She flips through the magazine, landing on the story.

"Oh, wow. Holy shit." She taps her finger against the page. "*In Your Hands* is number ten."

I run my hands through her hair and kiss her temple. "Well, shit. That's pretty fuckin' cool."

"Listen, listen." She taps my arm. "Some critics consider Kickstart's *In Your Hands* one of the last great rock albums."

"Last great rock album, huh? I'll take that."

She flips the page and giggles. "Vicious Vandals' second album came in at number twelve."

"How about that."

On the next page, Alvin left a post-it-note.

Still relevant!

I huff out a laugh and pluck it off the page, crumpling it and tossing it on the nightstand.

"Do you miss it?" she asks.

"Nope." I peer down at her. "You?"

"Hell, no." She snuggles closer to me. "Can you imagine with the Internet now and all the online gossip sites how many more shitty things would've been posted about us?"

"True." Every now and then some journalist tracks us down at our little estate outside of Kodack. Writes up a story, tossing in the same tired info about Jacob's death or the scandal of our

MC and mafia ties. All it does is reinforce what a good decision we made when we finally left Hollywood behind.

"At least it would've been easier to call you when I was out on the road." I brush my thumb over her cheek. "Touring would've been a hell of a lot easier if I could've called you whenever I wanted instead of always searching for a fuckin' payphone."

"That would've been nice." She wrinkles her nose. "You *know* some jackass would've stolen your phone and published all the risqué photos I sent you."

"Wait." I roll over and grab her little silver phone and flip it open. "I can't get you to send me a nude *now*."

"Yes, I have."

"Those barely qualify."

She clamps her hand over her mouth and laughs. "I'm afraid I'll end up accidentally sending one to the kids or my dad or worse, *your* dad. You just know I'd do something like that."

"Yeah, don't send me nudes." I pull the sheet back. "I prefer the live version."

She rips the sheet out of my hand. "I'm cold."

I glance at the magazine again. "Are *you* sorry you left?"

"Not for a second. We have everything that matters right here." Mallory strokes her fingers over my chest. "I'm happy exactly where we are."

"So am I, little dove."

Our home. The life we've built. I wouldn't trade any of it.

My heart's where it belongs. Right in Mallory's hands.

I click off the bedside lamp and spoon her soft little body, pulling her as close as possible.

"Sweet dreams, little dove." I press a sleepy kiss to her temple.

"You've already made all my dreams come true," she whispers.

"Then I guess we'll have to come up with some new ones together."

EPILOGUE

2 years later...
Devil Demons MC clubhouse, Western NY

CHASER

"What'd you find out?" I ask Tally as he steps into my father's office.

He closes the door before answering. "Lost Kings seemed to have cleaned house. Ruger supposedly went nomad."

"Bullshit." My father grins.

I don't find that as amusing as Dad seems to.

"They opened a charter downstate," Tally adds. "Sway's running it."

That wipes the smile off Dad's face. "They're going to make a play for more territory."

"You think they'll encroach on us?"

My father runs his hand over his chin, staring at the wall for a few seconds before answering. "That kid's in charge now, right?"

"He's hardly a kid," Tally says.

"We're just getting old." I sit up and punch Tally's shoulder.

Tally laughs and punches me back. "Speak for yourself."

"He came up under Grinder," I say. "Follows the more gentleman outlaw approach. Rock won't push into our territory."

"You want to bet your patch on that?" My father nods to the *Vice President* stitched into my leather cut, right over my heart.

I've run into Rock plenty of times over the years. I know he served time for his club, and never snitched. Loyalty—an important quality in our life. Not always easy when you're faced with a long prison stretch. He got out and from what we've heard, worked hard to clean up his club. Still takes care of Grinder and his old lady too. Do I want to bet my patch that he won't attempt to expand into our territory? Not particularly.

"They've got their own issues with Vipers MC right on their border."

"Fuck the Vipers. They're as bad as the Silver Saints. Both need to be put to ground. Permanently," my dad grumbles.

"So bloodthirsty, Pop," Tally jokes.

"Wolf Knights MC is right up in their neck of the woods too, right?" Dad asks.

"Jesus Christ, old man," I grumble, "Do I look like the Rand McNally of outlaw clubs to you?"

"Knowing all that shit's your damn job."

"Yeah, Ulfric's of the same mindset. Old school. Their club's small, anyway."

"We should invite 'em both to visit. Feel 'em out. See who's up for helping us get rid of Tyler's crew once and for all."

"You really wanna declare war on the Silver Saints, Prez?" Tally asks, all traces of humor wiped off his face.

"They're getting bold. Basically declared war on our Toronto brothers. Again." My father's pissed-off glare turns my way. "Your daddy-in-law ain't been real helpful there."

Ah, yes. I study the ceiling for a few minutes. Acting as the middleman between my club and my father-in-law never loses its appeal.

"Call Rock," my father says. "Use the excuse that you want to congratulate him on his new position. Remind him you've known him since he was a little punk. Hand out some fatherly 'proud-of-you' bullshit."

"Yeah," I answer slowly. "I don't see him falling for something so obvious."

My father dismisses my concern with a flick of cigar ash on the floor. "Whatever you need to say to find out what that second charter's about."

"Because he's gonna be real forthcoming with *those* details." I lift my chin. "You fucking kidding me?"

"You're smart. Figure it out."

A loud buzzing rattles from inside one of my father's desk drawers.

He pulls out one of the club's burner phones and glances at it. A slow smile crosses his face. "518 area code. Wonder who that could be?"

Empire, NY
Lost Kings MC clubhouse, Upstate NY

ROCK

FEW PEOPLE EVER SEE OUR STRUGGLES OR OUR PAIN. BUT everyone sees your mistakes. Revels in your misery. Passes judgment.

"That's my story, Rock," Trinity finishes baring her soul to me with lowered eyes and a voice barely above a whisper.

The things this woman has endured at the hands of her father's club leave fury boiling my blood. It took courage to spill her painful past.

"You've done the hard part, Trinity. I'll handle the rest now."

"Okay." The slight quiver of disbelief in her voice punches me in the gut. She's been let down so many times and by so many people, she doesn't know how to trust anymore.

Or perhaps she's waiting for me to tell her my club's

protection comes at the price of spreading her legs, which it doesn't.

The only way to earn her trust is to keep my word. Besides, Trinity's given me a kid sister vibe since the night we met when she teased me about my shiny new president's patch.

I work a more reassuring smile onto my face. "We've got your back. The ride goes on, right?"

She huffs a sad laugh. "My dad used to say that all the time. People change, the world goes to shit, but the ride continues."

"Bishop was a wise man."

I met her father once. A mean bastard of a biker, but a good man. Stabbed in the back by the same men who pledged to be his brothers.

Putting the Silver Saints MC to ground is looking better and better by the minute.

The Devil Demons MC is my best bet to take out the Silver Saints. Trouble's been brewing between the two clubs since well before I earned my colors.

"Your mother's still with a biker?"

"Maybe?" She shrugs. "I haven't seen her in so long..."

It shouldn't matter. If anything, it should motivate Stump even more once he understands the situation.

"If it's okay with you, I'll give Chaser a call."

A brief smile flickers over her lips. "I remember him. His ol' lady was always nice to me when I was little."

That doesn't surprise me one bit. Mallory's a fine woman.

"You won't...?" Her scared honey eyes silently plead with me.

She doesn't have to voice the rest of the question. "No. I won't share details of what you told me with anyone. I promise."

"Are you sure this is okay? You barely know me."

"I know enough. You're safe here, Trinity."

She finally seems reassured. "Thank you."

I stand and open my office door. "Go get settled. I have a few things I need to take care of."

She hesitates for a second before nodding and slipping out the door.

My vice president's waiting outside my office and watches Trinity with an interested expression that irritates the shit out of me. "Get in here, fuckface."

Zero grins, flashing a set of deceiving dimples. Dimples or not, he's as deadly a biker as one gets.

"'Sup, Prez?" He shakes his head. "Fuck, still feels weird calling you that."

I tap his almost pristine VP patch. "Same, brother."

He drapes himself over the chair Trinity just vacated. "She gonna be our new house mama?"

"Wrath's got his eye on her. They've been out a few times. Leave her alone."

He snorts. "Wrath's *never* claiming an ol' lady."

"Just leave her alone."

He shrugs. Between the girls at our strip club and the girls who wander in and out of our clubhouse, Z's not exactly hurting for female attention.

"What've you been hearing out of Kodack?"

"Demons still run the show. They're getting more pushback from Tyler's crew, though."

I growl at the mention of the sleazy fuck at the head of the Silver Saints' table. "Chaser's father-in-law isn't assisting them with that situation?"

"Nah, you know DeLova's too good for dirty biker business."

Yeah right. "You don't believe that for a second."

"Feds went at them hard for a few years. DeLova's keeping his distance."

"I think we should offer the Devil Demons our support."

The smile slides off Z's face. "Why are you eager to pull us into another war after everything we've been through?"

"Simmer down. Throwing our weight behind Stump's crew will benefit us down the road."

He glances at the door and I sense the question forming in his mind.

"Tyler's a piece of shit," I say to recapture his attention. "He needs to go. Grinder called it years ago."

"You gonna pay him a visit? See what he thinks?"

I cock my head, giving him the full force of my *are you stupid* stare. "Sure, why not? Seems like acceptable visiting hour conversation at good ol' Pine County Correctional."

He flicks his gaze to the ceiling. "You know what I meant."

"I'm not involving him in this. He's sacrificed enough for our club."

He sits back. "Call Chaser. Feel him out first."

With a heavy sigh I pick up the phone. I'm sure Chaser will be thrilled to hear from me. Then again, burying some bodies together is always a good way to solidify alliances.

"Chaser, it's Rock."

There's a beat of silence before he responds. "I hear you've made some changes in Empire, *Prez*."

My how word gets around. "A few."

"Congratulations."

"Thanks." There's not a whole lot we can say over the phone but I don't think that has anything to do with Chaser's reluctance to speak. "We're not moving beyond our existing territory if that's what you're worried about."

"Hadn't even crossed my mind, Rock."

Sure, it hadn't.

"Heard you established a charter downstate," he adds.

"It was...necessary." No, I won't get into the details of my own club's internal battles.

"Your club's squeezed tight." He lets the observation hang. He has a point. I've got my own problems right here in Empire.

"Yeah, but you know the feeling. Don't you?"

He snorts. Everyone knows about the war that's been brewing between the Devil Demons MC and the Silver Saints

MC for years. Involving my club might not be the best idea, but it'll establish trust with the Devil Demons MC.

Plus, there's the added benefit of protecting Trinity.

"Tyler still a thorn in your side?" I ask.

His low growl comes through the phone. "We've had some losses."

"Sorry to hear that. Been a while since we've seen each other. Think you and your father are up for a meeting?"

"Where'd you have in mind?"

"Name a location."

"Who are you bringing?"

"Just my VP. I'd like to keep things between us for now."

"Doesn't sound like a good start to your presidency."

"You'll understand why."

"I'll set it up and text you an address."

"Thanks." We hang up and I stare at the phone for a few seconds.

Z taps his fingers on the edge of my desk. "You're sure about this?"

The images left in my head from what Trinity shared won't be leaving anytime soon. One of Tyler's guys already tried to grab her once. Now that he knows where she is, he won't stop. "I'm sure."

"Chaser's a good man to go into battle with. Stump's a devious bastard and certainly no lightweight."

"Neither are you." I give him a weary smile.

"I'll follow you anywhere, Prez. Always got your back."

"Same, brother."

He nods and slaps my desk before standing.

I meet his ice-cold stare head-on. "Let's get ready for war."

Discover Rock's story and start the Lost Kings MC series with
SLOW BURN (LOST KINGS MC #1)
Also available in audio.

AUTHOR NOTES

A few readers mentioned the lack of author notes in the last two books. Thank you so much for noticing and caring. I usually write author notes as I'm preparing to publish. This year, I felt... drained and oddly out of words by the time I'd poured my heart onto the pages.

From the very bottom of my heart, thank you for buying and loving the Hollywood Demons books (I'm assuming if you're reading my author notes, you loved them. If not, carry on.) These books are incredibly special to me. Having grown up in the 80's, I was obviously heavily influenced by a lot of 80s-ish things (some of it incredibly problematic looking back at them now—yikes!) As a kid, I'd often write these wild, epic romances (oddly, also always three books long, go figure.) They were, of course, embarrassingly awful. But I so much wanted to capture that fun, adventurous, neon-colored spirit for these books. And yet, the story also covered some hard topics at times, because that's life.

It's probably obvious that some of the events were influenced by more recent stories coming out of Hollywood. I watched a few interviews with actresses who I'd always wondered "gee, whatever happened to her?" Now we know. They were chased out of the business in one way or another. I paid close attention to the stories of male actors who actually stood up for their female colleagues (spoiler alert—they were few and far between.) Not the ones who pretended they had no idea what was going on or "never suspected" a thing. *Fuck those guys.*

This is a theme throughout my books. I want my hero to always have my heroine's back—even if it comes at a personal cost. Nothing is more important or greater than the love and respect my couples have for each other. Poor Chaser and Mallory were a bit dickish to each other at certain points but it was always out of a frustration that they weren't together. When Andrew hits on Mallory, I suppose in some other world, he wouldn't have believed her, or maybe he would've blamed her, and they would've broken up. Or maybe Mallory would've said, "sure, let's bang!" But that's not who they are. I *love* a couple who faces the world and fights their problems *together.* I'm not into the angst of a couple doing horrible, hurtful, things to each other throughout a book. I'm just not. There's enough awfulness in real-life human relationships.

Even when Chaser's own father questions their relationship, Chaser stands up to him. A worthy alpha hero *always* defends his heroine. Although, it did plant that tiny seed of doubt that eventually worked its way out of Chaser's mouth in the heat of their argument over Andrew's actions. But he didn't let his pride stop him from making it right.

Oh, Chaser!

These two killed me. I just loved every moment with them. Maybe it's the horrifically challenging times we're living through right now, but I never wanted to leave their world.

It might surprise you to learn that I originally planned to kill off Jacob *and* Andrew. Andrew was such a dick. But a loveable one. Sort of. Somewhere in the middle of *Blow my Fuse,* he grew on me. I started wondering what his happy ending would look like. Does he even deserve one? Has he been redeemed enough? I still haven't decided.

Poor Jacob. It was traumatic for me to kill him off, even though I had been planning to do it all along. I reconsidered his death several times. But sadly, we've lost a lot of brilliant artists in similar ways and he was representative of that and all the complicated emotions the band and his loved ones would have.

For some reason, back in 2018 when I started re-writing *Kickstart my Heart*, I planned for Mallory and Chaser's story to be "three 50,000 word books." I based *all* of my "plans" around those numbers. I booked editing time and scheduled the audiobook recordings on those figures. I budgeted to pay for those services on those numbers as well. 268,000 words later...I am exceedingly lucky no one said, "What the fuck, Autumn?" when I handed in these significantly longer books and coughed up the extra money.

Although I've used *"True love stories never end..."* as my author tagline for a couple of years now, I can't think of a couple that it applies to more than Mallory and Chaser. Don't you think?

As I pointed out several times in my Facebook group, I have a span of like thirty *years t*o write books about Mallory and Chaser. We know they're still together and kicking ass in the present-day Lost Kings MC world. Surely, they must have had lots of exciting adventures in that time.

I *love* leaving little things unfinished or up in the air. I *love* the discussions my readers have about certain events that take place in my stories. I *love* leaving breadcrumbs for you to find and ponder. Not just the evil glee kind of love, but genuine affection and appreciation. Maybe I'm biased or you'll think this is obnoxious, but I am blessed to have some of *the most* incredibly passionate, creative, and enthusiastic readers an author could ever dream of having. The discussions in my Facebook group, in the spoiler groups for each book, the messages and comments I receive make all the pain and frustration worth it. Over and over readers tell me they re-read my books. I've always re-read beloved books. I still do. Not every book. Only special ones. So, I consider that one of the highest compliments. It also freaks me out because I'm always thinking, *"OMG! Maybe this time they're going to discover I'm actually a shitty writer!"*

And I'm self-aware enough to know that some of my readers don't care about the breadcrumbs and interconnectedness of the books and characters. You're not here for wedding books or baby books. You don't care what happens after the HEA. Sure, it hurts my feelings, and obviously I think you're missing out, but *I get it*. And I strive to write my books in a way that you will still enjoy the ones you *do* pick up whether or not you remember every last Easter egg or not.

I truly hope you enjoyed the Hollywood Demons. If you think I should write more in the series, by all means, let me know. I have more than a few ideas...Right now, my plans are to finish Rooster and Shelby's story in the Lost Kings MC series. It wasn't easy returning to the "present" time to work on their books. (Spoiler alert: You'll see Mallory and Chaser.) I had to make a decision about whether or not to include certain "current" events and ultimately decided not to. I think we're all getting a little too much "real life" now and we need books to escape into more than ever. Then, I want to release Grinder's book. He's already making me cry way too much and I can't wait to get to his happily-ever-after. He's really earned it.

If you loved this series, *please tell your book-loving friends,* and leave a review at your favorite bookstore. With this series, more than ever, I *really, really* need your help to spread the word. Your review doesn't have to be long or detailed. A few quick words about how the book made you feel helps enormously. Reviews left at *retailers, Goodreads, and Bookbub* are one of the only ways left to help authors obtain meaningful visibility for their work. Your words matter.

I hope you and your family are safe and well.

Please be kind to your fellow humans. A little compassion costs nothing and makes the world a better place.

I appreciate you so much.

xo,

Autumn

READING ORDER

I'm frequently asked where the standalones fit into the Lost Kings MC Series. Although the *Kickstart Trilogy* is not technically part of the Lost Kings MC series, there are some crossover characters. If you're so inclined, you could read my books in the *chronological* order in which they happen in the Lost Kings MC world. It goes something like this:

Kickstart My Heart
Blow My Fuse
Wheels of Fire
Cards of Love: Knight of Swords
Slow Burn (Lost Kings MC #1)
Corrupting Cinderella (Lost Kings MC #2)
Three Kings, One Night (Lost Kings MC #2.5)
Strength From Loyalty (Lost Kings MC #3)
Tattered on My Sleeve (Lost Kings MC #4)
White Heat (Lost Kings MC #5)
Between Embers (Lost Kings MC #5.5)
Bullets & Bonfires
More Than Miles (Lost Kings MC #6)
Unhinged (Iron Bulls MC #5) by Phoenyx Slaughter

Warnings & Wildfires
White Knuckles (Lost Kings MC #7)
Beyond Reckless (Lost Kings MC #8)
Beyond Reason (Lost Kings MC #9)
One Empire Night (Lost Kings MC #9.5)
After Burn (Lost Kings MC #10)
After Glow (Lost Kings MC #11)
Zero Hour (Lost Kings MC #11.5)
Zero Tolerance (Lost Kings MC #12)
Zero Regret (Lost Kings MC #13)
Zero Apologies (Lost Kings MC #14)
Swagger and Sass (A Lost Kings MC Novella)
White Lies (Lost Kings MC #15)
Rhythm of the Road (Lost Kings MC #16)
Lyrics on the Wind (Lost Kings MC #17)
Crown of Ghosts (Lost Kings MC #18)

And many more to come...

ABOUT THE AUTHOR

Autumn Jones Lake is the *USA Today* and *Wall Street Journal* bestselling author of over twenty novels, including the popular Lost Kings MC series. She believes true love stories never end. Her past lives include baking cookies, bagging groceries, selling cheap shoes, and practicing law. Playing with her imaginary friends all day is by far her favorite job yet!
Autumn lives in upstate New York with her own alpha hero.

www.autumnjoneslake.com

facebook.com/autumnjoneslake

goodreads.com/autumnjoneslake

pinterest.com/autumnjoneslake

Made in the USA
Monee, IL
25 January 2022

89845545R00277